About the Author

Bruno Noble was born in Beirut and educated at Oundle School and Southampton University where he read French and philosophy before moving to London. This is his first novel.

A THING OF THE MOMENT

A THING OF THE MOMENT

A THING OF THE MOMENT

BRUNO NOBLE

Dear Reader,

The book you are holding came about in a rather different way to most others. It was funded directly by readers through a new website: Unbound.

Unbound is the creation of three writers. We started the company because we believed there had to be a better deal for both writers and readers. On the Unbound website, authors share the ideas for the books they want to write directly with readers. If enough of you support the book by pledging for it in advance, we produce a beautifully bound special subscribers' edition and distribute a regular edition and e-book wherever books are sold, in shops and online.

This new way of publishing is actually a very old idea (Samuel Johnson funded his dictionary this way). We're just using the internet to build each writer a network of patrons. Here, at the back of this book, you'll find the names of all the people who made it happen.

Publishing in this way means readers are no longer just passive consumers of the books they buy, and authors are free to write the books they really want. They get a much fairer return too – half the profits their books generate, rather than a tiny percentage of the cover price.

If you're not yet a subscriber, we hope that you'll want to join our publishing revolution and have your name listed in one of our books in the future. To get you started, here is a £5 discount on your first pledge. Just visit unbound.com, make your pledge and type ISABELLA18 in the promo code box when you check out.

Thank you for your support,

Dan, Justin and John
Founders, Unbound

Super Patrons

Imad Abukhlal
David Ainsworth
Robert & Celia Barr
Lindsey Barraclough
Raffaella Baruzzo
Anna Best
Clive Best
David Best
Carol Bogle
Jeremy Bolland
Neil Burgess
Dominic Cameron
Sonia Cavalli
Julia Cavalli
Andrew Chapman
Michael Chappin
Simon Chester
Antony Christofi
Jas Chumber
Andrew Cochrane
Anne Cooper
Christopher Dizer
Angela Docherty
Amy Donoghue
Robin Eggar
Catherine Evans
Caroline Harding
Jim Hirschmann
James Horan
Art Hurwitz
Martin Hynes
Takeshi Imamura

Melanie Ireland
Jenny Jefferis
Virginia Jennings
Richard Jennings
Dan Kieran
Lorna King
Sheila Lenon
Margaret Lewisohn
Vikki Lindstrom
Catherine Lunshof
Susan Mason
David Matthews
Joe McDevitt
Kate Milne
John Mitchinson
Marc Noble
Caroline & Kevin O'neill
Sarah Patmore
Ann Patten
Jan Peters
Justin Pollard
Alexandra Robson-Hanafin
Justin Rose
Dean Smith
Rachel & Bernhard Speiser
Phil Spencer
Paddy Stone
Ashley Stones
Mairi Stones
David Stroud
Anthony Talbot
Mark Tattersall
Mark Thomas
Jill Tipping
Janice Troha
Jeffrey Van Schaick

Claudio Villa
Eva Sánchez-Ampudia & Cyrille Walter
Ole Wiig
Greg Wilkins
Laura Williamson
Mark Williamson
Claire Winning
Hugh Woolhouse
Kate Wynn
Mike Zelouf

With grateful thanks to Rachel and Bernhard Speiser who helped make this book happen.

The *I* is a thing of the moment, and yet our lives are ruled by it. We cannot rid ourselves of this inexistent thing.
– John Gray, *Straw Dogs* (2002)

Prologue

Isabella's mother hanged herself when she was six months pregnant with Isabella's sister. Isabella was nine years old and her brother Cosmo was two.

She discovered her mother's body hanging from the single beam in the garden shed, a pine kitchen chair on its side as though averting its face and a damp patch on the beaten earth floor a spotlight on a vacated stage. A butterfly, a male brimstone, had alighted on her mother's lips and flexed his yellow wings like a bellows, as though attempting mouth-to-mouth resuscitation. Moving closer, she could observe the brimstone's proboscis inserted in a corner of her mother's open mouth.

Actually, her mother wasn't there, Isabella said. Her body was, but her mother wasn't: a body that went from being her sister's source of life and sustenance to her coffin in two heartbeats. A doll within a doll, *matryoshkas* made of flesh. She felt her mother's absence, in the musky warmth of the shed, with all the intensity of a presence. She said she thinks that that was why she wasn't immediately upset – that, and the butterfly. That and the kernel of resentment that took seed within her immediately, tenacious like a foetus, ugly like a grey, knobbly puss moth chrysalis for its evident unfairness.

She would come to feel more alone in the world for the loss of a sister she had never met than of a mother who, she couldn't help but believe, had abandoned Cosmo and her. In her sister, had she been born and lived, she would have had an ally, a same-sex sibling whom she could have shielded from the worst of things and in whom she could have saved herself by proxy. She had anticipated her sister's birth with such longing that she felt cheated of the role she had prepared herself for and that her mother hadn't had the courage to assume.

Her mother, her dear hand-wringing, self-deluding mother, had believed that neither seeing nor hearing evil might guarantee its absence, that the world could be a better place by the power of hope alone. Isabella would come to think that her mother had died long before the day of the brimstone's embrace, at around the time she was pregnant with Cosmo, when life's baton had been passed from her mother to him. Then, when Cosmo and she had needed their mother most, she had left for good.

She could see her mother's logic: having failed Cosmo and her, she would save her baby. She could see her mother's desperate hope, too: having taken her own and her baby's lives, she would draw attention to her children's plight, raise questions about the probable cause of her action and, so, rescue them.

The deaths were in vain: it would be left to Isabella to raise a flag, and so she would begrudge her mother her unnatural death despite herself, old enough both to despise herself for doing so and to understand what only she, with the possible exception of her father, could guess to be her mother's motivation.

'You see,' she said, 'who I hated, resented, bore grudges against and forgave, who I loved, loved carnally, these were the things I would have control over. Sebastian, you wouldn't be here in bed with me otherwise.'

Isabella

My father was the elder son of a clergyman, theologian and lepidopterist, who, surrounded by his wife, sons and daughters, looked intently into my father's study from a framed photograph positioned on the left end of the study mantelpiece. My grandfather and grandmother are seated side by side in wicker armchairs in a large, luxuriant garden with their two sons standing behind them and their three daughters at their feet, all of them framed within the frame by the grey stone vicarage in the middle distance. Although taken in the 1950s, the photograph has a faintly Edwardian air in its formality, in the men's ties, in my aunties' billowing chiffon dresses that settle on the grass, in the leaky, fading colours. The picture contains its contradictions at closer inspection: it is a family photo in which no one is smiling; the garden appears lush and the bleaching noonday sun fierce, and yet the men wear their jackets buttoned up and my Aunts Mary, Linda and Patricia wear cardigans while, discreetly in the background, the vicarage chimneys smoke. My grandmother seems absent, perhaps embarrassed or even ashamed to be a part of this staid troupe; no matter how closely and frequently I examined the picture I could never catch her eye. Close up, her eye sockets, the spaces beneath pale eyebrows, are featureless and devoid of pupils. My grandfather sits forward, one hand gripping a chair arm, as though intent on missing nothing that goes on in my father's study, keen to hear every word, to see every coming and going and to savour every indiscretion. His eyes are black pinpricks below a centre parting. Behind him, my uncle James grips his father's chair as though he would overturn it and he and my father, too, standing uncomfortably in a tweed suit behind my mother, look at their father with a mix of hatred and contempt – or so it appeared to me. It was hard to tell, really: the picture quality was poor and contrasted with the opulence of the silver frame it rested in.

My mother's family was German, so my mother and I and, later, Cosmo, would visit her parents in Paderborn once a year. We would see my mother's older sister, who travelled South America to satisfy her wanderlust, and her younger one, who taught German in Japan, even less frequently.

On the rare occasions of paternal family reunions, which were held with a degree of reluctance and only, it would seem, for the sake of keeping up appearances, a sense of wariness and unspoken resentment would fill the air. My grandmother would retain a fixed smile as though in apology for an oversight or, perhaps, the perennially dry cucumber sandwiches and stale meringues, and would sigh whenever presented with her granddaughter to kiss, cuddle or commend. Every time I greeted her up close, I would start with surprise that she had eyes, after all. She would direct them somewhere either above my head or at my feet as she blessed me, my dear, and handed me back hastily to my mother as though anxious that I might regurgitate my lunch on her or she disgorge her secrets on me. Our family reunions were always in the summer and outdoors, as though to permit flight, as though in fear of the results of close containment, of what confinement might lead to. My father, uncle and aunts would circle their parents and each other cautiously, apprehensive not so much of what others might say or do but afraid of what they themselves might. They appeared as terrified of forgetting themselves in laughter and reminiscence as they were of finding themselves in pairs and open to confidences. They would wade through those hot summer days as though through treacle, deliberately and incapable of sudden movement, or as in an elaborate slow dance that my mother and her brother-in-law, Aunt Patricia's husband, were not invited to join. My father and his siblings orbited that central, stationary point of their father, neither daring to get too close to him nor capable of distancing themselves entirely from his pull. He was the sun and the father, the puppet master, the orchestrator of their poisoned lives from whom they had to buy the antidote repeatedly, thereby keeping revolt and hatred in check. His children beat their wings in vain against the slow death he had ensnared them in, illustrated so brilliantly by the rows and columns of butterflies behind glass in every public room of the vicarage that he would talk of with pride and no small degree of malevolence.

Well before my father and Uncle James had reached their teens, my grandfather had bought them each a fine denier butterfly net, a heavy-duty card display box, a magnifying glass and minuten pins and declared himself ready to instruct them in the art of lepidoptery.

I imagine they expressed enthusiasm, though whether feigned or sincere I can only guess. Whatever the case, my father's interest in butterfly collecting grew while his brother revolted against it at the earliest opportunity – on leaving home after school to take up an army commission, much to the chagrin of his father.

'Bloody butterflies. I hate them. No I don't. I love them. Why do we have to kill them to love them? That's what I don't understand. Bloody Father. He kills everything he touches. I know, I know. I joined the army. But that's because there were people I'd rather kill than butterflies.' Uncle James spoke in short sentences and in the clipped tones of a military officer even after his nervous breakdown and demobilisation.

Of all of my father's siblings, Uncle James was the nicest to me. He would stand to attention and then drop to his knees to talk to me earnestly, seemingly impatient for me to grow up – not in order to save his knees, one of which cracked as he knelt and stood, but to have me at an age at which he could uninhibitedly give me the guidance he was plainly aching to deliver. His eyes were like my father's, brown, but where my father's seemed to suck light in, Uncle James' seemed to emanate it; he radiated warmth and affection and concern only just held in check for form's sake. His goodbyes were extended.

'Look out. Look after yourself, won't you? If you ever need anything. You'll let me know, won't you? Well, you know where to find me. Take care. You have my number? Goodbye then.'

I hadn't Uncle James's number and I would have had no idea where to find him but I would nod, unable, such was the intensity with which he held me by the shoulders, either to raise my hand for a handshake, as instructed by my father, or to kiss him on the cheek, as encouraged by my mother.

My paternal aunts were indistinguishable from one another. They neither looked nor dressed alike, but all three wore the same anxious mask, of fear and of perpetual apprehension, as though a serpent lay behind every smile, a bear in every hug and a Boo behind every door. They evinced, at best, an indifference or, at worst, an antipathy to my mother; it was embarrassing to see her trying to ingratiate herself with her sisters-in-law whose contempt for her grew proportionately to her efforts to gain their favour.

Unfortunately, my mother's English was fluent to the point that one forgot she was German, so that her few errors jarred and made her appear stupid rather than clever enough to have learnt a second language so well. Her unforgiving sisters-in-law would exchange round-eyed glances and speak condescendingly to her in the same tone that they used with me. Aunts Linda and Mary may have considered Aunt Patricia's unexpected marriage to an executive of the Oxford and District Water Board a betrayal of their sororal ménage à trois but, if proof were needed that blood is thicker than water, Uncle Neville's enrolment in the Bicourt family provided it, in that the sisters' emotional ties proved stronger than the couple's wedding vows and he and my mother found themselves forever bemused outsiders to the Bicourt clan, frustrated visitors to a house with no doors.

Our house had doors but they were always kept shut, even the internal ones, on the pretext of excluding draughts; the air in the hallways was musty – made all the more so, or so I imagined, by people only exhaling in them if, like me, they took care to inhale deeply before entering. My father had bought the semi-detached red–brick Victorian house in Summertown, due north of Oxford town centre, furnished it, with the exception of one room, and, casting his eyes about him for the one last missing item of furniture, proposed to my mother. She had come to England as a German language assistant and, despite a promotion to teacher, had finished by finding employment in an administrative capacity in one of the university's many faculties. She had never enjoyed teaching as much as she had hoped, her love for her pupils remaining unrequited, and decided that if she couldn't improve young people's lives from the front line by teaching them the joys of the German language, she would assume her position in the supply train from where she would do her best to ensure their institutions of learning were efficiently run. A photograph of my mother and father on their wedding day rests on the right side of the mantelpiece in my father's study. She clutches his arm with one hand and holds a posy of flowers with the other and wears an elbow- and knee-length white wedding dress, white high-heeled sandals, a raised veil that hangs all the way to the small of her back and a childish expression that mixes relief, hope and anxiety. Her face is at the same level as the carnation in my father's buttonhole and nearly as white. His suit is blue, its trousers and his nostrils flared, its lapels and his grin wide, the latter in self-congratulation. He looks smug. He has the demeanour of a man who has successfully pulled the veil over his wife's and society's eyes, who has achieved his aims and ticked this next – the marriage – box on his way to ticking them all. My father had dutifully studied theology at university and, over the three years that followed, acquired a doctorate in philosophy, specialising in and, eventually, lecturing on 'the ancients' or 'the Greats' or even 'the Greeks', as he called them.

In between the photographs on the mantelpiece in my father's study are some pine cones, an earthenware candlestick, fossils of fish embossed on two pink stones and a postcard of a sculpture of a majestic bronze couple, massive in an English landscape, on the back of which is inscribed *Henry Moore, King and Queen* and, in Grandpapa's near illegible scrawl, the curious directive, 'To John, *read* Father and Mother.' The photograph has been taken from a low angle so that, despite their evident mass, the green- and grey-tinged regal couple, seen against a cloud-striated sky, appears to float above the moors, benevolent rulers of all it surveys. These are interspersed with out-of-date invitations to charity and university functions and brass medallions with famous philosophers' profiles in relief on them. Above the mantelpiece and on the entirety of the facing wall above a Chesterfield sofa are butterfly display cases that add the only notes of colour to the room. The two alcoves on either side of the fireplace and one wall are taken up entirely with bookcases; on entering the room, one has to open the door wide to squeeze past the fitted bookcase. Opposite, a big bay window framed by dark floor-length curtains accommodates my father's desk on which rest in- and out-trays and two framed pictures – not photographs of my mother, Cosmo or me but etchings of Plato and Descartes, angled not so that my father can contemplate them from behind his desk but so that casual visitors to the study cannot fail to notice them. Two Chesterfield armchairs on either side of the fireplace, on opposing ends of an oriental rug next to a hearth rug, two wicker chairs with embroidered cushions by the desk, a mahogany coffee table and a Turkish carpet beneath them complete my father's study. He entertains his men friends here, fellow dons and postgraduate students who gather for warm beer in brown bottles, cigarettes, cigars, pipes and philosophical debate that grows more raucous with the lateness of the hour. My mother never enters it and he rarely enters her room (unless to poke his head around the door and summon her or me), which he had presented to her empty as his wedding gift. He refers to it condescendingly as her 'parlour' and gives the impression, whenever he says the word, of making a gift of it to her all over again. She has furnished it comfortably, with fewer books than my father's study but with greater warmth, with several family photographs, with drapes over a settee and armchairs, with framed, colourful prints, including one each by Hokusai and Hiroshige, two by Picasso and two of Wagner's *Walküre*, with old advent calendars that she liked too much to discard, with coloured glassware bought from charity shops or in car boot sales and with bowls of chocolates, confectionaries and other *Süßigkeiten* that both she and I know are all the sweeter for being looked upon with disapproval by my father.

Having no communal room, my parents don't entertain together. The family meets in the kitchen around a large pine table for breakfasts that are relatively leisurely given our short commuting times to school, office and college, and for dinners that are consumed hastily on those evenings in which my father anticipates visitors. The kitchen is always warm thanks to a cast–iron range cooker that is kept permanently on at low temperature and a deep, springy sofa with cushions and throws to get lost in. The kitchen is where *Kuchen* and *Torte* are baked and consumed daily, where I and then Cosmo took our first steps, from the soft sofa to our mother's softer, cushioned welcoming bosom.

My father dabs the corners of his mouth with his napkin, pats his hair and, with no small degree of self-righteousness, declines my mother's offer of cake with his tea. Pushing the pine kitchen chair back, he pleads the pressure of work, the requirement for intellectual exactness, the need for untrammelled reflection, the demands of the philosophic activity that neither respects convention nor recognises the hour of the day, and makes for his study. I sense that my mother, too, is not unhappy when my father is out of the kitchen, when she can wash the dishes, bathe me and read to me before putting me to bed and writing to her parents, whom she misses.

Out of nowhere, at around the time my father considers it no longer inappropriate for me to enter his study when he is entertaining, on the pretext of bringing crisps or another glass or more beer, he begins to show great solicitude about my mother's enforced solitude when he has visitors. I become proud of my promotion to male adult company and am pleased with my father's sudden interest in showing me off, while he grows seemingly considerate of my mother and anxious to redress the neglect and loneliness he has exposed her to. He buys her evening concert tickets and signs her up for evening and weekend driving lessons, art classes, pottery courses and lectures and museum and city tours that consume her holidays. He presents them to her as birthday and Christmas gifts or spontaneous ones that express his love for her, so she can't refuse them. After a while she begs him to allow her some evenings at home: she works full days and is too exhausted to be ruled by an evening as well as a diurnal clock. She wants to end each day at her leisure and put me to bed later than is ordinary in England, as is the European way; she suspects that, once my father's gatherings are underway, my needs will be overlooked and she worries that if I wake with nightmares, my crying will not be heard above the animated discussion that takes place behind the closed study door. Finally, albeit timidly and apologetically, my mother puts her foot down and refuses to attend any more evening courses and concerts on her own; but this goes against the grain of her compliant personality and leaves her unhappier than before. Some months later, my father discovers what he refers to as 'a hole in the family finances' that it occurs to him my mother must fill by giving evening German lessons. My mother resigns herself to this; it makes her feel useful to be making a sacrifice and an important contribution to the good of the family. Besides, she is pregnant with Cosmo, another mouth to feed. By then, I am spending as many evenings with my father as I am with my mother – always with one or the other, never with both.

The earliest distinction I can remember making is between my father's lap and my mother's. Hers: soft, luxurious and padded, as she bounces me up and down and recites a nursery rhyme to a climax. '*Hoppe, hoppe, Reiter. Wenn er fällt, dann schreit er. Fällt er in den Graben, fressen ihn die Raben. Fällt er in den Sumpf, macht der Reiter, 'Plumps'!*' His: bony, uncomfortable and unwelcoming as he jiggles me from knee to knee and exhorts me to 'move up' to find a position tolerable for both of us; his breath, heavy with eggs, beer and cigarettes, coming faster as he tires of me. When he's not fussing over and petting me, an eye over his shoulder and a hand around my waist, he gives me books to read and then ignores me to the point of neglect. When my mother is absent, we spend our moments together between dinner and bedtime in silence, I in my wingback chair across the fireplace from his, the leather cool against my exposed legs that, too short to bend at the knee, stick straight out to either side like a doll's. When I look up, he looks down. I struggle with the books he gives me and come to understand that he has purloined them from his sisters. *The Twins at St Clare's*, *Malory Towers* and the *Nancy Drew Mystery Stories* are all 'girls' books', so they must do, and my mother tuts at my father's inability to gauge the age of such books' readers – all the while pleased that she has a reason to resume her teaching role, if only with me her only pupil. When she's not immediately by my side assisting me with new words and long sentences and expressing an overt pleasure in the discovery of new stories and sharing my excitement about the heroines' adventures, I like to call out to her.

'Mama!' I cry or, less frequently, when certain my father is out of earshot, '*Mutti!*' He looks upon my use of '*Mutti*' disapprovingly and will have neither my mother nor me refer to him as '*Vati*' under any circumstances. My mother and he have settled on 'Mama' and 'Papa' so long as, in his case, 'Papa' is said with the short, punctuated call of a bugle on the first syllable and the stress on the second and not, as my father considers it, the American way, with the stress on the first. 'Ma-*ma!*' I repeat.

'Yes, *Liebchen*, what is it?'

It is nothing. I delight in the mastery of my mother. One syllable, repeated once, and I have her full attention. It is only a little power, but it is mine and I relish it. 'It is nothing, Mama, nothing,' I say and resume reading and she talking.

Mama busies herself about the kitchen and prattles on of things seemingly inconsequential that, nonetheless, lodge with me at an indiscernible level, her words washing over and buoying me like a warm tide. When Mama talks to me, I learn something about inner worlds, about myself, if only that I am loveable and desirable, and about her, about the good in her and the values I must adopt if I want to be like her. Her chatter is redolent of maternal love; Papa's stinks of ulterior motive. A conversation with him is like a slow wade in an icy sea on a cloudless night, the subtext of his words submerged so deep that I am afraid to find it, sharp and jagged under my bare chilled feet. When he talks to me, it is to teach me about the outside world: table manners, formal means of address, famous philosophers, careers and butterflies; the longest conversations Papa has with me are about butterflies. I follow him on occasion to the greenhouse, which he refers to as his 'pavilion', that has been appended to the shed at the bottom of our garden. The whole forms one long, low apex-roofed bungalow that is the width of the garden, one third wood-panelled, with one solid beam spanning the central space, and two thirds single-pane glass and that, in spring and summer, is filled with hundreds of caterpillars, chrysalises and butterflies or, as I explain to my friends in a loud voice so that I can be sure my father hears me, larvae, pupae and Lepidoptera. Papa, who frets inordinately when Mama or I use inappropriate terminology, is strangely tolerant of my friends' errors of nomenclature. He stands behind me and runs his fingers through my hair, from my crown to the back of my neck, his fingers evenly spaced, his finger nails dragging against my scalp; and always, when he ceases combing, bunches my hair into a ponytail upon which he gives a little downward tug and so lifts my chin a touch, saying, 'I like your fair hair.' This time, he adds, 'We haven't seen Eleanor and Deborah in a while. You should invite them more often.'

Mie

My chin cupped in my hands and my elbows on my bedroom window sill, I could look down on dozens of telephone cables and wires that streamed to and from the junction point on the telephone pole just outside my parents' butcher's shop. From my north-facing vantage point in Sangenjaya I would follow them meeting and multiplying, converging and diverging all the way to the horizon.

Pushing myself up on my hands, tilting my head and crossing my eyes, I could manage the trick of moving one of the now two poles and one of the now two junction boxes closer to me, so close that I could imagine them emanating from my chest. I thus became wired to a web, hooked up to countless possibilities, plural lives and a multiplication of options. All I would have to do one day was to choose which telephone wires to follow and to decide where to have them take me.

How do swallows decide which telephone wires to sit on? They flock at sunset and darken the sky prematurely before settling on a small number, so that some wires have hundreds of swallows on them and others none. On one occasion, I saw a wire with just one bird on it and I thought, *That's me.*

Plane trails are visible in cloudless skies; unthinkingly, I would seek their parallels in the telephone cables and wires and always find one, one black cord among dozens, that was exactly parallel with the white jet stream above it.

The telephone wires hummed with conversations and spoken lives. I listened at my open window in the hope of overhearing confessions and shared secrets; occasionally, cheek in palm, I came to with a start after having drifted into reverie, thinking I had heard something only to realise that indeed I had but it was only the chatter, the voices from the pavement immediately below. Leaning out over the wide sill, I could look down on the heads of the passers-by and of my parents' customers. From directly above, they were distinguishable from one another only by virtue of a hat or umbrella. Stationary as they

13

waited to cross the road, they seemed like bacteria in a Petri dish. In motion, they resembled amoebae under the microscope. My heart swelled with a sense of superiority; I could not conceive of any resemblance I may have had to them.

When I raised my eyes, I would see, across the road from me, a baker's shop. My mother turned her nose up at what she told me was reproduction Louis XVI furniture in the café section by the shop window and, after she had explained to me who Louis XVI was, she and my father would giggle about the sign over the shop front: *Fresh Cakes. Since 1872.* My friend Michi had the first–floor bedroom above the shop. Her father was the baker and her mother, as my mother would say ironically, the *pâtissière*. Michi would occasionally serve customers or take her turn behind the till. My parents suspected her of being the shop's greatest source of leakage: she was as round as the pastries she packed into paper bags. On most days, Michi and I would wave to each other from our open bedroom windows. Next to Michi lived my other friend, Keiko, above her parents' electrical supplies shop. She was tall for our age, and thin.

Over a dinner of whatever meat my father had failed to sell that day, he would tease, once we had finished reviewing the day and I had recounted everything my friends had said and done, and say something like, 'So, what do you think they say about you? That you're as tender as Kobe beef? Or that you're as red as a sirloin steak? Or that you're a silly old moo?' Then he would laugh heartily out of one side of his mouth – the other still chewing a wad of, more often than not, *shabu shabu* – before slowly wagging my cheek between thumb and forefinger. His hands smelled of disinfectant and were red and rough, but he was never anything other than gentle with me.

My mother would smile and, anxious to assure me that my father was only jesting, would squeeze my arm with, 'She's as sweet as a lamb!' or, 'She has the heart of an ox!'

She needn't have worried.

One particularly hot summer, my parents took me to a swimming pool complex, having packed the picnic hamper we typically only used once a year for *hanami*, when we'd picnic under blooming cherry trees in the spring and remark on the intoxicating smell of the blossom, so sweet after the metallic odour of cold meat and bleach. We carried rice balls, pickles, fried chicken, and cucumber and egg sandwiches, green tea and fruit juices and our towels, swimming costumes, tanning lotion and, for my mother and me, inflatable rings and arm bands.

We queued for the train and we queued for access to the swimming pool grounds. Tickets in hand, we stood in line for the changing rooms and then joined the mêlée for the swimming pool.

The crowd had a mind of its own; we couldn't fight it, we could only follow where it led, a succession of rubber rings and perspiring backs and shuffles of flip-flops under a sun unchallenged by any cloud. From a vantage point, we saw teeming people surrounding other people corralled in a rectangular space that, my father guessed, contained the principal swimming pool. We were three among thousands of identically dressed – or undressed – hot, thirsty, sticky bodies. By two in the afternoon I was crying with hunger and thirst and with shame at having wet myself, as, I guessed, others had too, perhaps counting, like me, on their urine mixing with the sweat and suntan lotion that ran down backs and stomachs into swimming trunks and down legs to form puddles around our feet. The smell was overpowering, especially to children, whose nostrils are that much closer to the ground and to crotch height; my eyes were level with sweaty navels and hairy backs, the sweat-saturated tops of swimming trunks and clutched inflatables and picnic lunches. I held my parents' slippery hands tightly, terrified that in this nightmare throng they might mistake another child's hand for mine.

My parents' hope of finding a patch of grass by a swimming pool had long evaporated but it wouldn't do to turn back, not that one could. Slowly, the wide eddy we were in got caught up with the one comprising people leaving the main pool so that, without our realising it initially, we found ourselves drifting back to the changing rooms. Suddenly, we found ourselves traversing a paddling pool with no space for a toddler to sit in and I saw my relief reflected in other people's smiles as, yes, we could indeed later tell our friends we had gone swimming and found a pool. The warm water lapped our ankles; lost flip-flops and discarded tissues and plastic bottles nuzzled and bumped our toes and heels.

We had our picnic at four o'clock on a shaded patch of earth outside the train station. The *onigiri* had disintegrated, the *tsukemono* had wilted, the *karaage* had dried and the sandwich edges had curled and hardened, but we ate them all.

We had three coldrooms that were set at a temperature of one degree Celsius and a fourth, a walk-in freezer, that was set at minus twenty degrees. The freezer contained a mix of prepared foods and uncommon cuts of meat; one of the two coldrooms held chicken and the other prepared foods and marinated meats. My favourite was the last and largest in which hung game and sides of beef, pork and horse-meat and in which Michi, having asked to be shown the coldrooms at about the age at which one learns that the meat on one's plate comes from an animal that bears little resemblance to the fluffy, stuffed and stitched package one hugs to sleep at night, had burst into tears.

Michi and I had come closest to falling out shortly after that visit, when we had attempted to play with our cuddly toys and dolls together. While she and Keiko were content to enact tea ceremonies, happy families and school lessons with the dolls, I favoured stripping them, disjointing them to the extent possible and hanging them from a piece of string extended from a door handle to a drawer knob, like sides of meat we could then offer for sale in a game of 'butcher's shop'. While they treasured their manicured, anthropoid puppets, I loathed mine for the audacity they had to mimic human form, however inadequately. When still very young, I demanded my mother rid my room of the insultingly empty, humanoid shells my friends saw fit to amuse themselves with.

The back room of our house on the ground floor, the one directly behind the shop, was the butcher's proper, the preparation room in which joints were filleted and meats generally prepared for presentation in the shop in metal trays. On the walls above the prep room's marble tops, wooden chopping blocks, mincers and many steels, cleavers and boning knives, were pinned posters of drawings of animals in profile that detailed, by means of dotted lines, the precise anatomical cuts of beef, pork and horsemeat – simpler, consumer-friendly versions of which decorated the shop walls in order to help my parents' customers with their orders. As a joke, Takumi-*san*, my parents' shop assistant, tacked a large sheet of paper to the prep room wall on which had been printed a stylised, heavily inked frontal outline of a man tattooed with his own dotted cutting lines that denoted fingers, hands, arms, chest, stomach and so on. The frontal, featureless outline had been very well drawn and the sheet laminated so that the whole held its own against the professionally executed posters of animal silhouettes. I found it strangely compelling and would stand there staring at it until I could see myself filling the thickly delineated space entirely and looking out at the prep room from the wall. One day, quite unexpectedly, it felt as though the outline had stepped off the poster and onto and around me, like a new, thick additional layer of skin. This sensation delighted me; I felt both highlighted, more real than others in the real world, and, too, the lead cartoon character in my own anime world.

'Does it amuse you?' asked my father. I hadn't noticed him watching me.

'I am invincible,' I replied happily.

My father appeared nonplussed.

'I am me,' I added helpfully.

'Of course you are!'

He squatted and hugged me, keeping his arms straight and his unwashed hands away from me, and kissed me on the forehead. I could feel his strength and the depth of his affection despite my newly acquired squidgy second skin.

I'm not sure that my father had welcomed having that picture of a dissected human being on the wall, but he had left it there in recognition of Takumi-*san*'s efforts; my liking it gave him an additional reason for retaining it, so there it stayed.

Not long after, Takumi-*san* lost the tips of two fingers in an accident in the prep room. My father teased that the outline of the man was Takumi-*san* and that he had been intending to use it as a guide to his own cannibalisation, starting with his fingers. Our customers joked that Takumi-*san* had lost his finger tips in the mincer when serving a customer, who had returned the following day to ask for more of that quite delicious-tasting mince.

My parents allowed me to wander in and out of the shop on quieter weekdays; my only instructions were never to touch a knife and never to run, for fear that I might slip on the prep room floor where, invariably, bits of meat, fat and gristle would be spilled like landmarks around miniature lake-like drops of blood. I liked the singsong greetings and farewells that accompany shoppers in my home country and loved adding my shrill soprano to my father's bass and Takumi-*san*'s baritone and to the ding-dong of a bell that signalled the shop door opening. On hot days, I would enter the coldroom that housed the disassembled herbivores and walk among them as they hung there in their declining, reducing state. Live and whole once, they had been killed, skinned, disembowelled and bisected after their heads and hooves had been cut off. From here, they would be butchered neatly in our prep room, quartered, filleted and reduced to manageable sizes and recognisable portions, cut into ever-smaller pieces until, soon, we'd hold a morsel of them between our chopsticks before digesting them in an irreversible reduction that ensured their elimination. As they hung there, pink and purple in the grey-blue light of the walk-in fridge, I couldn't help but consider them at the start of their lives, not so much in vitro but in limbo, this room an ante-chamber from which they'd be released into the world and would grow heads and hooves and gambol, graze and gallop in rich green fields. I knew I was just confusing them with me as I hung in a stasis of seasons, school terms, play dates and homework, waiting for my real life to begin.

'Mie-*chan*! What are you doing?' The panic and incomprehension in my father's voice startled me so that I nearly lost my balance on the pile of boxes and crates I had stacked in the midst of the thicket of hanging meat. I saw him through the animal corpses, framed in the open doorway, and I saw myself through his eyes and felt foolish, although I didn't think I had actually done anything wrong. He pushed his way through the sides of beef and horsemeat that thudded as they hit each other and made the butchers' hooks jangle. His livid, pallid face looking up to me in the artificial light was ghastly and his hair stood on end.

'Come here.' He held his arms out to me and felt around my neck – finding no rope, to his relief. Helping me off the rickety stack, he exclaimed, 'You are freezing to the touch!' He walked me upstairs, wrapped me in his coat and sat me on his lap. 'What on earth were you doing?'

I could detect no hint of reprimand in his voice; just anxiety, fear and a desire to understand.

'I was just wondering what it was like to be one of them. You know, what it's like to be hanging there, waiting for your life to begin, waiting for that next step in your life. There's no need for you to be so worried.'

Later, at the coldroom door, I would understand my father's concern, his visceral fear. The overhead light failed to penetrate the tangle of carcasses so that the lower part of the room remained in shadow and the boxes I'd been standing on must have been quite invisible to him. That night, I hugged him ever so tightly and said, 'I'm sorry to have frightened you, *Otoo*–san. I would never, ever…' I didn't know how to finish the sentence, how to tell my father that his daughter was so arrogantly certain of herself, of her being, that she would harm others before she'd harm herself.

Sharon

I had the smallest bedroom in our terraced house in south-west London. It was easy to understand why. Mum and Dad had to share a bedroom, so they had to have the biggest one, and even then it was not big enough for them to have a bed each; they had to share one. It's like tennis: a doubles team needs the bigger doubles court to play in. Sherah had the next biggest bedroom, obviously, as she was the oldest of we children and needed the space for her dolls, her old records and new CDs and her clothes; besides which, she was untidy and needed a big bedroom because how would she otherwise have found anything? Seamus, being the youngest and smallest of us, needed the next biggest bedroom so that he had the space to grow into, evidently.

I suspected that Sherah kept her better dolls for no other reason than she knew I wanted them. I had Sherah's old dolls, unloved by her and dirty from our having played in the garden with them. Hers, for the most part, were in national costume and remained in the cartons they had come in, lightweight cardboard coffins of which one or two sides were sheet plastic and arranged on two shelves of a bookcase. *Beautiful doll from Holland: doll can be undressed*, read one such box. I would have loved to undress Lieke but I never dared.

Sherah's bedroom door closed and with the palm of my hand pressed against it, heart beating quickly for fear that she might catch me in her room and the top of my head barely level with the light switch, I would stand at the end of the two rows of dolls and consider myself their equal. I was just another, bigger version of them in the international dress of a young girl: plimsolls, short skirt, T-shirt, hooded sweatshirt and ponytail. Like them, I was in suspension, waiting for someone to breathe life into me, to flick the switch that grated against the back of my head and spark me into existence, give me definition, a role, a drive. If I knew who I was, I would know what to do. I would stand quite still, unblinking, then, when I raised my head, my eyelids would fall, quite deliberately, just as Lieke's did. If I knew what others wanted me to do, I would know who to be. When I lowered my head, my eyes opened again.

I am, more often than not, up and down before anyone else. I empty the dishwasher and lay the breakfast table.

'Who else ever lays the breakfast table?' asks Sherah. 'Where on earth did you get the idea to do that from?'

'From an American soap on TV, I bet,' says Dad from behind his newspaper.

'Well, if you're going to do it, do it properly,' says Sherah, waving a spoon at me. 'You know I don't like these round soup spoons – ever – I only ever want to use the dessert spoons, even for my cereals. Go on, get me the right spoon.' Sherah throws the round soup spoon at me that I fail to catch. 'Clumsy clot!'

'Sherah.' Mum's not a great talker first thing in the mornings.

'No! Don't put it back in the drawer,' says Sherah. 'It's been on the floor. Put it in the dishwasher.'

'I wasn't going to,' I protest.

'While you're up, Sharon, put some toast in the toaster for me, will you, please,' says Mum.

'For me too,' demands Seamus, without looking up from his colouring-in and join-the-dots books.

'It's not toast that you put in the toaster,' says Dad, still obscured by his newspaper. 'It's bread. Toast is what you take out of the toaster. If you've remembered to push the thingy down, that is.'

'Funny bloke,' says Mum.

Dad reads the sports section of the newspaper first, then the business pages, then the obituaries, then the op eds, as he calls them, and the news only last. 'The news is always the same even when it's different,' is what we hear him say to anyone who cares to listen. He seems proud of the fact that he doesn't read the same newspaper consistently and says to anyone who is still listening, 'A man should choose his newspaper like he chooses his friends, in order to challenge him in his opinions rather than to confirm his prejudices.'

'But you've got no friends,' said Mum once, to which Dad just smiled.

For years I thought that my family consisted of me, my brother, my sister, my mother and a newspaper on legs. At the end of one term I went with my primary school to see a play. When the curtain rose, the audience was presented with a domestic scene I recognised immediately: a round pine table set for breakfast, at which was seated to one side behind a broadsheet newspaper a man, whose outstretched, ankle-crossed legs and newspaper-gripping knuckles alone were visible. I knew him at once and stood and shouted, 'That's Daddy!' Everyone laughed and many children turned their heads and looked at me appreciatively. When the man eventually lowered his arms I saw that it wasn't Dad, just someone pretending to be him, but I was pleased that I had entertained others and, thinking about this, I missed much of the first half of the play. I missed much of the second, too, as it dawned on me then that there were people inhabiting other people's skins and the realisation of this thrilled me. When the actors took their bow, adults and children alike on their feet and clapping enthusiastically, I felt a mix of admiration and, I had to admit to myself, acute jealousy.

When Mum came to pick me up, a teacher recounted the story to her and my Mum laughed and patted me, and when Mum told the story to Dad, I stood by his side proudly, smiling in anticipation of his approval and laughter. The palm of Dad's hand came down across my cheek and mouth casually, not forcefully yet firmly, painful only for its being so unforeseen, in what he called his forehand. 'Don't ever make a joke at my expense again,' he said quietly, almost indifferently.

Mum hissed at him and pressed me to her. 'Honestly!' She stroked my hair.

Dad backed off and, keeping his eyes on Mum, held his hands up in apology.

I lined my dolls up by the fireplace and re-enacted the play – well, my version of it; I was as taken with my actors' costume changes and the colour combinations of their clothes as with the story. 'You naughty girl!' said one doll to another and he hit her in the face. A sudden chill descended like a stage curtain and I looked up to see Dad staring down at me from above his newspaper in horror.

Dad's unfinished face resembled the papier-mâché heads children make at school, while Seamus and Sherah already looked the finished article. Dad's chin was like a roll of plasticine that, attached, had yet to be flattened and shaped and his nose was like a blob of clay, the maker of which had been called off to playtime before addressing its contours with a palette knife. I imagined that while Dad kept his newspaper up, some force was at work finishing his features and, every time he lowered it, I anticipated the change that never came. My sister's and brother's hair was dark and wiry like his; mine was blond and straight like my mother's. Standing in front of the full length mirror on the inside of my parents' wardrobe door, I would reflect on a friendly-looking, green-eyed girl of perfectly average build and shape who, I would think, was the real, fuller me. Our fingers would touch, first one hand, then the other, and she would stay on her side of the mirror neither inviting me in nor refuting me, just smiling back at me, solid, complete and self-possessed in a way in which I wasn't.

If Dad caught me standing there, he would say, 'Admiring yourself again?' Or, 'Have you got nothing better to do?' Or, 'Get your own mirror.' Once, though, I saw him looking at me, not at me but at the girl in the mirror, as though she was someone else, and I took my hand away from hers and he took his eyes away from her and left the room without saying anything.

Mum, if Dad wasn't around, would come up behind me, place her hands on my shoulders and plant a kiss on my crown and I would lean gently back into her while I placed my hands on hers and looked at my larger twin in the mirror.

'Mum, why don't I look like Dad?'

'Don't be silly, of course you do!'

'But I don't!' I thought she was joking.

'You do.'

'Sherah and Seamus don't think so.'

'You do.' Mum gripped my shoulders.

Isabella

Eleanor and Deborah live two doors from us. Deborah is my age and Eleanor two years older. They look like twins even though Eleanor is fair and Deborah dark; they are of the same height and build, Deborah being that little bit tall and Eleanor short for their respective ages. They love visiting the 'butterfly house', as they call it; it's the only thing that can compete with their dolls for their attention. I am proud to show it to them, along with my father at his best: interested and interesting, kind and attentive, patient and tolerant in a way that Mama and I rarely witness. Mama is so anxious about saying the wrong thing – of confusing insect orders and butterfly species with families, of muddling larvae and caterpillars with pupae and chrysalises – that she no longer visits the pavilion.

Papa drops to his knees in an eerily precise visual echo of Uncle James' genuflections and places his arms caringly around Eleanor's and Deborah's shoulders, their three pairs of eyes immediately level with the two rows of wooden-framed breeding cages, flower pot cages and flower pots that run the length of the greenhouse on trestle tables. Above them, black netting cylindrical cages hang along the middle of the greenhouse. Butterfly nets and bait traps, collecting boxes, tubes and other types of container, an assortment of magnifying lenses in their steel and brass swivelling cases, store boxes and display cases, killing jars and setting boards are ordered tidily in the shed end, in which garden tools are consigned to the one, dark corner. An old bathroom cabinet, long relegated from the house, contains boxes of pins, field reference books and bottles of ethyl acetate, isopropyl alcohol, ethylene glycol, relaxing fluid and wing repair cement. The door that permits access to the shed from the conservatory is kept open by one leg of a pine armchair that belongs to the set in the kitchen and that Papa sits on when consulting his books or admiring his butterflies or – on those occasions when I mistakenly stray to the far end of the garden, emulating Mama, poorly – bouncing me up and down on a lean lap in an activity that, I am certain, gives him more pleasure than it does me.

Still squatting, Papa directs Eleanor's and Deborah's attention to a flowerpot cage crowded with pale pink flowers on slender, upright stems that shove against the fine nylon netting that forms the cage.

'Look closely,' he says. 'Can you see?' He has in one hand the stork-bill forceps with which he handles larvae and he uses them to point to tiny orange and grey orange-tip eggs and the pale green, near-translucent orange-tip larvae, no longer than a fingernail, on the stalks of the cuckooflower. Deborah is momentarily distracted from looking closely by the conjoined end of the forceps that Papa, trembling in his enthusiasm, waves close to her eye. Eleanor, though, is transfixed and leans forward so that her fair hair escapes from behind her shoulders and so that, for her better to see, Papa must raise his hand from the small of her back and with one hooked finger lift her lock of hair from her field of vision and tuck it behind her ear. He lowers his hand and, cupping her bottom, heedful that she not stumble and fall, continues, 'See? See these caterpillars?' He indulges my friends by using the more familiar terminology, as he does me by sticking to butterflies' English names, as his father did with him. 'These caterpillars came from eggs just like that, and do you know what the first thing they did was when they hatched? They ate the eggs they hatched from.'

Neither Eleanor nor Deborah appear impressed by this, but lift the dolls they carry in each hand so that they too can observe the eggs and caterpillars. 'Then they eat and eat and eat until they're about' – and, here, Papa places the forceps on the trestle table and holds his thumb and forefinger apart as far as he can – 'about this long and then' – and, here, he stands and looks about him and leads my friends by the hand to a wooden-framed breeding cage in which, I know, painted lady pupae, inch-long knobbly brown sacs, hang from nettle and thistle stalks – 'and then they will form a chrysalis much like this! And then,' says Papa, raising his voice, fearing he'll lose Eleanor's and Deborah's attention in front of the plain, unattractive contents of this particularly dull breeding cage, 'and then, these, these chrysalises turn into but-terflies!' Papa waves his arms to take in his pavilion, the butterflies in the hanging cages and those without who beat their wings against the bigger glass cage until they either make their escape by means of the roof or side vents or door or fall exhausted to join their predecessors on the beaten earth greenhouse floor. 'Look,' he says. 'Just put your hands out. Let's see if you can get a butterfly to land on your hand.'

'I don't want to,' says Deborah, both hands and clutched dolls behind her back while she shuffles butterfly corpses with one sandaled foot.

Papa drops to one knee and encircles Eleanor's waist with one arm while, with his free hand, he holds her arm outstretched, the palm of her open hand up, having forfeited one of her dolls to him. 'This one's a large white,' he says, indicating a mainly white-winged butterfly with black markings that flutters close and then far and, pointing to a pale yellow one that alights on the outer side of a near hanging cage, 'and this one's a brimstone.'

But the butterflies appear uninterested, much as bored and unco-operative zoo and circus animals sometimes do, and drift languidly on light breezes that carry them either out of the greenhouse and away, or to the bowls of rotting fruit and vegetable peelings my father leaves out for them to feed on and that fill the greenhouse with a sickly sweet and heady odour. Eleanor lowers her unrewarded hand and what small hold my father had on the girls is lost, but he doesn't give up without a last try. 'Look! Look here!' he cries breathlessly, and his excitement sounds genuine, even to me. 'This one's a red admiral and – look! – he's feeding!' We peer closely at a dish of rotting rhubarb and other food waste and watch the brown-, orange- and black-winged butterfly unfurl and furl his proboscis in search of sugar. The proboscis resembles an obscene, inverse beckoning finger that summons us closer, closer, until our heads touch. The heat of the greenhouse, the butterfly's sinister probing procedure and the cloying, fetid smell of the fermenting sugars become all too much.

'Yuk!' exclaims Deborah, standing and shaking her head as though to clear it.

We all stand too.

'Let's go and play with our dolls!' suggests Eleanor, and Deborah and I follow her, running into the garden, leaving Papa alone in his pavilion with one of Eleanor's dolls, looking after us with longing, absent-mindedly brushing the doll's hair and pleating its skirt with his fingers.

Mie

Keiko, Michi and I go on our *tsuugakuro*, our walk to and from school together, along a strictly established and well-rehearsed route, with me in the middle. I think that Keiko and Michi conspire, whether subconsciously or consciously, to have us walk this way because their walking side by side would only emphasise the unusual skinniness of the one and the dumpiness of the other. Such is the pressure to conform – in body shape as in everything – that I can't help but think that they resent me for my not so much perfect as average figure. In the mornings, we school children form tributaries: at the end of our street, Keiko, Michi and I become seven, then fifteen at the next crossroads until we converge on school in waves of identikit, uniform school children.

On one occasion, I catch sight of us in the glass floor-to-ceiling windows of the modern school hall and can't find myself among the hundreds of sunlit children reflected in its mirrored surface. No matter how hard I look, I am nowhere; the harder I look, I am everywhere. Girls in green pleated skirts and white blouses with green collars and big red Girl Guides' knots below the throat. Girls with white socks and brown polished leather shoes, with school bags over their shoulders – straps over both shoulders, never just one – and with two red bows in two ponytails. I have disappeared, drowned in a sea of uniformity, and sit down to my first class of the day with red eyes and barely dry cheeks.

I share the horror of the morning with my mother in whom I recognise a fellow spirit. She had studied French and even lived in Paris before, and was heavily influenced by Europe's spirit of revolution and individualism that blossomed in the 1960s, exercising her independence of mind by marrying for love and so, incidentally, to the shocked fury of my maternal grandparents, marrying beneath her.

'She broke the traces of convention and hurdled the fences of class divide only to prepare *basashi*,' quipped my father, who forewent the university education he so much wanted in order to assume the family business and to follow his father's exhortation that he must know and keep his place.

'If I had loved you less selfishly I wouldn't have married you,' I hear him say to my mother, as the distance between her and her parents grows and the silences between them extend to months. Where other parents press their children to conform to norms and consider any expression of individualism a terrifying eccentricity, mine revel in personality. They invest me with purpose and reinforce my sense of uniqueness while being careful to instruct me to conceal its manifestation outside of the home. My mother ties one ponytail with a blue ribbon the following morning in a calculated risk.

'That was my idea,' states my father proudly as he unlocks the shop door to let me out and the day's early deliveries in. 'Now, you need only look for the blue-ribboned girl in the reflection!'

Keiko and Michi disclose what that their parents say over dinner in what seems to me to be an assumption that the bonds between friends are greater than family ties. I'm surprised to hear from Michi that her parents consider my father a poor businessman – he extends credit too frequently and is too ready to make a gift of a rasher or offal to regular customers. I guess that at the heart of their criticism of my father lies his carefree and careless approach to the card game bridge that my mother learnt while a student in Paris, and that Michi's and my parents play together once a month. Occasionally, when one parent is temporarily indisposed, I am asked to make up a four, but I bridle at the thought of being the dummy, and Michi's parents struggle to hide their irritation and contempt when my father or mother – for whom bridge is just that, an aspirational bridge to the West – laughing and impervious to any ill feeling, look at my cards in order to assist me and still manage to lose. I can just picture Michi's parents shaking their heads over their soup as they express a fear that my father may not be in business long. This criticism is couched in terms of concern. Michi asked them, if my parents could ever no longer afford to keep me, if I could live with them; to which they'd replied that of course I could. However kind the sentiment, it irks me. I imagine myself in Michi's bedroom looking across into mine and seeing the new girl who has moved in who, to my mind's eye, looks just like me. Impossible! I shake my head to clear the picture. Keiko's parents apparently consider my mother aloof. Both Keiko's and Michi's parents consider mine irresponsible for not having fixed bars across my bedroom window, as they have across their daughters'.

Keiko and Michi, unable to lean out of their windows, communicate over the fence that separates their yards or by means of taps on their adjoining bedroom wall, for which they have developed a code. Occasionally, on a walk to or from school, they'll use it – ever so briefly out of consideration to me, I'm sure; but I feel excluded nevertheless. 'Tap. Tap, tap, tap,' one will say and both will giggle, and I set my face in a smile and refuse to ask them to share their code with me and they never offer to. Of course, on warm and sunny days they can talk from open window to open window, but without seeing each other until it occurs to them to borrow their mothers' vanity mirrors. Arms extended through the bars, they angle the mirrors to look at each other and up and down the street. I wave and look upon their intimacy enviously.

On one occasion, Keiko and Michi conspire to angle their mirrors so the sun is reflected directly onto me, onto my face and into my eyes. It's truly blinding and I am beaten back from my window. We don't mention this on our way to school the following day, but my pride is such that I allow a small rift to form between my friends and me that takes a term and its following holiday to heal.

Isabella

'Bridget,' says Papa, who likes to arrive early at church, 'hurry up. We risk being late.' He never calls Mama by her proper, German name but by its English form. Church, for us, is St Michael and All Angels. I sit on a pew with Mama to my left and Eleanor and Deborah to my right and we kneel, stand, sit and sing as instructed. The service over, Eleanor, Deborah and I play in the church gardens while Mama and Mrs Baldock talk. Mrs Baldock is probably my mother's best friend. I consider her forgiving and non-judgemental, as she never raises her voice and she addresses her children and me equally. Forgetting himself on occasion, Papa dismisses Mrs Baldock as, 'Too alternative. She's a hippy.' He does a passable imitation of her breathy manner of speaking. '"Hi. I'm Samantha but you can call me Sammy." The way she dresses! And what she's doing bringing up those girls on her own, I don't know. God knows what she's doing in church.'

To this, Mama's reply is, 'He probably does.'

Papa's look of irritation is brief as he stops himself in time from saying something irrevocably divisive and says instead, 'Of course, of course. Live and let live and all that. And the girls are such good friends to Isabella. No, keep it up, keep it up. Don't stop them coming around, whatever you do.'

While Mama chats and I play, Papa ingratiates himself with the vicar and the rest of the church community who have heard all about Papa's theology degree and his father's sermons and who cannot fail to be happy to count this Oxford don as one of theirs. The vicar struggles to hide his irritation when my father, taking a stand by the church door, greets or bids farewell to members of the vicar's congregation as though they were his.

We walk home along pavements just wide enough to accommodate Mrs Baldock, Mama and Papa side by side and, some distance behind, Eleanor, Deborah and me. Mama and I are in the middle of our respective rows of Sunday strollers. I cease hearing how Eleanor and Deborah intend to spend their afternoon and focus, instead, involuntarily, on Mama's bottom and waist, struck, first, by the grace of her movement and the natural, pleasing rhythm of her gait and, second, by her size. Next to Mrs Baldock, whose height and slendour – she is indeed splendid and slender – are emphasised by a caftan both elegant and brightly coloured, and next to Papa, whose stature and slim build is accentuated by a brown corduroy suit that is too small for him – the green of his shirt cuffs flashing (as he swings his arms) and the red of his socks blazing (as he raises a heel in preparation for the coming long step) contradictory signals of encouragement and warning – next to them, Mama appears fat. My immediate thought that I would like to see Mama dance is followed by the fear that Eleanor and Deborah might have made the same observation about her girth to themselves and then, all of a sudden, with a rush, as though hurtling at great speed, I am pulled away from myself and back to where I walked only ten seconds earlier and I experience the giddying ability to see myself from behind, sandwiched between my friends, both of whom clutch dolls and one of whom, Deborah, has me by the arm. I am so taken by the extraordinary novelty of this sensation, of this precipitous, unforeseen power, that I note only dispassionately that I am indeed wider around the waist than my friends (and, in partial compensation, a head taller) but take excessive pleasure from the symmetry of our two consecutive rows and of the spatial and temporal reverberation I form of my mother. I acquire a sense of my history for the first time, one so strong I can taste it, like a *Zwetschgenkuchen* that fills the mouth with plums, cinnamon, sugar and cream while sparking the mind and sickening the heart; a sense of ownership of my past, one that is mine and yet transcends my body, persisting as it does through my antecessors; a belief that I also have a future that, while I have first use of it, will belong to my progeny too; and, strongest of all, a sense of the present, the undeniable being of it, its perpetual death and renewal, that, somehow, however temporarily, I am a spectator of and not a participant in. I have a heightened awareness of the quality of light and of birdsong, of passing traffic and of domestic noises that waft from open windows and doors but am deaf to Eleanor's and Deborah's chatter. Eleanor nudges me in the side and, with that, I am instantly propelled forward and into myself and back in the moment, formulating my embarrassed apology to Eleanor who has stated petulantly and rightly, 'You're not listening!'

I attempted to follow the sisters' conversation but was distracted most by, of all the thoughts I had succumbed to in that short walk home, my first conscious self-image, by the fact that I had had it and by what it was. I deduced I must have had a subconscious one previously because this new, unbidden one, this image of a large girl, didn't fit with whatever image had preceded it. While not so much displeasing as unexpected, I had to admit the picture was more distasteful to me than appetising and I decided to put it to the back of my mind like a sherbet lemon sweet to the back of my mouth, for later exploration and consumption. It occurred to me for the first time that I could eat less cake and fewer sweets and this idea, the idea that I could quite literally shape myself should I want to, coming as it did on top of the day's other revelations, was too rich with potential for me. I slipped my free arm through Eleanor's, skipped so as to get in step with the sisters, and asked them what we were going to play that afternoon.

Mrs Baldock and Mama had pulled the kitchen chairs out onto the patio and sat on them heavily, as though weighed down by the heat, their dresses pulled up to their thighs and Mrs Baldock with her caftan's sleeves pushed up over her elbows. The doors to Mama's room were open onto the patio and reflected Mrs Baldock and Mama from the side and the back so that, at first glance, the patio seemed crowded with seated figures perceived from different angles and, at a second, brought to mind the Picasso prints in Mama's room. Butterflies and other flying insects, Eleanor, Deborah and I made our way in and out of the garden, in which our dolls had paused on their walk home from church, and in and out of the room in which cake, lemonade and tea were collected on the coffee table. Papa's jacket and tie hung over the back of one chair. Mama indicated Papa at the far end of the garden who, in his green shirt and brown trousers, couldn't have been better camouflaged, and to whom Mrs Baldock had said, 'If it isn't Robin Hood!', much to his ill-concealed annoyance.

'Would you mind,' requested Mama, 'asking Papa if he would like another cup of tea?' At which all three of us – Eleanor, Deborah and

I – raced to the end of the garden, each in the hope of getting there first but each attempting to run nonchalantly so as to make it appear, if arriving second or last, that one hadn't been racing at all.

'I won,' said Eleanor, flashing Papa a knowing, cocky smile.

I asked, 'Would you like some more tea?' first, to which Papa didn't reply but beckoned us follow him into the greenhouse and to the flowerpot cage he had shown us the last time the sisters had been visiting. Papa crouched to bring his eyes level with it, and Eleanor, Deborah and I stooped, hands on knees, our faces just inches from the cage's fine mesh. The cuckooflower flowers had been consumed and the stalks formed an abstract geometric pattern interrupted at multiple places in organic convulsions by the purple-tip larvae that had indeed, as Papa had said they would, grown into long, lithe, green-hued caterpillars. The four of us observed them in silence a moment, but then I noticed that Papa's attention had switched to Eleanor and I watched him watching her. It was hotter in the greenhouse than out, despite the open vents and door. The beads of perspiration on Papa's upper lip resembled caterpillars' abdominal and thoracic segments. They vanished with each slight smile as they met and merged and broke with surface tension and as sweat trickled from Papa's forehead and down his nose and cheeks. With a folded handkerchief, he mopped his brow and eyebrows that he himself had once described as poplar grey larvae-like. Rings of perspiration formed around his armpits and spread to his chest and shoulders and to his shirt collar, where butterflies alighted, attracted by the serendipitous salt deposits. The caterpillars in the flower pot cage propelled their anal and rear abdominal segments forward and their front abdominal segments up by means of their stubby prolegs and then their thoracic segments forward and their front abdominal segments down by means of finer true legs, contracting and extending like organic accordions.

Deborah frowned. 'What's he doing?' she asked, jabbing with a finger and tucking her brown hair behind her ears so as to not impair her vision as she leant closer.

'He's pushing,' I said.

'He's kissing,' giggled Eleanor.

We looked more intently and I became abruptly aware of a profusion of kissing or pushing larvae, of the fact that they were all, if not kissing or pushing, being kissed or pushed.

'Actually,' said Papa casually, 'he's eating.'

Deborah's frown deepened.

'Eating,' repeated Eleanor.

'Yes. You see, when there's not enough food for them, when they run out of their favourite food, they'll have a nibble of anything and, funnily enough, because other caterpillars of the same family have eaten the same plant for food, they'll taste like it, like the plant, they'll taste like their favourite food, which makes it very unlikely that a caterpillar is even aware that he is eating, well, his own family. And, of course,' Papa went on, warming to the sound of his voice, 'there are advantages to this. At moments of food shortage, you not only acquire nourishment yourself but you eliminate the competition and address the problem of food scarcity at a blow.'

We looked closer yet. Our knowledge transformed what in our ignorance had been an assortment of dull plant stalks and slothful insects into a cannibal battlefield. One caterpillar, its back arched, was intent on chomping its way through another's midriff that had its head and tail end raised as though in pain and surrender. Another, in pulsing concertina, was consuming another from the tail end and yet another had raised itself on its prolegs to better assault another from above. One luckless caterpillar was being consumed from both ends at once. I shuddered.

I could see through the fine mesh of the cage that Deborah's eyes and mouth were open wide.

'But why don't you just give them more food?' asked Eleanor.

Papa smiled and shrugged, displacing a butterfly from the back of his neck as he did so. 'Well, it's more interesting this way, don't you think?'

Deborah stood straight and shrieked. 'Urgh! I think it's disgusting!' We watched her run out of the greenhouse and down the garden to her mother. I went from having been shocked, to intrigued, to sickened and to bored. Deborah had given me a chance, so I took it.

Crying, 'Me too!' I ran out, regretting the insincerity in my voice that, in poor imitation of Deborah's horror and indignation, sounded hollow, out of the stifling heat and down the cooler garden and into Mama's embrace, insisting she hug me and comfort me as Mrs Baldock did Deborah.

Momentarily, Deborah and I outdid each other in repetitions of how 'revolting' and 'disgusting' it had all been, but we tired of the game and went indoors to finish the lemonade, having assured Mama that Papa hadn't wanted any more tea.

From the cool sanctuary of Mama's room, I looked out past the patio where the two friends sat and down the length of the garden to the shed with the appended greenhouse and I drank my warm, sticky lemonade. At the same moment that it occurred to me that I could see neither Papa nor Eleanor in the greenhouse, I heard a cry, I registered Deborah's, Mama's and Mrs Baldock's heads swinging around and up and I saw Eleanor run out of the shed into the greenhouse, the length of it and, in turn, out into the garden, the length of it, and to her mother. Her distress, to my surprise, was greater than Deborah's and mine had been. She flung herself onto her mother, sobbing, her fair hair fanning out onto her mother's chest. Mrs Baldock smiled above her daughter's head at Mama as though to say, 'Impressionable young girls, hey!' and held her daughter with one arm while patting her back with her free hand.

In the doorway between the shed and the greenhouse, Papa appeared, or at least his shirt did, Papa's face flashing intermittently between the hanging breeding cages as he made his way down the greenhouse and to its door where, instead of stepping out, he stopped. Given the distance, it was hard to see the expression on his face. He waved, dispersing butterflies, and I was the only one to wave back and then he waved again but this time with what seemed like a shoebox in his hand and appeared to shrug his shoulders. 'Now, now,' said Ms Baldock. 'There, there. It's only caterpillars.'

'It's only caterpillars,' repeated Deborah. 'Come on,' she added in a grown-up's voice.

Eleanor lifted her face from her mother's chest, her own convulsing as she struggled for breath. She shook her head. 'It was. It was. Such a big caterpillar,' she said.

Mrs Baldock, who had been running her fingers through her daughter's hair, stayed her hand.

'He said, did I want to see a really big caterpillar? It was in a box. And he held the box in his lap. And he said, did I want to touch it? And it moved. It was horrible.' And Eleanor wailed and burrowed her face in her mother again.

Deborah stood behind her mother and placed a hand on her shoulder as if in gentle reminder that she was there too and Mrs Baldock covered it with her own, gently patting Eleanor's back with the other.

'You know,' said Mrs Baldock, 'I think we should be going.' She stood, laboriously, still holding Eleanor to her. 'Come on, girls. Get your dollies.' It had got to late afternoon; the south-west-facing patio was in shade. There was a cooling in the air and a chilling in Mrs Baldock's manner. She moved with the deliberation of someone reluctant to accept a new idea, as when the body has acknowledged it before the mind has. It was as though a smell had offended her and she wanted away from it without causing offence to the injuring party. Papa had stayed at the far end of the garden, his discarded jacket and tie his formal representatives at the house end of it, emphasising his absence. Mama didn't protest. She stayed seated and reached to squeeze Mrs Baldock's hand as she and her daughters made their own way out.

That was the day I lost a mother and gained a sibling – virtually speaking. It was the day Mama's eyes glassed over, much in the same way as a shop's shutters might be lowered and padlocked or a house's windows' curtains be drawn and front and back doors locked and bolted while the owners go on extended leave. It was the day she told me that that little lump wasn't lard but love, that soon I would have a little sister or brother for friendship and company. I could tell that Mama spoke with reservation, with apprehension in place of joy, fearful that the gift of apples she had brought her child might hide a snake.

'Mama,' I said and sought to turn her head towards me and force her face me.

'Yes,' she replied, removing my hand from her chin and placing both of my hands with hers on her tummy. 'You can't feel anything yet but you will be able to soon.'

Papa walked up. 'They've left,' he observed.

'Yes,' said Mama.

'You've told her,' he stated, looking at our hands on Mama's belly.

'Yes,' said Mama looking into the distance, unable to meet my eyes and unwilling to meet his.

Papa picked up his jacket and tie and walked into the house.

Sharon

Miss Crossbank stood on the dais at the front of the class like an actor on a minimalist stage, her blackboard, desk and chair her only props. Every day, another controlled improvisation, another captivating performance. A roll–call of interchangeable pupils' names but just one enduring, enviable actor.

We children considered Miss Crossbank old but I knew that Mum and Dad thought her young. She was the first adult whose dress I had noted: a buttoned cardigan, a knee-length skirt, flat shoes, hair in a bun and no make-up that I could detect. She radiated warmth, certainty, fairness, modesty. Through her, I recognised the power of dress: dress as communication, as armour, as shape, as projected persona.

When I reached the age at which I noticed breasts, I prayed to have discreetly sticky-out breasts like Mrs Crossbank's and not embarrassingly protuberant ones like Mum's.

Isabella

It was an evening in which Mama was out. She had protested weakly and clutched her distending stomach pointedly, but Papa had assured her that she would 'enjoy it very much'. Besides, he would be poor, nay, non-existent company for her: he had a meeting, the first of the new academic year, at which I could serve drinks and offer crisps around and listen quietly for an hour or so before making my own way to bed.

'A meeting,' had said Mama, not a little sceptically.

'A gathering, if you prefer,' had said Papa haughtily, conceding some ground.

'A soirée,' had said Mama mischievously.

'No, a gathering will do,' had said Papa coldly, decisively.

Papa drew the study curtains closed and switched the lights on: the desk lamp with a butterfly-embroidered shade, the built-in bookcase lamps and the overhead picture lights that illuminated not pictures but butterflies, the wings' shadows of which made the butterflies appear larger than they really were and highlighted them in surreal, funereal outline.

I was patted and petted by four men, three of whom I knew by sight, and who, I could tell, considered themselves Papa's equal by the volume of noise they were unafraid of making, by the relative familiarity they exhibited and by their occupation of the comfortable Chesterfield sofa and a spot by a wingback chair and the fire place. I was ignored by two startled postgraduate students who had clearly had no expectation of finding a six-year-old girl in attendance, and who gave themselves away as junior by directly assuming the two least comfortable chairs in Papa's study and by only taking crisps when offered them. Professor Rennet was the oldest of Papa's guests and held himself at a distance, examining the things on the mantelpiece that he had seen before, one by one, before turning to stand with his back to the fireplace and staring at me appraisingly. Behind him, my grandfather stared angrily out of the family photograph at Professor Rennet's back, his view of half of the room now obscured.

My grandfather seemed to regard Professor Rennet with disapproval, perhaps objecting to a goatee that did a poor job of disguising a long chin and swollen cheeks, to long, greasy hair swept back from a low forehead and to a pince-nez that Professor Rennet kept in a breast pocket with a handkerchief when he wasn't peering through it. As though unwilling to assume a seat before Professor Rennet, Papa stood by the mantelpiece too, one arm on a wingback chair, the other reaching occasionally for the glass of bitter he had placed on the mantelpiece, obscuring his wedding photograph.

'So, Dr Bicourt, you're a butterfly collector,' observed the new man, raising one hand languidly in the general direction of the butterfly display cases on the walls.

Papa smiled affably and delivered his stock reply: 'A lepidopterist, actually.'

Dr Dearman said, 'Brian, I should have warned you. Tell John he's a butterfly collector and he'll correct you with, "A lepidopterist, actually." Tell him he's a lepidopterist and he'll correct you with, "A…" – oh, what's the word? It sounds like a rhinoceros. But it isn't, obviously.' He waved his hand in the air in invitation to Papa to interpose, and drank some beer.

'A rhopalocerist,' said Papa contentedly, and continued to explain, as though to a child, 'I don't do moths. Only butterflies.'

'And – remind us – why's that?' asked Dr Dearman, while the students nodded as though the distinction were evident. Dr Dearman tugged at his waistcoat, a habit he resorted to in order to give his rhetorical questions added significance. His eyes, set so wide apart that a canopy of brown, bushy eyebrows failed to shelter their extreme corners, gave him a bovine look that was dispelled by a smile that was sinister for revealing only his canines. His aspect of a malevolent bull was only just more amusing than it was disquieting.

Papa shrugged. 'The thrill of the chase. In the case of moths, you set a trap in a field in the evening and go back to it in the morning. At least with butterflies you have to chase the damned things. And you get to be out and about on a sunny day.'

'First you chase them. And then you breed them. You breed them too, don't you, John?'

'I must admit,' said Papa, not answering the question, 'that the display cases in here aren't mine, but my father's. The smaller ones in the hallway are mine, as are others upstairs. I was going to assemble some more, but where to put them?'

'John,' said Dr Faben, who, sandwiched between Dr Dearman and Brian, had to lean forward with some effort every time he wanted to lift or rest his glass and had decided to hang onto it. 'On the way here I was trying to tell Brian why you maintain that philosophy stopped with Descartes.' Dr Faben wore large, thick-rimmed glasses that, slipping to the end of his nose with his every movement, were only arrested by a wart of sorts and a moustache, the ends of which collected the froth from his beer and that he would suck once his beer glass drained. His thin, colourless hair lent him a weedy, sneaky look.

'It began with Descartes,' interceded Dr Dearman, raising a finger. 'After all, he's not referred to as the father of philosophy for nothing.'

'But that's Plato,' said Brian.

'Tosh!' said Dr Dearman. 'John, the floor is yours.'

'Indeed it is!' said Papa, looking down at his carpet, his floor, and then up with a smile for everyone that lingered, just longest, for the professor. 'But let's ask Messrs Baden and Lewis. What do you think, gentleman? With whom did philosophy start and end?'

'Psht! It's no use asking them!' exclaimed Dr Dearman. 'They're bound to say, with Frege and Wittgenstein or some such nonsense.'

Messrs Baden and Lewis looked at each other and said, 'After you,' simultaneously.

Dr Dearman insisted, 'John, go on, you're the Greek authority.'

'The *Greeks* authority,' corrected Papa immodestly. 'The last time I checked, I was English.' He shifted on his feet and stood straighter. 'It's like this. Plato took us apart and Descartes put us together again.'

'Not forgetting a little help from God,' said the professor.

'And the pineal gland,' proposed Brian.

'Isn't there more to philosophy,' asked Mr Baden or Mr Lewis ever so tentatively, 'than the mind and body split?'

Emboldened by the moment's reflection his friend's question engendered, Mr Lewis or Mr Baden cleared his throat. 'I would say that logic tells us that one can't reach a conclusion from the one premise and that, consequently, the *cogito ergo sum* argument fails to satisfy.' He drained his glass. 'If indeed it is an argument,' he stated to the silent room.

'Carry on,' said Papa.

'It draws a conclusion from the one premise. A and B therefore C, all right. But A therefore B is a nonsense unless B is contained in or identical to A and vice versa, in which case what we have is a tautology and not an argument.'

'What did I tell you?' exclaimed Dr Dearman exultantly, jumping up and down in the sofa, to the extent that he could without spilling his beer. 'Are you Russell men?' he asked the young men aggressively.

My father raised his hand and addressed the young men equably. 'So, tell me, you see Descartes' problem – how would you reconcile the mind with the body?'

'I'm not sure I would want to separate the two in the first place,' said Mr Baden or Mr Lewis.

'Too late,' said Dr Dearman. 'Plato has already done so.'

'You remind me of the tourist who asks the way to Donegal and is told, "If I were you, I wouldn't start from here!"' sniggered Dr Faben, addressing the postgraduate student.

'Crisps,' said my father, looking at me. 'And beer, please.'

'Let's ask Isabella!' suggested Dr Dearman, as I rose to replenish the empty bowls.

I stood, pleased to be included in the conversation.

'Do you have a body?' Dr Dearman asked me very seriously, perched on the edge of the Chesterfield.

'Yes!' I replied, delighted at the ease with which I answered the question.

'And what a lovely little body it is,' remarked Dr Dearman, before adding hastily, 'And do you have a mind?'

'Yes, of course!' I giggled.

'And is it the same as your body?'

'No!' I found the line of questioning hilarious.

'There you have it,' said Dr Dearman, reclining with a handful of crisps and looking pointedly at the young men, who laughed loudest to show that they took this all in good humour.

Dead butterflies in display cases followed me from the front door, along the corridor and up the stairs all the way to my bedroom, the second room on the first–floor landing, after the bathroom. Then came an airing cupboard, Mama's and Papa's room and then, around the L in the landing, the spare room that was to be Gaia's, should my mother give birth to a girl, or Cosmo's, should she have a boy.

I looked dispassionately around my room to see what toys and books I could divest myself of and place in my sibling's bedroom as a welcome present to ease the transition from cosseting womb to, as yet, empty room. The whole thing – how the mind chose the body to carry it or how the body selected the mind to fit it – remained a mystery to me. I had dolls, of course, none of which I felt particularly attached to. It had occurred to me that I played with them not only to pass the time and to relieve boredom but because it was the thing that young girls were expected to do. I couldn't animate them in the way that Eleanor and Deborah could theirs. I could assign them names but I couldn't endow them with personalities and give them consistent characteristics. My dolls remained, for me, plastic or, occasionally, china or wooden mannequins with which I could acquire the taste for power and only briefly indulge in the illusion of control and reinforce learned habits of behaviour. Such was the conviction with which Eleanor and Deborah acted their dolls' lives out, however, that I would grow convinced that their dolls were in some way better and more alive than mine; and I would play with theirs only to realise, by the time Mrs Baldock told me it was time to return home, what I already knew – that their dolls were as inanimate as mine and that the charade I had manufactured with such appetite would fool me only while my suspension of disbelief held.

Eleanor and Deborah spoke to their dolls in exactly the same manner, in the same tone and with the same gentle admonishments, as those with which their mother spoke to them. Their dolls were all assigned throaty, gravelly voices, spoke slowly to one another and, when one had to tell the other off, did so in a voice heavy with disappointment. When I heard a new tone of voice or a grown-up's clever remark for the first time, I would store it mentally and try it out with my dolls at the first opportunity.

'Have some more crisps,' said the biggest doll in a circle of dolls on my bedroom floor, to no doll in particular.

'A, B, C, D and because E, F, G,' said a doll.

'Don't be silly!' scolded a second doll.

'Do you have a body?' asked a third.

'What are you playing, *Liebchen*?' enquired Mama gently. She stood contentedly in the doorway, leaning against the door jamb and cupping her bloated belly with both hands.

I smiled.

'Come.' Mama stretched out a hand. 'Come and keep me company. I'll tell you if the baby starts kicking and you'll be able to feel it. Come and read to me while I get dinner ready. I'm out again this evening and I won't see you after dinner.'

Things lose their detail and their colour at night. I fall asleep and wake to shades of grey.

My curtained window formed a black rectangle framed with a pale contour and a faint bisecting furrow where the curtains met. My dolls, books and clothes and the items of bedroom furniture they rested on were featureless two-dimensional ashen shapes distinguishable from each other by only the barest of outlines.

'Mama,' I said to the form above my bed, unsure if I were awake or dreaming.

'It's Papa,' said Papa, faceless in the absence of a strong light. 'Mama's gone out, remember?'

I must have been awake and fallen asleep again because I later woke distinctly, my legs cool and bare, exposed to the night air and a moist sheet. 'What is it, Papa?'

'Isabella,' said Papa's silhouette with a shaking voice, 'you've wet the bed.'

I thought again that I might be dreaming; I hadn't wet the bed in a very long time, not in years – in fact, maybe not at all: I had never had an accident that I could remember.

'You've been a very naughty girl,' scolded Papa, speaking hesitantly and slowly from a mouthless oval outline above me. His voice frightened me. I feared he might be right. I must have kicked my bed covers to one side of the bed and now lay still, aware of a damp sheet and of a nightie wet in patches, of moisture cooling my legs as it evaporated from them. Struggling to wake fully, I apologised repeatedly, 'I'm sorry, Papa, I'm sorry.'

'There, there,' said Papa, leaning over me to stroke my hair. 'You were asleep. You couldn't help it. But Mama will be upset.'

In reply, I could only turn and press my face to the pillow.

Papa tucked my hair behind an ear. 'I'll tell you what,' he said. 'I'll help you clean up and we won't breathe a word to Mama. Shall we do that, Isabella? Shall we do that?'

Not trusting myself to speak, grateful to Papa for his offer of assistance and complicity so as to spare my embarrassment before my dear mother, I nodded and wept into the pillow.

Papa leant further and fumbled for the switch to my bedside lamp, the light from which breathed warmth, colour and definition into my room. I saw Papa's empty beer glass on my chest of drawers, nestled between the legs of my big doll that sat upright, arms outstretched as though reaching for it. I saw Papa who had sat down beside me, his hands shaking despite being clasped firmly on one knee, his eyes wide and blinking in the light's sudden assault. He turned and, deliberately and ever so gently, he raised my bottom and pulled my nightie from under it, raised my arms, one by one, and pulled my nightie off over my head and, leaning, having turned it the right way out, lay it over the back of my chair. 'It will be dry by morning,' he said. Naked, the chill only a minor penance for my misdemeanour, I lay on my back, the tears trickling down either side of my face, wetting my ears, the back of my neck and my pillow. Tenderly, parting my legs, he cleaned me, thoroughly, lifting each leg and resting it on each of his shoulders in turn, softly with balls of cotton wool, meticulously, taking great care to dry, after, the parts he had cleaned before. 'There,' he said, 'there,' and stood, trembling, saying nothing more, as though not trusting himself to speak.

'I'm sorry,' I said, for the twin humiliations I had subjected him to of having to clean his daughter and of having to witness her humiliate herself, for the trouble I had put him to, for the imposition of a secret he could not share with his wife.

'Here,' said Papa, his voice choking a little so he repeated himself. 'Here, move to where it's a little less damp and make sure you pull the bedroom covers well back in the morning so the sheet can dry. These,' he said as he tucked the bed covers around my chin, 'have stayed dry, fortunately.'

I turned my pillow over so as to sleep on its dry side. 'I'm sorry, Papa,' I said, overcome with a desire to take refuge in sleep.

'Well,' said Papa, 'at least we've got you cleaned up.' He took his empty glass in one hand and reached for the light switch with the other. I was asleep before he had switched the light off.

Sharon

We were a sporty family. Mum and Dad had met on a charity run. Dad loved telling the story of their meeting. 'So, when I run, I always select someone who's going to be my pacemaker, you know, someone I'm going to overtake going into the last straight. So, I thought to myself, well, I'll happily follow that bum around five Ks! But, wouldn't you know it, try as I might, I just couldn't overtake her! And I thought, you know, if you can't beat 'em, join 'em, so here we are, joined at the hip! Well, in unholy matrimony, anyway!'

Mum was a runner and a tennis player. Dad had tried his hand at every sport and settled on squash and tennis. This allowed him to complain that the one messed up the other and bemoan the fact that his generation's sporting prowess had been handicapped by the transition from wooden to metal squash and tennis racquets. 'You grow up with one grip and then it's all change; you have to learn another.'

Sherah had a good eye for a ball, as Dad would put it; she was a hockey and a tennis player. As for Seamus, he was ball mad: irrespective of a ball's size or shape, he'd want to throw it, kick it or hit it.

'What sport will you want to do, Sharon?' asked Mum, when we were considering my transition from gym and rounders to other sports in the final year of my primary school.

'Rowing,' I replied.

'Rowing? Trust you,' said Dad. 'Always looking for a place to hide. What's wrong with tennis and hockey? There's nowhere to hide when it's one on one and nowhere to hide on a hockey pitch when you receive the ball.' He swung his arm in a poor imitation of forehands and backhands before bending his knees to wave an imaginary hockey stick around.

'Rowing and tennis,' I said.

'Do hockey and tennis instead,' insisted Dad, bored with make-believe hockey–ball dribbling. 'You can have Sherah's old hockey stick and kit – it'll save on buying new rowing gear. Besides, have you seen the time you'd have to get to the boathouses in the morning? There's no way I'm getting up that early to drive you there.'

On Saturday mornings we would play tennis on one of the municipal tennis courts on the other side of the railway line from where we lived. Dad would ask, 'Anyone for tennis?' I would never answer first because if it were just me, Dad would either find a reason to change his mind about playing – 'It looks like rain!' – or would play so aggressively against me that it would knock my confidence. However, if he needed a fourth, he'd cajole me into playing – 'Come on, Sharon! A little bit of rain never hurt anybody!'

I best liked the days when four of us wanted to play – they were typically sunny Saturday mornings in which the greens of the Astro-turf tennis courts and of the surrounding lawns and trees, the cries of tennis players and children in neighbouring playgrounds and the sound of passing District Line trains formed a shiny bubble in which we lost ourselves in pursuit of balls, victory, love and self-esteem. The last was hard to come by when we all five turned up, racquets swinging, as Dad, more often than not, would say, 'Okay, Sharon, you be ball girl.'

'But Dad!' I would remonstrate.

'Go on Sharon, be a sport.'

'But why does it always have to be me?'

'Seamus has got to get as good as you and Sherah's trying for the first team. She's got an important match coming up. Come on, think of others for a change.'

Dad had to be on the winning team, which he nearly always was so long as he played against Seamus rather than with him. As I grew older, I realised that Dad was neither as good as I had thought he was, nor as good as he'd pretended to be. When he started losing and saw that he was going to lose, his tactic would be to clown around so that he could claim he hadn't lost really, as he had only been having a bit of fun. This involved accidentally hitting the ball across several courts in all directions and then telling me off when I didn't fetch it quickly enough.

'No! Don't just chuck them at me! Stand feet together and put your hand with the ball up. Straight arms! Don't slouch! One bounce only. Come on, do it properly!'

After the first set, Mum would hand me her racquet and say, 'I'll sit the next one out,' and she'd wander over to the café to read a news-paper in the sun.

If Dad had lost the set, he'd say, 'Right! New teams! Let's start again.' If he'd won, he'd say, 'A substitution for the losing team – they must be feeling the pressure!'

On one occasion, Dad said, 'You three play, I'm going to join Mum for a coffee.' He slung his racquet over his shoulder and followed her.

Seamus practised cricket strokes with his tennis racquet.

'Stop messing about, Seamus,' said Sherah. 'Come on, let's have a game.'

'How can we have a game when there are only three of us?' asked Seamus.

'Easy,' replied Sherah. 'Come around here to my side. Right, so it's us against Sharon. That's only fair, isn't it, Sharon, as, on average, the two of us are your age?'

I supposed that it was.

'Right,' said Sherah. 'Sharon, we have to hit into the doubles court and you have to hit into the singles court, all right?'

I thought about this. 'Hold on,' I said. 'Shouldn't I be hitting into the doubles court?'

'No,' said Sherah, 'because there's only one of you, right, so you get to hit in the singles.'

'Yeah,' added Seamus, 'and there's two of us and when there's two you hit in the doubles.'

'Besides,' said Sherah, 'Seamus has never played singles before so he's never hit into a singles court.'

'There's something wrong about this,' I said in between games, panting.

'You're doing fine,' said Sherah, who had got something in her eye and had to keep turning away from me.

Isabella

The absence of a garden shed and conservatory at the far end of the Baldocks' garden made it appear longer than ours. Eleanor, Deborah and I were using the extra space to ferry their dolls from one imaginary world to another on the backs of two bicycles and a tricycle. A dolls' house by the dining room's French doors was Earth, a late-blooming Madame Alfred Carrière rose that was halfway down the garden (and that Mrs Baldock amused me by referring to as either 'Madame' or 'Alfred', depending on her mood) was Limbo and the cotoneaster evergreen hedge that marked the garden's far boundary and that still retained its red berries (that the sisters had been forbidden from eating for as long as I could remember) was Heaven. Eleanor had been learning about different religions at school and the game had been her idea. She stood by Heaven and admired the dolls at our feet. We had garlanded them with the rose's pale petals and had scattered red berries about the dolls; to me, they seemed no happier than on Earth.

'Mummy!' Eleanor had to shout.

Mrs Baldock, standing framed by the doorway to the garden, raised one hand to her brow in signal that she'd heard her daughter or, maybe, just to shield her eyes from the day's bright light.

'Do Catholics go to heaven?'

Mrs Baldock shouted, 'Yes!'

'I told you,' said Eleanor to Deborah.

'Mummy!' cried Deborah.

Mrs Baldock raised her other hand to provide shade for her eyes with both hands.

'Do prostitutes go to heaven, too?'

'Protestants, you idiot,' snorted Eleanor.

'Protestants!' shouted Mrs Baldock. 'Protestants!'

'Do they?'

'Yes!' came the reply.

'But they don't go to limbo,' said Eleanor decisively, as if ready to win that argument too.

Deborah opened and closed her mouth and thought for a moment before saying, as though casually just checking, 'So, we won't go to limbo?'

'No,' confirmed Eleanor and the three of us, she standing and Deborah and I squatting in shaded heaven, looked halfway down the garden to the sunlit, sparkling, creamy white-dotted rosebush that was limbo and that appeared more appealing and pleasant than both heaven and earth. 'Well,' she said, in an attempt to ameliorate our situation, 'it's only our souls that go to limbo, anyway.'

'How do you know if you have a soul?' asked Deborah quickly.

'Oh, that's easy,' I said brightly. 'It's when you, you know, you see yourself from the outside.' I faltered. I hadn't tried to explain this before and found myself trying to put an intuition to words for the first time. 'When you see yourself from the outside, it's your soul that's doing the seeing.' The dolls at our feet, it was clear to me, had no souls.

Eleanor and Deborah looked at me, then at each other and then back at me impassively or maybe a little forbearingly.

'I mean, how do you know if you have a body?' I added helpfully.

'That's silly!' said Deborah, laughing, and Eleanor joined her in her laughter and I joined them in theirs and we all delighted in the absurdity of my joke.

We cycled up and down the garden either clutching dolls in one hand while we steered our bikes, or filling the barrow attachment to Deborah's tricycle with them. Mrs Baldock, who had asked Eleanor if her curriculum included Buddhism, informed us gravely that she was contemplating conversion to it and encouraged us, in this game at least, to embrace the spirit of reincarnation lest the heaven-bound dolls leave earth unpopulated. While we turned this idea over in our minds, while we pretended to give this metaphysical notion serious consideration, when, I suspect, we had simply tired of the game or, at least, of the hejira from and back to earth and heaven, a butterfly flew by, doubly surprising for its appearance in the relative lateness of the year and for the speed at which it flew. It landed on the dolls' house and graced it momentarily with an unfolding and folding of its grey-brown hind wings and its black-spotted orange-brown forewings before disappearing over the garden fence.

Eleanor and Deborah looked at each other and then at their mother and said with one excited voice, 'Can we visit Isabella's butterfly house?' and looked from her to me slyly and, as their mother replied and they protested, increasingly knowingly.

'No,' said Mrs Baldock.

'Why not?' asked Eleanor.

'Mrs Bicourt is out and we don't want to disturb Professor Bicourt.'

'I don't think there are many butterflies left to see now,' I said.

'Oh, please!' begged Deborah.

'I don't really want to, anyway,' said Eleanor.

'Besides,' said Mrs Baldock, indicating the garden with a sweep of her loose-sleeved, colourful blouse and a thudding tinkling of wooden-beaded necklaces, 'look at your dolls out in the garden. You can't leave them in limbo for ever, you know.'

Mama picked me up on her way home. She didn't stop for tea, and frowned when Mrs Baldock told her I hadn't had a drink once that afternoon, not even of lemonade. She waddled slowly beside me, the two of us hand in hand, and told me that, while she would be out this evening for the last of her German conversation classes, she had no further commitments and she looked forward to the next few days and maybe even weeks with me, just me, before we'd be joined by my baby sister or brother, when family life would get even better.

Papa saw Mama to the taxi and instructed the driver to be solicitous of her. No sooner had he shut the front door after her than he said, 'Come on, my hostess!' which he considered a joke of sorts. 'My guests are asking after you.' We entered the study in single file, the space between the edge of the bookcase and one end of the Chester-field sofa being too small for two abreast, even though one of us was a slight girl.

Papa said, 'Will you offer the crisps?'

Professor Rennet said, 'Ah! The empiricist!' He took a crisp and then drank from his glass that he replaced to one side of the family photograph. Grandfather looked on approvingly.

Dr Dearman said, 'Isabella, you are the single best profferer of crisps ever!' and patted his lap so that I might sit on it and he empty the bowl of crisps while making piggy noises to amuse me.

'Dr Faben,' said Papa, 'has a glass that needs refreshing, I see.' I assisted Papa briskly and willingly, so eager was I to make up for the inexplicable increase in my embarrassing bed-wetting.

'Those pins,' observed Dr Faben, standing with a full glass in front of a butterfly display case to one side of Papa's desk, 'with which you crucify these poor creatures, they have no heads.'

'The butterflies have no heads?' exclaimed Dr Dearman, pretending, in order to amuse me, that he had misheard.

'Crucify? Hardly; impale, I think, would be more accurate,' offered Professor Rennet. He made a jabbing motion with his pince-nez.

'Mount, actually, is the term. Or pin,' said Papa authoritatively.

'They have no heads,' repeated Dr Faben and, in a swift succession of movements, he placed his glass on Papa's desk and lifted me up so that I too might see, his hands under my armpits; and then, with a second brusque hoist, I was sitting in the crook of his arm, his hand clasping my knees for stability and his other hand pointing indiscriminately at the butterfly display case.

'I know,' I said, a little angry at something so familiar being explained to me and yet anxious to humour my father's colleague.

'Minuten pins,' said Papa. 'Exactly. The intention is that they interfere as little as possible, visually, with the insect they pin.'

'So they have no distinguishable head, no added width.' Dr Faben trembled with the weight of me.

'Or their head is the width of their body.' Professor Rennet looked fiercely at Dr Faben.

'Now, that's interesting,' said Dr Dearman, flashing his canines and moving to the edge of his seat. 'Very.' He lowered his head and looked around the company and asked, 'Does it have any implication for the how-many-angels-can-fit-onto-the-head-of-a-pin argument?'

'Aha,' said Papa gravely.

'Remind me,' demanded Professor Rennet of Dr Dearman, still looking as fierce. 'What is the argument?'

'Well, well,' mumbled Dr Dearman, taken aback by Professor Rennet's withering look. 'It is, it is, well, it's just that, that question, how many angels can fit onto the head of a pin?'

'Actually,' said Papa, 'it's dance. Dance on the head of a pin.'

'A question is not an argument,' glowered Professor Rennet.

There was a moment's reflection in which Dr Dearman, Professor Rennet and Papa drained their beer glasses and Dr Faben, seeing this, put me down and did the same.

'Now what do *you* think?' said Dr Dearman, addressing me. I liked him for remembering to include me in their conversations, despite his eyes and his teeth. 'You're a little angel. How many of you could we fit onto the head of a pin?' he asked, ignoring Papa's correction.

'I can't fit onto a pin!' I replied incredulously. Really, Dr Dearman was just too funny.

'Of course, of course,' said Dr Dearman, allowing himself to fall back into the depths of the Chesterfield. 'What can I have been thinking?'

'These butterflies,' said Dr Faben, who had remained standing by the display case and who was examining the butterflies it contained very closely, 'are very much like angels. Fallen angels.'

I dreaded falling asleep as much as having to drink. Not only recognising that I had to drink but desperate to quench my thirst at times, I rationalised that I should consume all the water I could in the mornings and none in the afternoons and evenings, so that I might have passed it all by bedtime. Sleep was a different matter. I couldn't sleep during the day, tired though I was for having fought sleep during the night. My sentiments with regards to Papa were mixed. As grateful as I was to him for his not having revealed my dirty secret to Mama, I couldn't help but resent his having shared it with his friends. He had on more than one occasion had Dr Dearman watch or assist him as he'd cleaned and dried me, their downstairs conversation – save for the occasional pithy but not unsympathetic comment about my predicament from Dr Dearman – carrying on in my bedroom, as though nothing were more natural than his presence by my bedside. 'Dr Dearman is simply keeping me company,' had whispered Papa by way of explanation for his breach of my trust, while I lay with my legs parted and my eyes open only enough to register my bedside light reflecting off the white of Dr Dearman's nearest eye and protruding side tooth while he sat on the wicker chair in the recess between the window and the chest of drawers. When he moved in it, I feared he'd break it.

Papa always entered my room with a drink in his hand. If I was awake, he'd raise the glass to his lips and whisper, 'Sweet dreams!' If I awoke to his ministrations, I'd see the empty glass on the chest of drawers, always just out of reach of my doll's clutches.

I lay on my back feigning sleep as Papa dried me. It saved his and my embarrassment that way. I must have actually fallen asleep because I woke with a start to light from the landing and Mama's grotesque, bulging silhouette in the doorway to my room. Lit directly from behind by the hallway's hanging light bulb, her phosphorescent hair lent her an otherworldly look. She appeared in outline, a warrior in a golden helmet carrying a large shield before her, a *Valkyrie* come to my aid. My relief at my finally being able to share my shame with my mother was as great as the shame itself. Mama looked from me to Papa who handed me my nightie and helped me tug it over my head and down. He pulled my bed covers over me and made a show of gathering wipes, tissues and cotton balls that he held up by way of explanation to Mama who shook her head unceasingly and who, I could see as my eyes grew accustomed to the light, was pulling hard, up, on her distended stomach with both hands.

'*Mein Gott!*' Mama had found her voice. 'What on earth is going on?'

Papa huffed, 'Well, we hadn't wanted to tell you – had we, Isabella? – so as not to worry you but' – and his voice dropped a register – 'Isabella has been wetting the bed.' He bent his head and sent me a look as if in apology for having our secret forced from him.

'*Unsinn!*'

'Oh, she has!' said Papa defensively, but not altogether convincingly.

'Nonsense!' There was pain in Mama's voice.

Papa attempted to invest his voice with some authority. 'It's a well-known thing, you know. Attention-seeking first-born resents the intrusion of the younger sibling into the family nest and all that.'

'Yes. *After* the younger sibling is born. Not before!' Mama's voice quivered and rose while she teetered and slumped, steadying herself against the doorjamb. 'Get out.'

Papa protested ineffectively.

'Get out! Get out!' Mama made no attempt to get out of Papa's way so, having switched my bedside light off, he had to squeeze sideways around her, the hand that carried the tissues and wipes held high at her eye level either to make a point or to distract her from the other hand, held by his side, that carried his empty glass. Mama made as though to step into my room and then groaned and leant against my bedroom door.

'I must lie down,' she said, as if to herself, and then, more loudly, 'Are you alright, *Liebchen?*' She managed a smile. 'Don't worry. I'll see you tomorrow.'

With some effort, she pushed herself off the door jamb and staggered her way to her bedroom without once having seen Dr Dearman seated in my wicker chair, nervous grin at the ready with, no doubt, a convincing reason for his presence in my bedroom should one have been needed. An eye and a tooth winked at me, in pale reflection of the landing light. I closed my eyes in the hope that when I opened them again Dr Dearman would be gone and when I did, in the morning, he was.

Mama was rushed to hospital in an ambulance.

Papa and I followed by bus.

A doctor knelt to look me in the eyes and said, holding my hands in his, 'Don't worry about Mummy. She's going to be all right. And – who knows? – she might even have a gift of a baby sister or brother for you tomorrow.' There was something reassuring in his manner, in his white coat, in the parade of coloured pen tops that lined his breast pocket. I wished Uncle James were with us. The doctor placed one hand on my shoulder, in part as a pat and in part to steady himself as he stood and said to Papa, 'She'll be fine. False starts are frequent. It's back to the starting line and on your marks all over again. Still, best to keep her in. We'll keep her under observation. She's clearly a bit stressed. The second should be easier than the first. We'll expect you tomorrow morning and will call with news if we have any.'

Papa appeared preoccupied. He held my hand across the road and didn't let go. He walked us to the bus stop and past it without stopping. Halfway home, he paused, as if only then realising we'd had a bus to catch, and shrugged and we carried on, still hand in hand. Mama and I would play a game in which we held one hand high, above our heads, and the other one low, by our knees, and then compared them to see which hands had lost and gained the most blood, which were the paler and the redder. Mama would say that I won because I had the best circulation and, indeed, the contrast between the colours of my hands was the greatest, as one would appear to have been drained of blood and the other dark red with it. To Papa's irritation, I insisted on swapping hands with some regularity as we walked in order to ensure my hands benefited from an even blood supply, an explanation that he found more aggravating than informative.

At times, as we threaded our way along residential streets, our steps the sutures that stitch our selves to the towns and cities of our past and present, it felt to me as though I were leading him rather than he me and, at others, I had the sensation that no one else existed other than the two of us; and, yet, the most persistent though faintest of feelings I had was the one of my being alone as I watched, from some distance behind, a father and a daughter walking along a pavement that became a path in a wood that became a tunnel in which only they were lit, that became a vast sky at night in which the stars were, at close inspection, not stars after all but butterflies. I looked at Papa, certain that if he was seeing what I saw, it would be reflected on his face in smiles and joy but, if he were, he gave no indication of it.

Papa said little all afternoon and spent most of it in his study, occasionally popping his head into the kitchen where, glad of the warmth, I read, did my homework and made 'Welcome Home' cards for Mama and a baby. Papa made me tea, as he called it, or supper, as Mama called it, and told me not to worry. He, too, noted that I drank little, but then occupied himself with encouraging me to look forward to having a baby in the house, not in the spirit of family love and affection that so clearly filled Mama, but as a parental reflex, as though he had hit upon this notion as being something a parent should promote. Papa's newfound concern was touching and trying in equal measure. Really, what did adults fear? That older children would eat their baby siblings? My mind, as Papa and I sat across the kitchen table from each other, kept drifting from what he was saying. It occurred to me that I had never heard him talk so much with me as his only audience, and then that he was doing so to mask his anxiety, his concern and love for his wife and as yet unborn child. This moved me, and he mistook my tears for tiredness; and all of a sudden I was tired. With a voice that quivered with what I assumed was the repression of a yawn, Papa suggested bed. He supervised my brushing of my teeth, my getting undressed and dressed for bed and, having run his trembling hands through my hair, he rested one on my bedroom light switch a moment and wished me a good night.

My first thought on waking was that Papa must have finally lost his patience. He was being rough with me. Having removed my nightie to better clean me, he turned me over and pulled me down the bed, neither of which he had ever done before. My second was that his shushing me in response to my mumbled, repeated apology was quite unnecessary: there was, after all, no one in the house for us to disturb. My third was that the bed wasn't wet. I felt all over it for a wet patch and couldn't find one and went from begging forgiveness in a half-waking state to attempting to inform Papa of his error, but too much was happening for me to find the words to do so. A multitude of thoughts then came and went indiscriminately. I considered my pillow, out of my arms' reach at the very top of the bed and reflected that that was a very pointless place for it when my head was halfway down the bed. I couldn't understand how Papa could hope to clean me in this way. Having pulled me well away from my pillow, he was attempting to push me to it while preventing me from reaching it, an unusual form of punishment for my misdemeanour. With every push, he pressed down with one hand on the small of my back and pulled my bunched hair with the other. I wanted to tell him to stop pulling my hair, to stop either pushing or pinning me down. Papa's hands on the small of my back hurt. His entire weight seemed to be concentrated there. The tops of my feet rubbing on the carpet at the foot of my bed hurt. Feeling the carpet with the tops rather than the soles of my feet was confirmation that something was wrong. If I lifted my feet, my legs hurt. The bed headboard banged against the wall in metronomic keeping with Papa's pushing. I wanted to apologise to Papa but had lost the power of speech; I had to concentrate all my energy onto holding onto the bed covers. I felt that it wouldn't do to fall off the bed, that I would be letting Papa down even more if I fell. I wanted to comfort him, to let him know of the tremendous guilt I felt at having driven him to such levels of voiceless, panting desperation, to let him know that I knew that I deserved my punishment fully. And, yet, to beg him to stop, to stop, please stop. The weight of him on his hands on my back. I lost all sensation below that point. He pushed. The caterpillars pushed. The purple-tip larvae pushed and pushed, arching their backs, they pushed. They pushed each other and they pushed me. Of course! They were eating one another. Papa was eating me. There was to be another mouth to feed. Papa was eliminating the competition for scarce resources. Eleanor and Deborah stood by the side of my bed, watching impassively, peering closely at my side, hands on knees, not without some element of curiosity. Theirs was disinterested, scientific observation. He's kissing, he's pushing, he's eating. Of course! That's the proboscis causing the stabbing pain, furling and unfurling, breaking and entering, sipping and sucking, sipping and sucking. Confirmation that I had been consumed from the waist down. I felt nauseous from the incessant, rhythmic shaking and confused by the extraordinary images that I couldn't shake off, visions of millions of caterpillars on beds and of caterpillars with proboscises. I felt ill and opened my mouth to beg forgiveness, to say I understood, to call Mama, to scream, to be sick – oh, how I wished Papa and the caterpillars and the butterflies would stop thrusting and probing! I opened my mouth wide to emit vomit, a cry, a request and Mama opened wide and Papa pushed, pushed, pushed and Mama was told to push, push, push and Mama and I were open wide and my mouth was open wide and out, having started as a flutter in a copse in my heart, emerged a butterfly.

Unused to walking on six legs, I stayed motionless on the bedsheet a moment, looking back at me, my body, basking in its hot, gasping, shuddering breath, flexing and drying my wings, inflating them with blood. I looked at myself, face pressed to the bedsheet, eyes looking back at me in wonder and love and joy and I opened my wings wide and drifted, up, up to the curtain rail where I rested a while and then, feeling stronger, around my room and, more confident yet, beyond and out and up and up. I flew above the house in which Eleanor, Deborah and their mother slept, the sisters sharing a room and their mother in a double bed although all on her own, above the hospital where Mama lay exhausted and content amid a profusion of sheets, watching a midwife in a crisp nurse's cap that contrasted with her soiled apron clean Cosmo and place him, exhausted too, in a linen cloth on Mama's chest, above our house where Papa buttoned his trousers, gathered me in his arms, sat me wordlessly in my wicker chair and covered me with my blankets. In the light from the landing, he stripped my bed of its puke-puddled sheet and fetched a clean sheet from the airing cupboard on the landing. He made my bed and lay me back on it and cleaned me, as tenderly as he had formerly done, he apologising to me as I did to him, me assuring him that I understood that that punishment had been my due and he telling me no, not at all, it was just one of those things and begging me to shush. He fetched me a clean nightie and helped me into it and fluffed up my pillow and placed it beneath my head. He gathered my sheet and nightie that were destined for the wash and left my room.

Sharon

I shone at school. Miss Crossbank praised me. I did well in all subjects. I excelled at sports. I loved the stage and the stage loved me back. The looks of others defined and shaped me, they gave me substance, meaning and colour that would have drained out of me by the end of my walk home that was all downhill.

On the last day of my last term at primary school I returned home with a school report that was so good that I considered it impossible for it to be overshadowed by Seamus' and Sherah's reports. That evening, as Mum was cooking and Dad had their reports out on the kitchen table, I pirouetted around the kitchen and read bits of my report out to them.

'Very good,' said Mum distractedly, over the noise of the extractor fan. She had her hair up in a bun when she cooked and wisps of it were being drawn up by the draught of the fan when she leant over the hob, as though she had an electric current running through her, and her top-lit head gave her sunken eyes with big shadows.

'Sherah, your report is the same as last term's that was the same as the term before that,' said Dad in his exasperated tone of voice. 'Sharon, pipe down! I can't hear myself think in all this racket! And stop prancing around – you're making me dizzy!'

'It's no worse than Seamus's,' said my sister, chewing on a strand of hair so curly that, extended, it was three times the length it appeared. 'In fact, it's probably better. Must try harder – his report is full of must-try-harders!' And she pulled the report out from under Dad's nose.

'Give it back,' said Dad, snatching it, and added, 'Seamus responds to gentle encouragement whereas you –'

'Oh! The carrot and the stick is it! Seamus gets the carrot and I get the stick! Go on, spank me!' Sherah stuck her bum out, provocatively.

'I don't like carrots,' said Seamus.

'You'll get more than the stick if you carry on like that,' said Dad, enjoying Sherah's pantomime despite himself.

'Shall I read some more of my report out, Dad?' I asked.

'There's no need. I'm sure it's very good, as usual,' sighed Dad. He had one arm around Seamus and held his report in his free hand. 'Oh, that's good,' he said. 'A two for effort in English.'

'And a D for achievement,' squealed Sherah, looking over Dad's shoulder. 'Thicko! What would you rather have, Dad, a son who tries hard but is useless –'

'I'm not!' protested Seamus.

'– or a daughter who has Bs for achievement and fours for effort?'

'Or a daughter who has As and ones?' I asked, seizing my chance.

'Who asked you, you swot?' spat Sherah.

'Yeah,' said Seamus.

'What I would like,' said Dad, looking at me, suddenly looking drawn, 'is to have my dinner and for someone to lay the table.'

'In that order?' asked Sherah, bending lower to stare provocatively at Dad at eye level.

In reply, Dad put Seamus's report on the kitchen table and, placing his free hand on the back of Sherah's head and pulling it down towards him, placed a slow soft kiss on her forehead.

'Lay the table, Sharon, would you?' asked Mum.

I laid the table.

Isabella

Papa considered it necessary to say sternly to me of Cosmo, though whether in jest or all seriousness I couldn't tell, 'He's not a doll, you know.' Of course I knew that. Dolls' eyes are dead while Cosmo's were alive with love, laughter and mischief, blue moons to his grandfather's dead stars in the photograph on the mantelpiece, with pupils like dark pools that exerted a pull on me as I cooed and cuddled him; it was so much more amusing for me to play with him than with my unresponsive, spiritless pretend people. True, I enjoyed lying Cosmo on our deep kitchen sofa and lining my dolls up on either side of him in order of size and addressing him as though he were one of them, or them as though they were many of him, but Cosmo knew that it was just a game of make-believe, as did Mama whose sloshes and plashes at the kitchen sink composed an alto accompaniment to the treble of Cosmo's gurgles of pleasure. In a matter of months, Cosmo ascended the doll hierarchy to become larger than them all, by which time he had inserted all their toes and fingers into his mouth as well as his own and whatever else he could lay his pudgy clutches on. After Cosmo had achieved his first roll, Mama, for fear that he would roll off the sofa, took to placing him on a play mat on the kitchen rug where Eleanor, Deborah and I would lie on our backs too and amuse him, Mama and ourselves by imitating him – toe-sucking, giggles, goo noises and all.

Eleanor and Deborah were besotted with Cosmo and would look on in envy as he burbled and squealed with joy when I held his hand and traced my finger around his palm before running it up his arm and tickling him, reciting, 'Around and around the garden, like a teddy bear. One step, two steps and a tickly under there!' They would shriek louder than Cosmo in request for their turn to tickle him, and would beg their mother for a baby boy of their own.

'Fat chance,' would say Mrs Baldock, sitting on a kitchen chair by the back door so she could blow her cigarette smoke outside; and she and Mama would exchange looks and then Mama and I would look down at Cosmo with pride.

I looked on in controlled jealousy as Mama fed Cosmo her breasts, first one and then the other, marvelling at the extent to which they had grown in motherhood. Cosmo ate my mother with a ferocity that would have been frightening had it not been so comic. I never heard him cry other than to summon food or to signal that his nappy needed changing; his cries were more informative than plaintive, expressive of an inclination to communicate rather than complain.

I wondered, did Cosmo have a butterfly in him too? I pressed my ear to his chest to hear a flutter behind the heartbeat, and Mama had to help me prise his fisted fingers from my hair. I looked as closely in his mouth as he'd allow without his sucking the tip of my nose, and saw only the snowy white crests of the milk teeth that lined the ridges of his gums. I peered into his eyes but could only see the adoration that he had for me and, reflected in them, that I had for him.

My butterfly fascinated me. Its species was a mystery to me. Its reflections eluded me; no mirror, no pond reflected it and so I couldn't see myself, my colouring, my wing shape. I was a clumsy flier, unable to master my wingbeats to fight drafts of air and to hover. I couldn't quite make it – or her or me – appear at will but could become it when I sought an escape of sorts, when Papa visited me at night on those rare occasions that he could now that Mama was home all the time, or when older, bigger pupils at my school bullied me for no reason other than because they were older and bigger, or when my peer group at school teased me because my breasts had begun to show before theirs. Sticks and stones can break my bones but words will never hurt me. When I was a butterfly, no one could touch me.

In the space of a couple of years, all our relatives had come to see 'the new baby' with the exception of Papa's parents whom, it occurred to me, I never saw once outside the boundaries of their vicarage and garden. We drove Cosmo to them in a second–hand car that Papa had acquired and that served as the excuse for his torrid temper, on account of the fact that he had overpaid for it.

My grandfather cast his grandson a cursory look without so much as inclining his head to better see him and said to me, 'Golly, you've grown.' His face expressed no surprise but bore a smirk directed at my father, as though in search of plaudits for having so knowingly pronounced a platitude. This was typical of the conversations my father had with his father – exchanges, of a sort, in which all critical information lay between the lines, in which so much was left unsaid; communication comprised of hidden semaphore that only the male members of the family were privy to.

By contrast, like a negative to its print, my mother and her mother-in-law had, whether wilfully or otherwise, a dance in which their eyes never met for fear of what they might reveal; instead, they spoke in code of children, weather, tea and cakes. My grandmother, as usual failing to meet my eyes, said to me, 'Bless you, my child,' and of Cosmo, 'Well, he certainly looks like you,' but never made it clear whom she was addressing.

My grandparents' was a house of animate human cadavers and of inanimate lepidopteral ones, a house in which there were always gauntlets of butterfly corpses to be run, in which the temperature was always lower in than out, a house of secrets and of unspoken pain, of clenched buttocks and gritted teeth. It was to me, on that visit, as though the pinned butterflies in the display cases that lined the internal, chill walls of the house had been ripped from former and future generations of Bicourts, and as though my grandfather, despite himself and in spite of his occupation, lived his life in denial of our being so much more than our physical forms.

We sat in the conservatory on rattan furniture and sun-faded cushions, each partially obscured from the others by the fronds of potted palms and other plants. I sipped a sour lemonade grown warm while the grown-ups toyed with fine china cups of milky tea gone cold. Cosmo slept on Mama's lap. I cradled his feet in my hands.

'Don't we all have a soul, Grandpa?' I asked my grandfather, turning from Cosmo to him abruptly.

'Of course,' he replied, surprised a little at my addressing him so directly. Regaining his composure, he went on, 'And of course you know that the ancient Greek word for the soul and for a butterfly are the same, don't you?'

'No!' I was delighted by this, having not wanted to say soul, but having feared being misunderstood if I had said butterfly. 'And do you inhabit your soul in the same way that you inhabit your body?'

'It's *psyche*,' said Papa, smiling around him at us.

'I'm glad to see you taking an interest in matters spiritual,' said Grandpa wryly to me.

'Surely, it's the soul that inhabits the body,' suggested Papa.

'So, really, you are your soul. Your soul is you,' I thought to add helpfully.

'Well, I think so,' replied Grandpa.

'So, if someone hurts you, hits you, then they're not really hurting you, they're not wanting to hurt you at all, just your body?'

'What a strange girl,' observed Grandpa.

'Strange?' said Mama defensively, more loudly than she had intended, and Cosmo started in his sleep.

I felt indignant at not being taken seriously. 'What I mean is, are we two or are we one?'

'An interesting question,' noted Grandpa, appearing a little perplexed.

'*Do not fear those who kill the body but cannot kill the soul*. Matthew, chapter 10, verse 28,' offered Papa, placatory and pompous.

'*You shall love the Lord your father with all your heart and with all your soul and with all your mind*,' countered Grandpapa. 'Matthew, chapter 22, verse –'

'Thirty-seven. Yes, I know, I know,' interrupted Papa quickly, as though already regretting what he had started. 'And it's God, not father.'

I could feel Cosmo's pulse on the inner side of the ankle, a determined rise and fall below two of my fingers, an affirmation of the body while the mind slept, and I thought to try again. 'So does that mean that the mind is different from the soul and that we have not just bodies and minds but souls too? And if, as we said earlier, we are our souls, then – oh, I find it so confusing! Does our mind die with our body?'

'Really!' exclaimed Grandpapa.

'What I mean is,' I said, in an attempt at clarification, 'are we mind or body? Or…' – as an afterthought – 'mind and body? Are we two or are we one?'

'I suppose this is all *your* doing,' said my grandfather to my father resignedly. 'This is what happens when a theologian has a son who considers himself a philosopher.' He snorted the last word.

My grandmother, unmoving, hands on her lap and eyes staring into the garden's middle distance, said, so quietly so that I was unsure whether she was talking to us or to herself, '*The son shall not suffer for the iniquity of the father, nor the father suffer for the iniquity of the son.* Ezekiel, chapter 18, verse 20.'

My father and grandfather bowed their heads in consideration of this command–turned–aphorism for a moment until my father rose, slowly, pushed a leafy branch aside and stepped out of the conservatory and into the garden where he went for a turn, hands behind his back, stopping occasionally to admire a flower or to reflect. My grandfather followed him out and the two of them ambled along their respective paths, never together and never crossing the other, not once exchanging a word, my grandfather watching my father all the time and my father never once meeting his father's gaze.

The telephone rang. Mama answered it. It was Oma. Opa was in hospital. Mama had to leave for Paderborn at once.

Mama replaced the telephone in its cradle and stood by it, looking around the kitchen with unseeing eyes at Papa, at me, at Cosmo who, exulting in being allowed in the garden in poor weather on condition he were appropriately dressed, had just run in from it, his galoshes' muddy footsteps following him in, like a trail of clues that led conclusively to a criminal. He stood beneath his yellow, sopping sou'wester that doubled as a sun hat in the summer and in its matching slicker from which rainwater dripped onto the kitchen floor, twigs in one muddy hand and half an old doll in the other, and showed surprise if not disappointment at not having received his usual reprimand.

'Of course, you have to go,' said Papa.

'Of course,' said Mama, looking sick.

'Don't worry about them,' said Papa. 'Don't worry about us,' he added with forced jollity. 'We'll be all right, won't we?'

Cosmo burbled in reply and presented Mama with the muddy, mutilated doll, which she received distastefully with her fingertips. Cosmo's burbles troubled Mama; she was increasingly concerned about his inability to articulate basic words – to produce little, vocally, besides pops and whistles. His vocabulary wasn't simply behind that of an average two year old; it was non-existent. And yet he had walked before the age of one and demonstrated the understanding of a four year old when Mama had had him seen by a speech and language therapist. She dropped the plastic torso in the kitchen sink, ran water over it and washed her hands. Having dried them, she leant back against the sink and, in an unthinking gesture that I had last seen nearly three years ago, placed one hand above and the other below her slightly swelling belly. I understood then that she was pregnant again and impulsively went to her and hugged her – her and my foetal sibling.

'You'll be all right to fly,' said Papa to Mama.

'I'm sorry your *opa* isn't well,' said Mama to me, running her lemon soap-smelling hands through my hair, stopping to work her fingers gently through its knots.

She flew to Germany the following day, after she had made arrangements for Cosmo and me to spend two days and nights with Mrs Baldock.

'That's not necessary,' Papa had objected.

'If you're too busy to come to my dying father's bedside, you're too busy to have the children under your feet,' she had replied.

Mrs Baldock spoilt Cosmo and me while Eleanor and Deborah spoilt Cosmo, competing, to his evident glee and pleasure, to dress, feed, play with and generally fuss over him to the point that Mrs Baldock exclaimed, 'For God's sake, girls! There happens to be a real person inside there! He's not a toy!'

'You should come more often!' cried Eleanor at dinner. 'We don't usually get apple crumble on weekdays!'

'And cake for tea!' added Deborah.

When Mrs Baldock escorted Cosmo and me home on the third day of my mother's absence, she stopped by the front garden gate; from where she said to Papa, who stood by our open front door, 'So, how is she? Is she back yet?'

'Soon. Soon,' said Papa, crouching low to pick his son up by the armpits.

The Oxford don and the hippy eyed each other with a profound antipathy.

'But you are expecting Brigitte back today, this evening?' asked the hippy.

'Oh yes, this evening. Bridget should be home this evening,' replied the don, the father, the philosopher, the man who held me by the hand and who itched – I could sense it – to be rid of the hippy and to be with his children.

'Well, goodbye, kids,' said Mrs Baldock reluctantly.

'Say goodbye and thank you,' instructed Papa.

'Goodbye, Mrs Baldock, and thank you very much,' I said.

'Goo,' said Cosmo, waving.

Mama called in the late afternoon. She was still in Paderborn. Opa was not expected to last the night. She spoke to us in turn, Papa appropriately sympathetic, Cosmo marvelling at his mother's voice emanating from a Bakelite handset that he gripped with both hands until I took it gently from him, me unable to concentrate on what she was saying, uncertain whether I felt sorry more for my mother for the loss of a father, or for myself for the loss of a grandfather – or for Cosmo and me for the absence of our mother. I handed the telephone back to Papa who concluded the call with, 'No. Of course not. Not at all. It's quite all right. Absolutely not. I'm quite capable of looking after my own children.' I heard him say the same to Mrs Baldock when she knocked on our door ten minutes later, adding, 'We really can't exploit your extensive kindness any further,' and then, as if capitulating, 'Well, if you really don't mind, if Bridget decides to stay on after the funeral – I may have to be out of town for a conference so I'll bring them to you then.'

That early evening, Papa busied himself with some excitement for the arrivals of Professor Rennet and Drs Dearman and Faben. He tidied his desk and drew the study curtains tight and allowed Cosmo and me to set glasses and beer bottles out on trays and to pour crisps into bowls, withholding any protest when Cosmo ate more crisps than he decanted from the large paper bags they came in, and thrilling him by blowing the bags up and popping them with a slap of his hand. While Papa built the fire, I changed Cosmo into his pyjamas and changed into my nightie, accepting Papa's rationale that, as I would no longer need to change, I could stay up later than if I remained dressed. The introduction of Cosmo to Papa's gatherings elevated my status somewhat. An old hand, I bossed my younger brother about to the extent that I could. He and I straightened the oriental rug and the smaller hearth rug and shook the embroidered cushions on the two wicker chairs by the desk, Cosmo copying my every move as precisely as a mirror image. Papa cleared the mantelpiece of mail, keys, rubber bands and other deposits. From his armchair in his garden, Grandpapa admired our work with satisfaction, leaning forward as though hoping to peer round the corner of the picture frame that held him or anticipating a play that was moments from beginning. Henry Moore's king and queen looked on impassively. Just-married Mama and Papa looked into the future with hope, although not necessarily for the same things. Having lit the fire, Papa placed the fireguard in front of it. Cosmo stood by it, mesmerised by the kindling flames that licked the larger logs. I twirled in my nightie, fanning the fire. The doorbell rang.

Professor Rennet and Dr Faben squeezed into the study one after the other, the latter saying, 'Hello, hello, who do we have here?' as he considered Cosmo and me through his thick, black-framed spectacles that almost met his moustache on either side of his nostrils, and the former pulling at his goatee with one hand and at his waistcoat with the other. Cosmo, having absorbed my instruction to offer the crisps rather than eat them, stepped forward, a full bowl in each hand.

To this, Dr Faben said, 'Hold on! Give a fellow a chance to sit down!'

Professor Rennet, seeing the disappointment in Cosmo's eyes, helped himself to a crisp, saying, 'Thank you very much, young man!' He adopted his usual station by the fireplace only to find that, the fire lit, he had to move to one end of it, much to the satisfaction of Grandpapa whose view, from the photograph, would remain unimpeded.

The second peel of the doorbell announced the arrivals of Dr Dearman and, much to my surprise and Cosmo's delight, a girl who, although a little shorter and thinner than me, looked to be about my age, and who was introduced to us as Dr Dearman's niece Kimberley. There were similarities between the two of them but where he was bullish, she was bovine; where he seemed sinister, she appeared benevolent, coming across as simple and pliant, as though never having possessed an intense emotion or a will of her own. Dr Dearman helped her out of a coat that was too big to be hers beneath which she, too, wore a nightie. She wore not shoes but slippers that she removed and placed by the bookcase where she stood, quite nonchalantly – composed despite her unfamiliar surroundings, registering nothing when Cosmo went to her and held her hand. He offered her a crisp that she accepted with neither reluctance nor enthusiasm, and then another that she also took with equanimity. For a moment, the only sounds were of Kimberley crunching crisps and the crackle of the fire, and then the grown-ups all talked at once.

'Very nice,' observed Professor Rennet, pince-nez in hand. 'Very nice.'

'I hope you two will be good friends,' said Dr Dearman to Kimberley and me.

'A man could die of thirst here!' exclaimed Dr Faben exaggeratedly.

'Say hello to Dr Dearman, Cosmo,' said Papa.

Cosmo lifted his hands to Dr Dearman's belt buckle that sparkled in the light of the fire.

'Steady on,' said Dr Dearman, pulling back and grinning sheepishly around the room.

'Only continental Europeans wear belts with suits,' stated Professor Rennet.

'Continental Europeans and Dr Dearman,' corrected Dr Faben and then, addressing me, 'What about our drinks, young lady?'

'Drinks!' cried Papa, clapping his hands.

I filled four glasses on the tray on Papa's desk and handed them around to the grown-ups.

'Have one yourself,' said Dr Faben pleasantly to me, an eye on my father.

'Me? No!' I looked at Papa too. Sometimes, his friends were very funny.

Papa, standing with his legs crossed and a drink in one hand while supporting himself with the other on the mantelpiece, was the epitome of nonchalance. He raised his eyebrows and shrugged. 'Why not? Just once in a while won't hurt.'

I couldn't believe my ears.

Cosmo had followed Papa's and my exchange with interest.

'Go on. Have a sip,' encouraged Papa.

'Kimberley will have one. Won't you, Kimberley?' Dr Dearman sought corroboration.

Kimberley nodded. She had yet to speak. I found myself wondering what she would sound like.

'Here,' said Papa covering the hearthrug in two strides and holding his glass to my lips. 'Have a sip of mine.'

Papa's beer tasted warm, flat, bitter, dull, belying the first, faint fragrance of fruits and sweet vegetal matter I'd smelt when he'd held his glass below my nose.

'What do you think?' enquired Papa.

I reached for another sip.

'Right,' said Papa definitively, decanting a bottle of the pale brown liquid into the remaining glasses on the tray and handing the fuller ones to Kimberley and me and the third to Cosmo. 'Cheers!'

'Cheers!'

'Gee!'

'Down the hatch!'

'Down in one!'

'Let's have another!'

Papa's study grew hot. Cosmo amused us by spinning around wildly and laughing grotesquely before bursting into tears; at times his inability to communicate became impossibly frustrating for him. Dr Faben held his arms out to him and, to my astonishment, Cosmo went to them and crawled into the space on the sofa between the two doctors, where he appeared to fall into fitful sleep, his face in Dr Faben's lap, his bottom and legs on Dr Dearman's. I observed that Kimberley swayed in time to a music only she was hearing, until it occurred to me that I was swaying or, perhaps, that we both were, the realisation that the one didn't preclude the other tipping me into a fit of giggles. The fire demanded my attention, it dictated my moves and thoughts, it was the conductor, Papa's study the stage and we the instruments. There was a universal symmetry that I was a part of, reflected in Papa's study either side of the sun in the grate: the picture frames at the two ends of the mantelpiece, the two men – Papa and Professor Rennet – at either end of the mantelpiece in identical postures; the two high, wingback chairs in front of which Kimberley and I stood barefoot and in nighties; Drs Faben and Dearman reclining deep in the sofa's remote corners, a blowing and grunting, tossing and turning Cosmo between them completing the circle. Above them, Papa's butterflies in their hundreds fluttered their wings in the flickering firelight as though in warning or to escape their glass cages. Grandpapa sat forward in his wicker chair in the garden in the photograph, looking on intently, approvingly. In the light cast by the agitating fire, the clouds behind Moore's king and queen ran across their sky. I found everything portentous one minute and uproariously comical the next, especially Papa's adding more logs to the already roaring, well-stoked fire, without being able to put my finger on why exactly.

'What are you trying to do? Roast us?' asked Professor Rennet rhetorically; intending to mop his brow with his handkerchief, he had dislodged his pince-nez that, hitting the fireguard, had fallen the right side of it and onto the hearthrug – to his evident relief.

Dr Faben moaned. The heat must have got to him. He rested a hand on Cosmo's head; his eyes were shut, his head lolling to one side.

'It is indeed hot,' stated Dr Dearman, patting Cosmo's bottom through his fine cotton pyjamas.

'I know – why don't we take our jackets off?' suggested Professor Rennet.

'That's a good idea, but what about those of us who don't have jackets to remove?' asked Dr Dearman, looking around him.

'It might be fairer if we each remove one item of clothing,' conceded Professor Rennet.

'I'm afraid it is indeed very hot,' said Papa apologetically. 'And when it's hot, one must drink.' He filled Kimberley's and my glasses for the third time and encouraged us with, 'Drink it down! Drink it down!'

Dr Dearman leant forward and held up a stubby finger, as though struck by a thought, and looked from Kimberley to me. 'But, hold on a moment, if we remove our jackets, what will you remove?'

I handed my empty glass back to Papa and exclaimed, 'But we've only got our nighties on!' Really, Dr Dearman was so funny! The entire room balanced on the tip of his finger. The floor of the room rocked. Its walls wobbled. By fixing my eyes on the upheld finger and sitting on the wicker chair nearest me, I could keep myself from falling.

'Well, off they go,' dictated Dr Dearman, extricating himself from Cosmo's legs, the depths of the sofa and, finally, his jacket.

'Off it goes,' concurred Professor Rennet, removing his jacket and hanging it over the back of Papa's desk chair.

Papa removed his jacket wordlessly, looking at me complicitly as though to say, *What a lark!*

'And you two!' exclaimed Dr Dearman, in what I considered mock seriousness. 'Play the game! Maintain your end of the bargain!'

Kimberley crossed her arms and leant forward to catch her nightie by its hem. She pulled it off slowly and gracefully, naturally. She stood still, held it in her hand a moment and let it fall by her side in a pastel puddle of cotton on the Oriental rug. Her shoulder-length hair rested on her shoulders, just. Her fringe courted her eyelashes. The firelight that played on her slender form lent her the illusion of movement. Our admiring looks clothed her naked form in adoration and approbation. I felt it imperative that I join her and stood and divested myself of my nightie too, though with less dignity and more haste, reluctant as I was to not be excluded from this wonderful game for a moment longer than I could help.

Papa clapped his hands again. 'More drinks!'

Dr Dearman looked at Cosmo by his side and said, 'Poor Cosmo. It's so unfair. He still has his pyjamas on.'

Dr Faben's eyes swam in his glasses. He pushed them up, off the wart on which they had rested, and searched in his pocket for a handkerchief that he used to wipe the spittle Cosmo had deposited in his sleep, and then his own mouth and moustache.

'Down in one,' commanded Papa to Kimberley and me.

The beer was warmer now than at the first time of my drinking it, and headier.

'Now dance,' said Professor Rennet who had removed his waistcoat as well as his jacket and loosened his tie.

Papa's study floor rocked like the deck of a ship in a squall, the Oriental rug rising and receding like a fine, frothy wave. Kimberley's and my shadows cast by the fire raced up the butterfly-festooned walls and onto the ceiling and back. And up again and back, to and fro, up and down. Professor Rennet clapped his hands. Dr Dearman sang a ditty. Papa looked on, a grin fixed above his hand-cupped chin. Dr Faben helped Cosmo out of his pyjamas and to his feet. Cosmo stood, a little unsteady, and swayed and waved his arms in imitation of Kimberley and me. I, too, was copying Kimberley, unsure of the extent to which I was succeeding in actually dancing like her as opposed to just staying on my feet and not keeling over. The room shrank in the heat. Dr Dearman's teeth and Dr Faben's moustache grew larger. Dr Dearman's breath was warm and smelled of salt and vinegar and cheese and onion crisps; Dr Faben's of beer and cigarettes. Their tongues, rasping and wet, tickled me where they touched me and their fingers and palms, clammy but firm, supported me when I risked falling. The shudder and slip of Dr Dearman's teeth on my skin and the cooling of his saliva trail on my legs gave me goose bumps. I wanted to divest myself of my surface membrane like a worm casts its cuticle, to climb out of myself like a butterfly out of its chrysalis. Papa and Professor Rennet assisted Kimberley, attentively, closely, lovingly. Cosmo fell asleep where he had slumped, curled like a cocoon with his head on the Oriental rug and his back against the sofa. I found myself on the rug, too, my arm reaching to pat his. Dr Faben's ministrations as he moved from the small to the top of my back were those of a cleaning lady, the broom of his moustache preceding the mop of his mouth. Somewhere near my left ear, I could hear the professor panting. I noted the soles of Kimberley's feet in the firelight and the tips of her toes aligned with the sweetness and perfection of ducklings behind their mother. I wished Dr Dearman would keep his fingers still. He rolled me over. He had reverted to his larval stage and was using his fingers like prolegs and true legs, feeling and fiddling, prodding and probing, pushing and shoving. Momentarily, I thought we were in Papa's butterfly pavilion, the flicker of the fire's flames lending the pinned butterflies on the study wall the illusion of flutter and flight. The caterpillars chomped and chewed, bumped and butted. The caterpillars are hungry tonight. The butterflies had disrobed and displayed their proboscises with a hungry bravura. Kiss the proboscis. Kiss, kiss, kiss, push, push, push. We were playing caterpillars and butterflies but, this time, I was being consumed at both ends simultaneously and my butterfly's route out was blocked and I panicked and gagged and bit and spat and my butterfly finally flew. Dr Faben remonstrated. I rested on the fireguard where I dried my wings for a moment, my wings' shadows on the ceiling above me on the rug pulsing like angels' wings and then becoming smaller when I drifted up on the fire's hot air, across the glass cages of my fellow, imprisoned Lepidoptera, across the spines of Papa's many books until they, my wings and their shadows, met, up against the distant ceiling.

I flew up and out, up above the city that throbbed with the heartbeats of its inhabitants, that resonated with the steady drum of their footsteps, the city that, sonorously, below it all, as though deep underground, vibrated with its own life-supporting and -enhancing pulse. Concert halls, pubs and cinemas were emptying. Heartbeats and footsteps, laughter and chatter, bus and car engines formed the city's constant hum. People were walking and cycling, talking and listening, joking and arguing, pushing and shoving, slipping and slapping, juddering and blowing, panting and ceasing. People and caterpillars finished their dinners. Men dressed in the warm light of a dying fire and children were bathed and put to bed. It's better to give than it is to receive. Somewhere, far below me now, I had made a gift of myself to Papa and his friends. No, not of myself, but of my body. *Take, eat; this is my body, which is given for you.* You can touch my body but you can't touch me. I was out of reach. I couldn't be bought with warm beer, crisps and late nights. One day, I would want my body back. I fluttered high above the Brüderkrankenhaus St. Josef Paderborn where

Opa was leaving his, vacating his body with elegance and humility, where red-eyed Mama and Oma, heads bowed and seated either side of a grey-painted hospital bed, each held one of Opa's hands, Paderborn's drumming heart the undercurrent to Mama's sporadic sobs and Oma's ardent weeping.

And then, three months going by in a flutter of sorties. Months in which I lived more as a butterfly than as a schoolgirl, daughter and sister, given Mama's long absences in Germany where, despite her pregnancy and her neglected children's vulnerability to their predatory father, she assisted Oma in the immediate aftermath of the loss of her husband.

And then one more month, the sixth of her pregnancy, at the end of which I was flying above Horton General Hospital and looking down upon two mortuary attendants who contemplated Mama's swollen body in silence. They pulled back the sheet it lay under to reveal its blotched purple necklace and its swollen pale blue lips. I alighted and gave my mother's lips one last kiss. I wept butterfly tears then, globules of salt water as big as my eye segments that trickled down my thorax and abdomen before falling as rain on Oxford's gardens, droplets that weighed me down as they gathered and threatened to take me down with them before they broke and detached from me, after which I rose suddenly; tears that lent to my flying an odd, bobbing, fitful motion. Exhausted, I eventually fell to earth.

To my shame, I resented Mama's sudden departure, her abandonment of us, as though she were complicit with Papa, and I was fascinated by Oma's grief that had a terrifying, vicious quality to it, as though she too knew Papa to be the reason behind her daughter's violent, inexplicable death. Oma offered to take Cosmo and me to Paderborn but Papa, as I would have expected, and the other Bicourts, to my surprise, would have none of it.

'They'll be quite all right here,' said Papa, running his fingers through my hair, raking my scalp and bunching my hair up at the ends so that, holding it in one hand, he could tug it down, raise my head in so doing and, looking down into my eyes, ask me for confirmation. 'Won't you, Isabella?' Where others saw a gesture that denoted affection, a play of fondness between father and daughter, I knew it to be shorthand for his molestation and control of me, made all the worse by its public nature. 'Hasn't Isabella nice hair?' he asked the collection of Bicourts before releasing me slowly. I wanted to cut it and even to shave it off in order to spite him but, aware that were I to do so I would effectively be ceding absolute control to Papa in that he would have been the cause of my radical act, I didn't.

Grandmother was the only one to reply. 'Oh yes,' she said, 'just like her father's when he was a child, until he insisted he had it cut.' She cast her husband an indifferent glance, by now too weary and jaded to add venom to the look.

There had been a disagreement between Papa and Grandfather about whether or not my grandfather should minister at the funeral service, though whether he wanted to and Papa didn't or he didn't and Papa did, I didn't know. Following Grandmother's instruction, I had taken tea to them in Papa's study, where Grandfather had said, 'Our days are like the grass. We flourish like a flower of the field; when the wind goes over it, it is gone and its place will know it no more.' Although he had been looking at me, I felt he had been making a point to Papa who had requested, by way of equally obscure reply, that I place the tray on his desk. Grandfather, looking knowingly at Papa, had tapped the family photograph on the mantelpiece with a fingernail.

'It will be time for you to go soon,' said Papa to his father, attempting to look at his wristwatch without spilling his tea.

My paternal grandparents gave the impression of having drifted into Mama's and my sister's funeral and wake by mistake, and accepted the condolences offered them for the deaths of their daughter-in-law and granddaughter with the requisite melancholy and humility, as though in modest denial of the great affliction the loss was to them. They resembled actors who had stumbled onto the wrong stage but who had the good fortune to know the lines of the play they found themselves in and to have prior knowledge of the extras. Aunts Linda and Mary made sympathetic clucking noises; Aunt Patricia wrung her hands and, when not doing so, kept them clutched around her quite visible pregnancy. Clearly, the nature of Mama's sudden death was particularly disconcerting for her; she wouldn't let Uncle Neville from her side for a moment. Uncle James ruffled my hair and kissed my forehead and, leaning that little further, did the same to Cosmo. Such overt demonstrations of affection were unusual in the Bicourt family; reason enough, I sensed, for Uncle James to undertake them. He sat us either side of him during the wake while family, neighbours and Mama's former friends and colleagues drifted in and out of her room, the kitchen and the garden, and he said, 'Anything, anything at all,' and looked as though he might weep at any moment.

'Ging, ging,' said Cosmo and jumped down from his chair to follow Deborah to a kitchen table laden with cakes and sandwiches.

'What is the matter with him?' asked Uncle James, following Cosmo with his eyes.

'We don't know,' I said. 'Papa doesn't seem too concerned. He says that Cosmo will learn to talk when it suits him. When he wants something badly enough.'

'Does he now?' asked Uncle James.

'How are you, Uncle James?' I wasn't aping grown-ups. I actually wanted to know. He seemed sad to me, as though wrestling with someone else's guilt.

Uncle James sat with his elbows on his knees. 'I used to be a soldier. I learnt to fight.' He threw a playful punch at me and cocked his thumb in imitation of a pistol. 'Now all I can do is fight back the tears.' He hung his head again and, to my surprise, I found myself comforting him, patting him on the back as Mama had patted me.

'We're all sad, Uncle James,' I said.

'So you're Uncle James,' said a husky voice. Mrs Baldock sat down next to him and, as if in afterthought, extended her hand to him. She looked older, dressed all in black. Her style was the same, a caftan, a headpiece that resembled an elegant turban and a necklace of dark, polished wood. 'I've heard a lot about you.'

Uncle James shook her hand and looked from her to me.

'Well, not all about you. Just that you're Isabella's favourite.' Mrs Baldock spoke loudly, indifferent as to who might hear.

'Oh, and she's mine,' said Uncle James.

'How many nieces have you got?'

'Just the one.'

'That makes it easier, doesn't it? Have you got a cigarette?'

Uncle James shook one free from a packet, held it to her and lit it for her.

'You need to eat something, sweetie,' said Mrs Baldock, blowing smoke in the direction of the tea that had been laid out. 'Eleanor, take Isabella to get something to eat.'

I felt not a little guilty at the pleasure I felt at the attention I was getting, and placed my hand in Eleanor's outstretched one. We left Uncle James and Mrs Baldock together and headed to the kitchen. Papa and Grandfather were in the butterfly pavilion now, I could see, though at opposing ends of it. Aunt Patricia and Uncle Neville were seated and going on about the importance of her eating for two to a group of Mama's former colleagues. Grandmother was overseeing Cosmo picking up the cake he'd dropped from his plate. Aunts Linda and Mary stood arm in arm, exuding an air of anguish, either out of mortification that no one was speaking to them or out of fear that someone might.

Mama was dead and we were having a tea party.

There was no longer any place to hide. Mama's lap, bosom, apron strings, her embrace, her sweet voice were no longer there. The kitchen, her sitting room, the house were no longer the same. Her posters and paintings had faded. Any illusion that things would turn out all right was no longer possible to maintain. If Mama's wilful blindness to her husband's nocturnal transgressions had been a betrayal of her children of sorts, her death was a perfect perfidy, an absolute breach of her children's trust and of the security, love and comfort Cosmo and I had had every right to expect from her. Resenting her absence as much as missing the one person whose love had been deepest and unconditional was doubly upsetting for me.

I missed Mama most suddenly when my periods began: the time of my metamorphosis from pupa to butterfly, from child to young adult. I had thought I had known what to expect; Eleanor and older girls at school spoke freely about menstruation. But all the same it came as a shock, and I felt the absence of the one person to whom I would have turned for guidance and comfort sorely. My periods rooted me more in my body; I considered them abhorrent and fought futilely against that sentiment. Bloody tendrils, keeping me earthbound. Finding me bleeding, earthy, soiled, my butterfly would stay away in an undesired rebuttal of the physical me, of the woman I had become. But then, so would Papa, Drs Dearman and Feben and Professor Rennet and, realising this, I came to look upon my periods no longer as an affliction to be endured but as a benevolent force field. The men lost interest in me – not just while I had my periods, but in between them too; they had no appetite for a woman.

At a remove, in bed and yet aware of the activities in Papa's study, I considered that I was failing Cosmo. Not finding his Mama, he had turned to me. Assuming responsibility for what was happening to him was too much for me to bear.

Mrs McKey became Mrs Baldock's best friend. She was Irish – she sang when she talked. She had long fine hair and elegant, tapered fingers that were either pushing her hair behind her ears or lifting cigarettes to and from her lips. She and Mrs Baldock sat by the kitchen window, smoking, while Deborah and Sarah McKey tackled colouring-in and puzzle books and Cosmo and Sarah's brother, James, sulked because they had been forbidden from playing football in the rain. They slouched, hands in pockets, by the closed French doors to the patio, Cosmo copying the older James in his posture and attitude.

Mrs Baldock leant forward and laughed. 'Sarah! Just like Isabella!'

'What?' I looked up from my book.

Mrs Baldock addressed Mrs McKey. 'Isabella always did that. She did that as a very young child. Colouring in outside the lines. Look at your people,' she said to Sarah. 'They sort of bleed outside of the contours of their bodies. It's like they're emanating something.'

'It's like their bodies can't contain them,' concurred Mrs McKey, adding, to comfort Sarah and, perhaps, me too, 'It's nice. It's very modern.' She blew smoke out of the open window. 'I once had a red coat – bright red – God I loved that coat – and got caught in a thunderstorm some way from the car. By the time I got back to it, I was soaked right through, soaked to my skin. Anyway, we got in, drove home and, when we got out, we saw the colour had run into the upholstery – beige, it was, or cream – and the red had run into it, all over. I had left an almost perfect, scarlet imprint of myself on the passenger seat. Richard was furious.'

'Richard is never furious,' stated Mrs Baldock. She put out her cigarette.

'Well, he couldn't stay furious for long. He'd bought me the coat. Afterwards he said he liked it. The red smudge that was my shape. He said it was as though I was always with him, wherever he went in the car. The ghost of me.' She raised her voice. 'Do you remember the red stain in the car, James?'

'Yes,' said James, in a fed-up kind of voice.

'James and Sarah never liked it. They said it spooked them or some such nonsense.'

'Car,' repeated Cosmo.

If I had asked Cosmo and James to play with Eleanor's and Deborah's dolls, they would have considered my proposal with horror and snorted contemptuously – at least, James would have done so and Cosmo would have copied him. Which isn't to say that I disliked James; I liked him, particularly for ignoring Cosmo's speech impediment and for standing by him when other boys teased him about it. The two of them gave me an insight into what older male friendships could be: manly camaraderie in which little conversation was necessary and an understanding was possible despite the lack of a shared spoken vocabulary. I removed a number of dolls from the box they were in and began playing with them on the carpet near where the boys stood, attempting to create, admittedly a little clumsily, a comic domestic scenario.

'"Let's play football," said Daddy doll,' I said in my gruffest voice.

'"Okay," said Jimmy. "Golly, this is a strange ball!"' I said in a voice pitched just higher than mine. I had only a smaller doll's head as a ball.

'"Ouch! Don't kick me! Kick the ball! Ouch! Do that again and I'll punish you!"' I said in the gruffer voice.

I created goal posts as best I could and then Cosmo squatted and, holding a doll in one hand, swung its leg with the other at the severed doll's head.

'How dare you kick Daddy!' said the Daddy doll.

James knelt to play and I ceded the game to him and Cosmo.

Deborah and Sarah stopped colouring and looked on, smiling. The room had quietened as the drumming of the rain on the patio doors had lessened. Mrs Baldock rocked back in her chair and Mrs McKey bunched her long hair in one hand and tossed it over her shoulder. Eleanor appeared in the doorway to the kitchen and said, 'Hello, everyone.'

Cosmo and James entered their private worlds as I looked on expectantly. Deborah and Sarah resumed colouring. Eleanor gave her mother a hug and stayed still a moment, her arms and dark hair a multi-hued muffler around Mrs Baldock.

'Oh, my God!' said Mrs McKey quietly.

'Oh, my God!' said Mrs Baldock that little bit louder, the front legs of her chair hitting the kitchen floor with a clack.

Cosmo looked up. He looked at me, seeking reassurance that he had done nothing wrong. He had had the dolls kick the doll's head around for a while and then adopted another game that may have started as the punishment of one doll by another, before becoming yet another, revealing game in which he, however temporarily, had acquired the exercise of power and control over another – or, at least, its illusion. He had undressed the dolls and, bending the knees of the smaller one, had it kneel before the other, had it bury its head in the other, while he made slobbering and grunting noises. He had then turned and laid the two dolls down, the bigger on the smaller one, pushing and shoving, pushing and shoving.

I cried noiselessly as I met Mrs Baldock's look: tears of confirmation for her that her fears were true. She stood and went to Cosmo, knelt by him and beckoned me to join them in a hug, the first time I had received such a warm, loving, non-judgemental embrace since Mama's death. We all cried – each, I presume, for different reasons; Eleanor, Deborah, Sarah and James crying hardest because they did not know why their mothers and I were crying.

Sharon

The summer before I started at my new secondary school was a strange, dreamy one. I lost that thing, that place, the people I most identified with or, to be more precise, the institution that most contributed to my defining myself around points of reference I approved of. It was as though, cut off from tens out of ten and gold stars and absent from the admiring looks in sports and on stage of pupils and teachers, the strings that held me in place in the world had been severed. I spent that summer in what felt like a lazy freefall – not in a dizzying, anxiety-inducing sense but in a horizontal, gravity-defying passing through space that, though gentle, was too quick to allow me to latch on to anything to define myself by. The signposts and labels were there but either upside down or back to front and always just out of reach.

Those summer days turned us pink, red and amber. Sherah would examine herself critically before the mirror in our parents' room and gauge the effect of the sun's rays by the increased visibility of her bikini lines. Dad knew not to enter his own bedroom then but would argue with her from the corridor: she was not to wear a bikini in the park. It was indecent, in his view, to wear a bikini anywhere other than the beach. I was indifferent as to whether or not I tanned but I would pretend that I cared, if only in a deplorable attempt to endear myself to my sister and her friends. I would return my reflection's serene stare reticently and not without some envy that I couldn't assign a reason to. The girl with the sun-bleached hair in the mirror was becoming a stranger to me, slyly provoking me as she lifted first one arm and then the other to reveal light downy hair and then cupped the two tumescent perturbations on the front of her T-shirt with both hands. Seamus took his turn before the mirror one late afternoon, only because Mum had reflected on how red he looked and, not long after and for some time afterwards, he was crying with the pain of the sunburn. Sherah and I were both lectured on the dangers of sunstroke and severely reprimanded for having allowed him in the sun with, obviously, insufficient sun block. Sherah didn't argue back for once; she was clearly upset at seeing her brother so distressed. I was, too, of course, but all the same I didn't feel it was entirely our fault – the day's strong wind had helped mask the strength of the sun – and, perversely enough, I enjoyed being told off with Sherah for a change.

Mum and Dad were around that summer but rarely together, both begging work commitments, and Mum, wanting to train for an autumn marathon and to see her younger sister – who had moved to London from South Wales – settled in, was hardly home at all.

Aunt Wanda's arrival was the best thing that happened to me that summer, if not in my childhood, if not ever. 'Wanda from the Rhondda' or 'Rhondda Wanda', Dad liked calling her, even though, as Mum never tired of pointing out, Wanda was pronounced 'Vanda', Rhondda was pronounced 'Rhontha' and, strictly speaking, Mum and Aunt Wanda came from south of the Rhondda, from Cowbridge, a fact that Dad only remembered after arguments in which Mum had got the better of him, as in (muttering under his breath), 'Where do you come from? Oh yes, *Cow*bridge.'

Mum and I took the two stops up the District Line to see Aunt Wanda. I craned my neck in an attempt to see Seamus, who had been invited to play on the swings with his friend, but the train passed too quickly. My twin-glazed reflection sped along outside, looking in.

'Sharon! So kind of you to come to help me unpack all these boxes! Oh my God, do we have work to do!' Wanda released me from her warm hug and ushered Mum and me before her into her newly rented East Putney terraced house. 'Look! They put all the boxes in one room!' We stood for a moment, Wanda's hands on my shoulders, confronting packing boxes that reached the ceiling. Wanda was like water: she rushed in to fill the space made available to her.

Over the course of the day, I ran small boxes up the stairs to bedrooms and helped unpack the larger ones downstairs, placing items as directed by Wanda.

'I never realised you had so much stuff,' Mum said to her.

'I don't want just a house, I want a home,' said Wanda.

Wanda looked so much like Mum, only slighter, shorter and younger and, so, like me too. I liked our trio more than the one of

Mum, Dad and me, or the one comprising Sherah, Seamus and me. I had become aware that I was happier in relationships of three than of two, when I was always the more pliant, subservient one, except for, perhaps, in the case of Seamus; but even that was beginning to change as he grew older. Three gave balance, stability and provided the judgment and moderation of a third pair of eyes.

While we worked, Mum and Wanda chatted, the elder sister quizzing the younger on her employment prospects.

Wanda looked at me admiringly and said, 'I like your dress.'

'Thank you.'

Wanda had a way of making people feel good about themselves. 'Is it new? I don't remember seeing Sherah in it.'

'Well, it was Sherah's but I don't think she ever wore it.'

'But seriously,' said Mum to Wanda, 'do you think it will be that easy for you to find work?'

'Oh yes,' replied Wanda. 'I already have a few irons in the fire. Don't be surprised if I do something completely different – I mean, accounting and finance still, but not in a stuffy office for a bunch of stuffy old men.'

'Then where?'

Wanda touched the tip of her nose with a finger and arched her eyebrows.

'What next?' asked Mum.

Wanda looked around her. 'Okay,' she said decisively to her sister. 'Help me take these big boxes of books up and then Sharon can arrange the books on the shelves in the small bedroom that I shall make my office. Or study. Whatever.'

When Wanda and Mum leant over a packing case, their heads touched and their hair blended into each other's. Their hair was the same length and colour and for a brief moment they resembled a hairy one-headed, four-armed and four-legged monster intent on devouring a cardboard box, and I giggled.

'What's so funny?' They grunted under the box's weight.

I told them, omitting to describe the unbegrudging jealousy I felt as I watched the loving sisters, in the certainty that Sherah would never do for me what Mum did for Wanda.

The last box of books up, Mum and Wanda returned downstairs to the sitting room where more packing cases awaited them.

I knelt on a wool carpet that, brushed by my hand, released smells of carpet cleaner and disinfectant. Around me, to my kneeling head height, towered the nine stacks of, on average, seventy books that I had removed from the boxes they had been transported in. Six hundred and twenty-one books to be exact. I pulled some of the piles carefully towards me until I felt quite surrounded, protected, like an animal in a burrow. I leafed through some books at random, idly. With the exception of Wanda, we weren't great book readers in my family. Like Dad and Seamus and, to a lesser extent, Mum and Sherah, I didn't understand why people would read a book when they could be hitting a ball. Or performing on a stage. The only books I had taken pleasure in reading from cover to cover were the plays I had acted in – why read a story when you could perform it or, even better, dance it?

Besieged by the bank of books, I stood and moved some aside. I dusted the shelves and, reaching for the book nearest me, paused. I wondered how Aunt Wanda would want me to arrange them. I could do it in alphabetical order of the authors' names – obvious – or of the books' titles. I could separate the Polish from the English books – or not. I caught sight of an author's dates of birth and death on the back of a book and thought I could do it by date of birth, but that would be too time-consuming. I decided to ask Aunt Wanda what she wanted.

Performing a salsa in a series of side-steps to escape the towers of books in the room and the empty packing boxes in the hallway, I paused at the top of the landing by the open sash window to watch a District Line train trundle by. A few passengers stood; most sat. Although together, they seemed quite alone. Others might feel the same way I did, a fragile eggshell of a person, the yolk and albumen having leaked long ago. Humpty Dumpty sat on a wall. Humpty Dumpty, why did you fall? I pressed my forehead against the windowpane and looked down onto the road below, taking pleasure in the cooling draught around my waist.

The train came to a stop further down the line, at East Putney. I lifted my T-shirt to encourage fingers of draught up and around me. It was unusually quiet. Not a car passed. Not a bird sang.

Quite distinctly, as clearly as if I had been gifted with powers of extrasensory perception, I heard Aunt Wanda say, 'When are you going to tell the children?' It was as though those words had been whispershouted in my ear, gathering volume as they reverberated in my head.

Mum said, 'I don't know.'

I sat on the top step. Through the banisters, I could see, in the front room below, the edge of a packing case and, on a grubby magnolia wall and on the worn wooden floors, Mum's and Wanda's shadows. Wanda's shadow moved closer to Mum's.

'You won't be going back to him this time,' said Wanda.

'No,' said Mum. 'Not this time.'

Wanda's long-fingered shadow patted Mum's on a distended, pointed knee.

'Last time, it was…' Mum sighed. 'Different. Sherah was just a baby.'

Somewhere, somehow, someone had turned life's large volume knob up. Cries and the sound of car engines reached me through the open window and the chug-a-chug of a train picking up speed to Putney Bridge blended with the whoosh of the rush of blood from my head as I stood. I snapshot saw rather than counted sixteen passengers standing in the penultimate carriage and six in the last before I fell. Relaxed, I folded and unfolded down the stairs. My head met a cardboard box of soft furnishings destined for a bedroom.

Terrified, panic-stricken, solicitous Mum and Wanda fussed over me as, upside down, I looked up two pairs of nostrils above two double chins. Their hair as they bent over me and their hands as they searched for a grip around my arms and back tickled my cheeks and my armpits.

'I only wanted to know,' I said to Wanda, 'how you would like me to arrange your books.'

Isabella

It was a winter of unusually misty and monochrome days in which I would confuse the fug in my mind with the fog in the town, in which the difficulty I had in seeing to the end of my street and my inability to recall events with much clarity came together in a vague but persistent picture of greys and a sentiment of perplexity. Cosmo and I spent nights with the Baldocks and were shepherded along Oxford's wet and pea-souper streets during the day by Mrs Baldock or Mrs McKey to interviews with the police, social services, psychologists and doctors. Clothes were fetched for us from home. We received visits at the Baldocks' house, where adults conferred behind closed doors and made telephone calls from the hallway to – I knew, because I could hear them despite the hushed tones – our relatives, after which they would put the receiver down with a sigh and a disbelieving shake of the head. Cosmo and I were interviewed, together sometimes, alone at others. He found it all extremely difficult and was maddened by his inability to communicate until someone had the idea of presenting him with dolls again and with pen and paper so that he might draw.

To the astonishment of some people, Cosmo asked for Papa a lot. I understood, though, and would hug him as he clung to me. I felt curiously detached from it all, volunteering little information and answering questions economically, stopping answering them altogether when some clever clogs of a policeman suggested that Mama had been complicit in Papa's delinquency. Although it was never said to me explicitly, I realised with horror that Papa was blaming Mama for the abuse of his children and that it was he who had encouraged that particular line of questioning. This only added to the rage of conflicting emotions in me. I felt the confusion of loving Papa because I didn't know how not to, and yet hating him for his humiliation of his children and for slurring our loving Mama posthumously. Had it not been for Cosmo and for Mama's death, which had thrust a sister's responsibility upon me, I don't think I would have led Cosmo to expose Papa. I forced myself to confront the reprehensible and crazy idea that, at some outrageous, deep level, I resented Papa's rejection that had followed once my periods had begun. I had wrestled with this shameful notion and faced it down in the mirror but, lacking the courage to reach a definitive answer, had told myself that it was best to do the right thing even though it may, in very small part, have been motivated by the wrong reason. In the aftermath of my exploitation by Papa, of Mama's dying, of my monthly cycles commencing and, most recently, of this abrupt disintegration of what had once been a family, I felt my judgement failing me at every turn and considered anything possible. No matter how much I reasoned, Papa's treatment of me remained tied to the belief that he had administered just punishment for my bed-wetting – no matter that I may have never wet the bed. For some indefinable reason, I felt that I had deserved his chastisement and I had even wondered, as I had grown older, if I hadn't in some way asked for his physical attention even though I knew I hadn't.

Cosmo and I didn't see Papa, but it was clear from the things that the police and social workers said that the police had had numerous meetings and conversations with him. On occasion, the adults would speak to each other as though neither Cosmo nor I were in the room, and so I learnt certain things before we were told them formally – sometimes days later – and other things I was surprised never to be told directly at all.

After numerous consultations with speech therapists and examinations by doctors, Cosmo became the subject of a dispute. One doctor advised that he would require reconstructive oropharyngeal surgery, which meant that he would have to submit to several operations over a number of years to repair damage to his throat and palate that had occurred as a consequence of the repeated insertions of foreign objects into his mouth from an early age. The speech therapists assigned to Cosmo rubbished the notion.

We were told that we would be placed in a foster home, and were given the opportunity of meeting our foster parents before we actually moved in; a stage we never reached that day, because Cosmo, to whom it had been explained that the new man he was about to meet was to be his new father, had, eager to please, immediately tried to undo the man's belt buckle and trouser fly. The man and his wife had become very embarrassed and angry at social services for not having been given Cosmo's and my full histories. Much to the mortification of the social workers who had been assigned to our care, it was another month before we said tearful goodbyes and heartfelt thank–yous to the Baldocks.

Cosmo and I were welcomed into the Iffley home of Sonia and Gregor Bobeckyj, motivated to foster children despite having two of their own by the example set by, they said, the many European families who had sheltered Mr Bobeckyj; having seen his parents killed, he had made his way from Poland to England immediately after the Second World War. 'Just as we children of the war formed the peace of today, so the children of today will form the Europe of tomorrow,' he would say as Mrs Bobeckyj piled steaming pie and vegetables on our plates. Incapable of consuming the large helpings we were presented with, Cosmo and I would exchange guilt-ridden looks until Mrs Bobeckyj accepted that neither of us would eat as much as her son, Tomasz, who was a year younger than me, and her daughter, Zuzanna, who was a year older than Cosmo. Cosmo ate little for good reason: he was subjected to a number of operations on his mouth in the five years we stayed with the Bobeckyjs and, consequently, there were periods in which it was uncomfortable for him to consume solid food. Our hearts went out to him and we were full of admiration at the resolve with which he bore pain; but he and we could hear the benefits of the operations and the speech therapy he received, as his speech improved to the point at which, in short exchanges at least, no stranger would have guessed that he had a speech impediment. Of course, Cosmo had his coping tactics: his favourite words and a slight stammer were deployed to give the impression that he was thinking hard and weighing his words carefully.

My reasons for eating little were more psychological than physical, a truth I would only confront when awake in bed, when everyone else in the house, to the extent that I could tell, was asleep. The social worker and psychologist assigned to me had made things worse rather than better. Hampson Lafontaine was a well-meaning young woman who spoke with a plum in her mouth and always arrived with a basket of fruit for Cosmo and me. She set about her job as though it were a blend of charity work and research for a thesis. Armed with books that she would remove from a tote bag and leaf through prior to interviews, she would ask me leading questions or try to place words in my mouth that, I assumed, would conform to whichever theory was the subject of the books she'd been reading. She would sigh and consider me pityingly before consulting a book and dolefully asking her colleague, 'May I?'

Christian Johnston would bow his head, his hair falling forward, as though acknowledging his colleague's natural born right to lead.

'Did he tell you that you wouldn't be believed if you told?' asked Miss Lafontaine, conspiratorially,

'No,' I said.

'Did he tell you that he'd hurt you if you told?' she asked me in hushed tones.

'No.'

'What did he tell you?' she asked exasperatedly.

'That he was sorry.'

Miss Lafontaine looked lost for a moment. 'Did he tell you that you enjoyed it?' she asked with an uncomfortable mix of cunning and desperation.

'No.'

'Well, for goodness' sake! Why didn't you tell anyone?' Miss Lafontaine flung herself back in her comfortable chair.

I wanted to say that I had, eventually, in a sense; but instead said nothing.

Mr Johnston leant forward and parted his long, lank, greasy hair, which formed brackets either side of a face punctuated by the scars of childhood acne and an exclamation mark of a pursed mouth and plumb–line nose. 'And did you enjoy it?' he asked quietly.

'No!'

'It's all right, you know.'

'But I didn't.'

'You mustn't feel ashamed.'

'I don't.'

'You mustn't feel' – and here he sniggered – 'dirty.'

It had never occurred to me to feel dirty – dirtied, yes, but not dirty.

'You don't have to be so defensive,' said Mr Johnston.

It was hard to say that I wasn't without appearing so.

'It wasn't your fault. Unless.'

'Unless what?'

Miss Lafontaine placed her hand on Mr Johnston's arm and pulled him back. She interrogated the open book on her lap with a long fingernail and said to him quietly, 'You are at risk of confusing a perceived truth with an empirical truth. Remember, as far as the patient is concerned, only the perceived truth matters.' Louder, to me, she said, 'You've done nothing wrong.' She enunciated very clearly.

That was a conclusion I had reached for myself.

Mr Johnston appeared peeved and, lowering his head, disappeared behind the curtains of his hair.

It took Miss Lafontaine's and Mr Johnston's inept interrogations to force me to confront my feelings and face the extent to which things had happened around and to me that I had had no say over. The realisation of my former powerlessness, combined with a large degree of self-reproach for my slowness in reaching that awareness, sent me reeling and spinning as I lay on my back in bed; neither patterned wallpaper nor frilly bedspread and bedside lampshade arrested my dizzying descent into a sleep in which I dreamt of control and of the lack of it, of its loss and regaining.

Sharon

I sat cross-legged in the park in the last days of the summer holiday in shorts, halter top and trainers.

A recurring daydream was of a hole immediately before me that, somehow, has my shape. Leaning and peering in, I see nothing, just browns and greys that turn to black. I feel a tremor beneath my feet and fall back from the edge of the earthy rim as that hole that is me climbs out of itself, liberates itself from its substrata of stone, clay, sand and pebbles and assumes a form through which the wind and the light pass without obstruction. I want to comfort it and it me and we stumble and fall into each other.

'What are you hugging yourself for?' asked Dad, standing unknowingly at the very edge of the hole. 'It's not cold.' He hit the outstretched palm of one hand with his tennis racquet. 'Where's Seamus?'

Dad's face was against the light but I could tell from his tone that he knew I didn't know, so I said nothing but looked around me and at the milling, funning children on swings and slides.

'Yes,' said Dad gleefully, tapping the soles of his tennis shoes with his tennis racquet. 'You've no idea, have you?' He paused and when I said nothing he added, bored, businesslike and sarcastic in succession, 'I came to tell you that he's gone with Mum and Sherah to buy new school uniforms. To Kingston. Just in case you worried for him and thought of looking for him.'

Seamus was going to a new school, as was Sherah – to a crammer, in order to resit her exams. I looked up, resisting my desire to beg for a new uniform too, intent on disappointing Dad. The breeze picked up and I saw him through strands of my hair, as if on old, striated film, and he seemed as irrelevant and unconnected to me as the film stars in the black and white films he and Mum sometimes fell asleep to.

'You're okay, though, aren't you?' he said hopping from one foot to the next in exercise. 'You can wear Sherah's old uniform. It'll fit, won't it?' Dad knew that I hated living in hand-me-down clothes that were the fashion of some three years previously, that Sherah had frayed, stretched or discoloured. 'Won't it?' he insisted, testing the strings of his tennis racquet.

The goblins and elves of my parents' coming separation and my sister's antipathy lurked in trees and bushes, behind the children who swung to and fro and climbed up and slid down. They were too quick and cunning for me to see them out of anything but the corner of my eyes.

Isabella

No matter the superficial changes I imposed on my outer appearance, I remained a young girl, a teenager, and Tomasz was a young boy and a teenager too. I grew thin and tall and confident with my new sense of control and self-esteem; only recently made aware that I had been powerless, I stopped feeling it. As I ate less and more fastidiously, my stomach and my belly shrank to the same extent that my breasts swelled and, as my cheeks hollowed, my cheekbones acquired greater prominence. Despite what Papa had subjected me to, I was a young woman, had become one, grown into one with the physical appetites of one; my wings had dried and the time had come to show them off. Tomasz noticed it and I noticed him and his noticing it: the attraction was mutual.

I sought to justify my nascent sexual appetite to myself intellectually, by understanding my feelings in terms of the natural chemical changes a young woman goes through (as explained by Miss Lafontaine) and viscerally, more guiltily and yet pleasurably, by considering it a consequence of the manner in which I had been used and humiliated: having been used by men, I would use men in return, get my own back, get my power back. Sexual predation would be my way of rising above my personal history, of regaining control. And yet, such affirmative thinking only took me so far, so far as to fool around with Tomasz, to feed his infatuation, to tease and to flirt, to deliver parcels of promise. I was like an advent calendar to Tomasz but opening windows over weeks rather than days and, while opening some, closing others – to his frustration and yet secret delight.

It wasn't just Tomasz who noticed my transfiguration into palpitating womanhood but Mr and Mrs Bobeckyj too or, to be more precise, Mrs Bobeckyj who noticed her son and her husband noticing it, and decided to do something about it; though whether to safeguard her son's relative innocence or her husband's constancy, I was uncertain. I read the decision in her eyes on my 16th birthday when both father and son kissed me too close to the mouth and that little too long and held me that little longer than propriety allowed on the occasion of wishing someone many happy returns of the day, after which Miss Lafontaine and Mr Johnston paid me three visits in a fortnight, during the last of which they suggested I move to a sheltered home for older girls in Littlemore, just south of Iffley. I had crossed from north to south Oxford already and told myself that this was London exercising its inexorable pull, and so assented without objection. The move had been sold to me as something that would be good for me and good for Cosmo, as a boy of his age would replace me in the Bobeckyj household. Cosmo and I were close, as brother and sister, but our age gap and gender difference was at its widest in adolescence and I was neither his confidante nor even his close friend, our secret history having left a tart taste in our mouths and become unmentionable. Besides, Mrs Bobeckyj had become the mother figure for him, a role I had been relieved to relinquish to her, and he was discovering academic excellence at school – what with the confidence that accompanied the improvements in his speech – and great skill as an artist.

Sharon

In RE we learnt about Christianity, Islam and Judaism. 'There's more than one way to skin a cat, even if it's only a Cheshire cat,' said Dad. 'Protestant or Catholic, Sunni or Shia, Ashkenazim or Sephardim, take your pick. Double cream, full fat, semi-skimmed or skimmed, why not try goats' milk? You can have one one week and another the next.'

Mum glared at Dad in rebuke.

'Why not? I know people who've done just that. You know, chop and change, duck and dive.' Dad bobbed his head like a chicken when he said that. He claimed to be Church of England but when pressed as to why he never practised on a Sunday and went to play tennis instead, he could only muster a weak, 'What I need to practise is my tennis serve,' which in of itself was quite true.

We decorated the Christmas tree on Christmas Eve, a Polish tradition that Dad was happy to follow because he could wait until the very last minute before selecting an overstocked Christmas tree supplier and haggling aggressively. At Dad's insistence, we had our Christmas meal on Christmas Day rather than on Christmas Eve. 'That's the way we do it in our family. Turkey and a *vino rosso*. No *pierogi*, no fish and vodka, thank you very much,' was said to endear himself to Nonna, Mum's Italian mother.

Lunch would be spent trying to guess what the gifts from Dad were, on one occasion thinking of funny things the poorly wrapped bicycles marked Sherah and Sharon could be, as though we hadn't really known. Hula hoops and flying saucers had been the best guesses and they had been Seamus's. Of course, the correct guesses would have been a new bike for Sherah and Sherah's old bike for Sharon. 'It's as good as new after the thorough cleaning I gave it!' had said Dad, in response to a withering look from Nonno, Mum's father. 'Look, I changed the brake blocks, I fitted new ones,' he'd added weakly.

Nonno had left the room.

Dad's face had sagged, then crumpled, as though the effort of Christmas cheer were too much for him. His nose and eyes had collapsed and disappeared into his sharp, ridged chin that had slumped to his chest as though in defeat in a battle he had been waging under the winking green and red lights of the Christmas tree.

I liked being part of the trickle of churchgoers on Christmas morning that swelled as we passed the doors of other Christians. Sherah, Seamus and I had taken our Holy Communion under Mum's direction and yet we didn't attend church regularly. Mum had done her bit out of loyalty to one part of her family tree by giving us Hebrew names, Dad would joke, and to the other by bringing us up as Catholic; and yet, whenever I tried to engage Mum on such issues, she ducked them. She, I knew, had tried several Catholic churches around South London before settling on the one nearest us. I wasn't quite sure whether she had been actively seeking Polish congregations or trying to avoid them.

I walked alongside Mum, making a big show of checking the time on the digital watch she had given me. She was distracted, not herself, apprehensive. I held her arm tightly and chatted inconsequentially. I wanted to make her feel better but didn't know how. Neighbours greeted us and Mum pulled herself together, her absorbed air replaced by a masking smile.

Christ the King was a pale grey brick building of no architectural merit, despite its architect of note. It squatted at the bottom of a long hill at the top of which presided the Anglican St Mary's Church, emblematic of the country's attitude to the two religions, Dad had once said – the Protestant above the Catholic.

I liked the hymn-singing best of all and looked at the choristers and altar boys and girls with envy, wishing that church could be another performance event for me but afraid that the sentiment and emotion such engagement risked bringing with it would expose me as hollow, not spiritually worthy. I thought of the man Dad had read about in the paper who was found to have no brain, just a layer of brain cells around the inside of his skull, but emptiness where grey matter should have been. That was me, I felt, at a personal level: cut me in two and you'd find nothing, just an inner lining to an exoskeleton that walked and talked like a human being.

'Take this, all of you, and eat of it, for this is my body, which will be given up for you,' pronounced Father John, holding a wafer up for his congregation to see. He paused, then placed it on his tongue and swallowed it. The reflected light on his glasses hid his expression.

Father John reached for a chalice, the choir sang and the congregation queued. I stood in line between my siblings, uneasy not because I considered myself to have sinned and not because I hadn't been to confession, but because the doctrine of transubstantiation bothered me.

'Truly, truly, I say to you, unless you eat the flesh of the Son of man and drink his blood, you have no life in you; he who eats my flesh and drinks my blood has eternal life, and I will raise him up at the last day. For my flesh is real food, and my blood is real drink. He who eats my flesh and drinks my blood abides in me, and I in him. As the living Father sent me, and I live because of the Father, so he who eats me will live because of me.'

The idea of eating someone's flesh was unsettling, at best. That it was Jesus' struck me as idolatrous to an extreme. Father John offered me the wafer. I trembled and took it. Father John blessed me. The body of Christ tasted faintly of what I imagined to be starch and dishwater as it dissolved between my tongue and palate.

Isabella

I didn't hold my expulsion from the Bobeckyj household against Mrs Bobeckyj at all. She and her husband had been kind and sensitive, if slightly distant, surrogate parents and my leaving brought a tidy resolution to the complication that Tomasz and I had been knotting for each other, one that untangled only gradually over months of Sundays on which I was invited to visit Cosmo for lunch.

And then there was the care home and the novel company of a dozen teenage girls who, I would learn over the next two years, were blemished but beautiful butterflies, all the more admirable for having been damaged.

We had our own rooms and shared four bathrooms and two kitchens and a communal room across two floors. Mr and Mrs Bankes lived on the premises and either Miss Robbie or Miss Heverfet was there daily. It was as Miss Heverfet and Miss Lafontaine were introducing me to my new family, to use Miss Heverfet's term, or housemates, to use Miss Lafontaine's, that I found myself in front of a girl I hadn't seen in five years and yet recognised instantly, despite the massive change she had undergone.

'Kimberley!'

Kimberley said nothing and, blushing beneath lowered eyelashes, edged back into her room while Miss Heverfet moved on to her neighbour.

'You know each other?' asked Miss Lafontaine.

'And this is Frederica. She's been with us a month. Frederica, this is Isabella.' Miss Heverfet made the introduction loudly so as to preclude my reply, demonstrating an understanding of the nature of such encounters that Miss Lafontaine had yet to grasp.

'Freddie,' said Frederica once Miss Heverfet and Miss Lafontaine had departed, and shook my hand quite formally.

I had never met anyone like Freddie. She mixed tact and delicacy with candour and bluntness that I found disorienting until I recognised that she was open about herself and yet discreet about others. She was like the lemon sherbet sweets I had once been fond of:

initially hard and bitter and, later, sweet and effervescent. She didn't ask me how I knew Kimberley but, as though relishing being in charge and no longer the new girl, sat me down and made me tea and toast and spoke about the home, its timetable and rules, her routine and her aspirations.

Ambition, I came to learn, was considered a virtue in the home. When Freddie spoke it wasn't to explain why she was there but to talk about her future. As the other girls on my floor drifted in and out of the kitchen, welcoming and introducing themselves to me, it occurred to me that I needed neither a rescinded nor an alternative history but an intended future, a goal, an aim, something I had come closest to contemplating when it had been suggested to me that I stay on at school after the age of sixteen. In between cups of tea, preambles and digressions, I smiled and nodded and leant forward and back, doing my utmost to adopt a body language that spoke of my attentiveness and interest while I sought an appropriate reply to the question of what I was hoping to do should I be asked, but I wasn't; the girls tiptoed around my future with all the sensitivity they demonstrated around our personal histories.

'It's what Have-a-fit and Blobby go on about,' said Freddie, slumped in a kitchen chair. 'Ambition, ambition, ambition. They want you to look forward, not back. Ambition is their "thing". Choose your direction. One step at a time. Aim high, aim low – it doesn't matter. Aim high and reach your target – bravo! Miss it – well, at least you tried and are at a different place from where you started. Aim low and – succeed or fail – it doesn't matter: re-set. That kind of thing.' She sat up. 'It works for me.' She tossed her black hair back and bunched it with both hands, her armpit hairs, visible through her short T-shirt sleeves, surprisingly bushy. 'I'm going to be a singer. I'm going to go to music school in London. Opera.'

'Are they… nice?'

'Who?'

'Miss Heverfet and Miss Robbie.'

'Oh, they're okay. We call them that because Have-a-fit can fly off the handle sometimes and Blobby, well, she is a bit fat, you must admit. We don't call her that when Kimberley's around, of course.'

'She's not well, is she?'

'No.' Freddie frowned and looked into her mug. 'It doesn't work for her.' She looked out of the window, as though what might work for Kimberley were hidden in the flowerbeds and bushes that bordered the care home's garden. 'I think that, for some people, they have to look back. You know, to understand and accept. Therapy and all that. Come to terms with things. I think Kimberley has to do that first. Verdi and Puccini. You know, the opera I want to do.' She finished her tea, her eyes just visible above the lip of her mug.

I knew that Kimberley hadn't followed me into the kitchen for fear of what a public encounter might entail, what reaction it might trigger, and was grateful to her for it. I guessed that her embarrassment was greater than mine and her confusion more profound; neither of us had been prepared to see the other and both of us had to undergo considerable mental readjustment, to brace ourselves for the introduction of a daily reminder of our former lives. The shame we feel when we see ourselves through the eyes of others is of a sharper quality than the self-disgust we experience in front of a mirror, when we can allow our eyes to glaze over and add self-pity to the mix. I wondered whether social services had failed to connect the dots or whether they were intentionally reuniting me with Kimberley, Kimberley whom I had only ever seen in states of distress or undress or both, countless times for a number of years.

'You could knock on her door, you know,' said Freddie.

I did.

As Kimberley rose from her chair by the window to welcome me, the room grew darker and I noted that she was the width of her single bed. Her voice was a whisper, a spectre of a sound that contrasted preternaturally with the huge body and thick, bull-like neck it emanated from. The waif of a girl who had stood and swayed in Papa's study that first evening I had met her now resembled a minotaur, her widely spaced eyes and her ears protruding from her lank hair like nubbins of horn only adding to the likeness. We talked, she in her armchair and I on her desk chair, about the home, the routine and the staff. Our questions were on issues of little consequence, our pasts never referred to, our prospects not alluded to. Gradually, the light ebbed from Kimberley's room, so that I could no longer distinguish her features against the still pale sky and, yet, dark trees' and distant houses' silhouettes. She sat, an amorphous mass against the curtains and the back of her armchair, bleached of the personality and character a body imputes to a person, her voice carrying like the plaintive cry of pan pipes, expressive of pain, humiliation and despondency despite the banality of our topics of conversation.

Sharon

Dad hid behind the newspaper and Mum performed menial kitchen tasks while wearing a dressing gown and an abstracted look of anxiety. She opened and closed a kitchen cupboard without looking in or removing anything from it. She leant, her back to the kitchen sink, her head bowed, her shoulders hunched, her two hands wrapped around a mug of coffee as if for warmth.

Seamus pushed his chair back from the table.

'Just stay a moment,' said Mum. 'Dad,' she said to Dad, who hadn't turned the page of his newspaper in a conspicuous while. She put her empty mug in the dishwasher and walked deliberately to him. Slowly, firmly, she took away the newspaper, folded it and placed it on the radiator by the window. Sherah raised her eyes from a magazine and looked at Seamus and me. 'There's something we need to tell you,' said Mum, standing behind Dad with her hands on his shoulders.

Dad rubbed his face with his hands and untied and retied his dressing gown cord and looked up at Mum who gave his shoulders a gentle push.

'The thing is,' said Dad, 'Mum and I thought that… Well, you know, Mum and I love each other very much and we love you very much. However, well, you know, we thought we might live separately for a while – not for a long time, but just for a while, you know, just for a change.'

Seamus looked from Dad to Mum while Sherah looked at Seamus and me.

Seamus said, 'You're splitting up.'

'Yes,' said Mum.

'No,' said Dad. Then, 'Only for a short time. To begin with.'

'For a short time to begin with,' snorted Sherah.

'You've taken your time about it,' said Seamus. 'Is this the bit when you say you'll always love us and tell us it's not our fault? And that you'll be best friends? That's what my friends say you'll say. Is it you who's moving out, Dad?'

Dad, taken aback, answered, 'Only around the corner.'

'So we'll see you at weekends?'

'Yes,' said Dad. 'And at other times too, of course.'

'Cool,' said Seamus. 'At least I won't be the only one anymore whose parents are married.' He looked at me and Sherah. 'You both knew, didn't you?'

I didn't know how to respond, and was certain that my confusion was written on my face.

Seamus looked at Mum and Dad. 'Why am I always the last to be told anything?'

Mum and Dad protested weakly and looked from Seamus, who made no move to get down from the table, to me.

My parents looked pale in the wan December light. They maintained their positions, one sitting, one standing, like statues on a stage set, the play long over. I was overcome with love for them. They had drifted apart without my realising it was happening and I had taken the silences and the trivial disputes to be a normal part of family life, preferring to think with every passing day that I had misheard or imagined the conversation between Mum and Wanda or that Mum and Dad had changed their minds. Maybe, if they had separated once and got back together, they could do so again. Or, maybe, if I hadn't come along to complicate things, they might still want to be together.

I stood and hugged them, one arm around Dad's neck and the other around Mum's waist.

'I love you,' I said, 'and I hope it will be just for a short time,' and Mum, Sherah and I started crying while Dad patted my arm and Seamus looked on, surprised, as though he might have missed something.

Mie

It occurred to me that, for flight, where a bird needed wings, I needed a foreign language.

I spun the globe that stood on a shelf at the back of the classroom, east to west, to find that Spain is at the same latitude as Japan. I stared wistfully at the square Iberian peninsula; we were taught neither Spanish nor Portuguese at school. I didn't look east from Japan, the thought of losing myself more metaphorically than actually in the desolate blue expanse of sea quite terrifying. What are we when, silver-bulleted, we cross the ocean thousands of metres above it? The thought of flying above land, however, held no fear; I would remain rooted by the swiftly moving tendrils of my imagination. To the north of France: Britain. There was a symmetry I found appealing: Japan and Britain, insular parentheses either side of the Eurasian landmass.

Too proud to underperform academically, I did well in all my classes; the ones I really excelled in were language classes and, specifically, foreign languages: English and German. I loved the precision that language could convey when needed and, too, the ambiguity and poetry at other times. It became evident to me that I would study a language at university. I found German to be like mathematics; surgically, thrillingly precise with straitjacket-like qualities and an abrasive sound of metronomically regimented jackboots, not unlike our harsh, barked Japanese. Indeed, German was too like Japanese and, indeed, Germany too like Japan. Both languages place the verb at the end of the sentence and have polite and informal forms of speech. Both countries lost the last great war and, at some profound level, the more I learnt, the more I was put off German by the fact that the Germans, like we Japanese, wore the world war like a badge of shame. I didn't want to remain in a losers' club.

English, by contrast, was the language of victors; it was democratic, with the one form of address. It brought the verb closer to the subject with the emphasis on the subject doing the doing rather than the object being done to. English was active, not passive. It was liberating, with rules that only went so far. One needed a poem to remember how to pronounce tough, bough, cough, dough and hiccough, thorough, slough and through. There were no rules; it was down to you. It was up to me. *Aus, bei, mit, nach, seit, von, zu* take the dative but what rule governs English prepositions? Mrs Watanabe, despite her excellent English (or so we thought), only ever risked losing her composure when explaining prepositions that, in our language, had been subsumed into compound verbs that, in effect, made the learning of these almost automatic. Was I the only one to notice the silent plea she would make to the English assistant as she removed her glasses with one hand and ran the back of the other against her brow?

Our German language assistant was a big blonde farmer's daughter in pigtails, thick glasses and dungarees who desperately wanted to be liked. The more Ursula tried to impress us with the Japanese she had learnt and the more she tried to ingratiate herself with us, the more we disliked her. We had been brought up to revere our teachers but, as we recognised a mutual sentiment in the implacable Mrs Watanabe – who detected our malevolent attitude to Ursula and yet did little to discourage it – we grew to despise the stranger who had parachuted into our midst. Her Japanese language skills were her eventual undoing; we soon learnt that, easily frustrated with our reluctance to communicate in her native language, she would lapse into Japanese and, ultimately, as we watched her anxiety levels rise and enjoyed her total capitulation to explaining in Japanese what she had been so desperate to tell us in German, we learnt little.

Margaret, in contrast, appeared to understand not a word of Japanese and to be quite indifferent as to whether she was liked. Her hair was light brown in colour and of medium length and her face and hands quite free of make-up and jewellery. She wore jeans, woolly jumpers and Hush Puppies shoes and kept her arms straight and her hands clasped in front of her, whether standing at the front or the back of the class or leaning over our desks to assist us with our work. She spoke English a little loudly but slowly and clearly, and when spoken to in Japanese would reply, 'I'm afraid I speak no Japanese. Can you please repeat that in English?' Initially, we didn't believe her but she remained so benignly beaming when some pupils, out of earshot of Mrs Watanabe and keeping an innocent smile on their faces, addressed her as *busu*, *putaro* or *kusobabaa*, when she was anything but ugly, a tramp and a farty old woman, that we quickly decided that she could, indeed, not understand a word of our language. So we doubled our efforts to communicate to her in hers and, consequently, learnt English fast.

Sharon

Mum and I arrived at my school just before Dad. We stood on the highest of the seven concrete steps to what had once been a modern steel and glass school building and watched him park; he was always meticulous to ensure he parked exactly in the middle of a parking bay and that the front wheels were aligned with the back. He got out, locked the car and stood motionless, as though summoning energy and courage. Grey concrete steps, grey parking lot, grey cars, grey sky, grey dad.

The years since he'd left home had not been good to Dad. Sherah and Seamus rarely visited him, pleading homework, tiredness and extra-curricular activities so that what had once been a bland rental apartment gradually declined into a grotty and stuffy lad's den, reflective of the vicious circle whereby the less his children visited him the less he considered it necessary to tidy it and, so, the less they wanted to visit him. Sitting amid the dross of takeaway food cartons and soft drinks cans and laundry laid out on radiators and feeling sorry for their dad and angry with him too and guilty at feeling angry was not how Sherah and Seamus wanted to spend their weekends.

We would see Dad at school during the week or outdoors on weekends; he became our groupie, cheering us on from the touchline at school sporting events, driving us to and from away matches and applauding us at school plays and concerts. No sooner was I on stage than I would look for him in an audience, squinting against bright stage lights. Identifying him among the many parents' expectant faces, I could relax, fill my role, a little part of me always, no matter my dedication to the production and immersion in the part, surprised that I, who was nothing, could become something – someone – on stage, and conscious too that I performed at some hidden level just for him, for his approval, despite the fact that he never came to say hello before a performance or goodbye after it. Touchingly, Aunt Wanda never missed a play I was in, and I couldn't help but feel that Mum turned up to see and chat with her sister as much as to watch and support me. Mum spent what time she had to herself running.

A hole in the car park fenced off by once-white plastic barriers made a mockery of my aspirations to completeness. Dad skirted the dirty plastic barricade and walked to Mum and me where he climbed the steps laboriously. On the step immediately lower than the one Mum and I stood on, he was at the right height for an exchange of kisses on cheeks. As he and Mum stood eye to eye, the contrasting changes in my parents were startling. He looked as though he had found the years and kilos she had lost, and more. She was a sleek young greyhound to his wrinkled-jowl ageing pug. If anyone had not known which of the two had asked for the separation, they would now. Dad's face against a late afternoon autumn sky was featureless; his unpolished brogues and scruffy corduroy trousers, his ill-matching and tight herringbone tweed jacket over a stained jumper spoke of a battle lost. Mum, with a healthy complexion, elegant in her sharp shoes and sharper knee-length dress suit, tossed her long hair to one side and said, 'Right then. Let's go in and see what this is all about.' When Dad opened the door for us and turned to usher us in, I could see love and a sense of loss expressed conflictingly in his eyes and, for a brief moment, was pleased to have brought Mum and Dad together even if I were to suffer for it.

My co-ed school had only recently appointed its first headmistress, Mrs Baxter, who always wore a rich blue trouser suit and a grey bob that framed rectangular steel spectacles. She stepped out of her study to welcome us.

'Mrs Truss. Mr Truss. Sharon.' She shook each one of us by hand in turn.

She held the door open for us and indicated an armchair, on which were some papers and by which was a cup of tea, and a three-seater sofa; there was only one place for us to sit and we took it, my dad to my right and my mum to my left.

While Dad gazed around the imposing study that was decorated with some of the pupils' better art work and with framed photos of the school's sports teams, I could sense Mum and Mrs Baxter assessing each other. I hoped that their common ground – their dress, their composure – could form the basis for an affinity that would work in my favour and yet I feared that they might unwittingly compete with each other, and that Mrs Baxter would take it out on me.

Mrs Baxter removed the papers from the armchair and sat down; now she leant forward, legs crossed at the ankles and one elbow on a chair arm, and gave the appearance of studying us above her glasses. I was conscious that I hadn't sat between my parents on a sofa in years.

Mrs Baxter cleared her throat and stretched her lips in facsimile of a smile. Her large, quite uncluttered desk behind her spoke of authority, order and confidence. When she spoke it was quietly but distinctly and determinedly.

'Thank you for meeting me,' she began. 'There are two issues that I'd like to discuss with you. The first is Sharon's academic perfor-mance. As you no doubt know, Sharon once had an exemplary aca-demic record and was at the top of the class or very near it in every subject. Over the last three to four years, however, the quality of her work has declined such that it has failed to keep up, with both that produced by her peer group and her earlier high standards. I assume that none of this is news to you. My concern, now, is to arrest this degradation in performance before Sharon reaches a stage from which there is no return, academically speaking. I should say at this point that Sharon remains in some respects the model pupil she once was – her extracurricular contribution to school life, particularly in the areas of sport and of the performance arts, remains second to none – and that her popularity – well, that is something I will revert to. But we must discuss the question of Sharon's academic performance with some urgency. We need to either determine a course of action that will get her studying and working hard again, or agree that this school is no longer best suited to her if, for example, she seeks a career in sport or in acting. Sharon, is there anything you'd like to say?'

There was so much I wanted to say. Instead, I said, 'No,' before adding meekly, 'I'm doing okay in maths and English.'

Mrs Baxter looked from Mum, who sat motionless, to Dad, who struggled to extricate himself from the corner of the sofa and then, surrendering to its depths, mumbled, 'We hear you, we hear you.'

Mrs Baxter placed her folded glasses on the coffee table and asked, 'May I speak plainly?'

Dad said that of course she could.

'We don't want to lose Sharon. But I don't think the school can do this alone.' Mrs Baxter inhaled deeply and licked her lips, as though what she was about to say would be said at great cost to her. 'It is not uncommon for children whose parents have either divorced or separated to suffer a prolonged period of either behavioural problems or academic underperformance at school. In fact, I would say that at least one of these is to be expected and happens in the majority of cases.'

Mum stiffened.

Mrs Baxter softened. 'I've seen it all, you know. Children blaming themselves. Or punishing their parents. Or just wanting attention. Some attention, no matter if it's a scolding, is better than no attention at all, better than neglect and indifference when a parent's mind is understandably elsewhere.' She picked up her glasses and fiddled with them. 'Sharon sits her O levels next term. It would be useful to know what her ambitions are and what yours for her are.'

With that, she sat back in her armchair and pulled her skirt over her knees; clearly, it was our turn.

Mrs Baxter had been right: my marks had declined steadily and, truth to tell, I hadn't cared and still didn't. I had realised, when I was younger, that I did well because I was intelligent, and I knew, now, that intelligence without application would only get me so far; but I didn't care enough. Besides, good marks in class did little for me other than to produce a brief pulsing glow that was nothing compared to the acclaim of leading a victorious hockey team off the pitch or to the flush of taking a bow, curtain call after curtain call, as my peers clapped and whistled. And then there were boys who, funnily enough, reciprocated by noticing me at around the same time that I had started noticing them. At some point, with no one in my family besides Aunt Wanda realising, I had grown from girl- to womanhood. When Mum wasn't working, she was running. Sherah was always with her friends. Dad and Seamus were doing their own thing, sometimes together, but, anyway, they were blokes and there were some things I'd never discuss with my father or my younger brother.

Wanda, though, was different, in that she noticed everything. 'Look at you!' she'd say when I stopped by to visit, and she'd hold her arms to mine or have me stand with my back to hers or against the door jamb so she could measure me and, on one occasion after a school play after she had driven me home and I was having my first period, she hugged me close for longer than usual and, holding me at arms' length, said, 'Congratulations!' mischievously, conspiratorially, as though we were now members of the same club. Over the months that had followed I had looked at my arms and legs and my hips and breasts in wonder as they had grown and acquired tone, shape, delineation; and I had noticed boys looking too and, I had had to admit, I had liked being noticed.

Mum and Dad wrestled their ways to the front of the sofa.

Mum said, 'It would have been very helpful to have received advance notice of what this meeting was going to be about.'

Dad raised his hands and allowed them to flop down, wrists on knees, and said, 'No, the truth is that we have never discussed Sharon's future with her. We kind of, well, let our children decide their own futures. Instead of deciding for them,' he added.

Mum said, 'If I had known that this was to be a counselling session, I would have come better prepared.'

Mrs Baxter said, 'Come now, Mrs Truss. Remember, this is about Sharon and what's best for her; it's not about us.'

Dad said, 'Of course, of course. Sharon, any thoughts?'

Mum said, 'Mrs Baxter, are you saying that Sharon has failed to perform to the best of her ability or that she has lost all ability? Are you saying that she has underperformed because her father and I have separated or because we are – what were the words you used? – neglectful and indifferent to her?'

Mrs Baxter said, 'No.'

Dad said to Mum, 'Of course she's not saying that,' and, to me, 'Come on, Sharon, what do you have to say?'

The sun had set on the curtainless study. Dad, Mum and I sat in one pool of yellow light and Mrs Baxter in another while a green Anglepoise desk lamp lit the green baize of Mrs Baxter's mahogany desk. I thought of spectators at an evening hockey match on an Astroturf pitch, quiet in anticipation of the teams' appearing. I thought of a play in which the actors have forgotten their lines or their cue for their move into the spotlight. How I preferred sports and theatre to life! I received instruction and knew what my roles and lines were. What I did or said were someone else's decision and responsibility. If necessary, I could execute a reverse stick pass or ad lib in context. Squeezed between my parents and in the depths of a hideously uncomfortable sofa in a meeting that was all about me, I could think of many things I wanted to say but nothing that I wanted Mrs Baxter and my parents to hear.

Mrs Baxter blinked first: rattled by Mum's hostility, she raised her cup to her lips and replaced it, embarrassed to have found it empty.

Mum said, 'You had two issues to discuss with us. I presume the first was my daughter's work and the second her relationship with her parents. Is there anything else?'

'That wasn't the second issue,' said Mrs Baxter defensively. 'I am sorry to have been misunderstood. It may have a bearing on the second, though,' she added hesitantly.

'Which is?' asked Mum.

Mrs Baxter cleared her throat. 'You will have noticed that Sharon's form tutor is absent, although you might have well expected him to be present given the subject of our discussion just now. The reason is that, well, the subject I'm going to raise next is, well, that little bit more delicate.' Mrs Baxter tugged at her skirt. I admired her for not shirking what was obviously difficult for her. She continued, 'I mentioned Sharon's popularity earlier. Popularity is a good thing. Sharon has friends, which is good, of both sexes, which is even better, and retains her popularity despite not belonging to a clique or a gang, which I consider admirable.'

I could hear Mum and Dad either side of me thinking, 'Get on with it!' But not me. I knew what was coming.

As though hearing Mum and Dad too, Mrs Baxter said directly, 'The second issue for discussion is the one of Sharon's promiscuity.'

There. It was out there. The temperature either side of me dropped appreciably.

Mrs Baxter recovered the composure Mum and Dad at that

moment lost. 'I must say two things here,' she said. 'The first is that we are in no way passing moral judgment on Sharon. We are concerned for her physical and mental wellbeing. That's all. The second is that we should bear in mind that Sharon's behaviour is of itself not unusual or abnormal but that the extent of it is, well, let's say, at the extreme end of observed behaviours.'

'How exactly does her parents' separation have a bearing on this?' asked Mum very, very quietly, at the same time that Dad asked quite loudly, 'Behaviour? What kind of behaviour exactly? I mean, exactly what are we talking about here?' And he looked from my headmistress to me and back again to her.

I sat, centre stage, the main protagonist of a play in which I had the fewest lines.

Mrs Baxter chose to ignore Mum, if she had indeed heard her, and replied to Dad's question while meeting his perplexed stare confidently. 'In the sex education classes we give, we stress not just the mechanics of the reproductive system but the social and emotional consequences of sexual relations. We make it clear that what is done cannot be undone, that reputations once lost cannot be easily regained and that girls and boys have choice; that girls can say, *No.*'

There was no reaction from Mum or Dad.

'Look.' Mrs Baxter leant forward, elbows on knees and hands clutching her glasses. 'I know it's not what you want to hear and, I must repeat, this is not a reprimand. It's just that I felt I had to act,' she added almost apologetically and, after a moment's thought, as if by way of explanation, 'You've heard of the euphemism, the village bike?' She winced as she spoke. 'There was graffiti in the boys' toilet about Sharon being the school bike, amongst other things, until we had it removed.'

That was news to me. To my surprise, I found I didn't mind.

My parents didn't move.

'When Sharon turns 16, which she will very soon, it becomes potentially more difficult for us – for you – to have certain conversations with her, the school and doctors – about contraception, for example. I would like the comfort of knowing that these conversations have been had. Again, sexual experimentation is only to be expected in adolescence, but I believe that Sharon is taking it to an extreme that hints at a deeper pathology, or a cry for help, or a need to be noticed.'

'By her parents? Is that what you mean?' asked Mum in a small, steely voice.

Mrs Baxter sat back. 'Mrs Truss, believe me, we are not or should not be enemies. I've seen enough children and families to understand the complexities of family relationships, particularly when there are teenagers concerned.'

'What you're saying,' said my deflated and dejected dad, 'is that my daughter is a –'

'No,' interjected Mrs Baxter. 'I'm not saying that at all. I object to girls who are sexually active being assigned one label – typically, a nefarious, shameful one – while boys who are the same are assigned another typically commendable or estimable one. I am saying that the school has a duty to bring such activity to the parents' attention, particularly in the case of a minor.'

'I remember when I was Sharon's age,' said Mum. I didn't think any of us were expecting that from her.

'So do I,' said Dad.

'So do I,' said Mrs Baxter, and in that moment I sensed a bridge had been built between Mum and her.

Mrs Baxter stood and walked to the light switch by the door. The cold overhead light came on, converting us from players to spectators instantaneously.

'Can I say something, please?' I asked. It bothered me that my voice came out so thin and young when I was suddenly so certain about what I wanted to say. 'I'm sorry to have been the cause of so much trouble.'

Mrs Baxter came and stood by the coffee table, hands clasped, and Mum and Dad twisted around to better look at me. They looked drawn, tired in the white light.

'I would like to say I'll work harder, but I'm not sure that I will. The thing is I like the maths and numbers – I love numbers and I love the plays we do in English, and words on their own I kind of like more than I used to, but everything else, well... None of it really interests me. It's like all this information is floating by but there's nothing for it to catch onto. I'd love not to disappoint everyone but the truth is that I'd just rather not be in a classroom.' I experienced the delicious sensation of discovering what I meant as I said it. It was as though I had to speak in order to discover what I thought. So I continued, 'About the other thing. What can I say? I mean, like you said,' I said, looking at Mrs Baxter, 'it can't be one rule for them and one rule for us. The thing is, I don't like saying no.' I lowered my eyes. 'I mean, I don't say yes to everyone and everything,' I added hurriedly. I paused to reflect. 'The thing is, I like to please. But now I haven't pleased you and I hope… I hope you're not ashamed of me.' Shame only crossed my mind as I spoke and I saw myself through others' eyes and not just as a friendly girl who liked to please. I buried my face in Mum's armpit. She placed her free hand on my shoulder and Dad patted me on the arm and stood.

'I think it's time for us to go,' said Dad, and extended one hand to his adversary for a handshake and then the other to me to pull me up. Mum managed to stand up gracefully unassisted. Dad concluded, 'Thank you, Mrs Baxter. You did well to call us in. And not a moment too soon. You have given us a lot to think about and we have a lot to talk about. The three of us,' Dad emphasised. 'And what you need from us is a reply to the question of Sharon's further education; that's been noted.'

We stood in the dark car park in between Mum's and Dad's cars, all three of us uncertain as to how to conclude this unexpected reunion. Dad looked better in the dark, an imposing shape the shabbiness of which was obscured; Mum's vaguely luminescent features looked elfin beside his blunter shadowed ones.

'I'm sorry,' I said.

'You're sorry?' said Dad. 'How do you think I feel?' He looked at Mum. 'I need some time to take this in. Tomorrow's Saturday. Can I come over on Sunday morning?'

I had thought that Dad had meant that he was sorry for being the parent he had been, whether the absent dad or the bolshy dad, that he was apologising to me in his own fumbling way. And maybe he had been at the time but, when I saw him two days later, it occurred to me that he might have been sorry, too, to have learnt that his daughter had decided to exchange learning for sex.

Dad came around after Mum had returned from church and, for the umpteenth time, I wondered, as I made my parents a cup of coffee, what must it be like to be a guest in one's own home. While, ten years ago, the mildest of misdemeanours would have earned me a slap, today, my graver offences carried with them their own punishment – guilt, shame and, worst of all, a sense of having disappointed my parents. But no telling off. My parents were, I had to admit, more understanding than I would have given them credit for; at least, that was what I preferred to think – that they were sympathetic and caring rather than merely indifferent to me.

We blew on our hot mugs at the sun-lit kitchen table. Seamus had yet to return from a sleepover and Sherah was at college in Brighton where she was studying sports science, so it was just the three of us for the first time in as long as I could remember. Mrs Baxter's words came back to me. The idea that I had somehow, at some subconscious level, engineered this parental, familial reunion intrigued me. I considered it mistaken, but interesting. Still, I couldn't help but feel happy – contented had been Mrs Baxter's choice of word but smug might have been a more fitting one – that I had, if not actually manipulated Mum and Dad, been the reason for their sitting across the breakfast table with me in between them for the first time in forever. They had gone to the school because of me and they were here because of me.

Mum said, 'About your school work,' and we talked about that for a while, with neither Mum nor Dad seeming particularly upset. Mum said, 'Given that you're set on leaving school at the end of this academic year, on the condition that you work as hard as you can for your O levels, we'll pay for a year's secretarial college starting in September. If that's what you want.'

I said that I would and that it was and so, calmly and straightforwardly, the end of my school career, my life of formal learning, was decided on.

'Now, about the other thing,' began Dad, fidgeting and evidently uncomfortable at the prospect of a discussion about sex with his teenage daughter. 'Mum's going to have a bit to say to you after me but I just want to say something before I leave you two to it. It's one thing being liked but you have to be liked for the right reasons. Being liked for being... Well. You know. Easy. That's not being liked. Being liked is being... It's being respected. It's the same thing, almost, anyway. You can't be liked if you don't like yourself and you can't be respected if you don't respect yourself. I mean, it's all about self-respect. You've got to show that you have it, that you respect yourself and that means not giving away so much of yourself.'

I looked down into a mug as empty as me. How could I respect myself if I couldn't locate the self to respect? If there were none? How could I tell Dad that?

Dad patted my hand. 'Trust me, I know,' he said. 'I used to be a boy once and I know how boys think.' He gave my hand a squeeze and, looking knowingly at Mum, said, 'Right then. I'm off,' but he didn't move until, stepping suddenly towards me, he grasped me by the shoulders and said very seriously, 'You can't get the toothpaste back in the tube.'

Mum and I listened for the clap of our front door and sat in silence for a while, Mum, I thought, embarrassed as much as me by Dad's cliché until I realised she was so focused on the original source of her embarrassment that she hadn't even heard what Dad had said. I counted the tiles on the kitchen floor and the motes of dust in the air. I closed my left and right eyes in turn to better align the sash window's frames with the drainpipe and other verticals of the house we backed onto.

'What on earth are you pulling those faces for?' asked Mum. 'What are you doing?'

'Nothing. Sorry,' I said, and stopped.

'I can't do this,' said Mum and looked at her mug. Then she lifted her eyes to me. 'I'm not happy, Sharon. All this business. It's unthinkable. Thank God you're leaving the school.'

'Sorry, Mum,' I said in a small voice.

'What am I supposed to tell you? What was I meant to have told you? What can I tell you that you don't know?' Mum's hands were white against the porcelain of her mug.

'I don't know, I don't know,' I said, afraid that she or I might cry. 'What did Dad and you agree that you'd tell me?'

Mum waved her hand. 'So you're on the pill?'

'Yes.'

'And you never thought of telling me?'

'I wanted to but, you know... And you're not around that much.'

'Finally!' exclaimed Mum. 'Finally! I thought we'd get here! So it's all my fault? My daughter is the village bike and it's her mum's fault!'

'The school bike, Mum, the school bike.'

We stared at each other, surprised by the fervour with which I had corrected her.

Mie

I only learnt later, when I had spent more time with Margaret ahead of my university entrance exams to study English, that she had been able to speak Japanese all along. To amuse her, I would make English sentences using *gairaigo*, Japanese words that had their origin in English, much as, as I would learn later, the English borrowed words from the French. The entrepreneur had a rendezvous with the chef in the abattoir where they had an apéritif and hors d'oeuvres. The *kameraman*, looking *sumāto* in his new *janpa* and *torēningupantsu*, wiped the spilt *jusu* and *miruku* with his *hankachi* and some *kitchinpēpā*.

One afternoon found me sitting at a table in the sixth form room with Ursula and Margaret. Successive classes had not yet taught Ursula that love only follows respect and that a need to be loved only brings contempt. She looked gloomy, as only a friendless person who needs to be loved could be, and what I had to say made her shoulders sag all the more.

'Ursula-*san*, Maggie-*san*, I have reached a conclusion: I shall study English at university.' I fiddled with the hem of my green school skirt. Ursula's reaction made it clear that she considered this a victory for her rival. I felt the need to explain and tried to do so in a way that would impress and endear me to Margaret and not offend Ursula. 'I long to get away,' I said. 'To go somewhere really different, really foreign, and German seems closer in so many respects to Japanese than English does.'

At this, Ursula guffawed and her ponytails shook. 'My God! You think Japan is like Germany and not so much like England?' She adjusted her position to face both Margaret and me and slapped a hand on each trousered knee. 'You both drive on the left and you both have an unelected head of state, to start with. You are both island nations and' – here Ursula floundered – 'and you both eat a lot of fish!' She resumed her anxious, sorry expression and adjusted her glasses on the bridge of her nose.

I had never heard or seen Ursula so confrontational. Margaret appeared disinvested from the discussion and disinclined to come to my assistance. The distinction between sashimi and fish in batter served in newspaper was clearly not one she thought worth making.

'The thing is,' I began, in what I hoped to be a moderator's tone and with a forced smile as I noticed the decrease in the volume of the room's hubbub after Ursula's brief explosion, 'that I wish to escape not so much this country, that I love in so many ways, but its formalities, the many ways in which I feel that I, me, the individual, am subjugated.' I took inspiration from an essay I had scored high marks in. 'Both countries wear the yoke of failed military expansionism heavily and have withdrawn into, if not quite collectivism and socialism, a state in which the merits of the individual, that pure expression of selfhood, are somehow subjugated.'

Ursula looked at me incredulously; Margaret watched me impassively.

'I mean, in Germany, you have retained the formal way of speaking to people, you still have *sie*. England hasn't. England is less formal, it's more relaxed, it's cool.' Margaret had taught me not to say groovy. 'I mean,' I added desperately, 'look at punk rock.'

'Look at Berlin,' said Ursula, but without conviction and now quite deflated.

Margaret placed her hand on my knee, leant forward and said quietly, 'You are so wrong, you know. It's arguable that the English, following your line of reasoning, are more formal than the Germans – and the French. How to put it? You know the French *vous* and *toi*, their equivalent of the German *sie* and *du*?'

I nodded.

'Well, *vous* and *sie* are 'you' and *tu* and *du* are 'thou' – do you notice the similarities? It's we, we English, who are the formal ones – we dropped the informal thou, thee, thy and thine from the English language years ago and retained only the formal mode of speech.' She patted my knee. 'There. Now you know. I hope that doesn't disappoint you.' She sat back and fixed me with a look that suggested that she hoped it had.

I was speechless with that discovery and had to make a mental readjustment. To my surprise, Ursula's morose expression remained unchanged. 'Anyway,' she said, 'Who am I to talk?' She addressed Margaret directly. 'I am leaving at the end of this year, too, and, yes, I am going to go to England or America and, anyway, not back to Germany; so who am I to tell Mie-*san* where to go?' I realised that my hand was raised to my mouth just as Margaret's was to hers; her eyes were wide open. 'If I am honest, I have not made a success of my time here. The pupils don't like me, the teachers have never accepted or even supported me, and Japanese men are terrified of me.' She waved Margaret's protestations away. 'No. I know. Anyway, I have applied for jobs as a German teaching assistant at universities where I assume that university–age students who want to learn will be more forgiving of my weaknesses than schoolchildren whose interest in a foreign language goes only so far as singing along to Beatles songs.' Ursula smiled at me and leant forward conspiratorially. 'Who knows, we might even meet in England one day!'

For the first time, my heart went out to her. I saw her as a person and not as a foreign national. I felt ashamed to have contributed, no matter how little and how indirectly, to her unhappiness in my country. Her failure had been ours. We had turned the virtue of niceness into a liability.

Sharon

Was it that I was unfeeling or that I didn't dare to feel? Sorrow, shame, rejection were like so many clothes discarded in a heap at my feet for want of hangers in between scene changes. The theatre lighting technician swings a spotlight despairingly across a bare stage in search of its non-existent target. There's nobody there. Just stage boards and cross-shaped duct tape marking yet another place at which I don't exist.

At some point between the end of my last school term and the start of secretarial college, it had been decided that I would go and live with Aunt Wanda. As far as she was concerned, it was all going to be great fun; we two girls would have a laugh, I'd be the sister to her that her elder boring sister never had been and, she said conspiringly, we would spend the rent my parents were going to pay her on takeaway food we would scoff while watching wildlife documentaries. Besides, she made me see, it made sense: Sherah had left home, my mother's commitments meant her being away a lot, Seamus could move in with Dad who spent all his time ferrying him from home to school, training session, match and back again, the house could be let and I would have a shorter commute to secretarial college in the West End.

Aunt Wanda hugged me in welcome at her front door, a suitcase either side of me. My mother stood in her running gear on the short garden path, sheepish and embarrassed to be declining coffee and a chat with her sister and her daughter as she pleaded other commitments. I clung to Wanda, my nose pressed into her neck and into her fresh, rosemary-scented hair, who reciprocated with a gentle squeeze and talked to her sister over my shoulder and that's how I said goodbye to my mother: through Wanda, vicariously, hugging my mother through Wanda and Wanda knowing this and never minding.

Wanda helped me carry my suitcases up to the second bedroom that was to be mine. My mother, when she came to stay in between marathons and work commitments, would sleep on the futon in the attic. Having unpacked, I stood by the window, one foot in shadow, the other in sunlight, attempting to seize the buzzing sensations around me.

Mie

Takahiro Imamura-*san* had never stood out from the boys at my school until Margaret introduced us to one another in our final year.

Margaret had chaperoned a group of final–year pupils who had signed up to see a *kabuki* performance of *Macbeth*, which we were studying. At Margaret's invitation, I joined her in the front row of the bus. As the other pupils piled in, she indicated one of them with a nod and asked, 'Do you know him?' Takahiro moved down the aisle, a slightly long- and floppy-haired adolescent of medium height and build who wore a pleasant, open expression. He had a good complexion by the standards of a generation that was discovering milkshakes and hamburgers.

'Only by name. I've seen him around. He's neither a swot nor one of the cool guys, you know, who hang around in gangs and act tough and ask you out all the time.'

'He's your only competition,' smiled Margaret, reclining her seat so that I had to turn my whole body around to look her in the eyes.

'Competition? For what?'

'Oh, come on,' said Margaret. 'You know.'

I really didn't know.

'You and he are the school's top English–language pupils. It's you two by a mile. No one else comes close. The pupils know it. And all the teachers say so.'

The bus moved off and out of the school gates to join the slow-moving evening traffic. Men and women in black suits under black umbrellas lined bus stops in anticipation of buses stuck behind fleets of black cars. Windscreen wipers were set to work intermittently. Streetlights seemed only to add to the gloom that I perceived only objectively, in a complete reversal of the pathetic fallacy we had studied in *Macbeth*.

Margaret's comments were a revelation, a not unpleasant shock. I had never thought in such terms, never thought that, as I walked home from school or lunched in the school canteen, teachers, somewhere, as they readied themselves for home or opened their bento boxes, had said good things about me to each other, had lauded me and referred to me as a *top pupil* – me and Takahiro. I felt a strange kinship with him that warmed me before it discomfited me – doubly so, given that we'd never even spoken. Margaret's comments stimulated me: if I was considered to have competition, I had to ensure I would win. In the space of seconds, I had gone from not thinking in terms of a competition to being determined to triumph. I would have to get to know my adversary. I would have to meet Takahiro.

'I'll introduce you to him, if you'd like,' said Margaret.

Margaret made the introductions at the interval, by ensuring that all five pupils who had congregated around her, soft drink in hand, knew each other; which we did, if only by name. I immediately saw the group for what it was: three pupils with poor English in awe of their English language assistant and of two pupils with excellent English. Takahiro must have sensed this, too, for he replied readily, in order to save the others' blushes, to Margaret's question as to what we thought of the production; as though knowing that the others – and maybe I, too – would be too shy to say a word.

'Maggie-*san*, I would be very interested to know if, in your opinion, I am completely wrong in my analysis and beg you to tell me if so; anyway, it is this.' I was impressed and jealous of Takahiro's easy familiarity in calling Margaret Maggie. 'While I am enjoying the performance on, I must admit, a rather superficial level, I feel that the *kabuki* style of theatre is not suited to this particular play. I mean, Macbeth is interesting – a masterpiece – for its great psychological subtlety, and this *kabuki* performance, well, it renders everything one-dimensional.' Takahiro received nods and grunts of assent from us all, save from Margaret, who merely raised her eyebrows in encouragement. 'I mean, take Banquo's ghost. The scene of his appearance is played like a comedy. "Oh! Help! I've seen a ghost!" The actions are exaggerated and stylised such that there is no room for ambiguity. Such is the nature of *kabuki*.' Takahiro clutched his paper cup with both hands and shook his head, then continued, 'There's something else. The colour scheme is all wrong. When I read the play, the colour that dominated was red, all I saw was red; there's so much killing, and blood is mentioned so frequently. Here, all we see is white, the white *kabuki* faces, the white-sheeted ghost.'

'And black,' I felt compelled to say, and immediately wished I hadn't as Takahiro looked at me, looked at me properly, searchingly, as though seeing me for the first time; which perhaps he was. 'The witches are all in black, the soldiers and other men are dressed mainly in black and the minimalist stage is black.'

'Yes, you're quite right,' Takahiro assented. 'There's a lot of darkness but that, to me at least, serves to reinforce the impression of a monochrome world; one I didn't have on reading the play. Besides, having actors dressed in black as well as the *kurogos*' – the clearly visible stagehands – 'is confusing; but I can see that that may be considered to concentrate the psychological action on Macbeth himself.' Takahiro stopped there and we all looked into our cups.

From that day on, when Takahiro and I bumped into each other, we would wave and exchange quick *konnichiwas* and brief, nervous bows. In the sixth-form room, we chatted with increasing familiarity once the ice had been broken by his first, 'Do you mind if I join you?' Takahiro had the ability to make what one said seem interesting and profound and to make one feel clever, as though one had something of value to say. In contrast to most of our countrymen, he maintained eye contact when speaking and never interrupted with chirrups of encouragement. Believing that he was more interested in what I thought – in the concepts that I expressed – than in me, I was flattered by the intellectual attention and by his frequent lapses into English. He evidently relished speaking it in complicity with the only pupil who could hold her own with him, and I delighted in the pressure I felt to weigh my words carefully with him.

The stress all school-leavers were under at the end of that final term, to exchange addresses and telephone numbers with fellow pupils they hoped to stay in touch with, was absent in my and Takahiro's case: he was going to study English at the same university as me.

Sharon

I immediately liked attending the secretarial college.

For a start, I was commuting into central London, with the tide rather than against it, and I felt quite a grown-up, as though it were a rite of passage from child- to adulthood. I delighted in being allowed to wear Wanda's business suits, blouses and skirts. I learnt to do my blouse up when I had a seat, so that commuting men who stood in the aisles couldn't peer down my cleavage, and to stand by the doors rather than in the aisles when I wore skirts and didn't get a seat. There was a quality to being ogled by adult men that was different from being lusted after by teenagers.

The thing I missed the most about school was the acting, but this, the commuting into central London, was the real thing, the opportunity for me to act the young adult, the commuter. With every journey I took I played the role differently, depending on my dress, on my mood and on who was in the carriage around me.

I needed formation, a persona, opinions, so I bought different newspapers on the way to college in the mornings that not only gave me something to hide behind but also political and social views and perspectives. But I found them confusing and, to tell the truth, boring. I couldn't keep up with the disparity of views between the left and the right wings on the battles between the unions and the government and on AIDS, famine, market crashes and US foreign policy. I couldn't help but agree with every leader I read and every opinion voiced and eventually had to admit that my newspaper experiment was not delivering the new, adult personality I sought. Defeated, I read fashion magazines.

And then there were the girls, my college colleagues, teenagers and twenty-somethings looking for a fillip in life. We were ripe for reinvention; we could leave our short lives' baggage, reputations and old school uniforms at the door and either disguise or reveal ourselves in make-up, in new clothes, accents and hairstyles. Hanging over us, I detected a thin, grey cloud of academic or social failure – after all, we were the girls who hadn't gone on to finish a formal formation, alike in that we were caught between a higher education that we had been deemed incapable of and full-time employment in the service of others. After a while, though, I came to realise that this cloud hung over me only, that most of the others who tugged skirts as they sat and removed pens and pencils from their cases at 9.30 every morning were pleased with their achievements in having reached this point in preparation for the workplace. Emboldened, I decided to be like them – to no longer, when asked what I was doing, mumble defensively that I was attending secretarial college; to take pride in the course and in myself for taking it, and my cloud drifted away to leave clear blue skies.

To my surprise, perhaps because of the absence of boys, there wasn't the bitchiness among us that there had sometimes been among the girls at school; we were supportive of each other, tender and warm on the whole, even though one or two of the girls preferred their privacy and kept their distance. We fell into loose cliques, broadly defined by our commute – who, once college finished for the day, walked to which station or bus stop – and by our other commitments in terms of family, boyfriends and even, in the case of a couple of girls, babies.

And then there was the course itself that, I realised, I had signed up for with no expectations and that, maybe for that very reason, I found myself enjoying. We were taught on the second floor of our liftless school building, amid the clang of an old heating system, the hum of traffic on the West Cromwell Road and the squeaking and groaning of a post-war conversion of two now-conjoined residential apartments yet to settle. We were taught to type, to write in shorthand, to take dictation, to manage diaries, to make and receive telephone calls, to format and write letters and envelopes, to assist in preparing presentations, to organise meetings, take minutes, book restaurants and travel, to manage expenses and – most exciting as far as I was concerned – to maintain a ledger. I signed up for extra classes on the rudiments of accountancy, of book-keeping, and I stood out for my head for numbers: I didn't so much love numbers as was loved by them. Everything fell into place for me as far as they were concerned; even though I didn't really understand the meaning of assets and of liabilities, of the advanced principles of VAT and of book-cost accounting, even though I found the principles behind them tedious, my numbers somehow always ended up in the correct column and added up as they should. I would talk to Wanda most evenings after work and amuse her with stories of my new friends, sharing my day with her in a way I never had with Mum or Dad. An accountant herself, she was interested to follow what I referred to as my numbers work and exclaimed, after dinner one night, 'Sharon! You have such a gift! You should work in a bank.'

I settled into a routine that was only punctuated by Mum's visits. At times, Dad and Seamus would take us out for pizza and, at others, Wanda cooked dinner for us. I went out with my new secretarial friends on a Thursday or Friday night for a drink or dinner and a nightclub if we were feeling flush. There were nights in with Wanda watching wildlife documentaries and every week an evening or two on my own, when Wanda worked nights.

It occurred to me that Mum and Wanda had reversed roles; Mum now felt like my visiting aunt. She made a better aunt than a mum. She – and Dad – felt guilty, I knew, but they were adept at putting their guilt to one side and developing a relationship with me that was more adult. For so long the black outline of a girl in Seamus's old colouring-in books, I looked in at myself with a vested curiosity as my parents finally, albeit unknowingly, picked up colouring pencils and began to colour me in, from the feet up and ever so slowly. Mum asked me questions about college, about the course, my new friends and living with Wanda. The last was difficult to answer, as I didn't want her to feel that Aunt Wanda had replaced her.

'So how often does Wanda work late then?' We were sitting in front of the TV with the sound down low.

'Once or twice a week.'

'What do you do then?'

'Nothing. Cook or bake. Sometimes I'm out with friends.'

'Do you ever come home together?'

'I'm normally back before her.'

'So where does she work exactly?'

'Here and there. I think she does the books for small businesses.'

'Yes, but since when does an accountant work nights?'

I shrugged. It had never occurred to me to ask that question.

Mum extended her arm to give my elbow a nudge. 'Has she got a boyfriend?'

'No! Not that I know of.'

'Come on, you can tell me if Wanda has a boyfriend.'

'Mum! Actually, we were wondering if you had.'

'Me?' She shook her head. 'Find out where she works when she's out late at night. I'd be interested to know.'

'Well, you could ask her yourself,' I said to Mum boldly.

'Yes, I suppose I could,' she said quietly, her eyes on the television and one hand on my arm. Animals gathered around a watering hole. 'Do you have a boyfriend?' she added, still quietly.

'Me? No.' I couldn't help but blush. Another, unspoken question hung between us. 'I haven't been out with any boys, Mum. My friends and I, we go to clubs and such but, you know, it's just dancing and that. Just fun.'

'Sure,' said Mum.

Fun. That's what Gavina Belchamber, Sarah Henn, Monica Massit and I decided we wanted out of life. We carried no histories. We had no edge: we were warm, loving and fun-loving. After college, we four would make our way to Earls Court tube where Gavina and I would head south to Wimbledon and Sarah and Monica west to Ealing. That is, when we weren't heading east to Gloucester Road tube and on to London's West End. On those evenings, we swaggered arm in arm in knee-length boots and above-the-knee skirts, unbuttoned or low-cut blouses, glass bead necklaces and second-hand sheepskin or brocaded jackets or coats. And hair, lots of hair, piled high or left undone, and mascara and lipstick and sweet-tasting anticipation. At such moments, my friends and I poured out of and into each other, indiscriminately, I became them and they me, we were an intermingling of personae, me never feeling so much myself as when feeling I was someone else. Happily and loudly we strode, taking up the width of the pavements, breaking step and unlocking arms only at the last second in order to dodge trees, lamp- and signposts and parking meters, to overtake slow-moving pedestrians and make way for oncoming ones. Raising my head I could see the poised, watching gargoyles that lined the tops of classical red–brick mansions, echoes of the gremlins and goblins in the park of my child's mind. Incandescent in the setting sun, they were furious that I was escaping their clutches for the welcoming arms of my dear friends. Malignant though immediately harmless, I never quite forgot their presence.

'Watch where you're going, Sharon!' That was Gavina. 'Sorry!' she called on my behalf to the pedestrian I had nearly walked into. 'She's a bit ditsy this one!'

Sarah and Monica cackled in syncopation with the slap of our heels on the pavement.

'What a noisy bunch we are!' exclaimed Gavina. 'We're like those noisy birds, you know –'

'Jackdaws.'

'We're noisy and we're birds.'

'Parakeets.'

'A flock of birds.'

'A flock of secretaries.'

'No! What's that called, you know, that word for a large number of something?' asked Gavina.

'A collective pronoun,' I said.

'Yes, there must be one for secretaries.'

'Let's make one up!'

'A gaggle of secretaries,' offered Monica.

'A shoal of secretaries,' suggested Sarah.

'A school of secretaries.' Monica again.

'A goosestep of secretaries,' said Gavina, raising her legs high with each step.

'A skirt of secretaries,' I proposed.

'Yes! That's the one!' chorused my friends and, pleased with itself and with the world, this skirt picked up its step.

We ate in a cheap unlicensed Italian restaurant off Cambridge Circus that welcomed diners who had brought their own wine, bought, we could tell from the brown paper bags, from the old wine shop on Old Compton Street. Next, to a pub in Covent Garden and then down to the Embankment, to a club into which girls were allowed free and boys could only gain entry if escorted by a girl.

'Stop saying girls,' instructed Monica with a shake of her hair, when we wondered without complaining over this inequity. 'We're women now.'

True, I thought to myself, though still unused to the idea and to the terrifying responsibilities that accompanied the exile from childhood. It had taken me so long to come to some idea of who I was, only for it to have to change.

The deal was unwritten: if a boy asked you into the club and you accepted, he'd owe you a drink; if you declined the second drink or a dance, he'd have to accept the message and not approach you again. We queued and eyed the boys who eyed us on the other side of the street.

'What's the collective thingummy for boys?' asked Gavina.

'Oh, you and your collectives,' said Monica, fed up, tense – either, I assumed, hoping that a particular boy would ask her or that a particular one wouldn't.

'A bogey,' I offered.

'Anyway, I told you, they're men, not boys. Look at them,' continued Monica as four of them stepped out of the shadows and into the street.

'A bogey of boys,' I repeated, but no one was listening.

'Hello,' said one, as he and his friends approached us.

'Hello,' we replied, running our hands through our hair and shouldering our handbags.

They were clean-looking, friendly, polite and only a year or two older than us, so we accepted second and third drinks and dances, fast and slow. I never quite understood how couples formed on those occasions; in quick time, we each – Gavina, Monica, Sarah and I – had our boy and he had us, an arm around a waist and endearments in an ear. I never made a choice; I was always chosen or maybe simply allocated by default. We laughed and shouted and screamed and talked and mooched head to head, coloured blue, red, purple, yellow and green by rotating lights and glitter balls and all the time I forgot myself, who I was and who I wasn't, and then it was all over and we were outside the club, music ringing in our ears and the steam from our breath and hot bodies mingling with cigarette smoke under street lamps so that the street felt like an extension of the club, eyeing the entrance to the tube a hundred yards away and all too conscious of the need to make the last tube home.

I could hear Gavina saying to hers, 'No way, my father will kill me if I don't make it home!' and, 'No way! Take you home with me? My father would kill *you*!'

And me saying to mine, 'Sorry, no, I live with my aunt,' and letting him kiss me because he hadn't been drinking and tasted of chewing gum and smelled intoxicatingly of aftershave and fresh sweat, all the time worrying that if I left it at this I wouldn't be keeping my end of the bargain and that maybe I should have done or be doing more for him and, why not admit it, for me too but then thinking that it was just a little bit creepy that none of them had been drinking alcohol at all while keen that we should and thinking, too, that maybe it's best I left my old reputation at school and didn't allow it to follow me here and colour my relationship with my new friends, or maybe not, and then hearing Monica shouting at me to come on and Sarah tugging me by the elbow.

We four girls and Monica's Kevin and Sarah's Liam stood squeezed in the aisle of a crowded carriage of the last underground train of the night and Monica commented on the happy coincidence that Kevin and Liam lived in Ealing too. 'Oh yeah!' mouthed Gavina when the train's swaying brought her close to my face, but I didn't care. Who was I to judge? The last train home. The last refuge of party-goers, drunkards and pukers who carried on their partying from whichever club or pub they had left. We clung to the leather straps that hung from the handrail and swung, bumping into each other, trying to avoid the knees and toes of the seated passengers around us. My two friends with their beaus tried unsuccessfully to suppress their smiles when each clackety shake brought them together.

'There must be a hundred people in this carriage,' said Kevin in attempt at diversionary conversation.

'Actually, it's closer to two hundred,' I said. 'Give or take five.'

Kevin and Liam were good-looking, I admitted, even in the artificial overhead light that flattered no one.

A seated elderly woman in a coat like a quilt and whose grey hair escaped in wisps from a hand-knitted bobble hat clutched a stained Gladstone bag on her lap and talked to herself loudly, making little sense.

'Talking to yourself, are you?' asked Liam.

'First sign of madness,' said Kevin.

They hung onto the straps above her, grinning down at her.

'What I have in my bag is none of your business,' snapped the old woman, looking up. The overhead light shone directly onto her face, exposing dirt-filled wrinkles. The shoulder of her coat where her Gladstone bag's strap rested was quite worn through.

'Oh! Cheeky!' replied Liam. 'And which home are you returning to this evening? I'm surprised they let you out in the first place!'

'What I have in my bag is a secret, you know,' she said, wide-eyed and slowly, but loudly enough to be overheard by other passengers who had ceased their own conversations to listen to this one. Suddenly conscious of an audience, she added coyly, 'She's dead, you know!'

'Really!' exclaimed Liam incredulously, hanging from two straps as the train slowed. 'I was going to say, if it's the Regent's Park zoo you want, change at the next stop but maybe it's a prison you need!'

'No, definitely the loony bin,' said Kevin.

A young woman who had been leaning her head against her book-reading partner's shoulder raised it and barked righteously, 'Stop it! Stop talking to her like that. Show some respect.' And all in our end of the carriage craned their necks to look at her while, I guessed, feeling guilty for having enjoyed the exchange.

Kevin and Liam, their confidence shaken and swagger diminished, made big eyes at the young woman who glared at them in return, shoulders hunched in self-importance, when the old woman rounded on her. 'You shut up!' she scolded. 'You stop it! Don't you tell them to stop talking to me! At least they talk to me. No one else does. It's no good the likes of you pretending I don't exist. You mind your own business.' She then turned her head back and up to Kevin and Liam and said, coquettishly almost, outrageously, flirtatiously from below heavily lidded eyes, 'You were saying?'

Kevin and Liam were as delighted as the rest of us were dumb-founded. 'Yeah!' they roared in unison, rounding on the young woman. 'You mind your own business!'

'Here we were,' continued Kevin, 'having a little chat with our friend and you butt in.'

'Don't you want her to have friends? Is that it?' queried Liam. 'She's not good enough. Condemn her to a life of solitude?'

Perplexed, betrayed, indignant and close to tears, the young woman turned to her partner who had slipped down his seat and whose face had disappeared behind his book. 'Go on. Say something,' she commanded. 'Stick up for me for once, will you?'

'What?' he said sheepishly, lowering his open book only slightly, as though quite unaware of the exchange that had taken place. 'Sorry?'

'Oh, for God's sake!' she exclaimed, snatching the book from him, 'You're so weak!'

'But what exactly would you like me to do?' he complained meekly.

Lightheaded with laughter and drink, Gavina and I and half the carriage spilled out at Earls Court, where we waved our goodbyes to our friends and waited for our train south.

The young woman and her partner were still arguing as they climbed the stairs to the exit. Gavina yawned and said, 'You liked her, didn't you, that batty old woman? I wonder what was in her bag.' She rested her head on my shoulder and fell asleep on her feet.

Mie

To my surprise and slight horror, Keiko, Michi and I were asked, when shopping for our school graduation party, if we were sisters. Keiko had stopped growing when she was relatively young. Michi was no longer the fat weevil my father jokingly used to refer to her as (in a nod to the insects my mother occasionally found in the flour she bought from Michi's parents) but, to use Takumi-*san*'s phrase, a Bambi doe. I gazed at our many shop window reflections on our walk home and had to concede that we had grown more alike than not over the years, at least as far as external appearances were concerned. Keiko had stopped growing up and Michi had actually grown in; our bodies had unconsciously obeyed the national imperative to conform. Internally, however, I believed strongly that we had remained as different as the kimonos in our carrier bags.

We had been fitted for our kimonos four months ago. We all three carried *furisode* kimonos, but Keiko and I had chosen a *ko-furisode* each with sleeves that were as short as an unmarried woman's kimono could be, and shorter than Michi's *chu-furisode,* the sleeves of which were as long as an unmarried woman's kimono could be outside extremely formal occasions. It was ironic that the pupils whose parents I considered better off than mine thought nothing of hiring the graduation kimonos they would need for only one day and that my parents, who while not poor were not particularly rich, had wanted me to own my own, to leave this chrysalis's shell for them to remember their daughter by.

I had put my foot down, however, and declined a *hakama*, the full-length apron one traditionally wears over the kimono on graduation day, and was pleasantly surprised when Keiko declined one too. For me, refusal was a major step in the process of separation and withdrawal from my native country. As far as rebellions go, it was minor, I admit, but a *hakama* would have been one more tie to home, one more ritual to bind me, one more item to leave in a trunk for my mother to pull out and feel from time to time once I had fled.

Sharon

'Are we Jewish?' I asked Aunt Wanda.

'Ha. In this family it's best you don't ask such a question.'

She was right. Mum's and Aunt Wanda's family history was a no-go area for us. We sensed, as children, the invisible boundaries that adults erected around certain topics and so had asked our parents and grandparents few questions.

'Anyway, it is a particularly silly question coming from someone who has had their Holy Communion and who attends a Catholic church.'

'Attended,' I corrected her. 'I only ask because Sherah used to say we were. You know, her curly hair and her nose. She says I got away lucky, that she was teased at school but that she never told anyone about it. Where do you want your coffee?'

Wanda rose gracefully from her knees and joined me at a wrought iron garden table. She held her secateurs in one hand, lifted the mug of coffee to her lips with the other and blew. Her garden faced north, so we sat at the end of it where a small patio accommodated the table and four chairs in whatever sunlight it received. I liked this intimate place of flowers, potted ferns and confidences and suspected that Wanda looked forward to our weekend chats there as much as I did.

Wanda said, 'Fair enough. That was not a silly question. It's just that it's not something we talk about.'

'You're telling me!' I said.

Wanda sipped her coffee. 'What would you like to know?'

'I don't know! I mean, I know so little, I don't even know what questions to ask!'

I considered Wanda's outstretched bejeaned legs and mine, bare in the morning light, their fine hairs catching the sun. We were so similar, I reflected, that we could be taken for sisters. I pressed home my advantage.

'Tell me about Nonno and Nonna,' I said, referring to her and Mum's parents. 'I know that Nonna was born in Emilia–Romagna and emigrated to South Wales after the war. And I know that Nonno

155

is Polish even though we call him Nonno but – I don't even know how and where they met.'

'As you said,' said Wanda carefully, 'Nonna came to South Wales after the war. There had been many Italians who had left and gone before her, economic migrants, leaving Italy because they could barely scratch a living there and going, well, all over the world. Nonna took a ship from Genoa to Port Talbot, where ships would refuel before making the transatlantic voyage to New York. She had a job waiting for her in Porthcawl, waitressing in some relative's restaurant. The Italians, you see, had spotted an opportunity for cafés, fish and chip shops and ice–cream parlours in a country of family-unfriendly pubs with limited opening hours.'

'And Nonno? How did he and Nonna meet?'

'You know he's called Nonno to spare you having two *dziadeks*, don't you?'

I nodded.

'Not that he minded. He was delighted to deny the Pole that he is and to assume the identity of an Italian.' Wanda looked down at her lap. 'Poor old Nonno.'

'Why poor, Aunt Wanda?'

'In the space of one year, 1939, Poland was invaded by Germany and by the Soviet Union and divided between the two of them. Many Poles were sent to forced labour camps, some in Germany and some in the Soviet Union. Nonno and Dziadek were among the lucky ones because they were sent to the Soviet Union, to Siberia; lucky because they were sent to work on a farm and because after two years the Soviets thought better of it and released the deported Poles so that they could form a new Polish army that would join the British Army in the Middle East for training, and then fight Germany. Conditions were awful at the camp, at least I assume they were because Nonno never talked about it and neither did Dziadek, apparently.'

'Hold on,' I said. 'Are you saying that my grandfathers were in the same camp? That they knew each other before Mum and Dad met and married?'

'Yes.'

'I never knew!'

'They and I don't know how many other Poles, thousands initially, walked from Siberia to Persia, to Iran – can you believe it? They begged lifts or walked when they were capable of it. It took them a year. They were freezing and starving and had to forage as they walked. Many, many died on the way. Your mother once showed me some papers that mentioned that Nonno had joined the Polish 2nd Corps that fought alongside the British 8th Army in Monte Cassino, but when we tried to find those papers again we couldn't. Nonno must have hidden them somewhere or destroyed them.' Aunt Wanda was silent for a while. 'After the war, Nonno boarded a ship bound for New York.'

'The same one as Nonna?' I interrupted.

'Well,' said Wanda, 'that depends on who you believe. When the ship docked at Port Talbot, Nonno went for a walk and by the time he returned the ship had sailed.'

'So he missed the boat?'

'Yes! Literally. The funny thing about your *nonno* is that if you tease him for having been so silly as to have missed the boat, he'll claim it was because he'd seen your *nonna* and fallen in love with her, but if you call him a sly one who left his boat to chase a woman, he'll deny it and say that the boat sailed without him after he had gone to stretch his legs. That's his first line of defence, see – get us stuck on his start in Wales and we don't dig any further back.'

'I like the thought that he left the boat to pursue Nonna best,' I said.

'You'd rather think of my father as a romantic than as an idiot – thank you!'

'But what is it with the whole religious thing then? I mean, I kind of knew that story – Mum had told us that much – but what's the religious mystery in the background?'

Wanda reflected. I waited. A District Line train went clacketing by. Wanda looked at me through narrow eyes that were brown but flecked with green.

'In 1939, your dear *nonno*,' said my dear aunt, 'was away from home, either studying or working, I don't know. At around the time he was sent to the gulag his parents were sent to Piotrków Try-bunalski, a newly established ghetto for Jews in Poland. They were deported from there in 1942, but where to I don't know, and I don't know if he ever learned what happened to them after that. Certainly, he hasn't said.'

'So Nonno is Jewish?'

Aunt Wanda held a finger up. 'I would say he *was* Jewish. Somewhere along or sometime during his long walk south he saw or did awful things that made him lose his faith. Actually, that's not quite right: he lost his 'Jewish' faith; he converted from Judaism to Catholicism. He'll tell you he did that in order to marry your *nonna* but she says he could have married her anyway. Nonna once said that Nonno had loved his faith but was so ashamed of what he had had to do to survive the winter of 1941 that he had felt unworthy of it.'

'What kind of things? Kill people?'

'No! The people were already dead.' Wanda shook her head. 'You didn't have to kill them. They died of hunger, disease and cold. Nonno and, I presume, your *dziadek* did what they had to do to survive.'

I didn't understand and I didn't know that I wanted to. What Wanda was talking about was so alien to our sunny patch of garden in south-west London that it required a tremendous effort of imagination to arrive there. Around us, the bushes in Wanda's garden were coming into bud and I saw in the shoots the incipient flower, the potential that each contained. Wanda sat with her elbows on her knees, her long fair hair hanging down. I couldn't see her face.

'There was something else, too,' she said. 'In the farms, in the Soviet Union, Poles were made to guard Poles.'

'Guard?'

'Maybe that's what turned your *nonno* away from his faith.'

'Why?'

'Because he loved his faith and saw Jews and fellow countrymen behave abominably? I don't know.' Aunt Wanda looked directly at me and said with an odd mix of relish and regret, 'Which leads us to your father's side of the family. Aren't you hungry?'

'No,' I said. 'To Dziadek and Babcia?'

'Yes, to your *dziadek* and *babcia*. Well, to Dziadek first. We think he was one of the guards.' Wanda inhaled deeply. 'Not only that, Nonno claimed that Dziadek only converted to Judaism to give himself a new identity, to throw people off the scent, to discourage questions. Your *dziadek*, of course, says he converted in order to marry your *babcia*. And even when your *nonno* grudgingly concedes that that might be the case, he argues that your *dziadek* did so out of love not for your *babcia* but for her money, her dowry. Which, as far as your father is concerned, is ridiculous; his mother never had any wealth.' Wanda stood and paced the small patio, abstractedly feeling the leaves of the bush that separated her garden from her neighbour's.

'Aunt Wanda, stop for a minute. I can't take all this in.' I had so many questions. What kind of a guard had Dziadek been to Nonno? What had they done to survive the long walk south? What had they seen each other do? Instead I asked, 'So Babcia is the only one of my grandparents who is really Jewish?'

Wanda shrugged. 'Well, I suppose Dziadek is if he converted. What a crazy mixed-up family! You have one grandfather who converted from Judaism to Catholicism and one who went the other way. But traditional Jewish law has it that once a Jew, always a Jew. And that Judaism is passed down from the mother.' She looked at me.

'So Dad is Jewish, then? But,' I said, 'he claims to be Church of England. And he doesn't consider himself Welsh or Polish, just English.'

'Exactly. He reinvented himself. Like both of your grandfathers, in a way.'

'In fact, if anyone asks, he says he's a Londoner.' I paused to think. 'So, by blood, I'm three quarters Polish and a quarter Italian. But really, I'm English, born in England to British nationals. By religion, I'm one half Catholic and one half Jewish. It's really confusing.'

Wanda looked at me closely. 'What are you?' she asked. 'What do you feel you are? In here?' She placed a hand on my chest. 'In your heart of hearts? If you listen to yourself and to no one else?'

'Nothing,' I said. 'I feel nothing. I feel that there's nobody home.'

Wanda picked up some cuttings from the garden table and held them together. 'See these?' she asked. 'This is what I want to learn to do. Graft. Make my own plants. Create new plants out of old ones. Hardy plants that have the strengths of two species and none of their weaknesses. That's us, you see. Immigration, it makes all populations stronger. You are healthy, beautiful, smart – never let me hear you say you feel nothing again. Come. Enough for one day!'

Cuttings still in hand, Wanda took me by the arm and steered me along her narrow garden path to meet our reflections in the French patio doors. We looked like bridesmaids walking down a church aisle.

Mie

I saw more of Taka in the summer holidays; he had taken to hanging out with Keiko so that, whenever I went to visit her, I would find him there, sorting through a collection of 45 rpm singles that were strewn around her portable record player and across the *tatami* mats on her family's sitting–room floor. Keiko could always welcome Michi and me to her bedroom but not Taka, who took to going around with such frequency that Keiko's record player took up permanent residency in the living room. It gave onto the stairs down to Keiko's parents' shop so that, in quiet moments certainly, Keiko's parents were able to hear everything their daughter said or did.

I first heard punk rock at Keiko's and enjoyed the spirit of individualism and defiance that the music carried with it, but I disliked the lack of clarity in the vocals.

'Unlike our friends, who know the words of English hits by heart without knowing their meaning, at least you and I know or want to know what the words mean,' I said to Taka. It occurred to me that he might well have been the only pupil in our year to have parents who listened to popular English language music to the extent that mine did. I had no way of proving this but thought it likely, such had my appetite for the language been whetted on my parents' spinning record player.

'Thanks, Mie, leave me out of it, why don't you?' said Keiko defensively from just below her diagonally-cut fringe. 'Just because my parents happen to be' – she struggled to find the word – 'patriotic, it doesn't mean I'm going to be any worse than you.'

When we weren't talking about music, we'd be discussing the foreign language films that showed in our local art-house cinema, which we preferred to the mainstream cinemas that showed monster and disaster movies. While Taka argued for musicals, French film noir, Ealing comedies and worthy English cinéma vérité, I preferred Westerns, in which the rugged individual would eventually triumph. Essentially, though, it was the moving image that I loved: film, any film, film that spooled past the fixed stationary point of me, that, moving, defined me in contrast to it. Films began and ended, faded under a strong light, were subject to interpretation and points of view whereas I, essentially, was there, unchanging, persisting, the rooted reference for every passing frame.

Keiko waved *Never Mind the Bollocks, Here's the Sex Pistols* at us one afternoon. 'So, who's going to translate the title of this LP for me?'

To my relief, Taka struggled to make sense of it too, principally because he was preoccupied with extolling the virtues of an English film we had been to see. Accepting the record from Keiko with one hand while sliding the door closed behind him with the other, in anticipation of our playing the record loudly, he said, 'Come on, you must have both liked the film. Mie, Colin is an individualist, like you. Keiko, he is a rebel against authority, like you.'

Immediately, Keiko's mother entered, *sumimasen*ing profusely as she looked for something she didn't find, before exiting, leaving the door open behind her.

'And you?' replied Keiko languidly, flattered by the rebel label in the knowledge that her rebellion, such as it was, was even less than skin deep. Pulling a black leather mini skirt down as far as she could over the tops of her thighs, she asked, 'Who were you?'

'Me?' replied Taka dreamily. 'I was the landscape.' It occurred to me then that he had won our competition. He was a greater anglophile than me. Everything he liked, he liked for good reason but, principally, he liked it because it was English. Me, it was the language I loved; him, it was the culture, the country, the image, the look, no matter that it was ever-changing.

I contemplated Keiko, dressed as a rather tame punk, with nothing that couldn't be removed so that she could be presentable in minutes, and I was certain that her embracing this latest English export was her way of endearing herself to Taka.

'Describe to us your stereotypical Englishman,' I challenged my friends, in echo of a question Margaret had asked us in class.

'Courteous, pin-striped suit, bowler hat and umbrella,' laughed Taka, record still in hand. This was the type of reply Margaret had received, after which she'd asked us why the violence at football grounds and the skinhead look that were reported in Japan's media did nothing to challenge that old stereotype we persisted in carrying with us.

'Rude, pins in trousers – and nose! – Mohican haircut and bulldog,' countered Keiko. 'Aren't you going to play that thing?' she asked, indicating the record that Taka had dropped on to the turntable. He switched the turntable speed from 45 rpm to 33, lifted the arm, blew on the stylus and dropped it onto the record and we looked at each other in wonder and incomprehension as Johnny Rotten declined a holiday in the sun.

Michi flounced into my bedroom one exceptionally hot day, carrying a pitcher of iced tea and two porcelain beakers my mother had handed her on her way up. Spilling it and apologising only perfunctorily, she placed the pitcher and beakers on a low table on the *tatami* in the centre of the room and flopped onto my bed, losing a sandal and shrugging her handbag off her shoulder as she did so. Beads of sweat decorated her arms, legs, neck and face. She resembled a pixelated version of herself; once cooled, she'd be covered in pockmarks of white salt. She raised the back of one hand to her forehead and groaned, 'Why is it so hot?' I could see droplets of perspiration in her armpit hair and had an urge to lean forward and look for what I knew would be reflections of me and of the window behind me in each droplet, in an echo of multiple universes in the least likely of places. She smelled sweet, of a perfume that had been applied excessively because, I suspected resignedly, without resentment, she was visiting a butcher's daughter in a butcher's house in which the smells of meat and cleaning agents waged a particularly brutal war in the summer. 'Ouf! At least it's cooler here than in my room.' Suddenly uncomfortable, she reached behind her and extracted from among the bed covers a bra I had ambitiously purloined from my mother. 'Don't pretend to me you fill this!' she exclaimed and threw it across the room. 'Ha, ha,' she added to show she had only been teasing.

I sat down heavily next to her and pushed her leg with mine. 'Go on. Budge up.'

'Hot pants,' she observed. 'I didn't think you were allowed to wear them.'

'Not outside the house.'

'I bet that poor old Takumi-*san* can't keep his hands off you. How did he lose those fingers exactly?' Michi sniggered.

My father's assistant had always treated me with the greatest respect and consideration, and I told Michi as much. She jiggled her leg and foot against mine in a successful attempt to dislodge one of my sandals. 'Well, he has more sense, I suppose, than to proposition the boss's daughter. With me, he's just an old letch. Anyway,' she said, propping herself up on her elbows, 'Guess what?' Her wide, manga eyes were inches away from mine; in them were reflected the open window and the rooftops and blue sky beyond. There was some news she was clearly desperate to share. 'You know Taka has been going to Keiko's a lot recently?'

'Yes.' The sudden thought that Keiko and Taka were going out together was like a stab. I felt foolish for not having suspected it, and immediately jealous of Keiko at the same time as doubly foolish, for I didn't think I was interested in Taka myself.

'Ha! How do you know that? Surely, you can only know if you've been going a lot yourself! And to see who, exactly?'

'To see Keiko, of course.' No more or less than for the last fifteen years or so, I wanted to add. Michi's delighted insinuation confused me. It was too much to take in in one go, so I simply said, 'I never suspected!'

'Hold on, hold on, not so fast!' Michi sat up and held my hand and patted it, and my leg felt intensely hot against hers. 'Apparently, Taka said to Keiko the other day when they were, you know, hanging out together, drinking lemonade in Keiko's back yard, "Where's Mie?" and Keiko got really stroppy and said something like, "Oh, for God's sake, Taka, why do you keep on asking after Mie? Every time you come here, the first thing you do is ask when she's coming over!" Michi squeezed my hand and paused in order to gauge the effect of her words. She delivered Taka's line with glee: 'And Taka said, "Why do you think I come here?" Then he realised how rude that sounded and had to apologise, of course.'

I managed to ask, 'How do you know all this?'

'Oh, from my mother. She was outside; you know how she likes to sit out for a while once she's closed the shop. Poor old Keiko.' Michi hugged herself and then me with delight. 'Come on, don't play the innocent. Why are you going around there so much if not to see Taka?' She tickled me gently.

I got up and limped, with just one sandal on, to the window. 'I feel sorry for Keiko.' I tried to explain to Michi that I enjoyed my friendship with Taka very much, but hadn't wanted a relationship with him for fear that it might have made things difficult for all three of us – Keiko, Taka and me. I allowed Michi to take my hand and pull me back onto the bed where we lay hand in hand on our backs. 'And you... You are such a gossip!'

Michi giggled with joy. 'If you look out of the window for a while, and then up at the ceiling, you get these kind of reverse, negative images of the window on the ceiling,' she said.

Somehow, this seemed a good metaphor for the situation I found myself in: my friendships turned inside out and slowly fading.

'Don't be ridiculous,' said Michi. 'You'll be okay,' though whether she meant me or Taka and me or Keiko and me, I didn't know. 'Remember, you're friends and you like each other – just don't lose sight of that.'

I squeezed her hand and turned to admire her. Her energy and sense of mischief had faded with the heat of the day. I had been right: I saw on her arms and shoulders miniscule dried salt lakes that glittered dully in the evening light. I sensed that if we looked west from my window we would see, above the multiplying telephone wires, a sensational sunset.

I remained friends with Keiko, who chose to study business with a view to eventually managing her parents' expanding regional chain of electrical supplies shops, and with Michi, whose food-related issues – which I learnt about once she had successfully overcome them – had made her want to study psychology. In the weeks in which we readied ourselves for university, Michi, Keiko and I saw each other little; when we did, Taka wasn't mentioned once; and in Keiko's conventional clothing, I saw no hint that she was still pursuing a strategy of winning Taka over by adopting what she considered the new 'in' English look.

I was proud of Keiko for having what seemed to be business acumen and vision, but it didn't interest me; however, it did make me wonder if my parents might be expecting me to join the family business. I raised this with them one Sunday afternoon. They were completing the shop's accounts and I was preparing for my first term of study by reading *Sense and Sensibility*, which was on my first–year reading list. In a moment that I rather self-consciously thought of as my Elinor Dashwood moment in my seeming readiness to place my parents' interests above my own, I closed the book and looked up.

'Ahem. Otoo-*san*, can I ask you a question? I have never asked you if you'd rather I join you in the family business than go to university. Or if you'd like me to join it after university, in which case I should consider studying something more practical than English.' At this, I bowed my head and waited for the reply. When my father said nothing, I looked up.

He had removed his glasses and was looking at me incredulously; my mother was staring at me too. She uncrossed her legs and padded across the *tatami* to kneel by me. My father's shoulders shook with suppressed laughter and my mother put one arm around mine as they looked at me in wonder.

'Absolutely not!'

'We forbid it!'

'We wouldn't wish this on anyone, least of all on our daughter!'

'Actually, that's not quite right,' said my father more reflectively. 'We have not had an unhappy life and our expectations were never that high, but this job is not one I would want my daughter to aspire to. Fly! Fly away! Be who you want to be!' he exhorted, waving his glasses. 'Early mornings spent taking deliveries, afternoons spent with suppliers and early evenings spent arranging and cleaning – and weekends spent doing this' – he indicated the sheaves of paper that covered the low table – 'leave you no time for much else, as you know.'

'What if my aspirations are to... go away?' I asked with a lump in my throat.

My mother squeezed my hand as my father said, 'Then you must go. Our contentment will lie in seeing you fulfilled.'

'Mie, you're not telling us anything new. It's not as though you've never said that you want to study English in order to travel and see the world. We've known this all along.'

'Thank you,' I sniffed. 'Actually, it's not so much the world I want to see as England, to begin with, anyway. I just want to go somewhere where I can feel really me, you know – well, I can't explain it exactly.'

'You can and you have and we understand. You are our daughter after all. Permit us to live vicariously through you,' said my father generously.

My university days were to be like my school ones, on the whole: unremarkable, as though I were going through a long gestation, just waiting for my real life to begin.

I sat waiting for my first lecture at the Tokyo University of Foreign Studies, one in over a hundred English language and literature students, the majority of them young women. I eventually saw Taka who, I guessed by the way he was also looking around the lecture hall, was searching for me. He didn't see me and I wondered if he ever really had; if what he saw when he looked at me was what I saw when I looked at myself in the mirror, if he knew just how different I was (or thought I was, he might say) to the other assembled students.

I tried to explain my thoughts to him some weeks later, as we walked, books in hand, to Tampopo, a noodle bar that was filling with solitary commuters who dined alone ahead of long train journeys home. We found a table for two and set our two piles of books down beside its two tea cups, two soup bowls and condiments.

'So, you really think yourself so very different to others,' Taka said matter-of-factly, once we had placed our orders and poured our teas. He had grown his hair and wore it with a centre parting that had the effect of making him more feminine and, curiously, more handsome.

'Not superior,' I wanted to make clear. 'Just different. I want different things.'

Taka nodded. 'What makes you think you're different? In what way are you different? What do you want that others don't want?'

'All these questions!' My impulse was to laugh, but Taka had asked me over a cup of tea he had brought to his lips and I could see that his hands were shaking. My body language mirrored his as, elbows on the table, I blew over my steaming tea, so that he blinked. 'What do I want? You know. I mean, we've talked about it often enough, listening to all those English records and walking back from those English films. I had thought that you wanted the same thing? You know – England. I thought you wanted that too.' My voice tailed off and I waved our immediate surroundings away, intending to indicate that I wanted away and fearing that what I had just said might suggest that I hoped Taka would go to England with me. I tried again. 'To be clear, what I want is to study English such that it is good enough to enable me to find a job in England, so that I can live there.'

'Forever?'

I didn't know the answer to that question. 'For some time, at least.'

'Easier said than done. Finding a job there, I mean.'

'You may be right. I don't yet know. I intend to apply for jobs with companies that have offices in England and then secure a transfer.'

'That could take a long time! But it's not a bad strategy,' conceded Taka, who seemed suddenly bored by the subject and sat back to accommodate the bowl of steaming noodles in broth placed in front of him. 'Tell me instead about your idea that you're so different from everyone else. How can you know? You can't read anyone else's mind.'

'I know, but look around you.' I waved my chopsticks just as he leant forward to slurp his soup from his *chirirenge*. 'Sorry.'

'You're not telling me how they're different,' replied Taka. 'We've all spent a day at work or in college and here we are all eating noodles and soup before we go home.'

'Yes, but their – our – mental lives are so different.'

'But, Mie, how do you know? How do you know that not everyone wishes to do something else or to be somewhere else?'

'Because they never do it and they never go there.'

'Maybe it's out of consideration to others, to family, to loved ones; not everyone can up sticks and live in a foreign country. Maybe they can't afford to.'

'Look at it this way, Taka, it may seem that we two are having the same, a shared, experience – we're here together, eating in the same place at the same table at the same time – but, really, that's far from the case. You are facing the noodle bar, the chefs, some other customers while I look out onto a street with cars, mopeds and pedestrians. And we're not even eating the same thing – *udon* for you, *ramen* for me. So we are eating, seeing, saying and hearing – thinking – quite different things.'

'Mie the solipsist.' Taka slurped his noodles and reflected for a moment. 'We probably hear the same things. But I guess you're right for the rest. In fact, do we even hear the same thing? I mean, we may understand different things by them. For example, when you say that both you and I want to go to England, do you mean me to understand that you want me to go with you – which is what I used to think – or, simply, that I should understand your need to get away?'

I placed my hands in my lap and looked into my bowl.

'It's okay,' said Taka gently. 'I think I get it now.'

As I had grown older and boys had become bolder, I had been propositioned, squeezed, fondled and petted by a number of young men, typically before an attempted, unsuccessful kiss. I had never enjoyed the encounters. Desiring Taka insufficiently to want to repeat those experiences and yet liking him too much to want to upset him placed me in the difficult position of wanting to demonstrate my gratitude to him without leading him on. I followed my instinct and squeezed his hand, hoping that it would be taken as a sign of friendship rather than of encouragement.

Taka withdrew it as though it had been scalded. 'Do you even know what you want?'

Taka and I stood shoulder to shoulder on the train platform, talking haltingly about our course, our reading list, our fellow pupils and our lecturers. Railway lines in echo of parallel lives underscored the silences in our conversation. Tipsy salarymen on their way home spoke loudly, as though to overcome their anxiety that the obscenities they were uttering were overstepping the mark.

If I wasn't going to make a go of things with Taka, who was intelligent, courteous and good-looking, and who shared many of the same interests as me, who could I have a relationship with? Loose, general ideas, the germs of which I realised I had carried for years, began to coalesce in my mind. I recalled the drops of blood in my father's butcher's shop prep room and the manner in which, when two of them touched and their surface tension broke, they were each obliterated and combined to become one bigger droplet of blood, and I shuddered at the thought of eliminating myself in another. I thought of Takumi-*san*'s excellent, thick black stylised silhouette of a man on the prep room wall, and again wore its contours like a suit of armour, a strange, unorthodox comfort blanket that defined and contained me.

'Are you okay?' asked Taka.

I wasn't. Adolescent, that bold outline had seemed to me perfect, closed and impenetrable. A young woman now, I had become aware of that suit of armour's chink, of its hidden flaw, of my sex's weakness, of that indistinguishable slit where the legs meet and the outline must at some point be split, penetrated and violated as it admits of some other. The sensation of men's tongues seeking mine was bad enough, but the idea of this gross act of trespass, this intrusive union with another's body, nauseated me, and the railway lines rocked and the wolfish salarymen were alternately above, below, behind and in front of me. I realised, from the pressure to one elbow, that it was only Taka's hold that was keeping me from keeling over and yet I wanted to withdraw from it, from him, in abrupt conviction that everything he did, like all men's calculated activities, was with the intention of inveigling his way in.

As if from a distance, I could make out the distress on Taka's face that was yet pressed close to mine. His voice mingled with that of the intoxicated salarymen who made crude remarks about my inability to hold my drink and about the success Taka was likely to have with me once he got me home. Torn between having me regain my senses on a platform bench and on the train that was pulling in as I wobbled, Taka opted for the latter, maybe as much for him, because he wanted to go home and discharge his unexpected responsibility, as for me. He offered to walk me home but I declined.

I turned a corner on my walk home that evening. I gave voice to the kernel of a sentiment that I had carried with me as a child and planted when Michi had visited me that hot summer day. By the time I had arrived home, inserted my hand through the letterbox and fished out the string with the front door key on it, I had made a decision. I had my parents and my friends, my ambitions to travel, to learn and to remain true to myself; I felt no need to follow form, no need for romance and the possible disappointment it involved, for marriage and compromise, no need for children. How different a kernel of an idea, that develops in one's mind into a life philosophy, from a parasitic seed, that grows inside one's womb, ruptures one and continues to suck on one's emotional, physical and financial resources, on one's reserves of personhood. I leant with my back against the door waiting for my second dizzy spell of the night to pass.

Isabella

Kimberley and I spent our time together in the confines of the home and its garden, the prospect of the outside world clearly perturbing her. The physical demands of excursions were beyond her, such was her obesity and breathlessness, exceptions being made for the short bus journeys to public libraries. Little by little, as though following a courtship protocol or playing a board game that required stops and starts and lucky card picks, we exchanged information about our recent histories and, more specifically, about our coping mechanisms and states of mind.

Kimberley had sought refuge in books and food. Literature had provided her with an escape route to the extent, she said, that the worlds of some books became more real to her than her own, to the point at which the knowledge of a book's imminent ending would detract from her pleasure in it, as she knew that she would soon have to suffer the interval that came between its end and the start of the next. Books provided vicarious travel – both geographic and temporal, given her penchant for Victorian novels – and, as importantly, a form of therapy by proxy: she was every heroine, every jilted lover, every mother, every sister.

Kimberley laid five fat fingers and a sweaty palm on my arm when she asked after Cosmo and, having listened to me tell of his gradual habilitation, squeezed it and said, to my immense pleasure and relief, in a voice in an even higher register than usual, 'Don't chastise yourself for it. You did what you could. He is lucky to have you as a sister.' She knew, she understood and, momentarily, I loved her intensely for it, although not without thinking that she was speaking like the character of a friend or confidante she had discovered in a novel.

We had been on a one-stop bus journey when she had said to me amid breathy giggles, 'Having read *Tess* and excited at the prospect of the Hardy books ahead of me and having determined to read them in order, I marched – well, waddled – into the library and asked for *Dramatic Recipes* and, when they said they didn't have it, I gave them so much stick! And – can you believe! – I'd got the title wrong: it was *Desperate Remedies*! Well, they were good to me, they didn't bat an eyelid though if I'd been them I'd have told me I'd obviously had enough dramatic recipes and didn't need another!' I loved her then, too, for her ability to be self-deprecating, for her admission of her errors and, frequently, for her forgiving what she referred to as my literary lacunae: it was she who made me realise that, having been ahead of my reading age when a child, I had stopped reading much when an adolescent, and she who pressed books into my hands whenever I left her room.

Kimberley preferred Victorian novelists because they addressed sex less openly, more obliquely – if she hated anything, it was talk of sex or its sudden, unexpected description in a book or depiction in a film. Sex, for Kimberley, was where books met food. 'I hate my body. I hate what they did to it. My body, well, it was just a sack of body parts for my uncle and your dad' – here, she placed a hand on my arm as if in apology – 'and for others to sift through. I thought that I could reclaim it from them, you know, make it mine again and, it's strange, but being fat made me feel safer, it was like I was making my body big to protect myself, making myself undesirable to them.' Kimberley wheezed when she talked at length. 'And look at you!' she panted. 'Skinny as a rake!'

'You and me…' I said. 'Between the two of us, on average, we'd have –'

'Two fat people!' interrupted Kimberley, wheezing and gasping in laughter. She lowered her eyes and I looked down upon the pale cream of her eyelids and long, fair eyelashes. For a moment she was the young girl in Papa's study. 'The thing is,' she said quietly, 'that I don't want to be attractive to anybody, but then it's not nice for me not being attractive to myself. The doctors say I should lose weight for my health but I am happier being overweight because I feel safer. But then…' She lowered her voice so I had to hold my breath to hear her. 'I'm letting them destroy not only my life but my health too.'

'It's just so unjust,' I said, more to myself than to Kimberley.

'Miss Heverfet and Miss Robbie have a plan for me,' said Kimberley abruptly. 'I'm to go back to school, go to sixth-form college, take my

English A level, study English at university and become an English teacher. And I'll walk to college to lose weight so that nobody teases me. And so that my health improves.'

The chimes of an ice–cream van two streets away were audible.

We were quiet a moment, sitting on the bench at the bottom of the garden that received the last warmth of the sun at the end of the day, Kimberley occupying half of the bench that creaked when she shifted her weight, our home and refuge in silhouette in front of us, its odd mix of pebbledash and mock Tudor gabling faint and blurred against the pale disc of the low sun as though observed through the fine mesh of a butterfly cage.

'What I really want to do,' stated Kimberley seriously, quietly, 'is to spend the rest of my life here, eating and reading.' The prospect of having to leave the home terrified her. 'Don't you see? Don't you see why? Why would anyone want to leave? I hate it that I have to have a plan to leave. How can you all seem so indifferent about leaving?'

'The thing is, about being here, for me, being in this home, any home, even my foster home, it feels like a punishment. It was Cosmo and I who were sent from the family home, not my father. It was as though we were being punished, as though we were the ones who had done something wrong. And then being sent to a care home from my foster home – that felt like another unfair punishment. I know it's okay here but...' I shrugged. 'And it's been nice to have you as a friend,' I added. I leant against her and the warmth of her body fused with the warmth of the sun. Her arm was the size of my leg.

Freddie approached us from the house. She was carrying a plastic bag in one hand and waved with the other.

'Freddie's going to go to London to become a singer,' said Kimberley, resignedly. 'What are you going to do?'

'I'm going to go with her. Once I've finished school.'

'Budge up,' said Freddie and handed us each an ice lolly.

Freddie had revealed her story only slowly, over months, in stages at which she'd measure our responses before, having deemed them appropriate, she'd reveal yet more of herself to us. What element of disbelief we felt lay, for Kimberley and me, in the fact that Freddie had suffered at the hands of a dissolute mother, an alcoholic and a bully, and not at those of a father who, contrary to Kimberley's and my experiences, had been his daughter's protector and companion and, ultimately, his wife's victim. This inversion of roles had been a source of fascination for me and I had quizzed Freddie about it as gently and considerately as I could.

Freddie's father had been a man who, receiving an income from a family trust, had devoted his time to listening to music, to music journalism and, eventually, to a wife who, reportedly attractive when tipsy during their courtship, had become monstrous when continually drunk in marriage. Freddie believed that the only thing that had attracted her mother to her father had been his wealth and its implications for a steady supply of gin, her propensity for which had risen on her realising that his income was not all she had thought it to be. The more forgiving her father had been of her depravity, the more she had taken advantage of his kindness and his purse, and the more tolerant he had been of her degeneracy the more she had despised him for it. Freddie, naturally, had sought sanctuary from her volatile and frightening mother in her father's company. Her happier memories were of the two of them in their sitting room, she cross-legged on the floor amid LP covers and sleeveless records, and her father standing, wobbling on a battered leather pouffe in passionate imitation of Arturo Toscanini or Sir Thomas Beecham, and the music loud enough to drown out either her mother's screams that they turn the music down or her cries in the throes of love-making in the bedroom directly above the sitting room with the men whom Freddie hated to cross on the stairs of her father's house.

One evening, recounted Freddie, as she had been hugging her knees on the sitting room's cream shag carpet and admiring her father's unsteady conducting of an opera while she followed the libretto open on the floor beside her, her mother had walked in and brought the sharp heels of her shoes down on the record player and faced her husband defiantly, a shoe in each hand. She had broken the record and the arm of the record player that had kept on revolving and, in the immediate silence that had followed, Freddie had become aware of its soft hum for the first time that had then blended with the commencement of her father's profound, welling bellow as though he had only then decided to express years of repressed hate and misery. After the fight that had ensued, of one conductor's baton against two stiletto heels, Freddie's father, having stabbed and nearly strangled his wife to death, had staggered out into the road and into the path of an oncoming motorcycle, blinded, it was later suggested, by the blood in his eyes.

Freddie had stayed mesmerised by a drop of blood that had arced through the air and fallen miraculously on one, and only one, thick fibre of the shag carpet that would forever, in her mind, remain an erect scarlet reproach in a turbulent creamy sea of her inactivity – not just then, as her parents had fought, but throughout her life, as she had neglected and shrunk from her mother and allowed the chasm that had appeared between her parents to widen.

Freddie had then been sent to a foster home and, when her liaison with her foster father had been discovered by her foster mother, to the care home. 'Mr Johnston said that I look for my father in every man I meet,' Freddie had said. 'Urgh. He's such a creep. He needs to wash his hair. And he doesn't understand. Anyway, who cares if he's right. It's not as though I ever shagged or wanted to shag my father. Sorry.' She had squeezed my knee and looked apologetically at Kimberley.

I think I became Miss Heverfet's and Miss Robbie's greatest disappointment. 'Going to London is not a plan,' insisted Miss Heverfet testily, but I could see no further than that. I saw myself escaping a butterfly pavilion for the great unknown. Only sixty miles away and yet so far. From Summertown, to Iffley and to Littlemore, five miles in the right direction across Oxford's suburbs in eighteen years, and now, any day soon, sixty miles in an afternoon. The hum of traffic on the distant dual carriageways as I lay awake was, for me, the big city's siren call.

The connectedness of everything material and external to me – that one could be in a bus on an Oxford street and only a little later be on London's Oxford Street, was magical and yet frightening. It mirrored the internal trauma I had undergone when recollections of the nocturnal activities in Papa's study had intruded when I had embraced Tomasz and, later, contemplated a greater intimacy with other boys.

I listened to two voices, one of which expressed its disgust that I could even contemplate a sexual act, no matter if it was borne out of an affection for a boy my own age, and the other that filled my mind with obscenities and encouraged me to promiscuity in order to demonstrate my liberation from Papa, to assert my freedom from his control.

The butterfly in me flew infrequently, having entered a long period of hibernation. Without daring to examine my motive too closely, I hoped that London would awaken it and coax it out; London, where I would discover whether I had the courage to embrace sexual liberation and unlock the cage of my body.

'But what are you going to do in London?' persisted Miss Heverfet. 'You can't just go there!' But I could. Freddie had a music course to follow, a part-time job and an apartment to live in that I could live in too. I had maintenance money from Papa that would continue until I was twenty-one and money from Uncle James who thrust it at me on his infrequent visits.

On the day Freddie and I took the bus to the coach station, the day of Kimberley's tearful farewell and the day after I had said goodbye to Cosmo, the Bobeckyjs and the Baldocks, I had everything I owned in two cardboard suitcases.

Sharon

I had exchanged school for secretarial college and left my parents in order to live with my aunt. I had given up acting, as a child, to act as an adult. I had swapped my school uniform for that of a girl about town. I abstained from casual sexual encounters and missed them. I had grown up English and Catholic only to find that I was not quite either.

Close to home, I'd wander Wandsworth Park, which borders the Thames, and, secretarial college finished for the day, further afield: Hyde Park and then Green or St James's Parks, losing and finding myself along gravel paths. The holes in the ground no longer materialised in mockery of me and the elves stayed hidden within the bushes' dense leaves, lying in wait for me to fall into a false sense of security. Could this all mean that I was finally becoming a person? I thought so; I hoped so, but what kind of one? I couldn't tell.

Secretarial college finished for good. I needed to find work and could think of nothing better than taking Aunt Wanda's advice to heart: I took my CV and newly polished shoes, shiny tights and best business suit to recruitment firms in the City where I applied for secretarial positions with the banks. The interview process was an interesting one: I, too, wanted to be on the other side of the desk in my ongoing attempt to pin down this green-eyed, nervous, humourless secretary-to-be whose hair was pulled back into a bun and who failed to progress in a succession of interviews. I, too, wanted to ask her questions that I knew she wouldn't have the answers to.

Wanda set me right. 'Don't be so defensive. Remember, they're interviewing you because they need you or someone like you. Your CV ticks all the boxes so, really, by the time you're sitting across the table from them, their only question is, *Do I want to work with this person?* So be the person they'd like to spend eight hours a day with and ask questions. Remember, you're interviewing them too. Show interest, and that where you work is important to you. And do your homework.'

'My homework?'

'Yes, your research. Research the company you're interviewing with so you can have some questions for them.'

There must have been something in Wanda's words, because I got the next job I interviewed for. Either that or the bohemian, vaguely cynical and confused air of the personnel manager, who seemed like a fish out of water in his black polyester suit in the City, was enough to make me relax sufficiently to interview well. Mr Self sat forward in a swivel chair holding my CV in both hands and said, 'Next, you're going to meet Jonathan, who's head of the UK sales team and then Curtis, Guy and Kate. Relax,' he added, and raised his hand as though to pat mine, then thought better of it. 'You'll do fine.'

Jonathan was a big bumbling fellow who immediately put me further at my ease. He emanated wordless apology for his clumsy manner and the space he took up in a room. He squeezed into the chair Mr Self had vacated. 'You know,' he said by way of preamble, waving my CV in the air as though it were an irrelevance, 'that the sterling market hasn't decimalised yet?'

I smiled.

'We still work in fractions.'

I nodded, unsure of where he was going.

'You're good with numbers, it says here.'

'Oh yes,' I said.

'So if I give you some fractions, will you be able to give me their decimal equivalent?'

'I think so,' I replied, uncertain.

'What are three–quarters expressed in decimal terms?'

'0.75.'

'What are five–eighths?'

'0.625.'

'Three–sixteenths?'

I halved an eighth and added it to an eighth and said after only a little delay, '0.1875.'

Jonathan pushed his glasses up on the bridge of his nose and said, 'You're in as far as I'm concerned,' and left the room bellowing for Curtis.

I stood as I waited for Curtis and looked through the glass partition wall into the trading room. It was as exciting and alien as it was alluring. Suddenly conscious of the increasing number of approving male eyes facing my direction, I turned to find I was no longer alone.

'Hi,' said a young preppy-looking American, who shook my hand and closed the door behind him before sitting down.

Pushing my CV to one side, he leant forward conspiratorially and I found my body language imitating his. 'Say,' he said. 'Nice shoes. And nice valise!' he added, fingering what I would have called my folder or, if I had wanted to impress, attaché case, which I had placed on the table. 'Are they genuine plastic?'

'No!' I exclaimed, reclining abruptly. 'Well the shoes aren't, but I don't know about – that.'

'Good. Now, tell me, do you give good back rubs?'

Astonished, I laughed weakly.

'On-ly kid-ding!' he sang. 'Good! You passed the sterling desk sense of humour test!' Curtis sat forward all of a sudden, serious now. 'What is a bond?'

'Er, an IOU.'

'What is a gilt?'

I thought hard, back to the research Wanda had had me do. 'A bond of the UK government?'

He didn't seem impressed.

'It's when the UK government borrows money,' I added.

'That will do,' he said. 'Do you have any questions?'

I could tell from Curtis's face that someone behind my back was making faces or signs that were amusing him, so I replied, 'Yes. What's going on behind my back?'

He grinned impishly and said, 'Good question,' and then a gleam came to his eye and he said, 'I tell you what, when I tell you to, turn around suddenly – now!' And to his delight some of his red-faced colleagues whipped away sheets of paper they'd been holding up, but not before I had seen a large red 10 scrawled on one of them. Curtis hooted with delight and, getting up to leave, said, 'Watch out for Kate. She's got teeth!'

When Kate entered the interview room after the longest wait, during which I had kept my back to the trading room, I nearly laughed aloud, as she wore her tightly curled hair either side of her hair band in the fashion of a cocker spaniel's ears and I fully expected her to bare a cocker spaniel's set of teeth. I only then noticed her clothes, which were of an elegance and cut that screamed expense and taste, and I felt cheap and shabby in comparison.

Kate stared humourlessly at the activities behind my back, and turning her attention to me, smiled ever so artificially charmingly, and said, 'Sharon... Sorry, that is your real name, isn't it?'

'Yes, of course,' I replied, puzzled.

'Oh good, good, how sweet,' said Kate. 'Tell me, Sharon, if I asked you to book me into a hotel in Edinburgh for two nights, which one would you choose? And which airline would you fly me there with? If I asked you to book dinner, in London, for an important client and me, which restaurant would you choose? Would you choose a different restaurant if my client's wife were joining us? How much float do you think you'd have to keep in petty cash for a week for the team? On what occasions would you book a car service for me instead of have me hail a black cab? Would you object to running errands, for the greater good of the team and of our clients? Tell me, is that your old school uniform you're wearing? Do you think you'd be capable of submitting my expenses the day I give them to you? It's been a pleasure, Sharon, such a pleasure.'

Kate hadn't stopped to listen to my hesitant replies. All of a sudden, I was exhausted, deflated, as though I had just put on the longest, toughest performance of my life.

I woke to Mr Self shaking me gently by the shoulder. 'I'm sorry to have kept you waiting so long,' he said, ignoring my embarrassment. 'But I have good news! Congratulations!'

In celebration, Wanda opened a bottle of champagne, and then another, that we consumed either side of a Chinese takeaway, sitting at the ends of the settee in Wanda's living room, our legs interlaced in the middle of it. Our mood passed from exuberant to contemplative, when Wanda took it upon herself to resume the mother's role and advise me on good working practices: the importance of punctuality, of asking questions rather than pretending to have understood instructions, of honesty, integrity and of managing one's managers. As much as I appreciated my aunt's guidance, I wished I could have heard it from my mother.

'Aunt Wanda,' I said sitting up a little. 'Tell me, what are the evening jobs you go to? Mum asked me to ask you ages ago, but I always forgot.'

Wanda held the stem of her champagne glass in both hands and replied, 'Well, you know, I do the books for some restaurants and other businesses and they ask me to help out in the evenings. From time to time.'

'Yes, I know that. But which restaurants and which businesses?'

'Well, you know I've done the books at Lo Scoglio for some time now. Massimo and Laura would rather have me in if they're short-staffed or need a holiday than a temp. Anyway, it's easy – I go in once a week to take care of the finances and stay on for a couple of sittings.'

'Yes, but that's only one night a week, if that. What about the other nights?'

'Hit a person when she's down, why don't you? You choose your moment!' Wanda extended a leg to tickle me with a bare foot, head lolling to one side to exaggerate her inebriation.

'What do you mean, hitting you?' My curiosity was suddenly aroused. 'Come on! Are you hiding something? Where are you on those Thursday and Friday nights?'

'Oh God,' said Wanda, placing her glass amid the empty foil containers and cardboard lids and bringing a hand to her head. 'This you do not tell your mother. I do front of house for another company I do the books for.'

'Another restaurant?'

'Well…'

'Come on, tell me. What's it called?' I clutched her foot.

'You don't want to know.'

'I have means of making you tock,' I said and raised a finger as though to tickle her sole.

'You promise not to tell your mother?'

'I promise.'

'Argh!' said Wanda, in feigned anguish. 'It's so unfair of you to ask me after I've had a bottle of champagne.'

She held her head in her hands.

'So. What is it?' I persisted.

She told me.

'But. That's a strip club!' I gasped.

'A gentlemen's club or a lap-dancing club but not a strip club.' She raised a finger. 'There is a difference. Or so we like to think. Anyway, now you know.'

'Aunt Wanda!'

She shrugged.

'I don't believe it!'

'You might as well.' She withdrew her foot and pulled her legs up under her. 'To tell the truth, I didn't either to begin with. But I'll tell you what, it beats visiting all these so-called respectable companies to do their books for weeks at a time and being followed into dark, dingy offices by their in-house accountants on the pretext of delivering forgotten files so they can touch you up and leer over your shoulder with their bad breath and roving hands and go on about nice figures. And then beg you to sign off on their dodgy accounts, their crooked expenses, their trips to Paris with mistresses and their lavish dinners with their mates. You know, not once have I not been felt up by someone in those supposedly respectable companies I've audited – and not once have I not found occasions of corruption. And I'll tell you something about the club: it's whiter than white. No deviation from a hundred percent honesty is tolerated. Every penny is accounted for. It has to be; the police, the Inland Revenue and the council are all over it. But, more than that, Pierre wants to do this properly, cleanly.' Wanda leant back. 'He's the owner. If the business is considered smutty then it has to be run cleanly.' She leant forward again. 'And, actually, the best thing about it is the girls. The girls who work there. They're lovely! Like a big family for each other – they look out for one another. And nothing goes on besides chatting to customers and topless dancing. No touching allowed. You know...' She shook her head. 'It's not what people think it is, what they assume.'

'But what do you do there, Aunt Wanda?'

'I do the finances. I meet with Pierre and talk cash flow, bank over-draft and interest rates. I sign off on the numbers he has for me once I've either counted the money or seen the bank receipts. Sometimes I accompany him to the bank. Sometimes I go without him. Then I have dinner. Then I'm front of house and welcoming customers at the door and taking their money and, sometimes, their coats if we have no one for the cloakroom, and then I might help the cashier if customers wish to withdraw money on their credit cards. Or I might just hang out in the dressing room with the girls, laughing with some, consol-ing others, mending costumes. You know how it is.'

'I don't, really.'

'Sometimes, when customers get drunk or aggressive, it's good to have a woman to defuse a situation. But fortunately that doesn't hap-pen very often.'

'I wouldn't have thought you'd be short of women there.'

Wanda stretched her lips into a smile. 'A woman not in a bikini, I mean.'

'This Pierre, is he your boyfriend?'

'No! He's too old for me and I'm too old for him! You know, you should come there one evening and see for yourself. It really is not what people think. I bet you would love it. Oh God, what am I say-ing?' Wanda brought her hands to her forehead.

Isabella

The executors of Freddie's father's estate had secured her a grant for a music course and approved her rental of a London apartment that she and I had wandered about in amazement before falling into each other's arms in fits of giggles, the thud of our suitcases hitting the bald board floor reverberating off the bare brick walls. We had the top floor of a former Victorian warehouse, a vast expanse of space immediately below the building's serially vaulted, high–beamed roof that required the support of two iron pillars at a regular distance between the room's side walls; each of these contained a door that led to a corridor off which were a bathroom and a bedroom. Freddie picked sides, choosing one bedroom and bathroom over the other, not because there was any difference between the two but, I suspected, in simple demonstration of her right to have first dibs. A kitchen, the only immediately visible concession to domestic occupation, had been fitted the entire length of the rear wall either side of the entrance door.

That evening, each sitting cross-legged on a suitcase immediately below one of three massive casement windows constructed from a multitude of panes of glass set in dirty leading, we ate our first Indian takeaway ever and listened, on Freddie's transistor radio, to a discussion about whether the discoveries of four incendiary devices in London over the last three days were evidence of the IRA's intention to step up their mainland bombing campaign. The Indian and the Irish brought elements of exoticism and excitement to our London move. Looking out over the roof of the Smithfield meat market and, in the middle distance, the dome of St Paul's Cathedral half–lit by a setting sun, we listened to a programme on the impending first anniversary of Germany's reunification, and the elation that accompanied the story of that country's rebirth was ours, too, as we made plans for the work I would find and the furniture we would buy and the manner in which we would decorate the apartment and the life we would lead. 'And I will pay rent, of course,' I had said, to which Freddie had replied sweetly that there was no hurry before quickly suggesting a price, which, I thought, indicated that she had already given the matter some consideration.

Freddie and I trawled the second-hand furniture shops of Clerkenwell and further north and east to furnish the apartment, and headed to Covent Garden and further west to, as I put it lightly to Freddie, furnish our souls, dipping our toes and noses into museums, galleries and expensive shops like timid tourists. Freddie, complete and self-assured as she was, was unimpressed, so I kept to myself the thought that with every rug, armchair, trestle table and hanging rail we bought and with every decorative jug and vase we filled with flowers and placed on tables and window shelves, I furnished a little bit of my person, taking further steps towards self-definition and self-knowledge.

I took jobs where I could, in cafés, pubs and sandwich shops that served City workers at lunch, while Freddie studied and gave children piano and singing lessons. We took our pleasure where we could, by day with friends made in Freddie's college and my odd jobs, and by night in Kings Cross's and Hoxton's burgeoning club scene, later breakfasting with club-goers and butchers and meatpackers who were finishing their shifts in the meat market. Exhausted and yet wide awake, sleepy and yet buzzing, we and our hangers-on would climb the endless flights of stairs to our apartment to sleep through the better part of weekend days, Freddie and I waking up in the afternoons to complete strangers in our beds and armchairs and on our sofas and floors.

Sharon

I recalled a summer holiday in Wales, staying with Nonna and Nonno in Cowbridge. My grandparents would drive us to Ogmore-by-Sea for fish and chips and we would stop en route to climb the ruins of Ogmore Castle and dare to cross the Ewenny River on a series of close-set stepping stones just before it joined the River Ogmore only a mile from the sea. A memory came to me of Nonno and me on the stepping stones and of Nonna and Seamus on the bank and her shouting, 'Be careful!'

'One stone at a time, bring your feet together on the one stone before you step to the next, regain your balance, that's right, take it easy,' instructed Nonno.

It was easy. I grew confident. I slipped. I fell between two stones and gasped with the grip of the ice-cold water on my chest and the grasp of Nonno's fingers on my wrist and with the not knowing whether to laugh or cry. By the time we had returned home, with me stripped of my sopping clothes in the car park by the castle and swaddled in an assortment of clothes my grandparents had spared, I thought the discomfort and fright quite worth it for the attention I received; Nonno got the ticking-off from Mum.

There was something of the time of year, the quality of light that brought this back to me as I crossed St James's Park lake; maybe it was the crossing of the footbridge with Whitehall's buildings to my far right, a visual echo of Ogmore's castle in its relation to the stepping stones. I was unaware I had stopped until a tourist bumped into me and excused herself. She was saying something else to me. Would I take a picture of her and her friend together?

They stood, their bags at their feet and their backs to Buckingham Palace in the middle distance and the low sun behind; their faces would appear dark in the picture, I knew.

I returned the camera and thought, this is what my life will be like, a series of memories like a series of photographs with nothing to connect them. A join-the-dots life in which the dots remain forever unconnected, as in the pages of Seamus's join-the-dots books he never got around to completing. A sequence of stepping stones with no guarantee that anyone would be there to save me by the wrist when I slipped and fell.

The bank was a circus, its trading floor a tumultuous riot of voices raised in excitement and exuberance when not lowered in despair and frustration. I sat across from Curtis and Kate and between Jonathan and Guy, my designated mentor, who showed patience when he needed to and trusted me sufficiently to leave me to my own devices when I said I'd understood something. Behind me sat the Japanese team: a loud, arrogant man called Yuuto and a rotation of his timid, terrified team assistants who never managed to stay for long.

On my first day, Kate stood by my desk; she was shorter than I'd remembered her to be. She said, 'You might as well hear it from me: I didn't want you hired. But I was outvoted. Anyway, as you're here now…' She held out her hand and I shook it. 'You'd better be good.' She padded back to her desk. To my surprise, I saw that she was barefoot; she'd kicked her heels off. That detail made her seem more approachable, less aloof, and I vowed that I wouldn't let her down.

As a matter of priority, I read the compliance manual's entry on expenses and I learnt who her clients were, the cities they were located in and the names of the best hotels and restaurants. I learnt how to complete trading slips in triplicate and who to take them to. Gradually, I learnt the names of the traders and of the salespeople in the other teams. Over a period of months, I learnt the names of all our clients too, and how to keep them on the phone until one of my team was available so that they wouldn't go to a competitor.

'Sharon,' asked Jonathan one day. 'Did I hear you flirting with my client?'

I blushed.

'Good. Let's hear more of it, please!'

'Kate, call for you on line five.'

'Who is it, Sharon?'

'Call for you. On line five.' I waved the handpiece.

Kate stood, one hand over the mouthpiece of the phone she held in the other, and shouted, 'Sharon, how many times do I have to tell you? You don't just say, *Call for you.* You say who it is, where they're calling from and what they want.'

'Kate, just please pick it up,' I begged.

'No!' shouted Kate. 'Who is it? And what do they want?'

Resignedly, I said, 'It's the department store. The toilet roll holder you ordered has arrived. They want to know if you'll pick it up or want it delivered.'

Kate's face turned crimson as she jumped on line five. 'Laugh all you want, you bastards,' she shouted to the trading room before relaying her instructions down the telephone line.

'Nice one!' said Jonathan, delighted with Kate's discomfiture.

I learnt everything, everything but what the team and the bank actually did. The mechanics of it interested me. I was part of the execution process, one cog of many, albeit a small one. I knew that the money was made by buying bonds at one price and selling them on at a higher one, but why or when anyone wanted to buy or sell was beyond me. The eager, desperate talk about inflation, GDP, interest rates and unemployment left me nonplussed. They were the terms of an extraterrestrial language.

A year after starting with the bank, I had found a new home, a place where I was appreciated and valued. My team was supportive, even protective, of me. Kate had softened and accepted me. Even Yuuto, who I had considered brutish initially, had no bite to his very loud bark and would lean back in his chair to share jokes with me that I could rarely understand.

The aisles were my catwalks. I would walk them with trading slips, memos and various errands and would greet traders by name and stop to chat when they weren't too busy. The traders were chauvinist, sexist, but, to me, more endearing than threatening, even when they howled like dogs if a woman they considered ugly was shown onto the trading floor. Pity the poor salesperson showing a female client around who got howled at – he had to think of a believable story to explain the canine noises away.

Sebastian traded options on bonds and he sat at the very limit of my universe, just before the equities desk. He kept his eyes on his screens and would extend a hand for the three slips I held. He would examine and sign them and hand two of them back. It was a year before he spoke to me at all and when he did, as I turned from him to begin my long walk to the back office, it was just, 'Hey.'

I had only just had my first-year appraisal. Jonathan and Mr Self had barrelled me into the conference room off the trading floor and had been very complimentary. They had said that I had surpassed all expectations, that my performance had been error-free and that I brought good cheer to the desk. I was a pleasure to work with. I would get a pay rise.

'Why on earth are you crying?' Jonathan had asked.

'That's quite all right,' Mr Self had said, whether to me or Jonathan I wasn't sure. 'This happens quite often, you know.'

Jonathan had reached onto the sideboard behind him, grabbed a box of tissues and slid it across the table to me. 'Quick! Dry your eyes,' he had said in mock panic, 'before people think we've fired you!'

'Thank you,' I'd said.

'For the tissues or the pay rise?' had asked Jonathan.

For the kindness, for the words, I had wanted to say, but I hadn't trusted my voice enough to reply.

I had left the meeting room and snatched a trading slip from a waving Curtis without breaking my step.

'So, what's up?' asked Sebastian.

For the second time that morning, I was speechless.

'Your eyes seem to have that extra sparkle this morning.' He leant back in his chair and surveyed me critically, maybe even approvingly, openly and confidently.

Sebastian's sudden, unexpected attention, his having noted my mild emotional agitation, his bright, bright blue eyes, the unexpected flash of a canine tooth when he smiled, the mane of fair hair, the long fingers that held trading slips out to mine – something about him threw me. I was, all of a sudden, the young girl I had once been, the girl who wouldn't say no to boys, the girl who was eager to please.

I slalomed back to my desk, swinging my hips as I skirted the chairs, desk drawers and gesticulating people that formed a gentle obstacle course, Sebastian's eyes on my back like two hands on my hips, steering and warming me.

Isabella

I took two cups of tea to Freddie and the man in her bed and one to another man who lay propped on one elbow on the sofa, his pale hair tousled and his yellow smiley face T-shirt crumpled. A girl lay curled in an armchair, her chest rising and falling gently, a smile on her face.

'Thanks. I'm Buzz. That's Johannah,' he said. 'I'm from Chicago,' he added, seemingly finding it necessary to explain his accent.

In the evening Buzz took Freddie, Johannah and me to a club behind Kings Cross, a vast warehouse space filled with sound and strobing light and packed with people who moved as though to their own music despite the persistent deep bass that infused the building with a pulse. From the club entrance, looking down, the floor was like a sea of surf and counter-currents, raised bare arms waving like fronds on a murky sea bed only gaining definition as we descended, the strobe light like a full moon's rays through water.

'Here. As promised,' shouted Buzz above the music to Freddie, who grinned at me impishly as Buzz handed us a pale yellow pill with a smiley face each. 'First roll, right? This one's on me.' Freddie and I nodded and held our pills between thumb and forefinger tightly in anticipation of popping them soon, as Johannah had done hers. Buzz wagged his finger at Freddie and me to indicate that we should wait. 'Follow me.'

We pressed our way through hundreds of young people who stood dancing from the shoes up, keeping their feet rooted but moving their waists, arms and shoulders extravagantly in a state of delirious happiness. 'This is the water station. Drink.' I could feel Buzz's hot breath on my ear. 'Drink a lot. It's free. It's important, okay? Drink, and each of you make sure the other drinks.' Wide-eyed with anticipation, Freddie and I popped our first rolls. 'Good!' shouted Buzz. 'Do you see the chill-out rooms?' He ran a hand through his hair and indicated some rooms I hadn't noticed, doorless doorways that led to rooms with low seating and low ceilings, soft furnishings and mood lights. 'Hang in there for a while. Get used to things. And don't forget to drink!'

Freddie and I stood by the safety of the water station for a time, held there as much by indecision resulting from our desire to be in a chill-out room and on the dance floor simultaneously as by paranoia with regards to the effects of our first Ecstasy pill. We stood close, touched then clutched each other, her hair tickling my bare shoulder and arm, the sensation of it bright, electrifying, a caterpillar playing the marimba up my arm. The music, that had been one pounding wall of noise, grew clearer by degrees until I could see each soft brick in it, each note crisp and distinct with its own smell and colour. Colours grew primary – I could see the reds and blues in the purples, the blues and yellows in the greens, the vibrant colours in the T-shirts, the make-up, the skirts and the shorts and sneakers. My mind was a radio, tuning and fine-tuning, a spectrometer, releasing the enprismed primaries. Sound and colour melded. I knew that I wasn't hallucinating but that my powers of perception had simply become extraordinary and clear. What I saw was there and what was there I saw. Colour patterns warped and pulsed; I could make Johannah and Buzz out among the hundreds of other people whose names I didn't know but whom I felt I knew, whose essences I knew. Names were an irrelevance, a trapping, a distraction. Freddie's mouth was moving, the redness of her lips near-overwhelming, her words visible on the escalator that was her tongue, the tongue that was the launch pad for her words, the coloured words that carried more than their dictionary designation: she spoke of the chill-out room and of water and I saw those ragged words take flight and swoop and embrace and enlace us in the finest and warmest of cloths. I heard love and friendship. The idea of the unconditional love that was possible between friends swelled me with happiness. Freddie and I hugged and kissed, there on an ottoman in a chill-out room, not as lovers but as friends in love with love and with each other and with everyone. Her touch sent me into raptures. I dissolved with the sensation of her fleshy tongue against my inner lower lip as love, kindness and humanism washed over me. With tremendous clarity, I understood that what I saw when I looked at her was not her but the relationship I had with her; that, really, that was all she was to me and I to her. And I knew that what did the seeing was not my eyes but my mind and soul and intuition too. The urge to move, to dance was irresistible. The air above the dance floor filled with the unfiltered joyous truths of the distillation of people who held the essence of their selves before them like masks at a Venetian festival and then, suddenly as if on a collective whim, flew them like kites on a string. I marvelled that all these beings did not alight on others' bodies and inhabit them out of mischief, for innocent fun: an unwritten social, metaphysical code for life on earth respected from the goodness of all of our hearts. Echoes sounded of Papa and his friends citing Berkeley's notion that only ideas in the minds of perceivers exist – if only as barriers between us and material objects – if material objects exist at all. How right Berkeley had been! The intuited revelation that Berkeley had taken Ecstasy was sensational – I wanted to share it with Papa. Papa! I loved and forgave him. He loved me too but had not known how to show it, had gone about it the wrong way. The joy I felt at forgiving so unreservedly and at understanding was immense, filling the booming cavern with its bright, white light through which lasers strode and tickled. I am love.

'Drink!' commanded Buzz, lifting a water bottle to my lips while Freddie reached to lick the tears of happisadness from my eyes, a cat lapping my cheeks with a tender tongue.

'May I hug you?' asked a stranger with what I considered excessive politeness.

'Yes!' I cried with genuine enthusiasm, afraid he might dissolve in a puddle of tears if I declined.

Our hug was exquisitely warm, thrillingly friendly, universal. I am energy. I am music. My body was the music, the music was me and I was everyone. I had been born to dance. The rhythm was my heart's and the city's and everyone's. The bass was in my feet and the trebles were in my fingertips. I experienced epiphany after epiphany and the irritation I felt at immediately forgetting what they were of evaporated when I realised that I had grasped the profoundest truth that I and we all were stars, our places in the universe fixed, clear and clean. My cheeks hurt from incessant smiling and my teeth and gums grew sore from ceaseless chewing, but the distant discomfort wasn't mine alone; it was shared in a great community spirit of unity and companionship. Buzz presented me with a gift of a stick of chewing gum, such generosity reducing me to emotional extremes of gratitude. The mint in the gum was a pinprick of cool in my mouth that gave birth to a butterfly, to me, a rebirth, a butterfly of multihued wings that soared among the disco light dots of mauve and red and blue and among the disco light-mauve, -red and -blue butterflies. Naturally, one of them was mine or I was one of them. I was delirious with the joy of being me again. The butterflies were us all. We danced and fluttered, never touching despite always coming close. Mama's butterfly was there but she couldn't hear me, of course, of course she couldn't, she was dead. And Gaia. The issue of my stillborn baby sister, of how I should come to terms with a sister who had died before she had lived, had been too difficult for me. I had quite consciously placed her, or the notion of her, in a recess of my mind, the idea of her still as stillborn as she had been. It was all so clear to me now. There was music, love and forgiveness in the air. There were butterflies masquerading as coloured disco lights, mine, Mama's, Papa's, Gaia's and Freddie's.

'Do you see?' I shouted above the music to Freddie.

'Yes!' she shouted back, still moving, moving, dancing.

The dawn air was cool. Stars and a pale quarter moon were visible despite the light sky. Puddles reflected two police patrol cars' flashing blue lights in imitation of the disco lights in the nightclub we had wearily climbed up from, and an assembly of policemen and -women watched us disperse. A grey-haired man in a velvet-lapelled overcoat stood next to a Crombie-wearing, capped chauffeur by a gleaming saloon car. He smiled genially as an elegant younger woman chatted to Freddie and Johannah, having given them and me business cards of a sort and urged us to call. I remembered her from the dance floor where she hadn't been dancing so much as observing, assessing.

Buzz had buzzed off.

Johannah yawned.

Freddie shouted to me, 'He'll give us a lift home.'

I shook my head, which failed to clear of the music we had danced to. My arms ached from having been held aloft for so long and my breasts and nipples were sore from having persistently chafed against my bra. I wanted to walk in order to retain the sense of communion

I had with the city and its inhabitants without the diluting interme-
diation of a car's upholstered seats and its insulating rubber tyres, in
order to hold onto Gaia, to not ever let her go again. I walked down
Gray's Inn Road still slick with the night's earlier rain, past buses
that disgorged the day's early commuters at their stops and swept the
night shift cleaners up in exchange, past office blocks and town houses
now settling down, adopting their customary, distinct facades for the
day. As wonderful as the experience with Ecstasy had been for me, I
knew that I would not want to repeat it. Alone, still exhilarated but
exhausted now, more bumping along than flying, I could see that
I needed a grounding for my body, not separation from it. I feared
that, given my predisposition towards disengaging mind from body,
I might never regain the connection. Is that what death was? I didn't
want to encourage it.

Left onto Holborn, past Holborn Circus with the early sun in my
eyes and then – and then a green-veined white! A butterfly, in London, in April! Elated, I followed it to a freshly rain-watered flower
box at the foot of a small gatehouse that fronted a cul-de-sac where
it and I rested a while, it sipping and folding and unfolding its wings
and I giggling and gawking, and then on, through an open iron gate,
down the cul-de-sac of terraced brick houses, following it with my
eyes as it bobbed, dipped and rose, ascending ever higher. I lost it and
turning around and around on the spot found myself before a recessed
terraced church.

'It was so unexpected. Then two men walked past me, not together,
one after the other, and one said good morning and they both went
in by a side door and I just followed them in.'

Freddie had asked me what I had got up to and where I had been,
but no sooner had I started replying than I sensed she had grown
bored and impatient to interrupt. 'He gave me and Johannah a lift
back. And Jemma. She was with him – is with him. Well, I don't
know for sure that they're together but she works for him.'

'I just sat there. People came and went. Prayers before work. It was
so peaceful, so full of being. Of presence. No one spoke. And the
stained glass windows! So beautiful and clear. Like the lights on the
dance floor in an understated way.'

'Wasn't it amazing? The E! Amazing!'

'Amazing. It was. Amazing.'

'I felt I could feel the colours, you know? And the love!'

'Yes! The love. The colours! The colours of the stained-glass windows. When I finally turned to leave, there'd been this huge stained-glass window behind me all the time, the fleshy cuts of pinks and reds of Christ like a carcass on this cross, so bright, like he was looking down at me but he wasn't there, on the cross, but all around me, in the church and all so real.'

'And the music!'

'And then, it was so strange, it wasn't him but my mother, you know, my mother there, hanging there, happy in my forgiveness of her, knowing I'd forgiven her before I knew it myself and it felt – oh, all so real!'

'What are you talking about?'

'I told you! The church I went into. The Christ was so real. The body of him there in the window and the spirit of him filling the church. And suddenly, it wasn't him but my mother, you know, she sacrificed herself for me, for Cosmo too, like Christ did for us all, and I'd never really understood that before, the selflessness of her action, not really really.'

'Oh, yeah. But last night. And now, it's like we're all better people. Like, everyone should do it. If the whole world did it, it would be amazing!'

'Yes! That's exactly what I thought! That, I remember, I can't remember, someone I know must have done it. Or something.'

'Yes. I wished my mother and father had done some E,' said Freddie and fell about laughing at the thought.

Johannah, pale under the light from the window on the padded bench that served as a window seat, slept undisturbed. Did she live with us? I was no longer sure.

'What was that about your mother?' asked Freddie.

'Nothing,' I replied.

The effects of the Ecstasy having mostly worn off, the impulse to candour had gone too, and I felt I needed time alone to follow my chain of thought. I felt altogether less forgiving of Papa, not least because I didn't consider it my place to forgive him for his abuse of Cosmo. Cosmo and I telephoned or wrote to each other regularly, monthly at least. His letters were brief, pretexts for the dark, complex and twisted drawings that would accompany them and that I would pin to window frames and doors and examine for clues to his state of mind with regards to his private, hidden history.

Freddie fingered the card Jemma had handed her and said, 'Jemma was so nice. She said we were the best dancers. Natural. Johannah and I are going to do it. You're going to do it too, aren't you, Izzy? The money's amazing. And we can do it as little or as much as we like.'

'Melanie,' said Johannah, her eyes still closed. 'Melanie.'

'What?' asked Freddie with a giggle and a frown.

'Jemma said we had to choose a stage name,' said Johannah, opening her eyes and lifting her head to rest it in the palm of one hand. 'Mine's going to be Melanie.'

'Oh yeah!' exclaimed Freddie. 'And mine's going to be Frederica.'

'Frederica? But that's your real name!'

'Freddie's my name and Frederica will be my stage name,' said Freddie with an air of finality. 'It's like I'm running back to who I was or I don't want to run away from who I was. Or something like that,' she added, embarrassed. 'Anyway, it's Frederica. And you, Isabella, what's your stage name going to be?'

Frederica, Melanie and Gaia presented themselves for work on a Monday afternoon.

We were admitted by the chauffeur who, I could see, doubled as a doorman and were welcomed by Jemma who was more officious, as she allocated pieces of skimpy clothing to us and informed us of the house rules, than when she had recruited us in the early hours of the morning the previous week. She introduced us to the grey-haired man and club owner, Pierre, whose interest lay chiefly in helping us adjust G-strings and bikinis, and to Wanda, Pierre's accountant, who required us to complete forms, sign disclaimers and relinquish National Insurance numbers and passport details in order to prove that we were 18 years old or over. We were each placed under the wing of a veteran dancer who, over the course of the coming weeks and months, improved our dance styles, raised our confidence levels and taught us what house rules could be broken as well as how and when to break them.

My feelings about the club were mixed. It grew to be home, of a sort: neither the plush velour bar at ground level, nor the downstairs dance floor (seedier and tackier in the naked white light the cleaners laboured under during the day than when intermittently lit by the night's mauve and yellow spotlights), but the girls' changing room, furnished with ill-matching lockers, theatre dressing tables, hanging rails and comfortable armchairs, where the girls dressed and undressed, preened themselves, gossiped and bickered.

As in the care home, the girls were discreet. No girl asked another why she chose to dance near naked for a living, but listened sympathetically when the information was volunteered, usually by degrees as trust grew. Melanie was candid: she wanted the money. She had fallen in love with a builder and the two of them wanted to build a future together. Frederica's motivation was more complex. I would have said – albeit never to her – that she had something of her mother in her or that she wished either to discover her mother in her or, by behaving like her mother, so understand and forgive her. She, more readily than either Melanie or me, broke the house's first and second rules of not seeing punters outside of the club and of not accepting gifts or money in exchange for sexual favours. As for me, Gaia, I could cease to be Isabella, the prepubescent girl who, ignorant, misled, flattered and intoxicated by turn, had danced naked for her manipulative father and his conniving friends and be, instead, the seducing Morgiana who held her future and fawning, smitten men's hearts in her hands. I could assume control, wrest it back from Papa, not only by dancing knowingly and sexually aggressively in a way in which I couldn't have as a child, but by going even further and assuming my sexuality, feeding my sexual appetite in a refusal to suppress it.

We debated feminism in the close, heated changing room but futilely, as we had no one to argue against, being all of the opinion that the feminists and anti-pornographers who campaigned to have the club closed down were mistaken in believing that we were being exploited. 'Who's exploiting who?' would say Jemima, who had taken me under her wing. She looked upon men contemptuously for being so ready to part with large sums of money for the unfulfilled promise of that little bit more than the odd fondle and fiddle when she knew that Pierre and Jemma weren't looking. She and her lover, Betsy, would perform a double act for their punters who were driven to extremes of excitement and lightened wallets as they realised that the performance, the exchange of affection between the two, was not staged but real. Jemima and Betsy had it sorted, as Jemima would say, pencil eyeliner in hand. 'Five more years and then it's off to our cottage in Dorset. Chickens, not cocks. Pigs in muck, not pigs in suits. But if he's a Yank, send him to me.' The Americans were our favourite customers; they made us feel better about our work. American businessmen would admire us candidly, applaud and appreciate us, would say things like, *Lady you have a great ass!* or, *Ma'am, you're a ten out of ten!* or, *Those breasts are magnificent!* True, they objectified us but they looked us in the eye when they spoke to us and had us believe that our physical qualities were not just random allocations assigned us by our genes. And they tipped handsomely. Englishmen, by contrast, if they were City bosses or of the managerial class, were sheepish and embarrassed and behaved furtively, as though they had stumbled into the club by accident, as though their and our activities were something to be ashamed of, something dirty. Believing they could salve their consciences by not 'paying for it', they extracted their wallets from their back pockets with gritted teeth. Worst were the English *nouveaux riches*, the wide boys, the barrow boys, the City traders, the boys who 'done well' and who considered themselves entitled to paw us, revile us and throw notes of money on the floor for us to pick up, rather than hand them to us.

Over a period of two or three years, though, things changed for only one reason that I could see: namely, that the balance of British and foreign girls was changing. East European and Asian girls were working at the club in greater numbers and bringing with them stories of abduction, abuse and forced prostitution by international criminal gangs. Feminism, body ownership and girl power were no longer discussed so openly and comfortably or, when they were, conclusions were no longer reached with such a high degree of certainty. Our *esprit de corps* was not what it had been. I felt simultaneously less certain of myself and yet more determined to impose myself, to assume control of those who had controlled me, and so I started to meet punters outside the club after hours for taxi rides to their hotel or to Freddie's and my apartment.

Sharon

I first visited the club on a Wednesday evening, after a rare all-family dinner.

My mother had tickets to take Sherah to a musical on the same evening that Dad was taking Seamus to a football game, which had presented Wanda with the unusual opportunity to bring the family together. Massimo had said he'd open Lo Scoglio's doors for us early, so that we needn't rush; so we sat, solitary diners, around a table by the restaurant window.

Dad: tired, as ever, but delighted to have the family together and evidently still or, perhaps, more than ever in love with his wife. Mum: quiet, indifferent, self-contained. My stranger of a brother who now towered above us all and who bored and impressed us with his knowledge of football. My butch sister whose sporting regimen on the south coast had filled her out even more and who took pleasure in letting us know that she didn't like musicals, in the knowledge that I did. My aunt, who tried hard to conceal her anger with her sister for having bought Sherah but not me a ticket for the musical.

I considered our mocking reflections in the restaurant window. If I stared long enough, I could convince myself that we were the caricatures of the functioning family outside, until a car pulled up onto our reflected dining table and our reflected faces blurred with those of the car's occupants.

'A strange family,' Wanda had said, after the others had left; I didn't know whether she included herself and me in that designation.

Dad had asked my mother about her new work in national athletics; Mum had asked Sherah about the direction she was taking in her sports education; Seamus had asked and answered his own questions on this evening's football match; Sherah had shown no interest in anyone or anything at all; it had taken Wanda to ask me about my work and to tell the others about my good review and my pay rise. My family had congratulated me politely.

'Let's walk,' Wanda had said purposefully, once she had paid and thanked Laura for the meal and the discount.

'You know, my love,' she said as, arm in arm, we joined London's evening commuters on its pavements, 'I think I need to accept that broken things sometimes need to stay broken, that if you piece them together you risk creating something worse than what was broken before.' We stopped outside a purple-fronted shop. The dusty display contained champagne bottles, corks and glasses and top hats, gloves and walking canes in front of a mauve velvet curtain on a big brass rail. 'Tonight is as good as any. If not better, as it's likely to be quiet. Hello, Tony.'

'Hello, Wanda,' said Tony, a stony-faced doorman in a Crombie coat that, like its wearer, had seen better days. 'Unusual to see you here on a Wednesday.'

'Oh, I'm just popping by. This is my niece, Sharon.'

'Pleased to meet you,' said Tony glumly, opening the purple entry door with one gloved hand.

'Wanda!'

'Jemma!'

Wanda hugged a young woman who was tidying up a cloakroom. Again I was introduced.

'Wanda!'

'Pierre!'

A tall old man drew a dark, heavy curtain back and I followed Wanda into a large, low-ceilinged, carpeted space with low tables, pouffes and comfortable chairs, and a long drinks bar down one side. Mauves and purples were the dominant colours; white roses and lilies brought relief.

'Pierre. Sharon, my niece.'

'Sharon. You are most welcome.' Pierre raised my hand and bowed to kiss the back of it while keeping his eyes on mine. Furrows marked the passage of a wide-toothed comb through oily dirty-white hair. I was simultaneously flattered and repulsed by his indefinably vulgar air; he managed to be obsequious and yet threatening. With quick, darting eyes that belied his smile, he appraised me coldly, professionally. Keeping hold of my hand, he said to Wanda while looking at me, '*Ma chère*, where have you been hiding her all this time?'

Wanda laughed and said, 'Come on!' and pulled me after her down a large circular staircase into yet another similarly colour-schemed space with low chairs, pouffes, divans and tables, a small bar, some open booths with mirrored partition walls, a dais and a stage with floor-to-ceiling poles. A man who was passing a vacuum cleaner waved his hand in greeting to Wanda but did not stop vacuuming.

'Through here,' said Wanda, and I found myself in a large, bright and yet immediately cosy room with comfortable chairs, ill-assorted mirrored dressing tables and stools, hanging rails filled to bursting and, at its far end out of the direct lights, old metal lockers that would have looked more in keeping in a sports club changing room. A dozen girls in varying states of undress were chatting or applying make-up to themselves or each other, or eating out of cardboard cartons.

'Wanda!'

'Hello, girls!' said Wanda who, clearly pleased with the warmth of her reception, stood smiling, exuding contentment and, I thought from the way she clutched her handbag in both hands, just a small degree of apprehension. Most of the girls stood, too, and milled around her, either kissing her in greeting on both cheeks or resting their hands on a shoulder or arm for a moment in intimate acknowledgement. To those who had remained seated, she waved and received waves, air kisses and hellos in return. 'This is Sharon, my niece.' Wanda took a step away from me and looked at me inquiringly and approvingly simultaneously.

'Welcome!'

'Have a seat.'

'Would you like a drink?'

I was fussed over, helped out of my coat, petted and seated. Overwhelmed by the attention, the competing perfumes and the rich fragrances of skin and foundation creams, the friendliness, the extent of exposed flesh and the unabashed, natural ease with which the near-naked young girls moved around me, I shook as I held my glass of water in both hands. My eyes at crotch height, I was treated to a giddying kaleidoscope of bikini and tanning lines, young buttocks, varying flesh tones and pubic hair lines and styles that I had never imagined existed.

Jemma put her head around the door and called, 'Wanda? Could I nab you for a second? Pierre wants a word, as you're here.'

Wanda walked through the door Jemma had kept open for her.

'Melanie,' said a girl matter-of-factly. 'What do you think?' She held a bikini up in each hand. 'Red or green? Red for Hands Off! Or green for Go?' Melanie bent towards me and held the green bikini to my face. 'Wow! Your eyes are greener than this bikini! Beautiful. It must be a bugger dressing, though. Green doesn't go with your complexion.'

I couldn't help but smile. Melanie was direct, but right. Green made me look sallow, pasty. I kept my eyes on hers so as not to stare elsewhere. A nipple hovered above the rim of my glass. I didn't dare move.

She reached a conclusion and stood straight. 'Red,' she said.

'Hi,' said another girl, shrugging a coat off. 'Are you new?'

'Oh, no,' I said. 'I'm just visiting.'

'Oh. Thinking of working here?'

'Oh, no! I've got a job.'

'Wanda's niece,' said Melanie.

Melanie's colleague flashed a smile. 'Oh, Wanda! I saw her upstairs. This is a good place,' she said, unzipping knee-length boots and kicking them off while looking at Melanie for confirmation. 'It's not full of scumbags like some other places. So I'm told. Where is it you work?'

I told her.

'Never heard of it. How does it compare to here?'

'Oh, it's not a... It's a bank,' I corrected her.

'A bank!' She brought her hand to her mouth to hide a grin. 'Sorry! I thought, you know...'

Melanie grinned too. She received her friend's top and turned it the right way around and placed it on a hanger before draping her bra over it and hanging them both up. She then perched on the arm of my chair and stretched her arm along the back of it, so close I could feel the intoxicating musky warmth emanating from her body.

'So why don't you work here?' The girl eyed me candidly. 'You look like you could do it.' Without waiting for an answer, she said, 'Does the bank pay really well, then? I suppose it depends on what you do. We get bankers in here. They have a lot of money to throw around. Sometimes they bring their female colleagues in, too. I feel sorry for them, the women. They have to pretend they enjoy it and then when they realise they do they go absolutely wild. Or they hate it and you can see them fuming and itching to leave.' She folded her jeans and placed them over the hanging rail. She removed her plain knickers and tucked them into one of the pockets of the jeans. 'Excuse me,' she said. 'I'm going to fetch my costume.' Her brown hair hung all the way to the small of her back and swung as she took two steps in the direction of the lockers at the far end of the room before doing an about–face and standing directly before me again. 'Oh, I'm Gaia,' she said, extending her hand. That's when she told me her name, naked and natural and beautiful, and I told her mine, overcome with shyness.

Melanie gave me a pat on the shoulder and raised my hand to look at my watch. 'Oh, is that the time?' she said. 'We open in ten minutes but it will be another couple of hours before we get anything like busy. Nice watch,' she added, after I had pulled my eyes away from Gaia's padding walk to look at my watch in turn.

'Thanks,' I said. 'My mum gave it to me.' My mother! I saw myself through my mother's eyes, as though she were standing by me, and I had to admit that I no longer knew what she would say, if anything – whether she'd care and whether, really, there was anything for her to care about. I stood and said to Melanie, 'I think I have to go and find Wanda.'

Melanie piled her fair hair high on her head and sniffed her shaved armpits as she held her hair in place. 'Not too bad,' she grinned, and added, 'See you.'

Aunt Wanda and I returned home both a little breathless, she a little sheepish and me a little cowed, overawed by the sudden plunge into an underground, adult world and by the girls' brazenness. Rather than talk in the crowded tube train, we stole glances at each other. I wondered if Wanda feared that she had changed the nature of our relationship for the worse, thought that she may have failed in her implicit duty as my unofficial guardian. Once home, over mugs of tea that we treasured in both hands, she attempted to explain herself by talking of the girls as family, of their histories and of the affection she had for them. 'But, you know, going in there with you this evening, I suddenly saw it through your eyes, a new person's eyes, and I remembered the first time I had been referred to Pierre and been shocked and nearly hadn't stayed and yet...' She shrugged and continued, 'What you don't see the first time is how damaged some of the girls are, and how they find this camaraderie, this togetherness.'

I extended an arm to silence her and said, 'Aunt Wanda, you don't have to be so defensive. There's no need. I'm so glad you took me. Really. The girls are lovely. I think I know exactly what you mean. And the way they love you, look to you, that was so nice to see. And the respect everyone has for you there and they were friendly to me because I'm your niece, it made me proud of you.'

Relief filled Wanda's features, and it occurred to me for the first time that someone else might care what I thought of them; that my opinion of them mattered, and I tingled with this discovery and almost wept with the pleasure of it. A power I wouldn't know how to use let alone abuse, it was a source of warm pleasure, all the same.

I went back to the club. A month later. Then a couple of times a month. Then once a week, either with Wanda or to meet her there. I helped where I could, behind the bar or in the cloakroom or bringing the food out that was served only on the ground floor where our customers would dine, either before or between visits downstairs. When it was time for me to leave, Pierre would extract a wodge of banknotes from his inside jacket pocket, lick his fingers and peel some off for me and see me out with a kiss on the cheek and pat on the bottom. After I learnt that Jemma was his fiancée, I felt both more at ease around him and less comfortable around her; after all, he was over twice her age.

Mie

I spent three years immersed in the English language and in English literature. I travelled through Sir Walter Scott's Scotland and Jane Austen's Hampshire, Charles Dickens's London, George Eliot's provincial England and Elizabeth Bowen's Ireland. These authors took me to places I would never visit, not least because they no longer existed but because they were set in a different past, as if in a foreign country where things are done differently. While the physical scenes of place and time – the hanging drapes of English meadows and Scottish heaths and of English and Irish country homes – pleased me, the emotional tableaux of unrequited and reciprocated loves intrigued and excited me. How and why Elizabeth Bennet and Maggie Tulliver throw themselves upon others – throw their *selves* away to others – fascinated me. I would reread novels' endings in the fantasy that they might change, that our strong heroines would stand resolute and learn from past mistakes.

University had been different from school in two principal respects. The first was that I no longer had to contend with the furtive, uncertain advances of insecure boys, but with the propositions of self-assured, cocky young men. The second was that I grew to love the English language that I had found so charming at school and began to plan exactly how I would use it as a springboard out of my country. Additionally, university had opened my eyes to wider Japanese society and, by bringing me into contact with students from outside my prefecture, helped me realise just how sheltered my upbringing had been and how unconventional and open-minded my parents were. However, that only really hit home after university, once I'd started my first full-time job, at Yumimoto.

The evening before my first day at Yumimoto, after I had pressed my regulation white shirt and black skirt and polished my old black school shoes, I stood at my bedroom window. To my left lay a decaying sunset, as though a last call for those heading west. Soon, I thought to myself. Ahead, Keiko's and Michi's lightless bedroom windows almost shouted their absence. Keiko had gone south immediately after graduation to be assistant to the manager of her parents' shop in Hamamatsu; she would board above it for the length of her secondment, returning to Sangenjaya only occasionally. Michi had been accepted for a master's degree in clinical psychology and school education at Fukushima University. West-, north- and eastwards spread a quietening town, settling down for the night like a dog in its basket, and telephone wires that still whispered to me and sought to lead me astray and away. I was still me, the young girl with the ambition to travel as long as she could remember, but the closer I came to achieving my goal the less impatient I became.

I knew that taking ownership of myself and of my public image in a new, different society could mean changing – a liberating, thrilling prospect of reinventing not my essential self but my superficies, similar to the identical modern steel structures that I witnessed rising all around Tokyo, which appeared so different on completion once their facades were clad in disparate materials. I, that inner nucleus of me, had an integrity that persisted, despite the fact that every day, I learnt something new and, probably, forgot something old. I made the distinction between that core, that essential *me*ness and the social coatings, postures and attitudes that I adopted but could discard like a raincoat, a glove or a hat.

While university had broadened not so much my horizons as my self-awareness, my new workplace would increase my appreciation of just how atypical and non-conformist my parents were. Yumimoto was to open my eyes as wide as they could, and to reaffirm my decision to leave Japan for a society that would be non-judgemental and allow me to be myself. I had made friends at university but had never moved past the level of acquaintance, principally because we lived too far away from each other to socialise off-campus, but partly because sexual politics managed to get in the way: the boys didn't understand that you wanted to keep a friendship at just that level, and the girls didn't believe that you weren't in competition with them. I made no attempt to dispel a reputation for being cold and aloof after I learnt that being interested in people could label you a tease, a flirt who reneged on implicit promises.

I stood at my open window and angled it at 45 degrees so that the reflection of the setting sun lay superimposed on Michi's and Keiko's bedroom windows, and I reflected on the fact that university had brought me no new, lasting friendships, no friends that I would value as much as I did Keiko, Michi, Taka and, unexpectedly, as if out of nowhere, Margaret.

I didn't have the degree of intimacy with Margaret that I had with the others, which made for a different quality of friendship – none of the children's history that tied Keiko, Michi and me, none of the courtship and relationship issues that had hung over Taka and me – but one that grew out of mutual respect, admiration and, I sensed, a recognition of each other's self-containment, detachment and independence. That Margaret never seemed to care what others thought of her and what impression she made on others influenced me greatly; I attributed this to her Englishness and assumed it was a quality all English people possessed. I considered her a kindred spirit, but never said as much to her; the irony of distinctive and independent spirits being kindred was not lost on me. No longer seeing me at school, Margaret took to visiting me at home and would dine with my family regularly, seemingly unaware that she was the only guest my parents ever entertained to dinner. She amused them by introducing herself as from 'the nation of shopkeepers', an image of England that did not match any of the images they had of glorious battlefields, misty moors, empire-line dresses, horse-drawn carriages and miniskirts, some of which they'd got from me. The facility with which my English friend appeared to have assimilated our etiquette – the way she kicked off her shoes and slipped on her slippers on entering our house, and kicked those off in turn before sitting *seiza* style for long periods on our *tatamis*, having unassumingly accepted her place in front of the *tokonoma* – made me proud of her.

Taka had accepted we'd be just friends, best friends, and was no longer David Copperfield to my Dora Spenlow. He had created a circle of friends of his own around which I orbited elliptically, occasionally bringing to his attention girls that I thought he might fancy or that I had heard had a soft spot for him. This, I got the impression, pained him, perhaps because it suggested that I needed to see him established in a relationship in order to consider myself safe from his affections, so I desisted. Taka may have had a fling with Keiko, either that summer after school or later; whichever, I detected a slight tension between them whenever we met in a group, but whether that was because of Taka's faux pas, as recounted to me so blithely by Michi, or because of a more recent affair between them, I never learnt. If I was extreme in my complete abstention from sex, Keiko was the opposite, reacting, I thought, against the strictness of her upbringing. Had I not known her so well, I would have assumed her to be making a political statement of sorts, but that would have been to give more significance than she did to the string of one-night stands that, to her, were just the scratching of an itch. She would go to rock concerts far from home and, with other like-minded girls, hang about major road junctions where she'd be picked up by men who would offer her a bed for the night. No money changed hands, but Taka would reprimand her all the same. Keiko would just reply, 'Who's using whom?'

Sharon

I came to realise that the club had its own cliques, much as school, secretarial college and the bank's trading floor had, but they remained contained and, to a relative outsider like me, less than transparent. Jemma patrolled the changing room and was quick to address any girl who stepped out of line; Wanda defused tensions before they had even started with sympathy and tenderness.

Every girl had her story. All stories were different and yet all shared a kernel of pain or rejection or ill fortune. Some girls told you their stories candidly, directly, as though confronting their demons openly was their therapy. Others were talked about in hushed tones behind bare backs. Melanie had left her convent education at 14 when her parents had died, and now worked in her boyfriend's construction business in the East End three days a week. She was saving enough money for a deposit on a large house in which she and her boyfriend would go on to have fifteen children, she claimed. 'All you ever need to know about sex, you'll learn it in a convent, believe me,' she'd said. 'Just think, the sisters banned long-handled hairbrushes, roll-on deodorants and certain shapes of shampoo bottles and all we could think of was, *Why*?' Honey, Melanie told me, had been trafficked from Laos to Manchester and had escaped and made it to London with just her passport. She lived in fear of being kidnapped again and worked to save for her passage back to Laos where she had left two children with her mother. We had watched Honey apply her make-up and put her glossy black hair up, and agreed that she was probably the sweetest person either of us had ever met and that it was hard to believe that she was over 14, let alone 18, and mother of two children. She had a complexion like silk. 'And nipples like benedictions,' had said Melanie, 'because anyone who sees them feels blessed.' Frederica was a music student, paying her way through university and saving for conservatoire. She sang and gave private music lessons and had danced topless for the father of one her pupils one evening, without his realising that she was his daughter's voice coach. 'But then,' had said Melanie, 'it wasn't her face that he was looking at.' Bella was a nurse; Angelica, an economics student. All I knew of Gaia was that she was English, and talked so much that it was only after she'd finished that I realised she hadn't actually told me anything about herself.

Jemima and Betsy were two of the older girls, close friends who applied each other's make-up and exchanged costumes routinely, and two of the few who saw topless dancing as a career. 'We're strippers, darling,' had said Betsy. 'That's what we are. So long as there's someone who'll pay us to strip, we'll strip. We're not afraid to admit it, are we, darling?' Jemima had smiled and shaken her head and continued to paint Betsy's eyelids a cornflower blue, one hand cupping her friend's chin. 'Try it. Admit it,' Betsy had continued to no one and everyone. 'Be honest with yourselves. None of this *I'm only doing it for the money today and I'll be prime minister and a good mother tomorrow.* Be who you are, darlings, and don't pretend to be someone you're not.' Betsy looked up at Jemima looking down at her and they exchanged the most tender of smiles.

If you are someone who pretends to be someone you're not, can you remain who you are if you stop pretending to be someone you're not? The question remained with me until the weekend, when I recounted Betsy's comments to Wanda. I asked, over the sound of a talk show on the TV, 'Do you think it's all nonsense, then, the stories they tell about themselves and the futures they claim they're going to have?'

Wanda rounded on me. 'You never question a story. You never ask if their names are real. You never destroy dreams and aspirations. The only thing you know for sure is that whatever they told you was bad, it was a lot worse in reality.' Gently, as though realising she'd been severe, she brushed my hair from my forehead with her up-held finger. 'The club is where they come to hide, to be someone else.'

I clutched her finger. 'It's where I could be someone else.'

'Absolutely not!' said Wanda, with panic in her voice and fear in her eyes.

'Why not?'

'No!' She held me by the shoulders.

I swayed my hips and rolled my shoulders, stepping closer to her in a parody of a sexually provocative dance.

'I forbid it,' she said, but her voice was weak.

I stepped away and around the kitchen table and put one hand to my head and the other to my hips, which I gyrated in poor imitation of the girls' dancing. I waggled my boobs. I stood on one leg and curled the other around an imaginary pole and raised both arms as though clutching it.

The talk show host introduced a rock band. I raised and lowered myself on one leg, repeatedly, my arms still extended upwards, surprised to find myself thinking that I wasn't as fit as I once had been.

Wanda sat on a kitchen chair with her head in her hands.

Mie

I had applied to Yumimoto, a multi-tentacled beast of a business with an empire that seemed truly global, because it had a subsidiary in England and had advertised for language skills. I joined its import–export division on the same day as Fubuki Mori, a pale and svelte girl of my age, next to whom I felt as Michi must have felt next to Keiko when we had been children. She and I were greeted by Mr Mizuka, the department's gloomy head of personnel, who escorted us to the 44th floor where he introduced us to Mr Saito whose greatest concern on this, our first day, was to ensure that we understood that he was our line manager and that our careers depended entirely on his benevolence. Once we had committed this extremely important lesson to memory and after we had completed innumerable questionnaires and signed all manner of employment documents, we were set, by Mr Saito, the task of memorising the names of Mr Omochi, the departmental manager to whom he reported, of Mr Hanada, the department's vice president to whom Mr Omochi reported, and of the department's president, Mr Fujimoto, to whom Mr Hanada reported.

Our first day passed slowly, with no one telling us when or where to have lunch and when we could leave for home. Fubuki and I looked at each other repeatedly, communicating with a rolling of the eyes and a shrugging of the shoulders, and plucked up the courage to make our way down to a food emporium in the basement after everyone else had left their desks at midday. Come evening, instinct told us it wouldn't do to leave before Mr Saito, so we read and reread the company telephone directory and an annual report that had been left on our desks and moved our stationery from the drawers on our left to those on our right until Mr Saito yawned and accompanied other colleagues who left the office with muttered *sayonara*s and *mata ashita*s.

On our second day, Fubuki and I were introduced to everybody in the department by Mr Saito and by Mr Mizuka who, with the demeanour of an undertaker, only ever repeated what

Mr Saito said. I had never bowed so frequently and so low in one day in my life and it occurred to me, as I contemplated the tops of the umpteenth pair of black polished men's work shoes, that we had been introduced to no women. This had struck Fubuki too, as I discovered when I followed her into the empty, immaculate ladies' toilets.

Fubuki finished inspecting herself in the mirror, turned around and leant back against the washbasins, crossed her long legs and said, 'Welcome to our office!' Indeed, this was to prove our little sanctuary. She added more seriously, 'Do you think they set out to recruit women when they hired us? Or is it just' – she sought the right word – 'coincidence?'

I shrugged. I caught sight of myself in the mirrored wall above the washbasins, standing there, gazing at Fubuki, she looking down on me patiently, bored, probably quite used to the effect she had on people. I stammered as I sought a reply. 'Er, well, they wanted linguists, and more women than men study foreign languages, so the likelihood was that they'd end up hiring women, I suppose.'

'But I don't speak any foreign languages,' said Fubuki.

'You don't?'

'No!' Fubuki laughed. 'Well, I guess that answers it!' She leant forward, so that I could smell her unexpectedly garlicky breath. 'We'd better be getting back – or they'll suspect we're plotting! By the way,' she continued in a more sombre tone, as I held the door open for her, 'why do you think we weren't introduced to the secretarial pool?'

'The secretarial pool?'

'You know, the secretaries, the typing pool on the 43rd floor.'

'I didn't know one existed.'

'You see, maybe we're not the lowest of the low, after all!'

Not bottom of the corporate heap, then. Not in a row of identically dressed, automaton-like women that I imagined the typing pool to consist of. I couldn't help but feel a smidgen of satisfaction that leaked from me progressively during an afternoon spent in repetition of the first.

On our third day, Fubuki and I were promoted, as she ironically termed it, to *ochakumi*, expected to make and serve tea to our colleagues in the mornings and afternoons. On our fourth, we were given some filing to do and, on our fifth, some photocopying, which turned out to be the height of our responsibilities and set the tone, the rhythm, of our corporate lives for the subsequent six months.

Sharon

I led for a while not so much a double life as two half-lives. I felt complete, as close to fulfilled as I had ever been. I spent Mondays to Fridays working in the bank and Friday or Saturday nights dancing in the club. There existed the veneration of money in both, an intense sense of its significance, though I could understand the banknotes in my fists better than I could the flickering green numbers on the bank's screens in their context of the fortunes of corporations and national economies. The same men, the same pairs of eyes on me: in the one, narrowed, darting, stealing glimpses of my cleavage as I deposited trading slips on desks and measuring my legs as I marched the aisles; in the other, admiring, candid in their appreciation of my nakedness. I liked being looked at and I liked being liked and rejected the sense of shame I experienced in admitting that to myself. I liked the thought that we – that I – gave our customers something to think about when they went home to their wives. I would picture them stumbling in the dark, locking their front door behind them, patting and shushing their dog, avoiding creaking steps, brushing their teeth, getting undressed in the dark, cuddling up to their sleeping wives and fumblingly lifting their nighties, all the while retaining an image of me, of whichever part of me had most done it for them. 'That's gross!' Bella had exclaimed, when Betsy had said that that was our job: the creation of mental pictures that held marriages together for another year. But I didn't see why.

One night a week seeing Gavina, Sarah and Monica and one night a week or Sundays with Dad and Seamus or my mother over home-cooked lunches or dinners or just pottering around Aunt Wanda's garden. One night in shared domesticity with Wanda, doing the laundry and ironing and baking biscuits that I would leave on my desk for the UK sales team to help themselves to. Saturday mornings, Wanda and I slept till late; Saturday afternoons, I would go clothes shopping, for myself initially but then for Wanda, my mother and my friends, who had decided independently of each other that I had a facility for buying good-quality clothes at low prices and for matching clothes from different shops and competing lines.

Mondays: Sebastian.

We had happened to leave work at the same time one evening; we had walked to Liverpool Street Station and boarded a Central Line train together. Some days after, Sebastian had just happened to finish a conversation with Curtis and head for the door as I finished switching my computer off and shouldered my handbag. On that occasion, we had gone for a drink in a pub. The following time, we had taken a train that we left at Holland Park and dived into a wine bar. The next time, we had left the wine bar for his flat.

I understood that it was a physical thing, our mutual attraction, and our seeing each other rarely relative to most other lovers added to the sweet, delicious tension of the days running up to our nights together. We barely spoke in the office. We gave nothing away. An observant colleague might have noticed that my handbag on Mondays and Tuesdays was larger than the one I took to work on other days; a nosy one might have observed that it contained a clean top and clean knickers on Mondays and a dirty top and dirty knickers on Tuesdays.

On Mondays, I would walk to his desk with trading slips in triplicate, have him sign one and then walk back to my desk via the back office, dripping with anticipation. It would start with hearing his voice on the hoot-and-holler when Kate and Curtis screamed through the static at him for prices. He replied calmly, he murmured and yet was heard, he spoke as though withholding laughter, yet remained collected and professional throughout the exchange. His words were intended for others but his voice, I felt, was meant for me. We would conspire to take the same train to Holland Park without so much as acknowledging each other, seated at different ends of the same carriage. He would hold the *Evening Standard* open and not turn the page. I would tick the eleven stops off mentally, one by one, groaning when what should have been a twenty-minute journey experienced delays. I would follow him up and out, along a short walk and then up a few steps into a stucco-fronted Victorian house, now divided into flats, the front door of which he had left open after him. A moment for my eyes to adjust to the gloom and up one flight of stairs to his apartment door, that he had also left ajar. A deep, dizzying intake of breath and the step into the apartment and the closing of the door. Grinning, we'd consider each other a moment before embracing, kissing and shedding clothes and inhibitions. I felt a lust as sharp as hunger and a need to satisfy and please as deep as my appetite for my own satisfaction and gratification.

He would shower and prepare dinner wearing an apron while I gathered our clothes. While he was frying and boiling the various foods he'd bought from the Saturday market, I'd drift along with the smells of his cooking through his apartment, weak from hunger and physical exertion, wearing nothing except for one of his shirts that, liking the scent of him on me, I'd lifted from his laundry basket. I ran my fingers along the spines of the books he kept in every room. Recalling my stacking of Aunt Wanda's books, I tried to make sense of the order he kept them in, but failed. I'd inspect the framed photos on his shelves and mantelpieces, carrying them to the window to better make out the people in them in the days' dying light. Parents and siblings were easy to recognise under their mops of blond hair; he got his blue eyes and his looks from his father, his height from his mother. Maybe his confidence from his father too; it takes a self-assured man to have a wife a head taller than him. There were photos of friends in frames or just propped against books; some were of ex-girlfriends and, maybe, girlfriends. For all I knew, he had a different girl every day of the week. I had realised from the beginning, from the absence of the mundane, hackneyed interrogations that formed the grounding of most new friendships, that his interest in me and, maybe, in people generally was not expressed conventionally. He never asked me where I lived, who I lived with, where I was from and the other usual questions. And he only revealed a little of himself or, more precisely, of a small part of his unorthodox family history on one occasion when he caught me unawares, coming up silently behind me in his sitting room, placing a hand on my shoulder and saying quietly in my ear, 'What do you think of the painting?'

The room had pale green walls and two sash windows that framed a round pedestal table with wicker chairs either side of it. A cream sofa faced a long coffee table and the fireplace, either side of which were floor-to-ceiling shelves of books, and above which hung the room's sole painting that I had been lost in contemplating when he had walked in. My arm was outstretched, my hand still holding the silver-framed photograph of his mother I had been in the act of replacing on the mantelpiece.

The painting was dark and menacing, the wooden-planked patch-work raft, its occupants and stormy seas painted seemingly furiously in a curious act of self-defence. It reminded me of a scene in a chil-dren's book Miss Crossbank had read to the class in which three chil-dren, gazing intently at a marine painting, get swept into the painting and its sea. I shuddered. The ragged shipwrecked crew appeared dead or nearly so, save the few whose supplicant arms were outstretched in signal to an invisible ship.

'It's a bit dramatic,' I said. 'Sad,' and, looking for longer, 'Terrible.'

'Oh, it's terrible,' he said. 'More than terrible. You don't even know the half of it. Or maybe you do?'

I craned my neck to look at him as if to say, 'How could I?'

'It's my mother's version of a painting that hangs in the Louvre. In Paris.'

'I know where the Louvre is.'

'Sorry. Have you been there?'

'No.' I didn't add that I'd never been out of England except to go to Wales. 'So your mother is a painter?'

'Yes. She started by drawing and painting things from life, and then got it into her head that in order to improve as a painter and to become as good as the old masters, she should copy them first. She began painting – reproducing – famous paintings.' He placed his other hand on my other shoulder and leant forward, and I could tell from the sweetness of his breath that he had been munching on raw vegetables as he had peeled and diced them. 'And then, having done that for a while, she continued reproducing them but chang-ing them, delivering the same image with an altogether different style from the original while ensuring the model remained recognisable. Like a cover of a song.'

'Is this one like the original?' I asked, my eyes having been drawn back to it, and up and down it with the movement of the sea and the ropes that held a listing mast in place.

'Oh no. For a start, it's a fraction of the size. I doubt the original would fit in this room, let alone above the mantelpiece. Then there's the style. The original is in a classical style, while the kindest thing you could say about this is that it's figurative.' He laughed. 'And then there's a figure missing.'

'What do you mean?'

'One of the figures in the original is missing from my mother's version.'

'Why?'

'Now we come to the terrible bit.' He parted my hair from my shoulder and kissed my neck. I could feel the slip of a tooth and a sliver of saliva cool on me. 'My mother became fixated on this painting. She must have painted a dozen versions of it. And always with a figure missing. Not always the same one.'

'Why?'

'The family story is that one of our ancestors was aboard the raft.'

'Really?'

He took me by the hand and sat me down next to him on the sofa from where we looked up at the painting, our feet placed simultaneously on the coffee table as though signalling an unspoken agreement that we wouldn't move from the sofa for a while.

'The raft was constructed from the masts and timbers of a French ship that had run aground on a sandbank many miles from land. The incompetent captain and some of the ship's company saved themselves in lifeboats, leaving 150 people or so to survive on the raft – it was some 20 metres long and not even half as wide. They had nothing to eat or drink to speak of.' He kept his eyes on the painting as he spoke. 'They were a rabble of a crew. They fought for the centre of the poorly constructed raft so as not to be swept overboard, and they turned on the officers and the officer class. By the end of the second day, half of them had been killed. By the end of the fourth day, the declining number of survivors resorted to drinking their urine and eating the dead. The fifteen survivors, who were picked up after twelve days at sea, told stories of hanging strips of human flesh on lines in order to dry it and make it more palatable. Of the ten who made it to Paris, only two withstood the intimidation and bullying by the ship's captain and remaining officers who tried but failed to get a public exoneration. To my mother's shame, our ancestor was not one of the two.' He stopped talking and we contemplated the raft a while, silently, side by side.

'So where does the shame lie? As far as your mother is concerned,' I eventually asked.

'Oh, you know, in both, I think,' he replied.

I looked at him.

'Surviving – having done what it took to survive. And taking money to keep schtum. Presumably.'

'Does it make sense to feel shame for something you didn't do? Shame for someone else?'

'My mother clearly thinks so. It's as if she's obsessed with painting him out of history.'

'Is she a good painter?'

'What do you think?'

'I don't know. The fact that this is a copy makes me feel less capable of judging.' I could feel the heat from his leg along mine. 'Not that I think I'm a good judge of these things, anyway.'

'She's okay, I suppose.'

'And have you never wanted to be an artist?'

'Oh, but I am! Have you never seen me at work?' He grinned and I stuck my elbow in his side.

Mie

I began to worry about the stagnation of my intellectual capabilities and the possible decline of my English faculties. The route to England seemed impossibly obscure from the perspectives of my desk and the trivial tasks I was assigned. Fubuki grew angry on a matter of principle. She followed me into the ladies' toilets one day where she grumbled that she hadn't signed up to be a *shokuba no hana*, an office flower whose role was to be pleasing to the eye in the execution of the menial but necessary tasks the department required. I hadn't the courage to tell her that she made the most beautiful office flower – that, if that were indeed to be her role, she would acquit herself to perfection. As though she'd been overheard, we had no sooner resumed our seats than Mr Saito stood, nodded at Fubuki and requested she follow him to Mr Omochi's office, after which he returned without her as though nothing out of the ordinary had happened. For me, this change in our routine was of seismic proportions, and I assumed it marked a first step into what could be loosely termed our – or at least Fubuki's – career development.

An hour passed agonisingly slowly before Fubuki returned, and another hour before she excused herself to Mr Saito to go to the bathroom. I followed, mumbling my own excuses as I stumbled after her.

'What did you have to do?' I could barely contain my excitement.

'I had to take down a letter.'

I felt a pang of jealousy. 'What about? And then?'

'You know, I can't even tell you what it was about! I was so nervous. I haven't practised my shorthand in three months. And then I took it down to the head of the typing pool who handed it to one of the typists who typed it out and handed it back to her boss, who proofread it and gave it to me together with its carbon copy to take back to Mr Omochi, who signed it and asked me to take it to the post room and to file the carbon copy.' Fubuki examined her nails, as though to deny, out of consideration for me, I was sure, that she had had her most exciting day at Yumimoto to date.

My agitation was such that I could think of nothing to say or, rather, I couldn't think of what to say first. Why had Fubuki been singled out for this singular honour? When would my turn come? What were the typing pool and the post room like? 'What's shorthand?'

'Shorthand?' Fubuki trilled and looked at the backs of her extended hands. She had a way of reposing, of leaning back on the washbasin unit with her legs crossed at the ankles that made her appear relaxed and dangerous simultaneously. 'Sorry. It's why I'm here. I can take down what someone says very quickly, at the speed at which they're saying it, so that I can take letters down or take meeting notes in real time, as it were. That's why I'm here.' My face must have registered my incomprehension. 'While you're here for your English, that much you've told me.' She read my mind. 'Don't worry. I'm sure your time will come. You're reserved for greater things, I'm sure.' This was said with a smile and, I felt, no small degree of condescension.

Fubuki was proved right, but not before she'd had three more letters dictated to her by Mr Omochi and a good half dozen by Mr Haneda, who seemed to have discovered a zeal for letter-writing. I feared my resentment would show and threaten my nascent friendship with Fubuki, and I tried to keep my demeanour agreeable so as to avoid a negative bearing on my career.

Sharon

'How can options not interest you?' Sebastian asked me over dinner one evening, and we laughed at the absurdity of the question and at the earnestness with which he'd asked it.

He raised his eyebrows and a bottle of wine.

I declined. I was drunk enough on a passion I wanted to enjoy for what it was, an infatuation that only one thing could defer and cool: Sebastian's compulsive need to wash up immediately after dinner. I found his reluctance to leave plates and pots and pans dirty, to leave the kitchen until it was spotless, amusing. I watched him at the sink, my braless breasts sensitive to the rough cotton of one of his shirts and my bare bottom cool on the polished wood of one of his kitchen chairs.

He dried his hands and pulled me up and guided me by the shoulders to the door to the second bedroom that doubled as a study: an entire wall was lined with books. The room was lit by one desk light that, I could see, would also serve as a bedside light for whoever occupied the bed.

'I've watched you walk the length of these bookshelves,' he said, 'and you seem to have been reading the books' titles but, other than a dictionary, I've never seen you lift a book off a shelf and open it. You've never picked a novel out.'

'Yes.' If there was a question there, I was unsure what it was.

'Ever been tempted?'

'To pick a novel out and open it?'

'Yes.'

'No.'

His thumbs massaged my shoulder blades and his fingers applied pressure to my collarbone. His breath warmed the back of my neck where he had parted my hair.

'When I read,' I said, speaking slowly in order to make sure I said exactly what I meant and meant exactly what I said, 'I feel uneasy. I become jealous of the book's characters.' Having Sebastian behind me and not having to look at him as I spoke made it easier. 'I feel under threat. I feel that for them to live, I have to give away a little of myself.' He couldn't see me blush. 'I'm afraid that they will leave me empty, with nothing. It's a kind of spiritual one-way traffic.'

His voice in my ear: 'That's a very interesting response to literature.' I said nothing, and he continued, softly, 'I don't think that what you give of yourself is finite and that it has to be measured out sparingly. I would say, think of it like love.'

'I know what you mean,' I said. 'I mean, I understand. But I can't think of it that way. I mean, it just doesn't work like that for me. It's like, I have hardly enough self for myself as it is.'

His breath ruffled the hair on the top of my head.

'You are a funny bird,' he said. 'If I am the sum total of every book I've read, what are you?'

'You mean, if I've never read a novel?'

'Yes.'

'Then I must be nothing. Well, I've flicked through dictionaries. Maybe I'm just a jumble of words. I've read the plays I've performed in. Maybe I'm just an act.' I reached behind him and me with both hands, pulling him up against me. 'Is that really how you think of yourself? As the sum total of all the books you've read?'

'Yes. More or less, and what I feel here, in you,' he said, moving his hands down from my neck and shoulders, 'is something far more substantial than nothing.' And he led me, the two of us walking backwards down the hallway, to his bed.

A joyous, guiltless voyage of self-discovery, the act of sex told me nothing of who I was, it just affirmed that I was. It wasn't so much, for me, a fulfilment as a *fill*ment, a filling, a completing, a providing of evidence that, if only for a moment, I existed if not for myself then at least for someone else. I liked the selfishness and the selflessness, the shared responsibility for contraception beforehand and the domesticity that came after, the rearranging of the bed sheets, the blushing and the affection, the kind, sleepily mumbled *Goodnight*s.

'Why,' Sebastian asked, 'are you changing the alarm?'

'It's so that we can, you know…' I said, straddling him in order to replace the alarm clock on his side of the bed and unable to keep the twinkle from my eye and the giggle from my voice, 'One more time, before we go to work. To see us through for the rest of the week.'

He flung his arm across his tousled hair and forehead. 'You're insatiable! It's all right for you. You don't have to be in for seven. You can just go straight back to sleep. I'm going to be knackered.'

Still astride him, looking down at him, I said, 'Yes!'

Mie

Mr Omochi stopped in front of my desk. Surprised, I failed to comprehend that he had come for me and not for Fubuki and only just refrained from blurting out that her desk was the one next to mine. Mr Omochi extended a stubby finger towards me and then furled and unfurled it in lieu of a spoken request that I follow him, which I did, in a state of extreme self-consciousness and of mixed emotions, terrified that he might expect me to have shorthand skills and yet thrilled by the thought of movement, career progress, new challenges and skills.

'Atashi-*san*,' said Mr Omochi, indicating with a wave of his hand a tall stack of papers on a chair by his desk, 'photocopy these for me by tomorrow. I thought that, as these documents are in English, you'd be best qualified to do this.'

'Certainly, Omochi-*san*.' I approached the pile and picked up what I could. 'Please allow me to come back for the rest, as I can't manage it all in one journey.'

Mr Omochi sat down behind his desk and played with his tie that failed to reach his trouser belt, leaving visible the buttons that strained to join the two sides of his shirt together. He already looked bored with his act of delegation. On both occasions of my return to his office he hadn't moved, that I could tell.

I spent a day in the windowless photocopying room, unstapling documents, photocopying the pages one by one and then stapling them together. I filled the photocopying machine with paper on numerous occasions and replaced the ink cartridge twice. By the end of the job, I was close to tears, not just because of the tedious nature of the job and because colleagues did little to hide their disgruntlement at my hogging the photocopier, but also because it had dawned on me, despite the initial boost to my self-esteem, that no knowledge of English was required to position sheet after sheet of paper on the photocopier's glass, close the lid and press a button. If one photocopied each photocopy in turn to produce, to the naked eye, an immeasurably paler imitation of the original and of the preceding copies, how many photocopies would it take for the original to disappear altogether and to be left with a blank sheet of paper? I felt that only a few days spent in repetition of this would efface my spirit.

Fubuki, whether out of a sense of commiseration or of curiosity, had waited for me before leaving for home. 'I mean,' I said to her after thanking her for having waited, 'it would have made no difference if the document had been in Russian and I Chinese. Is he playing a game at my expense or does he really think that it made sense for me to photocopy those English documents?'

Fubuki arranged her handbag strap on her shoulder and stepped into the lift. I had noticed that she always placed one hand on her stomach as the lift started its long drop to the ground floor. 'You know, it's best not to ask yourself that question,' she replied pragmatically. 'If he's being mean, beat him at his own game; don't give him any satisfaction and he'll get bored of it. If he thinks it's important, be grateful; he'll then send something more interesting your way. Who knows? Maybe this is a test and, if you pass it, you'll be rewarded with a job that meets your aspirations.' I recalled her wise words the following morning when, panting after my six trips from the photocopying room, I asked Mr Omochi where he'd like me to put the originals and their photocopies.

Mr Omochi, who looked as though he hadn't even moved from the day before, stared at me blankly before nodding his head in the direction of the filing cabinet in the far corner of his office. It was as tall as me, and as wide as I was tall. It had five drawers, four of which were empty, the bottom one containing shoes, ties and empty bottles of *saké*.

'Omochi-*san*.' I bowed. 'Which would you like me to file there, the photocopies or the originals?'

Mr Omochi looked at me languidly. 'File both of them.' He looked pleased at my start of surprise.

I couldn't bring myself to ask what point the exercise had if the copy were to be kept with the original and not distributed to a second party, if the two were to finish their brief lives in the graveyard of the furthest recess of Mr Omochi's office. Instead, I asked, 'Under what heading, Omochi-*san*?'

Mr Omochi, not without some effort, leant forward and propped himself up on his fingers – that were so short and stubby that I thought for a second he was resting on his knuckles – from which simian posture he grunted, 'Show some initiative, can't you?'

I filed them under 'Originals' and 'Photocopies'.

Sharon

Gaia said, 'I've watched you dance.'

'Yes,' I said.

'You dance like a housewife. Or like a schoolgirl. Like you're at the school disco or something.' Gaia put her hand on my arm. 'Pierre thinks it's cute and he tolerates it from you because of Wanda. Come on, don't get all put out.' She rested her head on my shoulder in a low, friendly, tender head butt. 'You need to dance like a tart. Like you mean it. Look at me next time. Don't go for the steel poles: they're too slick, too fast and it's difficult to create tension and to keep control. Go for the brass ones: they provide more friction, they're easier to hold and you can try something slower, more sensual. Has a customer asked you for your phone number yet?'

'No. Does that mean I haven't been very good?'

'Yes. But what are you going to do when you are asked?'

I opened my eyes wide.

'You need to think about it. Have your answer ready.'

'Do you ever give your number out?'

'In for a penny, in for a pound. What's the big deal? It's only sex. It's what's at the heart of every family, right?' She squeezed my arm. 'If you were a man, you'd ask for my number, wouldn't you?'

I returned the gentle head-to-head and we laughed. She knew she was right.

We remained seated for a while, the two of us squeezed in between the arms of the high-backed armchair, taking the two-hourly ten-minute break we were entitled to. The club was hot, the temperature kept high in order to keep us – the girls – warm and the customers thirsty.

Mie

Gradually, I filled the filing cabinet with documents and their originals, approaching the last drawer with some trepidation, worrying about how to ask Mr Omochi whether his shoes, ties and *saké* bottles took precedence over the documents and their copies. To my surprise, I never had to, as first the shoes disappeared, then the bottles and then the ties, with the end result that there was always the space I needed. The first filing cabinet full, Mr Omochi jutted his chin out at its neighbour and my heart sank.

I discovered the photocopier's automatic feeder, a technological advance that I suspected Mr Omochi remained unaware of, and decided to use the 'extra' time this gave me to read what I was photocopying and so use my English and learn more about the diverse nature of Yumimoto's extensive business. Inadvertently, my world geography improved, too, and the exercise took me back to Mrs Watanabe's globe as I read about Yumimoto's importation of cheese from Finland, solder from Singapore, fibre optics from Canada, tyres from France, jute from Togo, watches from Switzerland and fashion labels from England in exchange for our exportation of steel, cars and electronics.

Fubuki had graduated from taking down letters to attending meetings in the formal capacity of minutes-taker, while I faced imprisonment in an unventilated photocopier room having parked my intellectual abilities and hung my mind up on a tenterhook to wither and die, so little was it needed.

The days in the office passed like conveyor–belt sushi, evenly spaced, with little differences between them but always, if only at occasionally irregular intervals, coming around again, with Tuesdays following Mondays as certainly as the *ebi nigiri* on the pink-bordered saucer followed the *tako nigiri* on the black-bordered one. I considered the saucers proceeding slowly around the sushi bar, each piece of *nigiri* waiting passively for a diner to determine its fate, lifted a saucer off the slowly moving belt and, holding a piece of *tekkamaki* between my chopsticks, said to Fubuki, 'I need a strategy. I have to take my future into my own hands. I must,' I said, punning on the meaning of *nigiri* – which is 'grasp', as the rice is shaped by hand – 'seize the day.'

Fubuki had taken to socialising with some of the girls from the typing pool and had been good enough to invite me to join them. I found that I liked them and discovered that my parents and I weren't alone in thinking the way we did about certain Japanese customs. The girls confirmed that the pressure they faced to conform to their half of Japan's anachronistic family model of salaryman husband and stay-at-home wife was strong, and they railed against Japan's punishing corporate world that made it impossible for women to combine a career with a family. To my astonishment, they lived in fear of becoming long-term *parasaito shingurus* who, partnerless, reach their thirties and still live at home; and yet, seemingly in contradiction, not one of the girls claimed to want to get married, believing, apparently, that staying single was preferable to what they imagined marriage to be like.

'What's so hard to understand?' asked Fubuki, eyeing some *futomaki* on the conveyor belt. 'We can have a great life. We can go out with our girlfriends and buy nice clothes and pay for holidays.'

'Yes, but you're all terrified of being single at 25. So it's a bit of a contradiction.'

Fubuki sighed. 'Personally, I'm fed up with all the men who think I must be desperate just because I'm single.'

'Tell me about it,' I replied. 'I think I've been asked out by every man on our floor. Except for my superiors.'

'Actually, they're the only ones who've asked me out,' said Fubuki, naturally. 'I think I scare the others away.' She looked at me and arched her beautiful, quite perfect eyebrows. 'So, how many have you accepted?'

'You know. None.'

'Exactly. So there's nothing different about any of us. We don't want to commit to a life of domestic drudgery. We value our independence. We know better than to take our work to our bedrooms. And our men, if we're frank, are not worth the bother. If we must, a one-night stand will do. Personally,' Fubuki shrugged, 'I can't be bothered. Not often, anyway.' She stared down two young men on the other side of the conveyor belt and then looked at me and said, 'So. It seems to me we have got to exactly the same place but via two quite different paths.'

'Yes.' I nodded. 'But, for me, it's more about, you know –'

'Yes, I know,' said Fubuki, not unkindly, and leaned forward conspiratorially. 'But, tell me, how exactly do you plan to "seize the day"?'

I had to admit that I did not know.

'Atashi-*san*.' An agitated Mr Saito stood to attention behind his desk and requested I follow him, which I did, rattled by his formal use of my surname, past Mr Omochi's empty office and on to Mr Hanada's that admitted of a round conference table and a sofa besides Mr Hanada's desk, desk chair, visitors' chairs and filing cabinets. Mr Omochi stayed seated while Mr Hanada rose to greet us and invited Mr Saito and me to join them at the table. I believed I must have misheard him and remained standing on the doorsill, my feet unable to take the necessary steps to reach the one empty space around that table, my eyes desperately seeking Mr Saito's for help. Mr Saito leafed though a pile of papers while Mr Omochi looked on without interest, his remarkable girth such that, arms fully stretched, he could only just rest his wrists, bandaged in his blue shirt's white cuffs, on the table. Mr Hanada guided me to my seat and resumed his own. I kept my hands on my lap and my eyes downcast; they were like rocks in my head I could not lift.

Mr Hanada looked at me kindly from above his glasses and asked, 'Would you like me to start again, Mie–*san*?'

'Yes please, Hanada-*san*.' I inclined my head, gratefully registered his use of my first name and determined to pay attention to every word.

'We are to receive, a week today, much earlier than anticipated, a delegation from the Netherlands-based More Stage Services with whom we intend to enter into negotiation for the domestic distribution of the European sound and lighting companies they represent and, reciprocally, for the European distribution of the hi-fi brands in our electronics industry portfolio. A list of the European companies and Japanese brands and of every product in question is to be found in these briefing packs together with the names, job titles and biographies of both delegations – are you following, Atashi-*san*?'

'Yes, yes.' I nodded furiously.

'Marc Nobel and Allison Boonstra of MSS are native English speakers; the third in their delegation is Adam Johnson, their American London-based banker. Please familiarise yourself with every detail of MSS's business and with the biographies of every participant you will find in the main body of the text. Familiarise yourself, in the first appendix, with every detail of the brand names, of the products – their prices, margins and the volumes they sell in. Very important: please read through the second appendix containing the questions they may ask, the answers we may give, the questions we will ask and the answers they may give. Atashi-*san*, you will have to be familiar with these in both Japanese and English. I don't believe, Atashi-*san*, that your English language and literature course at university covered the high fidelity and information technologies?'

Of course it hadn't.

Mr Hanada closed the file and folded his hands together, leaning forward on his forearms. 'Atashi-*san*, the change in schedule has thrown us. The interpreter we would normally employ for an occasion like this is unavailable. However, Messrs Omochi and Saito have satisfied me that you are a Yumimoto Corporation employee at heart by now and' – and here he looked at his notes before looking at me again – 'Tokyo University of Foreign Studies gave you such an excellent reference – you were not aware? Your tutor wrote that he considers you the best student of English he has ever taught – that I feel sure you will execute your duties as interpreter admirably and make Yumimoto proud of you.'

The week went by in a fug of intense study. I cancelled the social engagements I had and, having memorised the briefing pack in its entirety at my desk during the day, in the evenings I criss-crossed Akihabara, the district in which Tokyo's electronics shops were located, entering every shop, asking after every product in Yumimoto's portfolio and on MSS's distribution list and acquiring their brochures and specification sheets. I asked the salesmen their opinions on the respective merits of the radios, cassette decks, turntables, speakers and all-in-one music centres and noted the prices at which they were on sale.

On the rare occasions when I wasn't thinking about the first important meeting of my career, I was worrying about Fubuki. She had expressed her delight for me in a manner that had not rung true. Her formal expressions of joy had been correct, but her eyes had held no warmth. Her altruism in deciding not to speak to me all week for fear of distracting me seemed unnecessary, and appeared, as the week lengthened, more cold than kind. I chewed on this at intervals before deciding to take her at face value, a decision that I felt was validated at the end of the week when she fell in step with me as we exited the Yumitomo building.

'Your big day on Monday!' she exclaimed, eyes wide open. 'I just wanted to wish you the best of luck – not that you'll need it. You noticed, I hope, that I've been as good as my word and stayed quite out of your way so that you could concentrate? Tuesday first thing, you'll have to tell me all about it!'

'Thank you, Fubuki.'

'It will be your day – seize it! Don't let an opportunity like that go by without making your contribution.' She leant forward and tapped me on the shoulder with a polished fingernail.

'My contribution,' I replied thoughtfully, 'will be to interpret everything as faithfully as possible.'

'Nonsense!' replied Fubuki. 'You are the only person who will be able to strike up any kind of rapport with the *gaijin*, so you have a crucial role to play there too. Not only are you the only one to speak their language – you are the only woman on our team to face off against the woman on theirs. Hanada-*san* couldn't spell this out for you, probably, so I'm glad I told you.'

I kept my eyes on Fubuki as she strode off, a head taller than the other commuters hurrying home on a Friday evening, and, as though sensing me watching her, she turned around and waved before disappearing down an entrance to the underground. Her words had galvanised me. They enabled me to admit something I had hitherto kept suppressed, namely, that much as I had been happy to have been given a role interpreting, I considered the interpreter's a passive rather than an active role, one in which I would speak not for myself but for another, in which I would count for nothing. What Fubuki had said, though, shone a light on Mr Hamada's closing words to me such that I understood them differently now. I knew that a great contribution was expected of me, above and beyond the literal translation of the spoken word.

On Monday morning, our delegation greeted that of MSS in the reception area by the lift lobby of the 44th floor. The lift doors opened and twelve of us bowed. Mrs Boonstra, Mr Johnson and Mr Nobel appeared surprised to be faced with twelve crowns, bobbed their heads and then leapt, index fingers poised, to the consoles to either side of the lift doors, only to be confused, I assumed, by the mix of English, *kanji* and picture signs, too late to prevent the lift doors from closing. A minute later they reappeared, we bowed, they bowed, Mrs Boonstra keeping one finger on the appropriate lift button until her colleagues had exited the lift into the lobby. Once in the board-room, there followed thirty-six exchanges of cards; a stack of business cards in my name had, as if by a miracle, appeared on my desk that morning. I translated Mr Fujimoto's welcome and introductions and then Mr Nobel's. Mr Fujimoto enquired about our guests' trip and the weather they'd left behind; I translated this, too, and our guests' replies. Mr Hanada then presented the day's agenda and asked for agreement; I translated them both. And so the morning progressed, a ping–pong of items queried, ticked, agreed upon or parked for later discussion, with moments in which both sides conferred in hushed tones or took bathroom breaks. I had done my homework well and was able to translate the technical jargon without difficulty.

We adjourned for lunch over bento boxes that Mrs Boonstra admired greatly and took pictures of. She was a handsome blonde with a ruddy complexion and a ready smile who would have scared most Japanese men. She sought me out at the first opportunity more, I guessed, because we were the only women in the room than because we had a language in common. She waved the agenda at me. 'Tonight's dinner. I hope to God you're going to be there!'

Messrs Johnson and Nobel stood by the floor-to-ceiling windows, bento boxes in one hand and chopsticks in the other, and looked out. 'You have a beautiful view,' said Mr Johnson to my colleagues nearest him and, a bit louder, with expansive arm gestures, 'A beautiful view.' Everyone nodded and exhaled and made general sounds of agreement while ignoring the breach of etiquette that standing with one's bento box entailed. Mr Nobel, I could see, was unfamiliar with chopsticks: I had to resist the temptation to help him and, instead, as discreetly as I could manage, using a paper napkin, I picked bits of food up from the floor by the window before they could get trodden into the carpet.

The afternoon progressed much as the morning had done, only more slowly; lunch had to be digested. Coffee was served and served again.

We reached the last of the agenda items, namely the price at which we would import a new English brand of esoteric, top–end stereophonic equipment. Mr Omochi argued that the recommended retail price was such that Yumimoto simply could not bid any higher; Mr Nobel pointed out that the manufacturer's and his, the distributor's, margins would be too severely eroded should they sell at a price lower than the one they had proposed. Mr Omochi requested Mr Nobel recall the many distributors, the many middle men, that require satisfaction in Japan's wholesale-to-retail business *modus operandi*; Mr Nobel thought it instructive to consider an American competitor's product that had a higher recommended retail price. I wondered if I were the only one to see the similarities between the two men: physically, they were alike, with Mr Nobel's goatee seemingly, on his business adversary, having climbed up the face and on to the head.

'Why would anyone want to buy a European hi-fi product at twice the price of an even better Japanese product, anyway?' grumbled Mr Omochi. He had clearly thrown in the towel. 'The product will never sell, so it doesn't matter what we agree. Certainly, it won't sell if our distributors won't earn anything on it.' He looked apologetically at Mr Hanada and then at me. 'Translate, Atashi-*san*.'

'Mr Nobel,' I began, my heart beating faster as I leafed through the notes I had taken during my expeditions to Akihabara, 'the competitor product you referred to sells nowhere near its recommended retail price. To be specific, in two out of five shops in Tokyo's main electronics district last week it was offered for sale at' – I made some quick calculations – 'about 80 percent of that price and, in the three other shops, at somewhere between two–thirds and one–half of that price. Anyway, this argues for a one–third reduction of the import price of this last item under discussion.'

I had seen my chance and taken it and now awaited the consequences. Both parties, I thought, were aware that what I had said was not what Mr Omochi had said, and the room of a dozen or so bored, tired people suddenly took on a subtle charge: now a dozen or so reinvigorated business people sat forward, arms and elbows on the boardroom table, looking expectantly at each other. The MSS delegation conferred in a huddle around Mr Nobel.

Mr Hanada asked me to translate what I had said.

I did so.

Mr Fujimoto looked at me as though seeing me for the first time.

The Yumimoto delegation held its breath.

Mr Nobel resumed his place at the table and said to Mr Omochi, 'Okay. We'll agree to your price but, if this is acceptable to you, for a three-year contract, as opposed to the standard five.'

Mr Omochi indicated that it was, and the afternoon concluded with expressions of mutual satisfaction and instructions for our guests to be in their hotel lobby at seven o'clock that evening, when we would pick them up for dinner. We walked them to the lift and bowed as they entered it; they bowed in response and stayed bowed until the lift doors closed – and then the lift doors opened again.

'God damn it!' I heard Mr Nobel exclaim under his breath.

'It's this one,' said Mr Johnson helpfully.

We exchanged a mix of bows, nods and smiles until the lift doors closed for the second time.

I returned to my desk, exhausted and not a little elated. I considered that I had executed my duties well, and had even made a contribution to the negotiations. From hushed conversations and covert glances in my direction, I believed that I was being lauded for all aspects of my professionalism that day. I sought relief and some privacy in the ladies' loos and sat there a while, drained but happy. For the first time in that confined space, I nodded off, waking up with a start to see that it was nearly six o'clock. I splashed water on my face and, refreshed, sat at my desk again, waiting to be summoned to the dinner. The summons never came. The office clock ticked past seven and the office emptied. I went home with my sense of achievement tempered by a feeling of apprehension and foreboding.

'Atashi-*san*!' Mr Omochi stood in front of my desk the following morning and bellowed, 'Follow me into my office, immediately!' I stood and bowed and had to practically run after him, Mr Saito immediately behind me and all eyes on us, with no attempt by my colleagues to disguise their excitement at this most public of ignominies.

'Explain your behaviour!' Mr Omochi stood behind his desk, blocking the light from the windows so that I could see him only in silhouette and had to guess at his facial expression. To my consternation, Mr Mizuka, whom I had glimpsed only once since my second day at Yumimoto, stood by the side of the desk. Mr Saito stood behind me.

'Omochi-*san*,' I bowed, 'please forgive me. No one had mentioned the dinner to me. I waited to be picked up from my desk by' – I couldn't say Saito-*san* – 'someone, but no one ever came, and I didn't know what restaurant to go to.' I was bewildered to see Yumimoto's head of personnel attend my reprimand and could only think, my offence being so slight, that his presence was a coincidence.

My apology made Mr Omochi apoplectic, his mouth opening and closing soundlessly as he grew wilder with rage. Only after some seconds did he manage to splutter, 'Restaurant? Restaurant! You weren't wanted at the restaurant.' He stood on tiptoe and punched the air with both fists. 'The restaurant was for employees of rank, of distinction, to bond with their counterparts over *saké* – we didn't need you for that, thank you very much!'

Suddenly exhausted, Mr Omochi gripped the back of his chair and looked from Mr Saito to Mr Mizuka, whose eyes had never left me and who said, as if on cue, 'Atashi-*san*, at worst, your action has been one of attempted sabotage; at the very least, it's an act of gross insubordination. How dare you imply that Omochi-*san* did not have the facts that you displayed at his fingertips and how did you know he was not just about to make the very point that you made? How could you have forgotten your place among the assembled company and assume the role of negotiator? By what right did you consider it appropriate to lead your superiors down a negotiating path with no clear signal from them that it was the path they wanted to follow? What has Omochi-*san* ever done to you for you to reciprocate with such a humiliation? What has the Yumitomo Corporation ever done to you to merit such treachery?'

Mr Omochi swivelled his chair around and fell into it. His back to Mr Saito and me, he said, looking at Mr Mizuka to his left and then out over the city, 'Atashi-*san* likes photocopying. She's good at that. It's what she'll do. Atashi-*san*, you will photocopy; every day, the department will give you things to photocopy that you will file. And your job will be to photocopy, to ensure you get noticed by one of our employees, to marry him and to make him very happy so that when he comes home after a long day at Yumimoto he has a warm dinner and a warmer bed waiting for him. There, that's your job and, if you don't like it, look' – and he waved his arm over the city – 'there are lots of other jobs out there and lots of salarymen waiting for you to make them happy. Look,' he insisted. 'Look!'

In involuntary accordance with the irrepressible instinct to execute a senior's command without contemplation, I stepped forward and looked. The city, seen from a vantage point of considerable elevation, was a lattice of horizontals crossing from left to right and back, of verticals screaming vertiginously down and of perpendiculars streaming to a distant endpoint to obliterate us all. In this vista of aerial and linear perspectives, we travel and toil, ride lifts and escalators up and down, journey in trains and cars here and there and beetle from home to conveyance to work and back. It was a picture, seen from the great height of Mr Omochi's double-glazed office window, of a silent metropolis in which all hope was expunged and the individual obliterated. We share neither the common purpose of ants nor the individualist grace and vacillations of butterflies. We teem in this city that dehumanises us and reduces us to our basic mechanistic, mineral selves, to non-identities that function according to biology, custom and physical limitations. I looked up and my faint reflection looked back at me sternly. I stood legs apart on the city and resolute, with little intention of allowing myself to be permanently subjugated.

I became the office pariah, the Icarus who had overreached and come crashing down to earth from the 44th floor but who had lived to repent of her hubris. Fubuki grew busier than ever and had less time for me. I hadn't had to tell her how the day of the MSS meeting had gone for me; she'd found out easily enough. Mr Saito threw me what crumbs of work he could that Mr Omochi would not find out about, while Mr Omochi himself was as good as his word, giving me photocopying to do and seemingly indifferent as to when I completed it, and yet anything but indifferent as to my dress, remarking daily on whether what I was wearing was 'man-catcher' material: the shorter the skirt, the better. Clearly, as far as he was concerned, I was as good as gone – whether to make a Yumitomo salaryman a good wife or to find employment elsewhere, he didn't care. Ironically, my new status of outcast made the former more unlikely: it would take a brave employee to befriend me publicly.

Sharon

I experienced a period of contentment that little had prepared me for. My friends were happy around me. My colleagues and customers were satisfied with me. I was a good listener, I was efficient, I was attentive. I enjoyed giving more than receiving. I discovered my virtuous cycle of happiness, a merry wheel of pleasing others while retaining my own cheerful disposition, a wheel that little could dent or buckle until Sebastian spoke, one Monday evening, his voice hesitant, emanating from the tousled blue bed sheets we lay recovering under, to announce that he would soon be leaving for Japan.

For a few days? A week? 'Have a nice time,' I mumbled.

Sebastian placed a hand on my shoulder. 'You haven't understood. I'm leaving. I'm relocating. I'm going to live in Tokyo.' He raised himself on one elbow and looked down at me. 'Say something.'

I could think of only two things. The first was that I might have fallen in love with Sebastian and that it had taken the prospect of his leaving me for me to realise it. The second was that he had said *I* and not *we* and that my dismissal was implicit in that *I*. Maybe the invitation for me to join him in Japan was to come. My bubble of joy was punctured. I felt rejected, dejected, desperate to hear him wonder aloud whether I might like to live in Tokyo. I thought I would. I decided there and then that I would.

'Say something.' Sebastian blew a hair from my face. He sighed and sought to explain. 'It's a promotion. I'm going to manage the derivatives desk in the Tokyo office. Three years, probably.'

'*I* am going to Tokyo, not *we* are going?' My voice was small.

'Oh, come on!' Sebastian opened his mouth as though to say something more, but then decided against it. He appeared embarrassed. He sat up and held the sheets to his chin and looked cautiously at me over them. 'I leave next week.'

I wondered if he'd had the vanity to choose sheets that so precisely matched his eye colour intentionally. I made an effort to speak. 'That explains it. I thought your flat was looking a bit tidy. Well, bare. You've packed some things away.'

'You're not too upset?'

'Upset at what? That you tell me now and not before, not when we got here? Or that after three years of a relationship, you're happy for it to end just like that?'

'Oh, come on!' He tried to make light of it. 'It's hardly been a relationship. More like, you know, just a bit of fun. A diversion. For us both. Hasn't it? Sorry.' He held his hands up. 'That's not quite what I meant.'

'What did you mean?' I could only just hear my voice.

'Did you really think –' He tried again. 'We're not really compatible, are we? I mean, we have a great time together and everything, when we see each other –'

I raised my hand to stop him. I didn't want to hear it.

Sebastian was right. He was intelligent and intellectual and I wasn't. He was better travelled, better read and more interested and informed than I could ever hope to be. He had self-knowledge and a degree of self-possession that I envied. I wasn't so stupid, though, that I couldn't understand what he, perhaps, could only feel, or couldn't bring himself to tell me. That the effort of his completing me wasn't worth it. The reward, simply, would be poor compensation for the bother. If I couldn't love myself – if there was nothing to love – I could hardly blame him for not loving me. He must have, all this time we'd been seeing each other, been seeing me for what I was: nothing.

To my surprise and, I think, Sebastian's, we found ourselves hugging each other and then weeping and kissing, as he tried to comfort me and I, perhaps, to persuade him of his mistake, to remind him of what he would be leaving behind and might miss. Our imminent separation added a spice to our lovemaking, a quality whereby we were simultaneously with a familiar and a stranger, an excitement and yet an underlying sadness that accompanies the most intimate of exchanges when it's undertaken without consequence.

Mie

I met Margaret one weekend in Setagaya Park, where we ate ice-cream while sitting on a park bench and watching children play. 'Have you noticed,' she remarked, 'that until a certain age, children don't play with each other but among each other. I must admit, I don't see the point of them.'

'That's a strange thing for a teacher to say.'

'True!' Margaret laughed. 'Well, until they're teenagers. Anyway, what's plan B?'

I had to admit that I didn't have one.

'You could write to Ursula.'

I didn't like that idea.

'Okay, so you can either try to get a job in England from here or try to secure accommodation there and then look for a job once you get there. Or you can try both and see which happens first.'

I admired Margaret for her pragmatism, her ability to distil a situation down to its essential, component parts and to act accordingly; and I told her as much.

Margaret's response to praise was to ignore it. 'What you need is a course of action. I get all the expat English language newspapers and magazines with job offers from back home, so I'll bring some to you next weekend.'

By the following Sunday, however, there had been a development, one that was to change everything for me and make Margaret's offer of assistance redundant. I had been at my desk one evening, having just finished filing the photocopies of European car brochures, when my desk telephone rang. It rang so rarely that I was surprised; I looked at it thinking it might stop ringing, as though the caller would realise that they had dialled a wrong number. Eventually, I picked it up and pressed the receiver to my ear.

'*Moshi moshi.*'

'Hello. Is this Miss Atashi?' The English voice with an American twang – or was it the other way around? – was familiar but I couldn't quite place it.

'Yes, this is Miss Atashi speaking.'

'Hello! It's Adam Johnson here. How are you? Do you remember me?'

'Mr Johnson! Of course! How are you?'

'I'm fine, thank you. How are you?'

'I'm fine, thank you.'

'Say, we were very disappointed that you didn't join us at the restaurant when we were over. Sorry, that wasn't meant to sound… you know – it's just that we missed you there. I guess we'd have all drunk a lot less *saké* if you had been there! You did a great job, by the way.' Mr Johnson paused as though unsure how to continue, and I realised that I was gripping the receiver with one hand and the telephone cord with the other as if to never let him go. 'Oh, I hope I'm not bothering you in any way. Is this a good time for you to talk? I'm not keeping you from going home at all?'

I looked around the office. Mr Saito and Fubuki were either in a meeting or had gone home for the day, and there was no one within earshot; not that it mattered, I supposed, if I was overheard speaking English. 'Yes. No, not at all. Please go on, Mr Johnson.'

'Well,' Mr Johnson cleared his throat. 'Forgive me for being so direct. I was extremely impressed by your language skills. I mean, I have been doing business in Japan for a long time and, well, I have never met anyone who was as comfortable and as capable in both languages – er, Japanese and English – as you are.'

'Thank you,' I said.

'Well, it's the truth,' proceeded Mr Johnson. 'Now, we've had an opening come up in our bank in London, in our Japan team, and I wondered if, er, you know, you might know of anyone, you know, someone you might have studied with, for example, or a good friend, anyway, someone who would welcome a full-time employment contract in the UK –'

'Mr Johnson.'

'– someone who would be prepared to relocate – for excellent compensation, of course –'

'Mr Johnson.'

'Yes?' Mr Johnson belatedly allowed me to interrupt him.

'I know such a person.'

'You do? Excellent! I'm back in Tokyo in three weeks' time when I would like to interview – that person. If I let you know where I'm staying, perhaps you could book a meeting room at the hotel for me?'

'Of course, Mr Johnson.'

'Call me Adam, please, and, er, while I have you on the phone, could I ask one more favour of you? Would you happen to have Miss Mori's telephone number?'

'Miss Mori? Fubuki Mori?' I couldn't keep the surprise out of my voice.

'Yes, that's right, Fubuki. Would you happen to have her number? I must have left her business card at the restaurant.'

I was astounded. So Fubuki had been pulled into the dinner in my place – or was it that it had never been intended that I go? Had she been there as company for Mrs Boonstra or as eye candy for the men? Fubuki spoke no English, but maybe Mr Johnson spoke some Japanese. My mind reeled with possibilities. Well, I would let him have her number, willingly, so she could have her nights in Tokyo with her American while I, if things panned out as I started hoping they might, could face a lifetime in London with, theoretically, my choice of Englishman.

Long after Mr Johnson and I had said our goodbyes, I sat there, at my desk in a dark and empty office, holding the telephone handset in one hand and the telephone cord in the other, thinking that this telephone cord was connected to telephone wires that, just as I had one day dreamed, had come to form my lifeline, my release from servility and orthodoxy, my path to self-realisation.

I said nothing to my parents and to my friends until I had met Mr Johnson, when he had, to my surprise, conducted a proper, formal interview, and I had received a written job offer and, with the assistance of my new employer, my work visa.

The following months passed in a blur of administration and goodbyes. I resigned, as protocol dictated, first to Mr Saito, then to Mr

Omochi and, last, to Mr Hanada. Mr Mizuka hovered at my elbow on my last day as I said good-bye to my colleagues; I pictured him behind me, dustpan and brush in hand, as though to sweep up after me and obliterate all trace of my passage through Yumimoto. What had I contributed to this mammoth organisation over three years, besides stacks of photocopies? Disappointingly little. The office good-byes were perfunctory and the good wishes for my future expressed not so much insincerely as indifferently with, to my surprise, the exception of Fubuki who, I think, belatedly realised she would be losing a friend, a same-sex ally, and regretted having cooled towards me since my backfiring demonstration of initiative. Her hugs, in the privacy of the ladies' loos, were tighter than they needed to have been.

Taka received my news in exchange for his: he had just got engaged to a young woman he'd met in his company's secretarial pool. Michi and Keiko were delighted for me, and they promised to visit me in London. Margaret, understated as always, simply patted me on the shoulder.

My parents' reactions to my news pleased me the most. Weekly telephone calls would be no substitute for the presence of an only child, but they put a brave face on it and did everything they could to be supportive of my going and to dispel any sentiment of guilt I might have had about leaving them. On the evening that I broke my news, my father opened some of his best *sake*, my mother played her English 45 rpm hit singles and I blinked back my tears.

Sharon

Mr Self stood behind me and shook my office chair lightly in order to attract my attention. 'Sharon.' He had to speak loudly to be heard above an ordinary day's tumult: the banter, the invectives, the quoting, the pricing, the pleading, the closing of deals, the fizz and crackle of the squawk box. 'Do you have a moment?'

I looked at Jonathan, who pursed his lips and gave a barely perceptible nod.

I followed Mr Self down the trading floor's central aisle to its meeting rooms, thinking how droll he was, this now balding, punk hippy of a personnel manager at the service of sharp-suited investment bankers, and into a room in which stood Yuuto and Mr Johnson. Mr Johnson and I had never spoken but I knew him by sight: an American who worked in a department different to mine where he did deals of a kind that I never quite understood. A limp, nondescript Englishman called David, absent on this occasion, usually followed him like a shadow in poor light.

We sat around a table in the same room I had been interviewed in five years ago. Mr Self crossed his legs, one knee against the table, and reclined as far as the swivelling office chair allowed. Yuuto gave a series of nods, as though reluctant and yet compelled to do so by the tic of his cultural, formal upbringing. Mr Johnson spun a biro on his fingertips. The contrast between the dapper, precise bond salesman and investment banker with the bohemian, unkempt personnel manager was striking. I envied each not his appearance, but his certainty. I considered my colleagues solid, rooted behind their costumes, but I felt vacant, hollow behind mine.

Mr Self uncrossed his legs and leant forward, crossing his arms at the wrists on the table, and we all, subconsciously or otherwise, did the same. A replacement for the last Japan desk assistant had been found by Mr Johnson. Yuuto was happy for her to be entrusted to me and he had undertaken to modify his conduct around her in the hope that she would stay longer than the others. Mr Self looked pointedly at Yuuto, who only grinned in return. I was to be her mentor, to guide her, explain everything to her, pre-empt and answer her questions, assist her to settle in and bring any unhelpful behaviour by Yuuto to Mr Self's attention. At this, Yuuto narrowed his eyes at me in what I took to be a smile, and patted his brilliantined hair.

'Her name,' said Mr Self, consulting some loose sheets of paper on the table before him, 'is Mie Atashi.'

'Mie,' corrected Mr Johnson, looking at Yuuto for confirmation. 'It's pronounced me-é, not my.'

'Her English is excellent,' said Mr Johnson. 'Quite excellent. Better than mine. Honestly.'

'Better than your Japanese,' said Yuuto, and laughed at his own joke.

'And she's quick. Sharp. She'll be a great addition. You'll see.'

Mr Self pushed the papers towards me. 'Here's her CV. Yuuto has a copy. She starts on Monday. I'll have her desk ready and, for the rest, well, you know what to do. We have absolute faith in you, Sharon!'

How I welcomed such words! They were my daily bread, the validation I needed.

Mie

Society can fool you into thinking you are what it tells you you are, and it can seduce you into trying to be what you think it wants you to be. Key to the manipulation of image, to the person you present to the world, is fashion. In Japan, because of the long distances we commute and because our homes are small, we socialise in public places and, as our homes are unavailable to convey whatever statements we wish to make, our clothes and accessories must do the heavy lifting. The tension between the social imperative for conformity and the individual's need for self-expression can be acute. For many, labels become the clothing equivalent of the bids made under the various conventions in a game of bridge: code that delivers a great amount of information succinctly, economically, to a partner – indeed, labels are aspirational and have an important role to play in the mating game, the selection of a life partner. For me, however, with no interest in encouraging suitors, clothes were my suit of armour, my first line of defence in repelling invaders. Labelless, I hoped they would say, *Leave me alone, I'm not interested and I'm not interesting. Look, I wear flat shoes and no make-up; my stockings end above the knee and my skirts below it; my blouses are high and my arms rarely bared.* In theory, I should have deterred all would-be beaus; in practice, I found myself approached by men who considered themselves similar to me: men like David, who were drab and grey, timid and introvert.

I was introduced to David by Mr Johnson, who greeted me warmly on my first day at the bank. 'Mie! You made it! Great!' He shook my hand vigorously. 'How was the trip? Did you find the apartment okay?' The bank had found me an apartment on a three-month let in Clapham, on the Northern Line for direct access to the City, where the bank was located. 'Here. Let me take you to human resources. John is expecting you.' We stopped on the first-floor corridor, one entire wall of which was glass that gave onto the biggest confined space I had ever seen. 'This,' said Mr Johnson, waving his arms expansively, 'is our trading floor. It's where you'll be. John will show you. Bonds, equities, foreign exchange, everything.'

The hubbub reached us through the glass. I considered my new colleagues, some in groups, some alone, some silent, reading papers or watching screens that teetered in piles on their desks, some talking, others gesticulating. I thought of my ordered classroom, of Yumimoto's organised import–export department, and of how neither had prepared me for a work environment of such teeming chaos.

'Just over 300 people. It's a quiet day today. No data out. Don't worry, you'll get used to it. Come on, one more floor. Okay. Here, we have origination. This is where I am. This is David. David works with me. David, this is Mie.'

I shook hands with a man some five years older than me. He was my height, which was unusual for a European male, and, despite appearing shy and too demure to hold my eyes for any length of time, he held my hand for longer than I considered appropriate. He had pale brown hair and sandy eyes. He smiled, more at the floor than at me, and, speaking quietly, said that Mr Johnson had spoken well of me and that he hoped I'd be happy in my new job. His suit and shirt were creased, his shoes were unpolished and his tie was a monochrome grey. He was a moth to Mr Johnson's butterfly and, in the space of that handshake, I understood I was to be the candle he'd singe his wings on.

Mr Johnson nodded in the direction of a man striding between the desks in our direction. 'Here comes John. This is where I hand you over to him. Again, welcome. I'm so pleased to have you with us.'

'It was nice to meet you,' called David after me, raising his voice above a whisper as Mr Self walked me to a meeting room.

Tieless and long-haired Mr Self, more in the manner of a university lecturer than a head of personnel in an investment bank, talked me through the formalities as he pushed various employment-related papers at me across the meeting-room table. 'So you'll be assistant to Yuuto Kawaguchi in the Japan fixed income team,' said Mr Self. 'Specifically, Yuuto will expect you to book his travel, hotels and restaurants and to mediate between the front and back offices.' I was fascinated by an open dark mauve shirt, the cuffs of which remained unbuttoned, and by silver chains around his neck and wisps of coloured string tied around one wrist. Undecided whether he was a punk or a hippy, I could only marvel at the contradistinction I could already tell he posed in this institution. Mr Self uncrossed his legs and leant forward with his arms straight on the table. 'Look, I'll be honest,' he said. 'We call it the Japan team but it's not much of a team, is it? No assistant seems to stay longer than a month, and Yuuto turns down anyone else we try to hire to grow the team. We want to put an end to this turnover of junior staff. If it all gets too much – before it all gets too much – do say. Yuuto has a way about him that, well, is not to everyone's liking. If anything becomes an issue for you, come and talk to me about it.' He sat back. 'We're going to place you under Sharon's wing. She's assistant to the UK team and you'll be sitting back to back, so do learn everything you can from her.' He stood. 'Come on, I'll walk you down and introduce you to the fixed income team.'

Sharon

There was a peppery irony to the fact that Sebastian left my life for Japan at around the time that Mie from Japan entered it. She was, for a short time, the prickly reminder of where or what I had lost him to, but I couldn't bring myself to hold it against her.

There was a quality to Mie that elevated her above Yuuto's other Japanese desk assistants. They had been either expats' daughters or expats' wives who had sought diversion or pocket money rather than careers, and who had allowed themselves to be overwhelmed by the pace and pressures of the macho trading room environment. The more uncertain and nervous they had become, the more irritable Yuuto had been, and the louder his voice behind me had grown when he either instructed them or told them off. The more make-up and the more ostentatious the brands and labels they had worn, the less time they had lasted.

The first time I saw Mie, I had to resist an impulse to laugh and brought my hand to my mouth, just like the Japanese assistants' did when they were embarrassed. She was dressed like a grandmother: in a below-the-knee-length woollen skirt, socks and sandals with an ever–so–slight heel and a plain, dark blouse. Over one arm was an ill-matching jacket; over the other hung a large, featureless handbag. Jet black, pomaded hair was pulled back in a tight bun above a plain face that was free of cosmetics. Initially, I thought her eyebrows had been painted on, so perfectly had they been plucked into crescent shapes.

Mie had a focus and a dogged commitment to the job that the others had lacked. She seemed to apply herself consciously even to walking and moving, as though every action were considered, executed only once properly deliberated and weighed. She never said as much, but gave the impression that, having left home and Japan for this job, failure was not an option.

At first, I considered her if not stupid then a little slow, because she asked questions about everything; I feared for Mr Johnson, who I quite liked and who I knew had stuck his neck out in hiring her. I came to realise, however, that her questions were good ones, that she never repeated them and that they demonstrated a desire to go beyond the mechanics of a task to a full understanding of the reason behind it. I didn't always have the answers and felt the blood go to my face when replying, 'We don't need to know that,' as an alternative to repeating, 'I don't know.'

To begin with, Mie shadowed my every move. I showed her how the UK sales team's clients were organised in my database and we replicated the same for the Japan team's clients. We wrote sale and buy tickets together, had the salespeople and then the traders sign them together and walked the carbon copies to the back office together.

'Sharon, what did Jonathan do just then?'

'He sold his client this... this bond.' I waved the trading slip at her on which I had written the names of the client and a company, a rate, a date, a price, an identifying code and the day's date and time.

'What is a bond, *exactly*?'

'I don't know!'

'Why did the client want to buy it?'

'I don't know!'

'Why did we want to sell it?'

'It's what we do!' I cried in exasperation.

'It's what we do on the UK desk,' said Jonathan, a phone on each shoulder and his back turned to Yuuto. 'I don't know about the Japan desk, though. I think there you'll only get to write lunch orders, Mie.'

Yuuto replied at length in Japanese.

'No need to translate, Mie!' said Jonathan cheerily. 'I think I got the gist!'

Mie looked seriously at the three of us in turn and then stood up. Yuuto looked at her from the corner of his eyes to gauge the effects of his words, but she seemed quite unfazed by whatever it was he had said. 'Come on,' she said, holding her hand out for the slips. 'Trading.'

We placed the slips in front of the trader for signing.

'Hello, darling,' he said to me as he signed.

'Excuse me,' said Mie to the trader. 'Why did you quote this price instead of another?'

'Are you questioning my pricing?'

'Come on, Mie!' I took the duplicate slips in one hand and Mie's elbow in the other. To the trader: 'Thanks!' To Mie: 'Now's not the time! Not while they're busy!'

'All right. So, back office next?'

'Yes.'

'What is the back office, exactly? Excuse me, what is it you do here?'

'What do I do?' asked a settlements clerk.

'Yes. What does the back office do?'

'It's where we settle the trades.'

'Mie!' I took her by the arm again. 'Save it. We can't be away from our desks too long. Not when phones need answering and tickets are being written.'

Mie walked, or had the appearance of walking, from below the knees only. She managed to glide and beetle along simultaneously, without bobbing. Seen across a bank of desks, when only the top half of her was visible, she gave the impression of riding a horizontal escalator, a moving stairway.

'How on earth does she do that?' reflected Curtis admiringly.

Mie was humourless but not unfriendly. She made me recognise that I used humour ingratiatingly, in order to gain approval and acceptance, and I was fearful that she would consider it a weakness. To my amazement, I discovered that men found this rather dour, resolute quality of Mie attractive. Yuuto seemed a little in awe of her, and Mr Johnson and his sidekick, David, supposedly to help her settle in, took to entertaining her in The George, a pub that was so noisy that its customers had to get close to hear each other speak above the din of City traders. Occasionally, I would join them and make up a four in which Mr Johnson would address us all animatedly, David would look doe-eyed at Mie with barely a word, and Mie would look gravely at each of us in turn before asking a question about the financial markets that Mr Johnson would answer at length.

I joined Mr Johnson at the bar in order to help him carry the drinks back to the table David and Mie had secured.

'So, how's she settling in?' he asked, having elbowed his way into an ordering position.

'I think she's doing very well,' I replied.

'Does she have many friends?'

'Outside of work? I don't think so. She's been too busy looking for an apartment. The company one was only for three months. Anyway, she's found one.'

'Oh good. Say, do you think you could take her out with your friends? Just a couple of times?' He looked apologetically at me and then down at his feet. 'You know.'

'Of course! In fact, I'd already decided to. And we have a date.'

Mr Johnson looked up at once. 'Oh, great! Thank you!'

Mie

At home, at school and at university, I had been content, pleased to have met people's expectations despite, I had to admit to myself, my early assertion that I was to be the only measure of my qualities and achievements. In London I was happy. I learnt bus routes and delighted in the freedom bus passengers had to hop on and off their open platforms. I discovered the city on foot, and the better I grew to know London's streets the better I felt I came to know myself. I moved to a long-term rental, still in Clapham, and learnt some of the complexities of financial markets as I explored an industry that became less opaque to me by the day. For the first time, I paid my bills, I decided what I ate and where, I chose how to spend my leisure time.

On weekends, I explored London's parks, museums, suburbs and cinemas. On one or two weekday evenings a week, Sharon and other fixed income teams' assistants and I would huddle around a bottle of white wine in one of the City's wine bars. Less frequently, Adam and David would have me sip bitter in one of the City's many pubs. I wrestled with the concept of what constituted me – was I Japanese? Was that relevant to life in a cosmopolitan city? In London, I felt like a citizen of the world, a hard-working professional who reaped the benefit, the investment of her hard work and her vision and who aspired patiently to a thing as yet undefined. Where telephone wires had once been my fantasist's way out to the world, the Northern Line and the rest of London's tube system came to form the web I travelled. I lived with the smell of brake dust; it accompanied me to and from work and, on weekends, home as I took the tube back with heavily laden shopping bags from Tooting's markets. While Clapham was vibrant, relatively young and trendy, Tooting was a world away. With virtually every step from Clapham South, through Balham to Tooting and, on a good day, on to Tooting Bec, faces grew darker, the shops more full of exotic produce and the prices lower. Indians, Bangladeshis, Pakistanis, Sri Lankans, Africans, Afro-Caribbeans in coloured dress smiled, bartered, bought and sold. Occasionally, I would see Far East Asians – Chinese, Malay – but no

Japanese who, I was told, congregated in North London. South Koreans, I learned, were colonising New Malden to the west. How different to the City at the other end of my Northern Line journeys, where white-skinned, besuited Englishmen with umbrellas and newspapers tucked under their arms conformed to Taka's stereotype! Admittedly, there were Europeans and Americans there too, but they, to my uncultivated eye, were not easy to distinguish.

For a while, Yuuto Kawaguchi became the most important person in my life. He, I realised, was a bully whose bark was worse than his bite and whose skill lay in knowing his clients and telling them what they wanted to hear. I listened attentively as he took the good news out of the latest economic report for the market 'bull' and the bad news for the market 'bear', as he discussed one client's children with him and, with another, the client's girlfriends and his nights out and, with some, kept the conversation purely formal and focused on markets and economic developments. *Know your clients*, commanded the compliance manual, but Yuuto knew them better than any compliance officer could have envisioned. 'Everyone is unique and everyone is the same,' he told me on one occasion. 'Everyone wants to be loved and admired and everyone wants to write a ticket; you just have to find their hot button.' I wondered whether that were true of me and what my hot button was, and bridled at the thought of Yuuto presuming to ask himself and answer that question of me.

Yuuto seemed to measure my performance by whether or not I succeeded in keeping his clients on the phone and in gleaning information about their trading intentions while he assessed whether or not to end the call he was on. If a client was calling to boast of his hangover and just wanted to chat, I'd open and close my hand repeatedly and Yuuto would draw his finger across his throat in instruction to kill the call, or would twirl his index finger in the air meaning that he would call him back. If the client wanted to deal, I would repeat his intentions loudly enough for Yuuto to hear while assuring the client that Yuuto was coming.

I wasn't authorised to deal but, if the trade were either large or beneficial in helping the bank get out of a position, I would call the trader on the squawk box and set the trade up for Yuuto. If Yuuto failed to get off the phone in time, so that either the client went elsewhere or the price had moved against him or the bank, Yuuto would scream at me in, fortunately, Japanese. How different to Mr Omochi's tantrums that would fill Yumimoto's library-like offices! Here, Yuuto was just one more salesman or trader shouting and no one batted an eyelid. Everyone, even Yuuto himself, knew that the display was to prevent his loss of face and that my role was that of the sacrificial calf, and he performed these admonitions with gusto, waving his telephone handsets above his head and mine with passion.

'What was all that about?' Sharon asked me, turning her chair to look at me after a particularly long rant by Yuuto that had only stopped when his phone had rung. 'What was he repeating his name for?'

I swivelled around in my chair to face her. 'He was reminding me that Yuuto means 'superior' in Japanese and that it's also the name of a constellation and that I must follow his star. Generally, he was reminding me that I am his slave and he is the master, that kind of thing.' I had my hand across my mouth in the hope of keeping my voice down, and I gave a shrug as if to say, *It's no big deal*, but Jonathan overheard me and burst out laughing.

Jonathan was taller than Mr Omochi and nearly as large. He resembled Oliver Hardy when he laughed, when he played with his tie and picked his fingernails in echo of Hardy's forever bringing his fingertips together in supplication. 'Priceless! And what does Kawaguchi mean? Big head?'

'Oh, no.' I was keen to dispel any such misapprehension. '*Kawa* means river and *guchi* means mouth so –'

'Big mouth! Kawaguchi means big mouth!' Jonathan stood and announced this to the thirty or so people within hearing.

No one cared except for Yuuto who, squaring up to Jonathan across the aisle and behaving as though he had temporarily forgotten the difference in their weight and height, shouted, '*Kuso kurae, debu!*' But he saved the worst for me, accusing me of being a traitor, reminding me that we, the Japanese team, had to stick together, asking me whether my father butchered people as well as animals and, slipping into English, requesting I either eat less sushi or shower more frequently.

'Steady on!' said Jonathan, who had sat back down and had the telephone wires from his two handsets trailing over his shoulders and his braces. He looked up at Yuuto, who still stood, spent but satisfied. Jonathan suddenly leaned towards him, conspiratorially. 'Tell you what,' he said, seemingly appeasingly. 'Do you have any naked pictures of your wife?'

Yuuto recoiled. 'No!'

'Do you want to buy some?'

'*Saitei!*' Yuuto stepped forward quickly and plucked Jonathan's trouser braces so they snapped back hard on his chest, and was halfway to the trading room door before Jonathan had moved.

'Ouch! That hurt my nipples! I'll get you back for that!' was said half-heartedly, the delight at having provoked so much anger outweighing the sharp sting of pain. He sat forward to examine his screens, absent-mindedly massaging his chest.

Sharon and I looked at each other and confined our laughs to our eyes. 'Have one,' she offered, and handed me a plate of biscuits she had made.

Sharon

I saw my family increasingly less frequently in what was a gentle separation of ways rather than a falling out. Work took over from family, friends and colleagues from parents and siblings. Wanda celebrated this – my forging, as she called it, of an adult life: she considered it confirmation that I had grown up, that I had found myself and created an identity of my own. It didn't feel that way to me; it felt more that the strings that had held me in place were being cut before new ones could finish being tied.

Mie's arrival on the scene shook things up for me. Her complete freedom and autonomy showed me the life I could be leading. Instead, I lived the independent life through her as I accompanied her to department stores and helped her furnish her apartment, but not altogether satisfactorily: she and I had different tastes and I often wondered why my recommendations, which were good enough for my other friends and family, weren't good enough for her. I found her conservative and old fashioned, not chintzy but austere: her finished furnished apartment seemed anything but to me. She made me feel frivolous.

My college friends welcomed Mie unquestioningly into our little group. She had an earnestness that they found amusing at times and perplexing at others. Over a drink or dinner Mie would quiz us on English authors we had more often than not never heard of or, if we were lucky, had encountered only because of a set text in our English O level curriculum. She'd ask about art-house films we might have caught on a rainy Saturday afternoon on BBC2, or about music and bands that we only knew from our parents' record collections. She would take guidebooks from the shabby handbag she insisted on keeping and ask our advice on whether to visit Bath or Cambridge on a coming bank holiday weekend. It wasn't that she showed us to be ignorant – more that she made us see how much everything we knew was contemporary, mainstream or local. Whenever we did happen to have a recommendation, she would write it down studiously, which had the effect of discouraging further contributions in case they turned out to be wrong in some way, or not as good as we'd thought. Without her meaning to, I was sure, she had the effect of making me feel less secure, as though the level of *me*ness that had been slowly filling up the form that was me had reversed its rise and was slowly declining as a consequence of my incomplete knowledge. Departing from us after the restaurant or pub, declining our appeals and invitations to join us in the nightclubs and scuttling off to the nearest tube, her back turned on fun and the opposite sex, she would leave me with a sense of inadequacy, of social and intellectual deficiency.

'You should try a Japanese restaurant. We could go one evening,' said Mie casually as she, Gavina, Monica and I were settling a restaurant bill. 'Next time.'

'Are there any in London?' asked Monica.

'There's one in Swiss Cottage,' said Mie.

'Swiss Cottage? But that's North London!' Gavina reminded me of Dad in her fixation on the South and North London divide.

On the rare occasion of our forays north of the river, Dad used to say, as we climbed into the family car, 'Right. Have we got our passports? I've checked the oil, the tyres and the petrol. Seamus, are the blankets and spade in the boot?'

Despite myself and in spite of Monica's and Sarah's liking North London for its cool music clubs and markets, some of Dad's prejudice must have rubbed off on me, as I heard myself saying, 'Surely, there must be a closer one.'

'I must warn you, it is expensive,' said Mie.

Monica expressed the most enthusiasm. 'What a great idea!'

A month later, the four of us sat down to a distinctly unfamiliar menu in a restaurant that appeared both functional and formal and yet warm and welcoming.

'How nice to be able to clean your hands on this fresh little towel after the tube ride,' I said, placing it on a wooden tray held by a waitress in a kimono.

'I might need some help here,' said Monica, staring wide-eyed at the Japanese menu.

'You can ask me anything you like,' said Mie, 'even though every-thing has been translated into English.'

A Japanese waiter bowed and stood to attention by our table.

Gavina closed her menu and said, 'I'll have a lasagne.'

The startled waiter repeated the word. 'Lasagne? We don't have lasagne.'

'Very well then, I'll have spaghetti bolognese.'

The bewildered waiter looked around for help.

Monica and I couldn't help but laugh and then I said, 'Come on, Gavina, make it easy for him.'

Gavina waved her menu about. 'I don't understand a word of this!' She opened it. 'Okay, what's this? I'll have this.'

The perspiring waiter leant over to read the item Gavina was point-ing at. 'The sashimi?'

'Yes. What is it exactly?'

The appeased waiter straightened. 'It's little pieces of fish, madam, raw fish.'

'Raw fish! I want mine cooked.' Gavina handed the menu to him.

'Cooked? Cooked!' The now extremely disconcerted waiter hopped from one foot to the other, refusing the proffered menu. 'Per-haps madam can choose another dish?'

Gavina huffed and puffed and rolled her eyes. 'All right,' she said. 'What's this?' – pointing at another menu item.

'Yakitori?'

'Yes, yakitori. What is it?'

'It's chicken on a stick with soy sauce, madam.'

'Is the chicken cooked?'

'Oh, yes, madam, very cooked!'

'Good! I'll have some cooked chicken on a stick,' decided Gavina, thrusting the menu at the relieved waiter.

That evening and the few subsequent ones when the five of us met were never quite the same after that. Mie, who had remained impassive throughout the exchange, had clearly taken offence, and despite Gavina's best efforts to make up for her interventions, what little warmth there had been between them cooled. Certainly, their relationship wasn't helped by the accounts of our adventures that percolated from Monica's lips over coffee at the end of our restaurant meals, during which she would have consumed a bottle of wine or two in addition to the Babychams and Cinzanos she'd knocked back in the pub. Monica had found herself a boyfriend and succeeded in airbrushing herself from our history of sexual conquest as she told stories in which Gavina was depicted as a floozy, single-mindedly in pursuit of men, and I not much better. I saw Gavina and myself through Mie's disapproving eyes, to my double discomfort: not only discomfited for being considered loose by her, I was unhappy with my ongoing inability to anchor myself in a value system of my own.

Isabella

After four years, Frederica and I had made more money than we knew what to do with. We hoarded it in shoe boxes, beneath floor boards and had even opened more than one bank account each to appease Frederica's concern about our attracting the attention of the Inland Revenue. We lived well and well within our means, unable to forget our care home parsimony and unwilling to forego the flush of unearthing a good deal in an antique shop and the camaraderie of lazy afternoons in North London's charity shops. Competing with our customers' wives and girlfriends in West End stores for overpriced luxury items held no attraction for us. We furnished our apartment with, we liked to think, choice pieces of glassware, porcelain and ceramics, all the sweeter for having been bought cheaply, and framed posters of films and art exhibitions. I longed to trace Mama's pictures and belongings, and passed that burdensome task on to Cosmo in a letter, suggesting that it would be easier for him to undertake the necessary detective work as he remained in Oxford. Besides, he was becoming an artist and I assumed he would be interested to learn about his mother's tastes and preferences in art and artists. Frederica believed that I was looking to replicate my mother's parlour; I suggested that she wished to recreate her father's study. She accused me of modernism, of being avant-garde, of eclecticism, all of which I was secretly rather proud, and I her of being Victorian, chintzy and old fashioned; we met at Art Deco and Art Nouveau. Our large living space was eventually finished with a mix of ill-assorted, heterogeneous furnishings that we had both liked or, at least, compromised on, and came itself to resemble a second-hand shop, while our bedrooms became the repositories for the things we had failed to reach agreement on and that I considered the purest expressions of our intrinsic selves. On our return from one of Camden, Notting Hill and Petticoat Lane markets, having spun around our extensive living space and debated where to place our latest acquisition, we would sit cross-legged over tea and biscuits and ill-assorted china cups and saucers and revisit one of Frederica's favourite topics of conversation.

'Do you still think that our clothes and our accessories, that our homes express who we are?' she would begin grandiosely. 'That we chose them, and not them us?'

'Aha! That is a very interesting question.' I would buy time, for our positions on this were not the same from one debate to the next.

'What are we if not material selves? And what is a material self if not the sum of its possessions?' Frederica would speak ironically, self-importantly, humorously and yet, I understood, sought my validation and approval.

I knew what she meant. The *objets trouvés* on the low tables, the sofas, benches and armchairs covered with throws and cushions, spoke of a shared aesthetic and language. The light from the virtually floor-to-ceiling window playing with the coloured, glowing glass on the wide window sill, the vases and jugs of dried flowers, the bric-a-brac and the knick-knacks, were evocative of a time and a place and of companionship, all together the summation of two selves, two lives to date, imparting comfort and familiarity. I loved our apartment. I loved it most when the rain fell, a sound like a wire brush on a snare drum washing over our south-facing window, the dome of St Paul's Cathedral visible in relief only as though seen through a butterfly cage mesh, occasional helicopters and planes on their descent to distant Heathrow remote, silent insects.

'We're not like the punters, are we? With their big, heavy watches and their long, thin, patterned ties –'

'And their fancy cufflinks.'

'– and their fancy cufflinks, who do they think they are?'

'And those huge phones.'

'Yes, and those bricks with aerials. They look at themselves and think – I don't know – that they're cool, sophisticated, attractive. But I look at them and think they're saps, fools.'

'They try to create an image, a particular image out of their accessories –'

'– while we have our possessions reflect who we are.'

'They base their choices, their likes and dislikes on the approval of others –'

'– while we know who we are and what we like.'

'Something like that.'

We looked around our room, at our possessions.

'Who are we, then?' I asked Frederica. 'Who do the punters see when we bring them home?'

'The punters see our arses and follow them to the bedroom and then, after, when it's all over, they just want to get out as quick as they can. They don't see anything!'

Frederica and I rarely discussed the men we brought home. We had a different approach to it, and despite our friendship, the topic was the one subject we did not broach directly but, on good days, did risk skirting around. I suspected that Frederica considered sex a commodity and was concerned that she was not as discerning as she should be for her own safety and mine about who she brought home, or whose hotel room she visited. I imagined her recumbent with one eye on her mental bank balance and the other on her wristwatch. The men I crossed in the sitting room or on the stairs to our apartment were rarely ones I would have chosen to spend any time with. On one occasion she had breakfasted with me with a black eye. On another I had heard her scream and had gone running to her room to find a man hurriedly pulling his trousers up and Frederica crying and holding a bleeding breast in one hand and the wads of notes he had thrust at her with the other. I had dabbed her breast and nipple as tenderly as I could with TCP-soaked wads of cotton wool and registered not only the weight of her breast but that, despite her pain and the risk of permanent scarring – highlighted by the antiseptic's yellow stain on the indentations made by the man's teeth – she was gauging whether the excessive amount of money he had left her had made it all worth it.

For me, the money was the least of it.

Sharon

Three years after Sebastian had left London for Tokyo, he returned.

The news trickled down the trading floor, from the derivatives desk, through to the traders and, last, to the sales team. On a day like any other he was just there, at the formerly empty desk next to his old one, and I was walking hesitantly up the central aisle in his direction, trading slips for him to sign in hand.

I stood by his desk perhaps a little closer than I did to other traders' desks and asked how he was. My concern for him was genuine: I really did hope he was well.

He said that he was indeed well and asked after me in a way that, too, I felt, was sincere and affectionate. When he raised his eyes to mine they were bluer than I recalled them, shockingly so, and sparked an ache of desire that knotted my stomach. I longed to run my fingers through his hair and to snatch the pen from his hands.

He told me that he'd had a wonderful time in Japan, wonderful.

I told him of changes in personnel.

He told me about his job in Tokyo, his daily commute and the holidays he'd been on.

Our conversation was like an amateur tennis game of arcing, slow shots, let calls and double bounces.

I left him with a 'Welcome back.'

He said he'd see me around.

I walked to the back office and back to my desk, my knees weak and my stomach hollow.

'Who's that you were talking to?' asked Mie.

I told her. 'He's just come back from our office in Japan. I should introduce you.'

'No,' said Mie quite seriously. 'That doesn't follow at all. And, anyway, I'm quite capable of introducing myself.'

Monday came and went without my going to see Sebastian after work. The rest of the week passed with no hint that he had expected me to visit, no suggestion that he was unhappy I hadn't. I assumed he had been relieved that I had stayed away rather than disappointed and too proud to say so. For all I knew, he was in a relationship. Maybe he was no longer living at the same address. Perhaps he felt that a renewed Monday after–work visit from me would have been a backward step.

Mie

To the outside observer, we 300 or more people in the dealing room must have resembled battery farm chickens, and yet I was never more certain of being uniquely me. My sense of self consumed me; it fed on itself and expanded within me, like the air in a balloon fitting the balloon's shape exactly. Admittedly, I was a Japanese woman in an almost exclusively male and Caucasian environment but, perhaps augmented by this singularity, my sense of self made me giddy.

Knowing that a life will be shaped by the incidences one highlights and places emphasis on, leaving others to sink from the memory's surface, I recalled every step that had got me to this point. It was odd to think that if I were the sum of those memory–building blocks I chose not to discard, among those rejected, abandoned memories – of experiences, thoughts, events witnessed – lay other, potential selves. Intellectually, I saw this; physiologically, I failed to.

One other person in the trading room stood out for me, in the sense that he too, I felt, possessed elements of the qualities I had previously considered exclusively mine.

I stood and watched Sharon weave her way to the derivatives desk and to Sebastian, who sat in front of his bank of screens, immobile in the tumult, the calm in the eye of a storm. My heartbeat quickened when I saw him, even though from a distance. Where others gesticulated, spoke or shouted, walked or ran, slumped forward or leant back in their desk chairs, he sat straight with his forearms on his desk's edge and his hands clasped above his keyboard in a posture that communicated a state of relaxed attentiveness. It wasn't his looks that alerted me to him but his poise, his aspect of self-assurance, of containment, of ironic detachment, his knowing quality that he was of the fray and yet somehow above it. He appeared neither proud nor smug but sure of himself, certain of his own existence, while willing to entertain that everything else around him was illusion.

For the first time in my life, I envied someone their self-possession.

I looked around a Soho cinema foyer decorated with black and white film posters on one wall and colour film posters on another, and thought of David and of Sebastian.

'Do you know Sebastian?' I asked David when he returned from the bar with a gin and tonic and a half of lager.

'The film starts in ten minutes,' he said, lifting his glass by way of explanation for the half. 'No,' he added simply.

It was David who had first proposed a film, and we had gone to the cinema about once a month after that. The one we were about to see had been my suggestion and David had only reluctantly accepted because, I guessed, my previous choice, about a girl and boy who get lost in the Australian outback, had shaken him. I had considered David demure rather than shy, private rather than quiet, but I was beginning to realise that his timidity – his seeming introversion – was something else altogether.

I entered the film, which stars James Fox, Mick Jagger and Anita Pallenberg in a blurring of identities, ideologies and genders, like a hand does a glove. David and I sat in the dark where, next to my elation, I couldn't help but feel him seeping unhappiness, as though the film were challenging him to his core. When Fox's character said, 'I know who I am. I am a bullet,' I reached for David's hand and he grasped mine for different reasons, neither of them romantic or sentimental. When the naked Pallenberg sat astride the naked, lipstick- and wig-wearing Fox and held the yellow-bordered hand mirror to one breast so that we saw hers reflected in place of his, I felt the thrill of Fox's identity crisis that David's shudder, transmitted through his tightening grip, told me was his as well. We were, then, no longer a couple holding hands in a cinema, but life's navigators, with me reaching overboard to hold the hand of a drowning man.

As the credits rolled and the cinema emptied, David and I sat still. He needed to compose himself and I needed to decide whether it was sympathy or contempt that I felt for him. We walked in silence to the tube and I pictured our black-lined silhouettes as children's cut-outs from a folded piece of paper of two people joined at the fist, with my sense of certainty of purpose overflowing into the hollow man by my side at that juncture.

Isabella

It was Sharon who inadvertently had me question myself most profoundly. She was an ingénue, a guileless, pretty young girl with striking green eyes, naïve but not innocent, curious but not nosy, inquisitive but not prying; she was giving, loving and fun-loving. Pierre and Jemma had abandoned the appointment of a mentor for new girls, whether distracted by a more challenging economic climate and increased competition or by their deteriorating relationship, but Frederica and I had taken to Sharon and assumed the now formally neglected role, enjoying her candour and pleased to mother her. This, however, did not please her aunt, who I suspected of scheming to supplant Jemma in Pierre's affections and business. Wanda pulled me to one side one evening and lectured me, warning me that I'd be out on my ear if I led Sharon astray. Dumbfounded, I had been momentarily unable to reply but, having regained my voice, chose not to use it, not to inform Wanda of her niece's proclivities, as they would have provided no real defence of my own conduct and, besides, I liked Sharon. She appeared to carry no emotional baggage, unlike me, her aunt and most young people I had grown up around, and interested me for that reason. She had an attitude to sex I considered healthy, treating no liaison as illicit, greeting all mention of even the most fleeting and superficial of sexual encounters with a tender complicity, with raised shoulders, a grin and a twinkle in the eye that brought to my mind my guilt-free and pleasure-rich dips into Mama's bowls of sweets.

I would leave the club with men I was happy to spend time and to breakfast with, men I fancied or who amused me. On the occasions when I returned home alone, I would stop to breakfast at Smithfield Market and would choose, as I wandered in the thicket of hanging sides of meat, through the forest of carcasses hung from Achilles' tendons and aitch bones, along the rows and columns of skinned, amputated and stamped bodies of quadrupeds, one among the bipeds – the bummarees, the cutters and the traders – one whose banter made me laugh and whose apron was not too bloody and who was neither so drunk nor so exhausted as to fall asleep on me. I took my recompense, when it was offered, however it was offered, whether in pounds of pence or of beef, pork or lamb, whatever the cut or its derivative. My reward lay not in financial gain but in the bodiless flight that came with sexual climax and, as I climbed the stairs to Frederica's and my apartment with a man behind me, I looked forward to the disengagement I knew would come. At times, Frederica, either alone or with a punter, having jumped at the chance of negotiating a supplement, would join us on the sofas, carpets and armchairs in naked, hedonistic indulgence in a cubist still life of limbs, elbows and pubic triangles, rendered all the more lusciously exciting in bringing both the voyeur and the bisexual out in us all.

When I had started working at the club, and seeing Dr Dearman's and Dr Faben's expressions on other men's faces, I had come to feel sullied and soiled; but then I had decided to embrace my sexual appetite, to accept what had happened to me and be positive in affirming who I was. I would be active as opposed to reactive or passive, I would make decisions and regain my power while acknowledging the paradox that I was using my body precisely to escape it. In part to obliterate certain memories and in part to gain vicarious revenge, I approached sex with gusto – aggressively, animalistically, insatiably, occasionally scaring men who expected women to be submissive and pliant with no sexual appetite of their own. I was called a lunatic, a nymphomaniac and a freak by men whom I labelled closet necrophiliacs, men who wished for no signs of life from their sexual partners and who might have been better satisfied by the meat market's corpses. I was called wonderful, astonishing and fantastic by men I considered self-knowing, -confident and normal, who I believed sought a sexual encounter between equals and satisfaction between consenting adults. With such men, who betrayed no panic and no concern about the give and take, the push and shove, the equitable, unselfish exchange of small pleasures and of physical contentment, I could go into my head and cut myself off, allowing my body to respond to caresses and penetrations, to fingers, lips and tongues. I felt caught in a circle that, vicious in its conception, was virtuous in its completion. Unwilling to be consciously present while having sex, I wasn't.

I disappeared into my head and, from there, flew elsewhere. Consciously needing the drug of mental release, addicted to my mind and body split, I required sex frequently in order to attain it, to be the free, independent woman I wanted to be. The sexual partners with whom I achieved this responded with pride and no small degree of arrogance that I found endearing when they weren't too demanding. Limp, drained and deflated and yet cocky, content and flattered, they would beg to see me again, and continued to press telephone numbers or money on me as I left their hotel rooms or showed them to my door. I didn't want to know so much as their names.

Sharon

One Friday evening there was a commotion in the club that made its way into the girls' changing room. Honey and Angelica tumbled in, holding onto each other in fits of nervous giggles, and announced the arrival of three Japanese men in the club. We all knew what that meant.

A story had been doing the rounds that a Japanese man had been frequenting the clubs and had been extremely liberal with his money, to the point that the girls had been very willing to indulge him in the most bizarre of fantastical requests. While our club had only semi-private, open booths at the other end of the room from the stages and poles, other clubs had cubicles that afforded complete privacy. One of this mythical Japanese man's less grotesque requests was to ask a girl to scream, a request that would be met with little protest, given the very loud music typically played in the clubs and the money he would throw at her for every shriek that was louder than the one before. Girls would spill out of the booths, hoarse and breathless and giddy with fistfuls of notes while their colleagues would look on jealously. Or the Japanese man would step out of a cubicle first, leaving the exhausted girl on the floor gathering the paper money he had thrown at her. And then there'd been one evening when the lucky girl he had chosen had screamed louder and for longer than other girls at other times and he had stepped out first, bowed, gathered his coat and left. After a time, another girl had wondered what was keeping her colleague so long and had gone to look for her in the booth, only to find her body on the floor and her head in an ice bucket. At every iteration of this story another detail emerged. It hadn't happened once but twice, once in Tokyo and once in London. It had happened not twice but three times – in Bangkok too. It was rumoured that one dead girl's eyeballs had been gouged from her head. Another had had her cheeks bitten off. Yet another, her nipples bitten off.

And so, believing in safety in numbers, pleased with the distraction from a familiar routine performed to a succession of interchangeable customers, we tottered in our high heels and our two-piece swimsuits out of our changing room and onto the dance floor to catch a glimpse of the ogre.

That was when I saw Yuuto, and he saw me.

On noticing me, one amid half a dozen near-naked girls, Yuuto jumped, legs straight as though pulled by a stage wire from his back, black polished brogues clearing the shag carpet and one hand brought to meet the other to better grip the glass he was about to drop. His mouth and eyes formed three perfect Os and opened wider as he looked from my face to my breasts, my waist and my legs and back again. Within a matter of seconds, though, he had regained his usual, nonchalant, sardonic poise, patted his hair down and looked around for a place to sit next to two men I assumed to be his clients. We exchanged neither a word nor another look and I danced at the end of the cavernous room far from him for the rest of the evening, nonchalantly, distractedly and poorly.

I anticipated Monday morning with some apprehension, but I needn't have: Yuuto gave me not so much as a wink. I would never have expected such a level of discretion from him. It made me think how little we can know others and wonder for what reason I had ever thought that we could.

Mie

I was impressed with the fact that Sharon had landed her job after having left school at 16. It was as clear to me that her team loved her as it was that she needed to be loved and, because her need was met, she was always happy, and happy to please. No matter how different she was from me – unintellectual, superficial insofar as she was always concerned to make a good impression and to be liked – I couldn't help but like her. There was something amusing about being taken under the wing of this young girl who had stopped her formal education so much earlier than I had and, after she had shown me the West End's bright lights and included me in her group of friends, I recognised in her a complete absence of artifice, a true generosity of spirit. There was one thing about her that surprised me: she had absolutely no interest in the job itself or, to be precise, in the nature of the financial markets we operated in. I had learnt that the bonds we bought and sold were IOUs, the values of which depended on inflation expectations, central bank rates, economic growth and the credit quality of the borrower. I grasped the nature of bonds' derivatives – futures and options, especially the latter, as Yuuto had a client who traded in those practically daily – and sought to understand why a client would choose a derivative instead of the underlying instrument, why the client would choose to buy a *call* option on a bond instead of buying the bond or a *put* option on it instead of selling it.

Sharon, however, did not care, and yet she executed her duties to perfection. Where I bothered Yuuto by asking him about a client's reason for a trade, she completed and processed her UK team's trading slips faultlessly without having the slightest idea what she was doing and why, and without ever enquiring after the investor's motivation. She had a system, she followed it and any extraneous information risked only impeding her. I sensed she was at her happiest as she sashayed up and down the trading aisles, dodging chairs, waving arms and telephones, and replying sweetly to the frequently sexist endearments she received. *Hello, darling. Hello, love. Got any biscuits? What are you doing this weekend? You're young enough to be my daughter.* The more pairs of eyes she had on her, the happier she was, and yet there was nothing cheap about her; she moved elegantly and dressed well. Next to her, I looked like a frump.

'A frump? But that's only because you want to!' she laughed. 'When you're ready for a change of image, just say.' She replaced a blouse on a hanging rail of the clothes shop we were browsing in one lunchtime.

I looked at its price and then considered the clothes she was wearing more critically. 'Sharon, come to think of it, how can you afford to wear some of the beautiful clothes you have? On our salary? I mean, it can't just be clever shopping. I don't mean to pry,' I added.

She led me out of the shop. 'I'll tell you,' she said, and she did. 'Only Yuuto knows. And he's been very discreet. Though I don't know if it's out of courtesy to me or to protect himself – because, you know, he'd have to say he'd been there. Catching flies?' She chucked me under the chin and I closed my mouth. 'Come on, it's not that bad. No touching allowed. All in the best possible taste!' Laughing, she pulled me by the arm. 'Come on!'

Sharon seemed unaware of her own indiscretion in having told me that Yuuto visited strip clubs. The fact that he did confounded me little compared with my astonishment that, not only did she work in one, but could disclose it with such facility. I had little time to dwell on either, because we returned to the office to find our end of the trading room in a state of excitement: unusually, Robert, our head of bond sales and trading, Yuuto, Jonathan and the rest of the sterling bond sales team, Adam and David were sitting or standing around a meeting room table on which were laid an assortment of sandwich trays, crisps and fruits, canned soft drinks and glasses and white porcelain plates and paper napkins. Adam, seeing us through the glass partition wall, raised his hand and beckoned us over. The air was close. With the exception of David's, ties were pulled down and top buttons and shirt sleeves undone. Adam exuded an air of satisfaction. For good reason: he and David had acquired the bank co-lead manager status for a sterling-denominated Japanese government bond issue. It was a singular honour, the accompanying excitement of which was immediately contagious. The deal would be announced as soon as the eurobond markets opened the following morning.

'Sharon, Mie,' Robert paused to finish chewing the triangle of sandwich he had put in his mouth whole, 'draw up a list of every sterling investor and of every Japanese investor we know. Divide each list in two: existing clients and prospects.' Swallowing, he said to the salesmen, 'They'll be gagging for this one and if we're going to let them have the paper, this'll have to be more than a one-off trade – we want the relationship. Kick the spivs and the flippers off the list. Yuuto, you're going to have your work cut out – our co-lead is bound to go after your clients hard; they're all they've got. We'll update you on pricing first thing tomorrow. Adam, David, anything more to add?'

Adam looked at David who was looking at Yuuto, much like actors looking at each other in a Michelangelo Antonioni film. David looked down at his shoes and shook his head. Adam said, 'No.'

David leaned against a low sideboard, an open sliding panel of which revealed more plates and glasses. In his posture, I saw a visual echo of Fubuki leaning nonchalantly against the washbasin in Yumimoto's hallowed ladies' loos but, where my attraction to her had been physical, mine to David was emotional. Of all the men in the room, David was the least remarkable. He didn't dress to impress. He was the least distinguishable and yet the most distinguished to my foreign eye. It wasn't lost on me that what was a great advantage and source of delight to me, namely, that in a foreign country people struggle to place you socially so that you can't help but meet them on equal terms, could prove a handicap as much as an advantage.

Jonathan clicked his fingers before my eyes. 'Are you with us, Mie?' I blushed.

As the meeting broke up, amid much clapping of backs and pumping of fists in anticipation of the successful distribution of Japan's new issue the following day, I looked from David to where he was looking: at Yuuto. Most quiet people, less looked at than looking, have a quality of observation that's profound, I had found; and, indeed, Yuuto appeared relatively subdued and his expressions of eagerness phony. Back at our desks, he accepted the list of investors I handed him without interest. In return, he handed me a slip of paper on which he had noted a derivatives trade enquiry.

Note in hand and heart beating faster, I walked briskly down two aisles of traders and salesmen, replying in kind to the salesmen's odd friendly, 'Hi, Mie,' and ignoring the traders' occasional fake-fawning, 'Me! Me! Me!' – stimulated, too, by the noisy room's heady atmosphere. The good news about the new mandate had percolated down a trading floor that hummed in anticipation of a glorious day. I stopped at the derivatives desk and, giddy with the sense of gaiety and levity that affected us all, as well as stirred by the prospect of some moments with Sebastian, sat in the empty chair beside him and handed him Yuuto's piece of paper.

Where salesmen had, typically, two or three screens and bond traders three or four, Sebastian, an options trader, had six, amassed in two stacks of three. There was an implied trading room hierarchy that placed derivatives traders at the top of the pile, which irritated some people but that Sebastian seemed impervious to. He kept his eyes fixed on one of the screens ahead of him for a moment, sat back in his swivel chair, turned his head to look at me and only then, after another moment, after I felt he'd considered me properly, did he look down at my outstretched hand and deliberately take the note from my fingers. He retained his air of ironic detachment, signalled by a perpetual half-smile, as if everything were a big joke that only he were in on and that, to my irritation, I couldn't help but feel I wanted in on too.

Sebastian unfolded and studied the piece of paper. 'What is it with this guy? Who does he think he is? What is it with his request for an offer on gilt puts in such size the day before the Japan deal? This industry is as leaky as a sieve. Gilts,' and he indicated a screen with a wave of his hand that showed predominantly red, blinking figures, 'are already weaker on the day, despite no "news".' He tapped his teeth with a biro and then sat up straight. 'It's clear. News of the Japan issue has leaked. He'll want to dump a ton of gilts on me to buy the issue. Sell UK, buy Japan. Why not? It's worked for cars and electronics.' He turned to his screens and keyboard and I studied his profile as he considered the many factors that would enter his calculations and, ultimately, the price he'd quote the client.

Sebastian had fair eyelashes that formed fine brushes either side of blue eyes beneath a shock of blond hair. The faint scent of his aftershave floated like a protective shield, a decoy from the sweeter, underlying fragrance of his body. I closed my eyes momentarily and inhaled deeply. The only sound I could hear was the mesmerising tap-tap-tapping of his fingers on the keyboard. It occurred to me with a rush that Sebastian could be the first person I had ever met to whom I might be prepared to subjugate myself and whose self I might be prepared to admit into mine. This new sentiment – my acceptance of it – intrigued me. I struggled with the possibility that I would have to deny my whole life philosophy in physical, biological response to someone foreign to me on so many levels. I had, somewhere in the back of my mind, allowed myself to believe that if – *if* – I were ever to have a relationship, it would be with an intellectual equal. I had never admitted of the possibility that the right combination of atoms at the most superficial olfactory or visual levels would have a contribution to make in my ultimate capitulation. I grabbed at what clues I could that my attraction to him was other than physical and, blushing as soon as the words escaped from me, indicated the books on his desk with a wave of my hand and asked, 'How come you're the only one here to keep novels on his desk instead of finance books?'

He looked from his screens to the books and back to the screens. 'Because I like reading.'

'But not finance books.'

'Markets are just people. Novels tell me more about people than finance books do.'

'So, what novel should an aspiring financier read?'

'Financier? It's traders and salespeople in here and investors and spivs out there.' He handed me back the piece of paper on which he had written indicative pricing.

I read what he had written. 'You've kept the price and the bid/offer spread unchanged from last week.'

He leant back in his swivel chair and turned to look at me. 'You've remembered and you've noticed. But you seem surprised – why?'

'Well,' I had to think about this. 'The market is up, so the first tells me you think our client might be a better seller than buyer and you don't really want to be hit with a ton of gilts.' I looked at him for confirmation but he said nothing. 'And the second suggests that you are, after all, I mean, despite all this serious literature' – and I waved the piece of paper in the direction of his books, my heart beating faster as I dared familiarity – 'a little macho.'

'Unreal!' He leant back further and laughed. 'See you later!'

I looked up and over at the trading room, at the rows of salespeople, traders and desk assistants and momentarily suffered the unexpected mirage of seeing Sebastian and myself replicated in a series of near endless contiguous mirrors. A faint pride and other emotions hummed above the trading room's hubbub.

Attraction that one dares consider reciprocated brings with it an increased degree of introspection. What did, could Sebastian see in me that I must preserve and nurture in order to maintain and grow his interest? I entered the underground at Moorgate in profound reverie and exited at Clapham South in the same intense, internally focused state of mind. I blinked in the evening light and apologised to a fellow commuter for having stopped dead in her path when I realised I could recall no detail of my journey. She glared at me; I was an obstruction to her. What was I to Sebastian? A sales assistant. A foreigner. At best, someone who played a small role in bringing him the information he sought in order to better manage his derivatives book and to service his bank's clients.

I ate lightly so as to be able to sleep and rise early; I wanted to be at the bank from the beginning of the distribution of Japan's sterling-denominated bond issue. My thoughts, as I fell asleep despite the sound of music and the buzz of televisions and of end-of-day chatter of families in back gardens, didn't trouble so much as entertain me; there was a novelty to them, as I, who had always been resolutely egocentric and for whom all points of reference had been mine to the extent that my background, culture and education allowed, found myself wondering how I appeared to Sebastian. I had no answer. I had the sensation of being the outline of a woman, thick, clearly delineated but opaque to herself.

On entering the trading room, I knew immediately that something was wrong. In place of the positive charge of anticipation was the negative aura of crisis. Heads were low, shoulders hunched and the ceiling oppressively close. The fixed income sales and trading teams and Adam and David had got in even earlier than usual and were clustered around Yuuto's empty desk. I immediately shared what I presumed to be my colleagues' irritation that Yuuto had chosen to celebrate what was to be his biggest, most important deal the night before rather than following its conclusion. A long day with a hungover Yuuto was not something anyone looked forward to.

'Yuuto has resigned.'

The shock was such that I sat down abruptly while my superiors all stood. I didn't even know who had spoken the words that I repeated mechanically to no one in particular. Today, of all days, no Yuuto was worse than a hungover one.

'It's straightforward,' said Adam. 'Jonathan, your team will have to do the heavy lifting among UK investors. David, we'll call the co-leads and increase their participation, which will mean cutting our own back. But so be it. Where has Yuuto gone? There's no way I'm rewarding a Japanese bank for poaching our entire, admittedly one-man, Japan bond sales team.'

'No,' I heard myself say. 'I'll place it. I know who to call and what order to call them in. I know what size they're good for and I know what they own that we can switch them out of if we need to. However, I'm not an authorised salesperson, so I'll need someone authorised to hand the phone to to confirm the sale. And someone from compliance or personnel to work on getting me authorised as quickly as possible. It may be a good idea to get someone from personnel down here anyway.' I put my handbag down and switched my computer screens on. I shrugged my jacket off and hung it over the back of my chair. 'What's the latest on pricing? Do we have a term sheet yet?'

For a moment, all was silence. Waves of anxiety, as I recalled my ill-fated intervention at the first and last meeting I had been asked to participate in at Yumimoto alternated with pulses of confidence as my screens came on and my investor databases slowly materialised; I knew I could do this.

'Here it is,' said David, stepping forward and placing the term sheet before me while exuding a strong sense of proprietorial pride, though whether in me or in the deal I could only guess.

'Go, girl!' said Adam, clapping his hands and then squeezing my shoulders.

'All right, everybody!' shouted Jonathan. 'Smile and dial! Sharon, get me personnel and compliance down here right now.'

The deal was placed in its entirety by midday. The co-lead banks and the UK team placed their share, as did I, call by call by call. By late morning, news of the deal was out on the wires and those of Yuuto's former clients I had yet to call were calling us, so that allocations to all but the best of clients had to be scaled back. In retrospect, Yuuto couldn't have chosen a better time to resign: the deal overshadowed his departure and his career at the bank was consigned to history. Unnoticed by me in the morning's mêlée, someone from personnel had quietly cleared Yuuto's desk so that at the day's end it shone bare, like a physical metaphor for the Japan deal that had so effectively been pillaged by our hungry clients.

I participated reluctantly in the champagne celebration that followed. I kept to myself the realisation that our Japanese clients would have bought the bonds at any price, out of a sense of patriotism that would have declared it a loss of face should any of Japan's bonds have remained unsold. The UK team had, in fact, had to work harder to place their part of the deal, as their clients' considerations had been purely economic and not patriotic. Telerate and Reuters announced the deal a success: Japan had raised all the money it had announced it would, and the bonds had only marginally outperformed gilts on the day, which suggested that the lead banks had got their pricing right and not made Japan's money-raising activity any more expensive than it need have been.

I spent the late afternoon completing trading slips and the paperwork necessary to secure my registration with the bank regulator. In one day, I had gone from desk assistant to bond salesperson and, in the space of a few months, I went from that to the bank's Japanese bond salesperson, attempts to recruit a formal replacement for Yuuto having petered out as my superiors came to recognise my competency and, I suspected, baulked at the price for someone experienced. I received a pay rise that I accepted, although I knew it to be less than what I was worth to the bank. 'In this business,' Adam Johnson had advised me, 'you're not paid what you're worth, you're paid what you negotiate,' but I didn't mind; I was in it for the long term.

Sharon

I had passed my professional secret from Yuuto to Mie and with her too, it would seem, my secret would stay safe – for a time, at least. I put this quality of consideration and reserve down to the natural good manners of the Japanese but wondered, as I contemplated myself without make-up in the mirror one morning, whether I had told her in order to have the secret spill out and so force a change in my life. I felt that I needed saving from – something, but I couldn't put my finger on what. I had renewed visions of self-mimicking holes in the ground and of elves and goblins that no longer hid in parks but disguised themselves as gargoyles and shop mannequins. To keep myself busy and my mind occupied, I worked longer hours in the bank, where I grew to love the security identifiers and the other long lists of numbers I wrote on trading slips, delighted by the order I would find behind their supposed randomness.

I was saved, distracted, initially, by Mie's immediate promotion. Her assured performance on the day on which she had so effectively risen to assume Yuuto's job was one that made all of us who liked and respected her admire her all the more. I embraced the additional position of interim Japan desk assistant happily, in order to support her, believing that the success of my ward reflected on her mentor, and I was delighted to accompany her on shopping trips once I had successfully persuaded her that she needed a wardrobe that would reflect her new status in the bank.

Mie followed me into the ladies' toilets, where she stood facing the wall mirror above a row of hand basins, and observed herself severely. It was the first time we had found ourselves alone together since she had become the bank's Japan salesperson. She held the hem of her grey, shapeless cardigan between her thumbs and forefingers, lifted it and let it drop before standing, palms out, arms and legs straight like a paper cut-out of a woman, and exclaiming, 'You're right. I can't see clients dressed like this.'

I nodded.

'I've put client meetings off as long as I can, but I have my first one next week. What are you doing on Saturday?'

'Going to the shops with you, at a guess.'

We stood side by side, my hand on Mie's shoulder, her arm around my waist, facing each other in the mirror. Black and blond. East and West. Tall and short. Chic and shabby. Mie would be my project, my walking, talking, living doll. I giggled with anticipation, with glee at the prospect of Mie's imminent metamorphosis and said, 'Just you wait. No one will recognise you. You will be a quite new person.'

'Oh no,' replied Mie seriously. 'Admittedly, I may look different. But I won't be. I'll still be me, but just wearing different clothes.'

'"The apparel proclaims the man,"' I said, still smiling.

'Are you sure?' asked Mie, turning from the mirror to look at me directly. 'I'd always considered it to be the other way around. How superficial a person must be for that to be the case.'

I began to see less of Mie outside of the office after what had been, for me, a joyous Saturday afternoon spent shopping, advising her and admiring her in a succession of smart trouser and skirt suits, blouses and shoes and, in department store changing rooms, in her underwear.

'What's the matter?' had scowled Mie in her knee-length socks, beige granny knickers and bra, more anxious and scared than angry, I had thought – uncertain of herself, perhaps because unused to being seen so nearly entirely bare. Behind her had stood my reflection, knees ever so slightly buckled, eyes wide and one hand over my mouth to mask a laugh, and the other clutching hangers and clothes.

What a contrast to Mie's old-fashioned underwear were the spangled bikinis, thongs and bodices that others and I wore at the club! I could hear Pierre's French accent in my ear, him breathing, 'She has a nice, well-proportioned body but her legs are – how do you say? – too bandy.'

'You're beautiful,' I had said.

Mie

Instinctively, I had known to upgrade my wardrobe. Sharon was delighted, and appointed herself as my personal shopping assistant and style adviser. What pleased me most was that, despite my change in title and my rising status in the bank, the nature of our relationship didn't change: she would hang from my arm – like the giggly school-girl neither Keiko, Michi nor I had ever been – as we tripped from shop to shop and added bag after bag to our fists of bags of shoes, blouses, skirts and jackets.

We were shopping for pencil skirt suits when a lady approached Sharon who, chin in hand and head to one side, was considering me critically as I stood before a full-length mirror in a knee-length skirt and matching jacket. The lady, impatient and waving me aside with one hand by means of apology, I presumed, while using the other to hold an article of clothing under Sharon's nose, reprimanded her with, 'I don't know why this store can't be more clearly marked and the departments better indicated. It's so frustrating. Anyway, can you please tell me where I can find more of these?' It was more of a command than a request.

Sharon, ever so helpful as usual, replied, 'Of course,' and walked two aisles of suits from where she had been standing. 'They're here.' She walked back to me and wrinkled her nose in amusement before contemplating me again. 'Oh, Mie, what makes it so difficult with you is that everything suits you!'

The lady was back. 'I don't want a blue jacket, I want a black one. Where are the black jackets?'

Sharon took a step back from the blue jacket that had been pushed uncomfortably close to her nose.

'A black jacket. Like this one, except black and not blue,' persisted the lady.

'I don't know,' said Sharon, looking at me with round eyes over the lady's fist. 'I could go and have a look if you want,' she added help-fully.

'You don't know!' exclaimed the by now extremely irate lady. 'You don't know! What's the point of working here if you don't know!' She harrumphed and stamped her foot.

'Oh, but I don't work here,' Sharon said, keen to rectify a misunderstanding.

The lady steamed. She raised her other fist, the one with her handbag in it, so that she shook both a handbag and a blue jacket under Sharon's nose, and raised her voice to shout. 'You don't work here? Well, why do you pretend that you do? If *I* wanted to impersonate someone, it certainly wouldn't be a *shop assistant*!'

'I was only trying to help,' said Sharon to the lady's departing back, as a confounded shop assistant picked the discarded blue jacket up from the floor. While I considered the scene amusing, Sharon didn't; her reaction betrayed her disappointment that she had been unable to help, and had caused offence instead. 'I didn't mean to upset her,' she said dismally.

I put my arm around her and gave her a squeeze. She gave off a smell of talcum powder and day-old perfume. 'Come on,' I said. 'Let me get out of this suit and buy us some dinner,' and I found myself holding her to me a little longer than I had intended to.

Sharon shook her head. 'I'm working this evening,' she said. 'It's a Saturday, remember?'

'Oh well,' I said, 'I might see if David is free.'

I continued to see David for cinema outings and for cheap, informal dinners during which, when we weren't arguing over films, I would quiz him on financial markets. I think he never gave up looking for a way in, as it were, but I kept my walls up, much as I clutched my handbag vertically on my knees. At the start of our friendship, he had been a willing teacher of the naïve girl from Tokyo and this had helped define him, at least in terms of his relationship with me; but as I learned more, I began to have my own opinions – on the eurozone, on the collapsed Japanese economic 'miracle', on monetary policies – so that he began to feel less useful to me. I told myself that I should hold back, keep my opinions to myself, but I struggled to do so. David accepted most of what I had to say and rarely argued a point. This was both pleasing and frustrating.

I found myself wanting David to want me to be more than a good friend, yet I was certain that I would reject his advances were he to make them overtly, and just that little bit less than certain that he was making them at all – surely, the occasional gifts of videos, the long sighs and the wistful looks constituted an approach of some kind, however timid? Was he too much of a gentleman to impose, or too afraid of rejection? Was he, to his mind, nobly rejecting the real–life role of Rex Harrison's Henry Higgins? I bridled at the thought. I felt, after so long at the bank, very much his equal and had come to realise that, while my career remained on an upward trajectory, his had stalled, as he had been looked over for promotion on a number of occasions. I felt sheepish harbouring these thoughts; when I had been a desk assistant, it had never once occurred to me that he was seeking to exploit any advantage that being a corporate banking executive had given him over me.

It was, then, doubly surprising to me when David asked me to marry him. His proposal came as the last throw of the dice of a desperate man, a despairing lunge at the handrail of a departing bus that risked leaving him behind, alone at one of life's windy, mid–route stations. I felt furious with him for having asked me with such forlorn defeatism, and for his generating in me the guilt that he was of course right to be less than optimistic. I was angry with him, too, for his poor sense of place and timing: a litter-strewn, draughty Camden bus stop at night after an Italian film that was based on a couple's separation and on the futility of any attempt at a man's and woman's shared existence, on our kind's essential solitude. Love, as in the love act, was portrayed violently, a power game, in which one seeks confirmation of one's own self in domination of the other's. I faced the discomfiting truth that, even if I had been going to reject him, I would have appreciated an extravagant dinner in a romantic restaurant and an offer on bended knee. I felt offended that a man too faint-hearted to so much as to try to steal a kiss from me could think I would concede to marry him. Unable to keep the incredulity from my voice, I said, 'What?'

David asked meekly, apologetically, 'Will you be my wife?' and fumbled unsuccessfully for my hand.

If I had been capable of marrying one of all the men I had

befriended up to that point in my life, it could have been David; my certainty and conviction of self would have more than made up for his weakness and deficiency of character. He would have made no demands of me and acquiesced to mine, I am sure. He would have accepted my stipulation that we maintain a perpetually platonic relationship, a forever unconsummated marriage. But, still, the thought of the conjoining of myself with another, even spiritually, sentimentally and intellectually, letting aside any physical coupling, filled me with revulsion.

Don't be ridiculous! I wanted to shout, but was saved from that tactless rejection by the arrival at the bus stop of two other couples and, soon after, the number 88 bus, the open–back platform of which we climbed laboriously, the weight of David's unanswered question hanging oppressively above us.

We took the winding, steep steps to the top of the bus and sat side by side behind a family that stretched across the bus's very front seats in parody of what the future could hold for us. The parents sat to the right of their children, who sat directly in front of us so that, looking straight ahead, David and I could see our reflections above theirs in the bus's wide windshield: a clear picture against the night sky. If this was David's vision of his years ahead, it wasn't mine.

I felt the pressure of having to deliver the response that David knew was coming and that I hated him for expecting, that he had known he would receive even as he asked the question.

Isabella

'Gaia.' Pierre beckons me, his eyes shifting left to right, along the dark and empty corridor, down and up, from my high-heeled shoes to my halter top, his cocked finger frozen in summons, his pupils black pricks in a backlit head, the silver halo of his hair interrupted symmetrically by two jugged ears, his mouth and nose grey scars on a wasteground, the whole a Rorschach inkblot the meaning of which is indubitably clear.

My immediate thought is that Wanda must be away.

The light from Pierre's office streams past and around him, finds me and pulls me in. I am back in Papa's study: the look in Pierre's eyes is the same as the look Papa had in his, the look of wanting something he shouldn't have, of having what he shouldn't want, of a man who has relegated shame and conscience to another time and place. The office is windowless and the couch in it stained. We both place our hands on my halter top; when he pulls up, I tug down. I clutch my breasts so that he can't.

'Don't be ridiculous!' pants Pierre. His exertion and anger in the artificial light lend him the illusion of having applied rouge. I can't help but see his point of view: when I sleep with so many, why not with him?

My point of view is clear to me: I am my own homunculus, I sit behind the bridge of my nose and look out of two clear blue windows the shades of which fall and rise as I blink. Pierre insults me, or tries to; what he says is mostly correct. My resistance infuriates him.

From my pilot's seat on the bridge, I manoeuvre towards an escape. I feel I am of my body but not my body, in it but not part of it; it is a craft to which I am essential but not it to me. I have to stand to better navigate and watch my feet below my lower eyelids' lashes. I am clumsy: Pierre protests I have hurt him and holds his hand to his lip. I need to get out of his office and to think. It occurs to me, on this the first occasion I have defended my body, that my body might be essential to me. I am desperate to think. I turn the office door handle.

Wanda contemplates Pierre and me. He and I run our hands

through our hair and pat it down at the same time, as though one were a mirror of the other. I smooth my halter top down. Pierre tugs at his shirt sleeves. Wanda's eyes are dead in the gloom of the corridor but I don't have to see them to know that I will have to find work elsewhere. Mrs Bobeckyj acted to save Gregor and Tomasz from me and, having deposed Jemma, Wanda will be ruthless in preserving Pierre for herself in much the same way. I look at Pierre who looks at Wanda who looks at me. We all know that we are what the other sees us to be.

I pull one lever and push another and turn, steady myself against the corridor wall and start to make my way up, driving forward and up, one mechanical step after the other, up.

Sharon

I saw less of Mie after our shopping trip. Increasingly, she spent lunch hours at her desk or in meetings and travelled and entertained clients over evenings and weekends. Months went by, long stretches of days in which our exchanges were limited to greetings, to business matters, to Japan desk assistant issues and to snatched conversations in the ladies' loos and sandwich bar queues. In the recess of my mind lay the thought that Mie had discarded me, having been promoted so significantly above me, but I refused to believe it of her. Instead, I acknowledged the realisation that, really, we had little in common and had only been artificially tied by our jobs. I rationalised that Mie had long ago settled into her new life and, of my roles as guide, mentor and friend, not even the last needed remain.

And then, quite out of the blue, she invited me to dinner.

Surprised, pleased, grateful, I accepted immediately.

'About tomorrow,' said Mie. We were getting ready to go home. It was just gone five o'clock on a Friday and already the trading room was nearly empty, many of the bankers having left early to beat the traffic on their way to weekend, country retreats. Mie was arranging her things in a new handbag she had bought independently of me. She clicked the clasp close before I had finished tidying my desk and stood, the bag clutched. She frequently gave the impression of looking at me above glasses because her head seemed permanently ever-so-slightly inclined, as though she were about to bow.

'Do you mind if David joins us?'

'Of course.'

'You do?'

'I mean, no! I don't mind. Of course, I don't mind.'

'I would particularly like him to see a Japanese film that will be on television. I thought that maybe, if you don't mind, the three of us could watch it after dinner.'

'I'd love to,' I said, even though I didn't share their interest in film.

Mie and David saw each other on weekends, I knew, but I didn't know how far he had succeeded in extending their friendship beyond the purely platonic. I anticipated some insight into a relationship that revolved, to the extent that I could tell, around cinema outings and inexpensive restaurants. There was a sense in which they suited each other very much. Externally, they gave the lie to the idea that only opposites attract. They were similar in that their comportment was considered and sober, as though it would take much to excite them, and, by City standards, their dress would be considered plain. Internally, though, to the extent that one can ever have an insight into what people are really like, they seemed quite different. Mie was the hot knife to David's butter. She had a steeliness, a self-confidence that contrasted with David's embarrassed self-effacement. It was to me as though David provided the overflow container for Mie's personality and, as such, was of some use to her.

Mie's apartment reminded me of Sebastian's just prior to his move to Japan, though, to be fair, while his had been simply bare, hers was austere, the apartment an objective representation of its owner's ordered mind. In the last of the day's natural light, we ate an Italian meal off lacquered trays on our laps, an antipasto, a pasta dish, some rice, some chicken and finely diced vegetables presented exquisitely and simultaneously in small bowls on the tray. David, in his evident pleasure in being in Mie's company, was more animated than I had seen him before. He told us all about the double bill, the past custom for cinemas to show two films consecutively and repeatedly so that cinemagoers could enter the cinema at any point in either film and watch the end of the first film, the entirety of the second and only then the beginning of the first, leaving, should they wish, at the point in the first film at which they had entered.

'But that's mad!' I cried. 'You might get to know that it was the butler who did it before you even got to know what it was that he'd done!'

'Yes, but it's also true to life in a way, don't you think?' asked David, who had said more in two minutes than I had heard him say in ten years. 'I mean, in life, sometimes, a person's motivation for an action is only revealed afterwards and, anyway, this way, you think more about the why and the how than the what and the who.'

While I thought David might have a point, he spoiled it by looking slyly out of the corner of his eye at Mie, as though to gauge the effect of his words on her. Mie chased some rice around her bowl expertly and said nothing.

'How come you remember so much about double bills?' I asked David. 'I only barely remember them. And then I think we only saw them on holiday in Wales.'

'David was teased as a child and would take refuge from his school-friends in cinemas, wouldn't you, David?' said Mie.

'They weren't my friends,' said David, deflated.

'That's why he grew to like films,' said Mie. 'He could cease being the victim and become the hero. Isn't that right, David?'

'Something like that,' said David with difficulty.

'He can be the dashing, romantic hero who goes down on bended knee and always gets the girl – isn't that right?'

David swallowed.

'Unless he doesn't,' added Mie nonchalantly.

David sat, emptied of his earlier enthusiasm, his wrists on his knees, his hands slack and his head bowed, his expression invisible to me.

'David proposed to me,' said Mie to me, seemingly by way of explanation. In the evening's fading light her features were as if dictated by a malevolent elf at a typewriter, the straight underscore of her unpainted lips, the acute and grave accents of her painted eyebrows, the faint circumflex formed by her nostrils.

I hadn't considered Mie to be capable of such cruelty. The slope of David's shoulders spoke of loss and hurt and humiliation. 'Tell us about the film you want us to see,' I said, desperate to give him some respite.

Mie considered David with an expression of regret so fleeting that I wasn't sure if I'd imagined it, in the dusk of the room. 'It's a black and white film,' was all she said. 'Let's have some fruit. Then we wash up. Before the film.' She stood and squeezed David's shoulder, moving her hand away only when he reached for it. She switched a corner lamp on, whose soft glow didn't subject David to the critical examination the overhead light would have done.

David and I helped Mie tidy the trays and wash the dishes in an activity that made me think of Sebastian and the sudden, improbable thought of Mie and Sebastian, together as an item, entered my mind for no other reason than they both had a compulsion to wash dishes as soon as they had been eaten from. I reflected on her professional relationship with him and wondered how I would feel if it grew into something a little more personal. The idea that she might have rejected David for Sebastian was fantastical, but it entertained me.

David and Mie sat on a sofa and I sat on a large floor cushion from where we watched two poor peasant women, a woman and her daughter-in-law who inhabited a spectacular, extensive reedy marshland, seduce errant peasant soldiers and survive by killing wandering wounded samurai and disposing of their bodies down a deep pit – a black, quite vertical hole in the ground so wide that it could only be cleared at a running leap – having stripped them of their extravagant body armour that they would then go on to sell. The film finished and Mie turned the volume down; we sat in the near dark watching the credits roll. While Mie praised its cinematography and David enthused over its percussive jazz soundtrack, I tried to free my mind from the images of the hole, the hole in the ground that represented life for the peasant women and death for the samurai, and of the violence and desperation of the sexual act that gave fleeting meaning to grey lives. Crazily, I suspected that Mie and David had conspired to identify my childhood fantasy and adolescent fears and to present me with them in cinematic format.

'So what did you think, Sharon?'

'Did you enjoy it?'

I had to struggle to rid myself of the notion that they were mocking me for my insecurities and my promiscuity, things, I had to repeat to myself, they knew little about. As soon as I had regained my composure and as soon as I considered it polite to do so, I left.

The black and white film shook me for days, for weeks; it leached my world of colour, I couldn't shake off the pall of ill feeling it left over me. The film and Mie's meanness to David. It's what I was thinking of as I rested in between dances one night, when Gaia asked me if I was all right.

'What's the matter?' she insisted.

'My heart's not in it,' I said.

She put her hand on my shoulder. 'Of course not, darling,' she said. 'Of course not.'

'Why of course not?'

'It's all a game to you,' she said wistfully, her arm around my shoulder. 'You have another life. This,' she said in a gesture that embraced London's West End, 'is just a distraction, a bit of fun, I know.'

This life: the once exciting but now worn, jaded and yet still cosy dressing room; the once young and fresh but now tired, clammy bodies of a kind and affectionate sorority of fellow strippers; the admiring and generous customers; the grabbing and mean customers; the loving aunt now in a sheepishly confessed relationship with the avuncular, sleazy Pierre.

The other life: the day job, now routine but challenged by changing faces, with only Jonathan remaining of the UK team, the others having been headhunted and replaced by younger, less experienced and colourful, more serious and self-important graduates; the slow dissolution of my secretarial college friendships, the fading remains of which provided Gavina and me with the pretext to pursue increasingly unsatisfactory one-night stands from London's nightclubs' poor pickings; the vestiges of a family: Dziadek and Babcia had died, my grandfather barely outliving my grandmother, dying from a broken heart, had said Dad, who, along with the rest of my family I hardly ever saw any more.

Gaia said, 'Come home with me. A walk will do you good. We'll stop for breakfast in Smithfield Market, we can watch the sun come up and then you can crash at my place.'

We walked east for half an hour, along Long Acre, Chancery Lane and Holborn, on pavements wet with dew and deserted save for the odd street sweeper, office cleaner and drunk. We entered and exited the streetlamps' pools of light in repetition, our shadows racing ahead of us on each occasion to the next, leaving me with the illusion that we were making no progress.

'So, what's the matter?' Gaia repeated.

What was the matter? My double life was exhausting me, my two half-lives catching up on me, each shining a light on the emptiness of the other. Not twice as fulfilled but half so, if that, and twice as tired. The repetitive filling of a bottomless pit with the daily grit of life's experience, the one-night stands, the near-naked provocative dances and the trading slips correctly completed and delivered. Tension at home, with Aunt Wanda spending nearly all her time with Pierre, aware of and unhappy with what she knew I considered to be the ludicrousness of her having shacked up with a dirty old man. I would bake cakes and biscuits for her that would remain untouched. Tension at the club with Wanda, now the manager too, having taken the business by the scruff of the neck. She became more brutally mercantile, more of a driven business director and less of an agony aunt to the girls; she focused increasingly on financial success at all costs, perhaps in a rational commercial response to the economic downturn, or perhaps already aware that it wouldn't be long before Pierre traded her in, and wishing to make a demonstrable improvement to the club's bottom line so that he might think hard about the nature of the figures he preferred over others.

'Something's got to give,' said Gaia.

'Yes. Probably. But what?'

'You're too nice a person to be unhappy,' she said.

Mid-step, I touched Gaia's shoulder with my head in appreciation of her modest tribute. 'I'm not unhappy so much as not happy.'

'You're too nice a person not to be happy,' she said.

We strode London's pavements shoulder to shoulder, occasionally parting company momentarily – for lampposts, street signs and stacks of full black bin-liners that had been piled high by shopkeepers where London's litter bins had stood before being removed in response to the IRA bombings – and converging again once an obstacle had been circumvented in a reflection of life's encounters, separations and reunions.

'Something's gotta give,' she sang with a deep voice and a sudden swagger.

'I know.'

'But what?'

'I don't know.'

'What do you want? What do you want? Out. Of. Life?' She assumed a tone of mock interrogation.

'I don't know. Yes, I do know. I just haven't gone about it the right way,' I admitted. 'Actually, it's not all I thought it would be. It's not enough.'

'I see,' she said gravely. She wrinkled her brow a moment and added, 'You could stop working in the bank.'

'Yes.'

'Or you could stop working at the club.'

'Yes.'

'Or you could reduce your working hours at the club. One night instead of two.'

'Yes.'

'Would the bank allow you to work part-time?'

'No.'

'That's out of the question then. You could consider taking a customer home, from time to time,' she said slyly, looking at me out of the corner of her eyes.

'No!'

'They're all dying for you, you know. I know they are. Now that you've learnt to dance properly!' She knocked me off balance a little with a nudge of her elbow. 'They're no different from the losers you tell me about that you and your friends pick up on your nights out. Correction. They are. They're richer. And you could be too. Stop a second.'

We stood outside Ely Place, a gated cul-de-sac off Holborn Circus. I followed Gaia through an unlocked pedestrians' gate next to a small quaint gatehouse, and down a short road of terraced Georgian mansions.

'A terraced church!' I exclaimed.

'Yes,' she said. 'Unusual, isn't it? St Ethelreda's.' She beckoned. 'Come on. It's sometimes open at this time.' She pushed on a door that led into a hallway. I followed her, nodding to a man with a broom who responded with a nod of his own and continued his sweeping, seemingly unperturbed by the arrival of two bleary-eyed women with smudged make-up and tousled hair in running shoes and skimpy tops and miniskirts under long coats. We turned right along a corridor, went up a flight of stairs and right again into the church. 'It's special, isn't it? So quiet. I love it here.'

'How did you find this place?' I couldn't help but whisper, and looked around in wonder. The church was dark, its indiscernible stained–glass windows, in the gloom, as solid and non-translucent as its thick walls.

Gaia chuckled and sat in a pew, sliding along it a space so I could join her. She exuded a familiarity with the place, a deep comfort that communicated a sense of ownership. I counted fourteen pews and five windows on either side of the aisle. Ten life-size indistinguishable statues on the walls in between the windows and in the two corners of the church facing me, either standing on indiscernible wall-fixed pedestals or with their backs fixed to the wall, presented us with the appearance of ghosts, of corpses hovering well above the floor, or of bodies hanging from the high arched roof.

'Do you believe in God?'

'Look.' She pointed at the stained glass. 'You'll see when the sun rises. He'll absolve you of all of your sins. He loves people like us.'

'This is a Catholic church, isn't it?'

'Oh yes.'

My eyes adjusted to the lack of light. The whites of Gaia's eyes were the brightest things I could discern. I felt warm in my coat. 'It's so different to our Catholic church. Ours is so much plainer. I thought they'd all be like that.'

'How many churches have you been to then?'

'Two, I think. Now. And our school chapel,' I added as an after-thought. 'If that counts.'

'Only two! And you're Catholic?'

'Are you?'

'I asked you first.'

'Well, my mother's mother is a Catholic,' I said, 'and my mother's father is a Jew who converted to being a Catholic. And my father's mother was a Jew and my father's father was a Catholic who converted to being a Jew.'

'Is? Was?'

'Yes.'

'I see,' she said, resting a hand on my arm briefly in condolence. 'Confusing! What does that make your parents?'

'My mother is Catholic and Dad thinks he's Church of England. And as for me...' My voice tailed off. I found it difficult to speak loudly and for long in this splendid place of hush. The symmetry of the church, of its nave, columns and windows contrasted with my internal disorder. The regularity and harmony of line and form, the church's perfection of structure and geometry existed in aloof rebuke to my patchwork, limping self.

'Yes, and as for you?'

'I don't know,' I whispered, resting my head on her shoulder.

'I knew it. Just a crazy mixed-up kid,' she said softly, and stroked my cheek.

'Yes. You know what used to really freak me out was Mass. When I was a child, when we were told we had to eat the body of Christ, I found it shocking. I was afraid that, having no idea who I was in the first place, if I ate someone else, I would become them! Was that stupid? Is that blasphemous?'

Gaia considered that sombrely, continuing to stroke my cheek, seemingly quite unconsciously. '*Hoc est enim corpus meum*,' she said seriously and then, by way of explanation, 'It's on one of the windows. You'll see,' stroking still, and immediately after, it seemed to me, she said, 'Open your eyes!', her voice swimming up from the depths of sleep to which I had sunk, her words popping like bubbles as I surfaced, reached in my confused state for elusive stepping stones and lifted my head from her shoulder.

The sun had risen on Christus Rex, seated amid angels and Mary and Joseph in fiery, technicolour magnificence. The formerly opaque east window emanated the most warm and yet brilliant light, the Christ figure splendid, serene and commanding, the red-clothed and yellow-winged angels adoring and obeisant. Gaia and I clutched each other. It was a second of the richest, most rewarding theatre, appearing unexpectedly before the raised stage curtains of my painted eyelids.

We sat a while, saying nothing, then rose and wandered the aisle before stopping at the west window upon which Christ, crucified, hung, hovering above an auburn- and chocolate-coloured temple on a crimson cross in robes of rose, magenta and pink lozenges, looking down on us in welcome and farewell.

Gaia looked around her. We were alone in the church. 'Would it ever occur to you to say,' she whispered haltingly, 'that Jesus committed, you know, suicide?'

'What?' I asked incredulously.

'In a way, in a sense,' she added hurriedly. 'I mean, he knew he was going to be killed and yet he did nothing to change that outcome – is not doing anything to prevent something from happening that different from actually doing it?'

'He *gave* his life,' I said. 'He didn't *take* his life.'

'Yes, of course,' she said quickly.

'He sacrificed himself, true,' I added, thinking. 'Maybe there's not that much difference.'

She squeezed my hand. 'Come,' she said, and we moved falteringly the way we had come, out of St Ethelreda's and down the corridor and into the early morning's bleaching light. Once at the gatehouse, I looked back, but the church, set in a recess amid its terraced neighbours, was hidden from view.

We tottered downhill and uphill to a confusion of lamp-lit lorries and busying bodies set before a large Victorian structure, the far end of which was lost in steam and the early morning sky.

'Not another church, Gaia?'

Gaia laughed. 'Not exactly! This is Smithfield Market! Are you hungry?' Her cheeks bore the evidence of dried tears.

'I'm starving.'

'This way, through the Poultry Market.' She took me by the hand as we barged through groups of men, some of them standing and smoking and talking in loud voices while others carted sides of beef and other animals, and others yet bought and sold all manner of cuts of meat. 'What's so funny?' she asked, after I had laughed in turn.

'It's like work!' I exclaimed.

'Work?'

'The noise, the people, the shouting. The bartering. It's like the club on a busy night, like the trading floor on a big data day!'

We ducked and dived and rolled out of the way of tradesmen who sold with the good cheer of fairground workers and of shoppers who bought with the determination of businessmen intent on a good deal. I allowed myself to be guided by Gaia who strode the centre aisle between the meat stalls with confidence, linking her arm with mine.

Chopped ox-tail, ox-feet, tripe, honeycomb, sweetbread, pluck, lamb head, chumps, shanks, back straps, fries, trotters, pork loin, pork trim and spare ribs were advertised on one board; topside, silverside, chuck tender, chuck roll, eye of round, rump tail, clod, feather blade, brisket, rolled brisket, sirloin, rump, rib eye, fillet and neck fillet on another.

'Why's it called the Poultry Market?' I asked.

Ears, cheeks, tongue, shoulder, hearts, liver, kidney, knuckle, flank, leg, shin, heel, boasted a precariously balanced blackboard.

'This way,' she said, pulling me by the arm, and no sooner were we out of the Poultry Market than we were down some stairs and not into a public lavatory, which had been my first thought as my eyes adjusted to the relative obscurity, but into a café or, on the evidence of the many pint glasses, a pub. We sat on coffee-and tea-stained upholstery at beer-stained paper napkin-covered tables among butchers and meat traders in bloody aprons and once-white coats, and ordered bacon sandwiches and tea. A layer of cigarette smoke created the illusion of a lower, false ceiling that a rheumatic ventilation unit strived in vain to raise. Gaia hunched her shoulders and screwed her eyes up in her endearing way of saying, *What fun!*

'Hello, Gaia!'

'Morning, Biffo!'

'Disappointed to find that The Cock Tavern is a pub after all, Gaia?'

'No, given that there's at least one prick here, Jimmy.'

'So, what's the fresh meat you've brought with you, Gaia?'

'Her name is Sharon.'

'Come here, darling!'

Again, the shrug, the squint and the smile that spoke in code of intimacy, friendship, confidences and shared experiences. I wanted to hug her for letting me in on my city's little secrets, its churches, its markets and Victorian streets and said, as we wandered through the now quieter, closing West and East Markets to her flat, that in exchange I could show her its parks and green spaces.

'How sweet,' was all she said without enthusiasm, and then, as though in apology, finding my hand with hers, 'Come, I'll show you my place.'

Mie

I knew that I had treated David badly but was more sorry for the low standard of my behaviour than for the upset I had caused him. I held a book I was reading up to my face like a mirror and was confronted with the inescapable fact that I had expressed frustration towards David in order to hide from the true nature of my feelings for Sebastian.

I had taken Sebastian to a meeting with a client he'd complained about. It had proved constructive: the client had come to a realisation of the issues Sebastian faced as a trader and Sebastian to a better understanding of the regulations the client had to operate within. Of course, what made sense for one company could make sense for another, so Sebastian and I embarked on a round trip of investor meetings in London and in Germany. We spent days together, in planes, in cars to and from airports and clients' offices and on foot crossing London's Square Mile and, in that time of journeying, pre-meeting preparation and post-meeting debriefs, I got to know him a little.

Sebastian knew all about Japanese etiquette following his secondment to Tokyo.

'So, you liked it?'

'Tokyo? I loved it.' We were walking to a late–afternoon engagement and had stopped at the junction of London Wall and Moorgate. 'Yes. Look. Here, in London, we have to cross two roads, to cross twice – first we cross one road and then the other. In Tokyo, you cross a crossroads diagonally.'

We crossed London Wall.

'Is that the best thing you can find to say about Tokyo?'

'What was there not to like?'

'Would you have liked to have stayed there longer?'

He pursed his lips and took me by the elbow to help me cross Moorgate in an action that surprised me by its familiarity. 'If you're asking me whether you've done the right thing by coming here, I think you have.'

Freeing my arm from his hold and irritated by his assumption, I replied, 'No, that's not what I was asking you.' Then I asked, in as a matter-of-fact a way as possible, 'So, how come I haven't heard you speak Japanese?'

Sebastian swung his slim attaché case as he strode among the other pedestrians. 'Ah! I was warned not to. "Sleeping" Japanese is what I was told I will have learnt, so I thought I'd keep my mouth quite closed so as not to give too much away.' He was referring to the name given to the Japanese that *gaijin* learn from their Japanese mistresses who will, at times, by virtue of their sex or status or both, employ grammatical constructions that are different to those employed by businessmen. Consequently, when a *gaijin* uses them, they will betray where and from whom he has learnt his Japanese. 'What's the matter?' he asked, trying to catch my eye as we parted to make way for people heading in our direction. 'Have I embarrassed you?'

'Of course not,' I replied and increased my pace, side-stepping quickly around some pedestrians who were slowing us down.

Having given our names at our client's reception, we sat in the dingy waiting room of a Japanese insurance company that, clearly, did not consider it a good thing to have one's shareholders witness the spending of capital on opulent office space. I watched Sebastian leaf through a newspaper on the coffee table and was unexpectedly filled with a sense of missing Taka and David, men with whom I felt more certain of myself. Normally fluent and collected in our client meetings, I stumbled and added little value, conscious that Sebastian was understanding so much more of my and my client's preambles, and yet uncertain of just how much.

Our meeting over, we considered it too late to return to the office and wandered westward instead, past St Paul's Cathedral and then along Fleet Street to Covent Garden and the West End, the sun in our eyes.

'Yes,' he said in reply to my observation that he enjoyed his work. 'That's true. I love my side of the business. Without meaning to sound corny, it's just that with options, your options really are open; you retain a degree of choice, if not quite control, at all times. In fact, you buy choice and freedom, both the freedom to choose and the freedom that owning insurance gives you. Come to think of it, it's like life. I like to run my options book like I like to run my life.' He looked at me a little smugly, but also as though he'd said too much.

'So you're saying,' I said, in order to say something, 'that your business somehow mirrors your life?'

'Well, you could say that. I think that one has choice always, and to ignore that is to deny whatever element of freedom is open to you.'

'But not everyone has a choice,' I replied incredulously.

'True, some have more choice than others. Wasn't it Spinoza who said that even a jailed man can exercise the choice to walk into his prison cell willingly rather than allow himself to be thrown into it? That to act freely is to act as you *must*, to act according to your essence?'

Not knowing who Spinoza was, I kept silent, but his words, the ideas they signified, gave me a thrill in the challenge they presented. The crowds of pedestrians we moved against were like so many ideas in counter-current to mine, and I struggled to keep pace with Sebastian; literally and intellectually, I felt I was plodding.

'But, more pragmatically, I guess I'm saying that we have more choice than we think we do. I mean, if in the evening I set my alarm clock to go off at six the following morning, and get up at six the following morning, it's not because I said I would get up at six the night before but because, that morning at six, I chose to get up. I think that was Sartre,' he added as an afterthought.

I needed quiet and time to consider his arguments and grew irritated by his name-dropping. 'But what's that got to do with options trading?' I shouted after him.

'I have no idea!' He swung his attaché case high in the air.

'Watch it!' A pedestrian ducked and stepped off the pavement and into the street to avoid it.

'Sorry!' He gave a smile and received a frown in return. 'Actually, I suppose it has more to do with the fact that options allow you to formulate a decision and to delay its execution, if not to postpone it indefinitely, and to manage its consequences better.'

We walked on in not uncomfortable silence for a while, the rush hour commuters and noise of buses now making it difficult to sustain a conversation.

I recalled hearing Sebastian explaining the difference between American and European options to a group of male new joiners at the bank one day. 'American options and European options are different in one thing only,' he had said. 'American options can be exercised at any time while European options can only be exercised at expiry.'

The faces around his desk had remained blank.

'Let's put it this way. If I buy an American three-month option to buy a bond, I can buy the bond at *any time* before the end of the three months. If it is a European option, I can buy the bond only at *the end* of the three months.'

There had been a shuffling of feet and a shifting of body weight to accompany the increased level of comprehension and one of the young bankers had said, to a murmur of agreement, 'How do you remember which is which? It's like those binary Trivial Pursuit questions. Which foot did Neil Armstrong place on the moon first? I can never remember!'

'That's easy.' Sebastian had looked straight at the speaker. 'In my experience, you can exercise an American girl at any time while, with a European girl, you will get there... but only in the end!'

It hadn't occurred to me to ask myself then, amid the chauvinist laughter, what I asked myself later, namely, *And Japanese girls? How long had he been made to wait before he had exercised them?*

I glanced at Sebastian now as he strode insouciant against the stream of ambulatory traffic, his blond hair bobbing in the setting sun and his arms swinging easily from his slightly sloping shoulders and thought, was that it for him? Was it all just about his keeping his options open? Was I a call option that would come to him when beckoned, or a put option he could discard once it had served its use? The sun lit a canine tooth that rested on his lip. I took six steps to his four to keep up with him. He dodged pedestrians, I noted, as adeptly and elegantly as he dodged personal questions; despite our time spent together in airport and hotel restaurants and in cafés, I knew little about him. Equally, to be fair, he never asked such questions; never asking them was, I realised, a good way of never inviting them. Which wasn't to say our time together was dull and awkward; quite the contrary, because, rather than ask after family, siblings and personal history, he would ask about favourite books (that he was very interested in) and films (that he was less interested in) when he wasn't answering my questions on finance, economics and politics – subjects he had taken over from David in my ongoing education. And then there was art. Art, I had come to realise was his 'thing', up there with literature and with options.

We stopped on Long Acre across the road from Covent Garden tube station where he squinted into the low sun and said, 'That was a good meeting, by the way. We have some follow-up to do.' He paused and I found myself hoping, for the first time, that he might suggest a drink or a bite to eat in what would have been our own time and not the bank's. Instead, he said, 'Well, see you tomorrow.' Did that 'well' betray a degree of hesitation?

'See you tomorrow.' How hard would it have been for me to propose a quick drink?

Isabella

I had proposed we get together for dinner before the club opened and Sharon had recommended a restaurant called Lo Scoglio so there we went, Frederica, she and I, choosing to huddle around a table for two for the greater intimacy it provided. Frederica continued to dress like the music student she no longer was, in jeans, casual shoes and a baggy jumper. Sharon had come straight from the office and wore a tight secretarial suit and her hair pulled behind her in a bun, her green laser eyes scanning her life ahead in the evening's half–light. She was greeted by the restaurant's Italian proprietors warmly; they brought olives, bread sticks and water to the table unbidden and offered us *aperitivi* on the house.

'So, what's this about?' asked Sharon excitedly and then, before I could answer her question, 'Where's Melanie?'

Frederica rolled her eyes. 'With her fiancé. Where else? She's not much longer for our world. I mean, if you ask me, she's going to take over his business.'

'I've found a new club,' I announced.

'Have you?' exclaimed Sharon.

'I'm giving up music,' said Frederica.

'Are you?' repeated Sharon.

'That's news to me!' I said.

'I've just decided,' said Frederica. She inspected an olive between her thumb and forefinger before placing it slowly in her mouth. 'No money in it. Maybe later, when I'm older, I'll go back to it.'

I waited to be asked about my new club.

'What about you, Sharon?' asked Frederica, swallowing and reaching for a packet of *grissini*. 'Any earth-shattering news from you?'

Sharon giggled. 'Not from me. Ever!'

'What about Wanda and Pierre?' suggested Frederica.

'What about them?' Sharon shrugged.

'What about your ex being back?' persisted Frederica.

'He's been back ages!' exclaimed Sharon. 'And he's just that. An ex.'

'You knew that, Freddie, that he's been back a while,' I said, a little put out.

'Well? Might you get back with him?' Frederica kept her eyes on Sharon and reached for another olive.

Sharon replied with a slow, 'No,' and looked down at the floor.

'I thought you liked him?' Frederica wasn't giving up.

'I did,' said Sharon wistfully. 'But it seems he didn't like me, not enough to take me to Japan with him.'

'Send him to me,' I stated simply, in an effort to be central to the conversation.

'Well! That was then!' Frederica sucked on a *grissino* before biting onto it.

'No.' Sharon shook her head. 'It's like I've moved on, finally, you know? It's like' – she looked up for inspiration – 'we're no longer the people we were before he went away, like we'd be trying to stick a broken plate back together with some of the pieces missing. Or something.'

'Is he the really hunky blond? I remember your talking about him. Have him back! Until you find someone else. Unless you have someone else?' Frederica arched her eyebrows knowingly.

'No!' replied Sharon to Frederica, and turned to me. 'Did you say to send him to you? What a nice idea!' She laughed.

'*Signorine!*' said the Italian waiter, notepad and pen in hand.

I felt peeved at my friends' seeming indifference to my announcement but at some point, after we had been served, Frederica looked pointedly at me and said, 'Go on, then. Tell us about your new club,' and I understood that she, in turn, had been vexed at my not telling her sooner, at having clearly made a big decision without sharing the process with her – my longest-standing friend and flat–mate.

'Oh, yes!' cried Sharon. 'Please do! And why?'

Mie

Taka's marriage had ended so, on his third visit to London, he came on his own. I was curious as to whether or not a spark would kindle between us, given this second opportunity. It didn't and, with some relief, we learnt to enjoy each other's company safe in the knowledge that we would be just good friends.

It was with Taka that I had stood before paintings in the Tate and in the National Gallery and it was he, whose interest had moved from the moving image to the still, who had taught me to consider paintings critically. The dissolution of his marriage had given him a quality of introspection that, to my mind, had found its counterpoint in his discovery of art and painting. It was as though, no longer certain of his life's trajectory, he no longer wanted the world to move before his eyes, as it did when he watched a film, but to stay still, so that he could better grasp it, examine it and understand it and, ultimately, make sense of his marriage's wreckage. I had suggested this to him but he had only shrugged and encouraged me to visit London's free museums more frequently.

So it was that one Sunday, not long after Taka had returned to Japan, I was standing in front of a painting in the Tate when I heard Sebastian's voice over my shoulder. 'Well, well.'

'Hello,' I replied in greeting. Blushing, as though caught in some illicit act or, perhaps, intuiting the painting's extreme yet corrupt intimacy that it would embarrass me to share immediately with him, I didn't turn to face him.

The label to the bottom left of it read, *Salvador Dali (1904–1989) Autumnal Cannibalism 1936 Oil paint on canvas*. The painting, about 50 centimetres high and as wide, is of two grotesque, near androgynous figures, of two legless, featureless, plasticine torsos in a heads–together loving embrace ('her' extended, bulbous, distorted head supported by a crutch) in which she gently sinks a knife into his butter-like shoulder and he lovingly spoons some of hers while raising a fork to her head and, with his third hand (he has gained the hand she has lost) he squeezes a fistful of her fleshy, creamy waist. She, to the left of the picture, resides in a shallow earthenware dish; his chest is a drawer (with another fork and spoon protruding from it) on top of what appears, in the very foreground, to be a desk that morphs, as it recedes, into a desert landscape with a house and rocks and mountains on the horizon.

'What do you think?'

What did I think?

'Do you like it?'

My critical faculties, when it came to Western art, were muted relative to literature and to cinema. I struggled for context, for history, for points of reference or, having them, they were useless to me. We studied the painting in silence, me aware that that I still hadn't turned to look at him and feeling silly for it. When I did, I was startled to note that this was the first time I had seen him not wearing a suit and I had to make a mental readjustment as I spoke – uncertain, in the immediate moment, as to whether I found him in his jeans, trainers, T-shirt and bomber jacket, in what appeared to me to be an imitation of Japanese trendy teenagers' dress, endearing or exciting.

'I do like it,' I said.

He looked at me for more.

'It's beautifully executed and, although the two forms are engaged in a most horrible act of eating each other –'

'There's a tenderness in their embrace.' He finished my sentence for me.

'Yes, it's like love consumes the lovers.'

His fair hair was relatively unkempt, and it occurred to me that he added something to it on workdays in order to bring it under control and make himself presentable. I fought against the impulse to run my fingers through it and to pat it down.

'Yes!' He appeared delighted. 'I'm so glad you like it. I love Dali. Art critics tend to dismiss him because he's occasionally sensationalist or scatological or' – he sought a word – 'vulgar in other ways but, in doing so, they do his composition, his brushwork and his palette no justice.'

We left the Tate and rambled, with the sun in our eyes, along Millbank and then turned onto Vauxhall Bridge and crossed the Thames. A long way ahead of us, on the other side of the bridge, was another couple, two people of indeterminate sex (from this distance), side by side like two inverted commas; we must have looked the same to them, and the bridge a long equivocal statement between two pairs of quotation marks.

'Are you in a rush to get home?' he asked.

'No,' I replied, turning to look at him. The sun was low in the sky and the light bright so that his face, framed in its halo of fair hair, remained in shadow; my eyes couldn't adjust.

'Let's go there,' he said pointing down the road to a lonely, tired–looking Georgian house that appeared out of place amid the jumble of building works that were going on around it. 'It's a strange place. A mix of architectural salvage and café.' We toured rooms full of reclaimed chimneypieces and fire grates, dining tables and chairs, lamps and chandeliers, glass and brass door knobs, kitchen dressers and obsolete kitchenware, pots, jars and cracked porcelain and old paintings and carpets before settling down and ordering tea and scones. He said, 'It's ironic, really.'

'What is?'

'Our meeting in front of *Autumnal Cannibalism*.' He pronounced the last two words distinctly.

Well, it was autumn. Still, I said, 'Why's that?'

He uncrossed his legs and leant forward. 'What is the only developed country in the world not to have outlawed cannibalism?'

'I don't know. You tell me.'

'Go on. Guess.'

'Japan?'

'Yes!'

'That's simply not true!' I retorted, uncertain of what my confidence was based on.

He held his hands up. 'Okay, not the only country. I was being facetious. Still.'

'Still what? Where's the irony?' Even if what he'd said was true, the fact that I was Japanese and had been looking at the painting didn't register as worth commenting on, in my view.

'Okay, maybe there's no irony,' he said and then, as though to justify himself, he added, 'But, you know, there's a long history of anthropophagy in Japanese literature. And I've long had this thing about cannibalism and Japan.' He stopped talking as tea was brought to the table, and allowed the waitress to pour once he had checked that it had sufficiently brewed. By way of explanation, he continued, 'My mother had a friend who studied in Paris, where she befriended a student who was murdered and in part consumed by a Japanese student.' He paused as though to gauge the effect this had on me. 'The police found parts of her body in his fridge. Anyway, he confessed to the murder. You must have heard about this.'

I had.

'It was in all the papers. They called him The Paris Cannibal. He never served much of a jail sentence and was acquitted on a legal technicality.'

I blew on my tea.

'You know, it's strange,' he conceded. 'My knowing the woman second hand, as it were, makes the story feel so much more immediate. I only later read about it. The man was clearly crazy, but this idea he had that someone could absorb some of the qualities of another by eating them – well, that's just mad.'

'There's this expression, that you are what you eat.'

'Yes,' he laughed, 'but I think that refers to food quality and provenance.' He held up a scone and said, 'I am a scone!' before biting into it. He offered me one. 'And then,' he said, having swallowed, 'there's another story –'

'A true story?'

'Oh, yes, a true story of a Japanese man who had, well, what would you call it, identity issues, gender issues? Anyway, he decided he would have a sex change but, not only that, he would cook his amputated private parts and serve them for dinner to six paying guests, and he put an advertisement in a newspaper to that effect.'

'No!'

'Yes!'

'And he did it?'

'Yes! He underwent his operation and sold six tickets for this dinner. In the event, only five diners showed, but about twenty journalists did, so this is well documented. Now, the authorities weren't too happy about it but they could do nothing to stop him going through with it. However, they felt they had to arrest him for something, and they did so: for indecent exposure!'

'No!'

'Yes!' He drank some tea, clearly still amused.

'How did he cook it? His, you know?'

'His meat and two veg? I don't know! *Coq au vin* perhaps?' He looked at me as though he found me curious. 'That's a question it would never have occurred to me to ask.'

The to and fro on a subject for which I had little enthusiasm, feigning an interest I did not have, had tired me. My shoulders sagged. I looked around me. I was irritated by Sebastian's comments about cannibalism and Japan; I couldn't decide whether they were simple observations or pointed in some way.

'I didn't mean anything by that, by the way. It's just, well, peculiar, I suppose. You know, it's funny seeing you out of your work clothes.' He looked at me appraisingly. 'I mean,' he added hastily, 'in clothes that are not your work clothes!'

'I know. I had the same thought about you,' I said, hiding ineffectually behind my raised teacup while reappraising my day's rather plain wardrobe of jeans, boots and a large woolly jumper.

We didn't go Dutch, as the English call it, *warikan*, as the Japanese do; Sebastian paid for both of us, for which I simply thanked him. While he waited for his change, I toured around a huge pine table on which were laid ill-assorted, second-hand sugar spoons, cake forks, fish knives, cruet sets, sherry glasses and cooking utensils.

'What have you found?' he asked, once again standing just behind me and breathing over my shoulder. Placed like boxes within boxes, like *matryoshka* dolls, were three slightly rusty, different-sized but otherwise identical steel cookie cutters. 'Cookie cutters,' he said. 'For gingerbread men.'

I was struck by the fact that these cookie cutters had precisely the same proportions as Takumi-*san*'s silhouette of the filleted man, as though that outline had climbed off the poster and down the wall and followed me to London with his wife and child where, shrunk by the long journey, he had rested on this old kitchen table waiting for me to find him. Dizzyingly, momentarily, the café and bric-a-brac receded and my nostrils filled with the smells of sawdust, congealed blood and bleach.

'You're not going to buy them!' Sebastian exclaimed, and I realised that while I was supporting myself on the table with the outstretched fingers of one hand, I clutched, in the other, the largest of those three steel-edged figures – so present, solid and, to my imagination, certain of themselves that I envied them. 'But you can get new ones – clean ones – at any department store!' he said as I paid for them.

Once home, I washed and dried my cookie cutter men and stood them one behind the other on the window sill above the kitchen sink. I had moved into my own apartment, the top–floor flat of a large Edwardian house on the north side of Clapham Common. I knelt, my chin just by the sink, so that, from that low angle, I could see through the gingerbread men's outlines in silhouette against the edges of an anaemic sunset. Their straight and fisted arms and solidly planted feet amused me; their posture echoed that of an obstinate child. There I was, the closest to me, my mother behind me and my father behind us. I rested my forehead against the cool sink. I should have called them today. I stood, considered my reflection in the window a moment and set about tidying my already tidy kitchen in a desultory way before ironing the blouse I'd wear tomorrow.

The day had unnerved me; Sebastian, I saw, risked disappointing me. Physically and professionally, I had long admired him, impressed by a manner more genial than slick with his colleagues and more capable than ingratiating with the bank's clients. When I had first known him, I had respected and applauded the extent to which he appeared to value his privacy and maintained his social defences – he didn't give himself away cheaply. I knew where his politics lay (little different to most other bank employees), which films he enjoyed (more mainstream than Taka, David and me) and which authors and genre of books he favoured. Here, he was different to most City employees who, to my surprise, read little that was not work related. Jonathan, leaning back in his chair and looking over his shoulder whenever I happened to be depositing my handbag's contents on my desk, would exclaim, 'A novel! Another novel! Now, what I want is facts!' in an unknowing caricature of Mr Gradgrind.

'Jonathan says he only wants to read facts,' I had told Sebastian.

'Good for Jonathan. He can stick to non-fiction books. They may deliver facts but novels deliver truth,' had said Sebastian, who, on every plane and train journey I made with him would read a novel, rarely by an author I knew. I had continued my literary education in England so that after a decade I had read all I could find of Evelyn Waugh, Graham Greene, George Orwell and E. M. Forster who, particularly, touched a chord with me in contrasting the English with the foreigners around them. Sebastian approved, once patronisingly telling me that he would let me know what I should be reading once I had finished my self-imposed syllabus. So I knew about him, but did I know him? I didn't know. I decided I would say as much to him.

Isabella

I never did tell Sharon why I had left Pierre's club and I suspected that Wanda, for reasons of pride, had never mentioned the incident with Pierre to her either. Instead, I had bemoaned the increased regimentation and commercialisation of the old place and talked favourably of the new club I was dancing at.

It billed itself as a modern strip club and not as a Victorian gentleman's club. Overt sexual provocation replaced seedy gentility and hypocrisy. Customers were encouraged to take the girls home, with the house taking its cut of the girls' earnings, and touching was not *verboten*. Its owner was an enterprising young German who mucked in with his staff, not a French letch who lorded it over his. Its location in increasingly gentrified Farringdon suited me better than the West End.

Godehard reminded me of my mother with his perfect English, just the odd German word peppering it here and there. He was slim, a quality disguised by his wearing trousers and shirts a size too large for him, the latter unbuttoned to reveal a silver egg on a silver chain in a nest of curly chest hair and with its cuffs never done up. A large, expensive-looking watch was on show on one wrist and a copper bracelet on the other. He wore his light brown hair straight with a side parting and black-framed glasses that the NHS had made so familiar to my generation, but that he insisted had been tailor-made for him by a specialist glasses manufacturer in Hamburg at great expense. Where Pierre had sought to exercise his *droit du seigneur* underhandedly, Godehard propositioned the girls he employed openly in a commercial transaction with no strings attached. He dispensed advice on the importance of managing one's money, on saving, on shares and other investments and bemoaned the fact that no one listened to him. He did the same on the subject of sex, too, advising on the importance of general hygiene, frequent exercise, a good diet and plenty of sleep, of the use of condoms and of regular health checks at the VD clinic, and he would listen sympathetically to the girls who told him about their gynaecological problems. He was, within the scope of my experience, American in his open and frank attitude to sex, but he spoke of himself as European in contrast to English. 'What is it with you limeys?' he would say to the English girls, and would stand to attention and do his shirt top button up while grimacing in what we understood was an attempt at stiffening his upper lip. 'So stuffy! So repressed! Hey, sex happens!'

Godehard guiding me by the elbow, the two of us clutching our coats at the throat despite our scarves, we crossed the road to Smithfield Market where we ordered tea and bacon sandwiches in The Hope. We had it to ourselves; at 2.30 in the morning the butchers and tradesmen were still at work. We sat at a table in the bay window watching, through the clear glass above the frosted frieze, the unloading of vehicles, admiring the industry of the steaming tradesmen as cow halves were hurried from the dark backs of trucks through flapping rubber and Perspex doors to the bright lights of the glimpsed butchers' stalls for further, final dismemberment. I found something contemplative in the repetition of the actions of the men in the backs of lorries and vans and of the men in chiaroscuro who dashed from vehicle to the market and back as though on a loop, the cumulative recurrence of which would deliver meaning. When not running, the men stamped their feet and blew into their hands, their breath forming speech bubbles in which everything had been left unsaid. I knew many of them by name. I had slept with some of them. Some stood in the half–dark, smoking and drinking from hip flasks by the doors, jollying their colleagues along. I could tell those who had been butchering lambs, that were placed on a block and cut towards the butcher, by their bloodier, grislier aprons.

'Heaven or hell?' asked Godehard of the scene.

I only smiled in reply.

We ordered more tea and another round of bacon sandwiches from a pale, wordless waif of a waitress who appeared, while corporeally intact, to have been filleted fully from her personality in partial counterpart to the massacred carcasses across the street.

'You're half German, I hear,' Godehard said to me.

I nodded.

'*Wunderbar! Welche Hälfte?*'

I bit into my sandwich.

'Now, tell me,' he continued, the smile leaving his face and his eyes looming large in their television-like frames. 'I've never seen you so unhappy. What's wrong?'

I said nothing.

'You've always been the cheerful one. Boyfriend problems? Money problems?' probed Godehard encouragingly.

'No boyfriend and plenty of money.' I smiled weakly. My knees against the old, clunking iron radiator were warm and my stomach, mouth and fingers, where they held my teacup, were hot; everything else was cold. When I had thought that I'd been answering London's call, it felt to me now as though I'd been running away from Oxford. When I had thought that I might have been running away from my father, I now had to accept the possibility that I had been running away from myself. There is a paradox about the self that when you try to grasp it you change it, that the unreflective self is no longer such when reflected upon. I failed to see the connection between me and the excited girl who had climbed the stairs to a rented apartment with Freddie all those years ago, and I could only just recognise the girl who had gone from fun-loving sexual encounters to prostitution at around the time Isabella had become Gaia. The change went deeper than a name, however; it carried with it a sense of shame, of latent disappointment not by my own lights but by those of my mother and her family and of society at large. But shame is born of pride, and what pride I possessed fed my revolt against what shame I felt. 'But I enjoy sex!' I wanted to proclaim; and that, to me, was sufficient justification for it before I even contemplated hiding behind the ready incestuous abuse excuse that well-meaning social workers had seemed so willing to allow me. Again, I grasped for that understanding of myself and wondered if one could ever be sufficiently honest with one's self to look where one knew it was hidden. I forced myself to look my reflection in The Hope's window in the eye and to admit to myself that I had enjoyed the consensual sex that had nurtured my butterfly in adulthood, that had unlocked me from within, liberated me, permitted me my orgasmic, cosmic escape. Latterly, though, sex had become perfunctory and had rooted me in the physical, in my body, leaving it invested with an inhibiting consciousness. Isabella's pale complexion looked back at me from The Hope's window. I missed Mama and Opa. And Gaia who I hoped would have forgiven me the misappropriation of her name. I missed Oma, Cosmo and Uncle James with whom I maintained occasional contact and who, I hoped, missed the me I had once been and who didn't know the me I had become.

'Hel-*lo*,' said Godehard, reminding me of his presence.

'Everything's fine, really,' I said. 'I'm just a little tired, I suppose.'

We made small talk about Paderborn that Godehard had once visited and about my grandmother.

Expressing surprise at the hour, Godehard stood to go. 'Take care,' he said.

I ordered a third cup of tea in the hope of regaining my earlier pensive, meditative state of mind.

Shoppers – butchers and retail, in their cars and in their vans – replaced the wholesalers who drove their lorries elsewhere, back home or to the railway depots. The animals that had gone to market as recognisable as they had been dead now left it amputated, disjointed, smuggled out in indistinguishable packages of plastic wrap.

Mie

Sebastian and I had taken a late afternoon flight to Hamburg from London City Airport and were the only people in business class. Our proximity, the small size of the plane and the dimmed cabin lights engendered an intimacy that I welcomed. As I leafed through the following day's presentations, double-checking for typographical errors and making notes of the contributions I would make in the margin of my copy, he read yet another book I hadn't seen him with before.

'*I Spit On Your Graves*. That's an interesting title.'

'It's an interesting book.'

I closed the presentation. 'What's it about?'

He closed the book. 'That's a good question. Ostensibly, it's about a young American who is one–eighth black and seven–eighths white, but looks quite white and who seeks to revenge his brother's death on "society"' – he described inverted commas in the air with his fingers – 'by killing a white upper–class society girl.'

'Why, what did she do, that girl?'

'She may have been implicated in his brother's death but, really, her only "crime"' – those fingers again – 'was to befriend him and, so, to patronise him – at least, that's what he feels.'

'So you know the end already?'

'Yes, I'm rereading it. I first read it ages ago, as a teenager, for its sensationalism.' He looked down at the book on his lap. 'It occurred to me recently that I'd missed something, that there was more to it than the schlock and horror.'

'Why? How does he kill her?'

He rolled his eyes and puffed his cheeks out and looked at me. 'Oh, you don't want to know that!'

'Why not?' I held my nose and swallowed in order to combat the discomfort of the barely pressurised cabin.

'Well, it's not very nice!'

I turned in my seat to better look at him. 'Try me.'

'Well.' He looked back down into his lap. His eyelashes, seen from my perspective with the soft overhead light, seemed extraordinarily long for a man's. He looked at his watch as though a specific time or event that was due to happen at a given time would relieve him from a difficult moment. 'Well, he forces himself on her. He pursues her into a field where he commits a sexual act on her in the process of which he bites her… out.'

'He bites her. Out.'

'Yes.' He flared his nostrils in remonstration. 'He bites her in a very sensitive place and she bleeds to death.'

We left the North Sea behind us. From my window I could see the night clouds lit from above by the moon and occasionally, more weakly, from below by the lights of industrial and coastal towns in the Netherlands and in north-western Germany. We commenced our descent to Hamburg that, so Ursula had lectured my fellow pupils and me, was Germany's largest port despite its being over 100 kilometres from the North Sea thanks to the magnificent River Elbe.

'So if that is what the book is ostensibly about, what is it really about?' I asked him.

He breathed deeply, as though relieved to be able to move the conversation on to another plane. 'It's about identity. About conforming to stereotype. The ironic thing is that, while he sees himself as black, his white friends don't and yet he ends up conforming to a stereotype that he assumes would be assigned to him because of his heritage, if it were known. Something like that.'

Through the plane window's triple-glazing, I saw, superimposed on the night sky and twinkling traffic and city lights, this poor dead rich girl with blood weeping down from her panties and over her thighs and, standing over her, an albino negro, with a blood-covered mouth and dripping chin; a trashy image from a B-movie poster. 'So, something like, are we who we choose to be or are we who people decide we are?'

'Yes, if you like.'

I liked. I looked at the book in his hands. It was by Boris Vian. 'Vian means meat in French, doesn't it?'

'No,' he replied. 'That's *viande*.'

We dumped our bags at our hotel and asked for directions to the nearest restaurant; we fancied neither the hotel's bland, tired dining hall nor a long walk under the one small umbrella we had. Side-stepping puddles and giving passing cars a wide berth as they drove through the ponds that collected around blocked gutters, we fell down some steps to the basement Italian restaurant we had been directed to. To scowls from a lugubrious waiter, we hung our sopping coats and umbrella on the hangers provided and watched as he removed the umbrella from its hanger and dropped it in the pool of water at the bottom of the umbrella stand.

'*Ein Tisch für zwei, bitte.*'

I had explained through my blushes, once when Sebastian had complimented me on my German, that I had felt obliged to do my best when learning the language in order to make up for how nasty my fellow pupils and I had been to Ursula.

Sebastian tore a packet of breadsticks open, offered me one and perused the menu.

'The aubergine parmigiana for my friend,' he said in German to the sullen waiter, 'and, for me, the Wiener schnitzel without the vegetables but with the spaghetti *vongole* instead.' He smiled sheepishly and raised his eyebrows as though to say, *Yes, I know, a strange combination.*

The waiter perked up at this and began to look positively pleased, as though having just remembered a piece of good news. 'That's not possible,' he said. 'The schnitzel comes with vegetables.'

'Oh, I know,' said Sebastian, 'but I'd like to have it with the spaghetti *vongole.*'

The waiter stared intently at the menu. 'I'm sorry, you can't,' he said finally.

'Oh, I see the problem,' said Sebastian. 'I'm happy to pay for both, of course.' He closed the menu and placed it on the table as though to signify that that was sorted.

The waiter, however, didn't seem to think so. He tapped his order pad with his pencil and shook his head and tugged on his moustache, as though genuinely apologetic. 'I'm sorry,' he repeated, 'but that's just not possible. You have to make your mind up between the two.'

'Ah, we have a problem!' Sebastian looked at me with raised eyebrows and wide eyes.

Then, turning to the waiter with an uplifted finger as though suddenly possessed with an original thought, Sebastian quietly requested to see the restaurant manager, a tired, greasy, uninterested man who emerged from behind a curtain as if bored with performing in the same play every evening and with whom Sebastian repeated the conversation he'd had with the waiter. They looked at each other, the fat, near-bald, moustachioed manager and the thin, curly-haired moustachioed waiter, as though quite willing to help but bewildered by the complexity of the request.

The manager shrugged and held his hands out, palms up. The waiter rolled his eyes and scratched his head with his pen. I brought my hand to my mouth to hide a smile – they were Joe and Tony to our Lady and Tramp!

Sebastian stood, smiling too, maybe stimulated by my giggles as much as by the absurdity of our situation. 'Thank you, gentlemen. This is for the breadsticks.' He placed some coins on the table. 'Have you ever wondered why your restaurant is empty?'

'It's late,' said the manager.

'It's a Monday night,' said the waiter.

We walked back to the hotel in a lighter rain and ordered food from the room service menu that we ate in the hotel's empty bar.

'Do you know what I love about Italy?' Sebastian asked rhetorically as we chewed our club sandwiches. 'There, when I order the same, an escalope with spaghetti *vongole*, they exclaim, '*Sei pazzo!* You crayzy!' and then they make it for me anyway, even if it's not on the menu. I could never live in this country. Did I surprise you by getting up and leaving?'

I thought for a bit. 'No.'

'So you thought that consistent with my behaviour? With what you know about me?'

'Yes.'

He laughed. 'We're always making choices. Even then, I quite consciously thought that I could either simply choose one of the dishes on offer or make my point and leave. On another night, or even five minutes earlier or five minutes later, I could have chosen to stay.' He wiped his hands on his napkin. 'Sorry for not consulting you, though.'

'Oh, that's all right. You really don't have to apologise.' *But it was nice of you to*, I wanted to add.

It was late, the bar was gloomy, I was tired and we had some client meetings to attend to in the morning. We parted in the corridor that led to our rooms, each, electronic room key in hand, saying good-night to the other, stepping into our rooms and shutting the door behind us. I removed my shoes, sat on the end of the bed, removed my stockings and, tugging my skirt from above the knee to the tops of my thighs, considered my outstretched legs. What did Sebastian think of them, if he thought of them at all? Why had there been no question of a nightcap, no possibility of his requesting entry to my hotel room or inviting me to his, no chance of a knock on the door? Was it professionalism, consideration or a lack of interest in me?

Isabella

Mornings. Movement, mutterings, a draught that sweeps my exposed back fleetingly, shadows and light perceived in red and white through my still–shut eyes. Apologies or excuses, thanks, endearments and goodbyes dimly heard. My hand out of the duvet and raised above my shoulder in farewell. I will never see him again. Already I have forgotten him. Money and a business card left on my bedside table. A used condom and tissues in the wastepaper basket. Alone in bed, I concentrate on filling my body as precisely as possible.

Sharon

My bank work was routine, automatic, as was my smile and good cheer. I had watched nearly everyone I knew there move on over the years, either gaining promotion or being headhunted, and had never achieved the quality of relationship with my new colleagues that I had had with my old ones. Jonathan had had a health scare and returned from a long absence for treatment thinner, sadder and quieter. Mr Self had fought against premature hair loss and lost. My annual review with them was an awkward one. Mr Self presented me with a glass globe paperweight and pressed me on my professional aspirations, as though torn between losing me and yet desperate for me to have some career development. I was formally promoted to a newly created post of desk assistant manager in recognition of the leadership I had shown and of the mentoring I had given new desk assistants, and I was given an above–inflation rate pay rise.

'Well done!' said Mie, when she heard the news from Jonathan. 'Does this call for a celebratory drink?'

I was so pleased and so confounded at the prospect of going out with Mie after work for the first time in years that my strangled reply was inaudible.

'I know, it's been a long time,' she said.

We revisited The George, which seemed populated by ghosts of a past life and lacked the atmosphere and promise of a decade ago when we had crowded the high, small tables with Adam Johnson and David but, of course, it was we that had changed.

We sat on bar stools on either side of the tall tables and watched the ice melt slowly in our G and Ts. I took in Mie's dress, her successful businesswoman's attire, and thought, *She's got it, now*.

'Have you kept in touch with Adam?' I asked above the loud music.

'No, not really. Well, we meet occasionally for lunch.'

'And David? Do you see him a lot?'

'No!' Mie sat back with a sudden look of distaste.

'Oh, I thought you were still friends? That you'd remained friends? Despite... you know.'

Mie pouted and shrugged as though to say that they might have, but no longer were.

'What happened there then?' I persisted.

'Nothing.' Mie met my look unblinkingly as she drank and crunched an ice cube. 'Are you still dancing at that club?'

'Yes,' I said. Discomfited by the direct question, I reached for my glass and took a long swig. I assumed it to be a reproach for my having broached the subject of David, Mie's way of telling me that the topic was not up for discussion.

Mie said nothing.

'It's good exercise,' I added, in weak justification.

'It seems to be,' said Mie, in what I took as a compliment.

'Mie,' I said, 'do you ever look back at, you know, your life or certain events and, while recognising that they happened to you, not really feel that they did? As though all along, behind you, there are just a series of people who were you or looked like you, but there's no continuity of you?'

'No. I never think that,' said Mie decisively.

I considered her enviously.

There was a finality to our evening together – the sense that it was the last time we'd share a drink and a private conversation was overwhelming. It was as though she had invited me out not to renew a tired friendship but to meet one last obligation, and to draw a line that ran from Putney through Clapham all the way to the City and along the aisle between her desk and mine.

Already, in the present, I was looking back as though through a series of windows that each presented a different scene, distinct tableaux of past lives into which she and I happened to have ventured: brief, framed moments in which we had coincided. While Mie remained resolutely unchanged behind the façade of her new wardrobe, constantly and recognisably Mie in each image, I had no notion of existing for myself for more than two or three seconds at a time. The only factor that contributed to any sense of continuity, however ironically, was the thought that this notion was familiar to me. While Mie glided serenely and purposefully across a bridge, in that way she had of walking by moving her legs from below the knees only, I advanced hesitantly from one stepping stone to the next, unable to ascertain whether, if the far bank were to be reached, it would be me who would reach it.

Mie had depressed me and shaken my confidence. A little ashamed of my fragility and wanting a friend's non-judgmental warm arms around me, that night I crashed at Gaia's.

Isabella

Sharon snuggled up to me, her body against mine cool. I grumbled, in protest as much as in welcome. She had taken to staying the night with Frederica and me (when, I suspected, her Aunt Wanda stayed at Pierre's and she felt alone in their Putney home), sleeping in Frederica's bed if it was empty and mine if it wasn't.

We dozed. At such times, I fantasised that it was possible to undergo an involuntary, inadvertent exchange of selves and bodies; I imagined my butterfly leaving me and alighting on Sharon, bearing my history with it, were she only to hold me tight enough.

'Do you ever imagine,' I asked, 'that your' – I sought the right word – 'your soul, your psyche, could ever depart from your body and reside in someone else's?'

'No!' was a murmur in my ear.

'Never?' I could sense her waking. 'Not that if you held me tight, really tight, something, some essence, could pass from me to you and vice versa?' I could feel her tense.

'Like, sex, do you mean?'

'No! The opposite, even. As though our bodies are incidental to us. Something like that.'

'I think you mean like sex,' persisted Sharon. 'That's the only way that what you said makes any sense to me. And not always.'

I said nothing. I found it hard to explain, even though back to front and not face to face should have made it easier.

'To be honest, there was this one time,' said Sharon enigmatically. 'All right,' she continued, as though having made her mind up abruptly, 'this one person.' She rolled onto her back and was quiet a moment and then she took a breath. 'And I never realised until it was too late.'

'Sebastian, do you mean?'

Sharon placed her hand on my exposed shoulder and squeezed.

'He's the only one whose name you've ever mentioned. Are you sure it's too late?'

'Yes. I don't mean that he wouldn't have me back if I worked at it. Just that the moment has gone. It's as though, to me, we aren't the people we once were, as though we're reinvented each and every day and today's people have chosen not to love each other.' Her hand stayed warm on my shoulder, its pressure increasing as she sat up. 'You asked me to send him to you!' she said as if just remembering. 'You know, I think you'd like him. And I think he'd like you. I should introduce you. Gift him to you.' She giggled at the thought. 'Would you like that?'

My back still to her, I patted her hand in reply.

Mie

It was a late Friday afternoon and my desk assistant had requested my permission to get an early start to her long weekend, so it was I who walked down the emptying dealing room to Sebastian. We had addressed the outstanding points of business and were rocking back in new office chairs, admiring the two new large monitor screens that had replaced his six old small ones, when he asked me what my plans were for the weekend. They were vague and included shopping on Saturday and, on Sunday, brunch with new Japanese acquaintances.

'I was thinking of seeing the Francis Bacon retrospective at the Tate,' I said.

'So was I!' he exclaimed. 'Do you mind if I join you?'

One speaks of a circle of friends; I had circles of them that I had initially, inadvertently, but then quite deliberately managed to keep separate. To my mind's eye I was the centre circle of a Venn diagram that overlapped with five other, alternately shrinking and growing circles that only occasionally touched. I was at the very heart of this universe, the one solid star; the others pulsed strongly or weakly, depending whose company I sought. Since my move, I had lost touch with former neighbours. Since my promotion, I had gone out less with Sharon and her friends and more with City contacts and their spouses. Since my cruelty to David, we saw each other only occasionally.

Sebastian and I met at the Tate and paid our way into the Bacon exhibition where we spent an hour, not conversing much, before he followed me out of the exhibition space, out of the museum, down the museum steps and onto the embankment overlooking the Thames. He was exhilarated as much by the exhibition as by what I think he sensed was my response to it. He was breathless from having run across the wide and busy four-lane road in pursuit of me. 'What is it?' he repeated.

The sky was blue grey, the sluggish river brown, sandwiched, at low tide, between wide strips of mucky taupe and, on the opposite bank, ochres and brick reds. Further downriver, Battersea Park's trees' saffron- and mustard-coloured leaves completed Bacon's palette that had followed me out of the museum and into the street in a dizzying, colour-leaking amalgam of the in- and outdoors. Bacon's paintings had been blows to my stomach and heart. And it was more than the rushing regression to my parents' butchers' shop stimulated by Bacon's sides of meat and meat-like sitters. *A mirror to the human condition*, Bacon shouted, *here we are, but flesh and bone and all alone*. Nothing had prepared me for this, not even *Autumn Cannibalism*, the frame of which was so defined that one looked at it as though through a window, at a remove. Bacon's colours spilled gently off their canvasses and formed puddles around my feet and legs, then pools I swam, saw and breathed through and, now, as I leant on the embankment wall, brushed my field of vision with hues and blushes that tinged the external world while singeing the internal one. Anti-religious – *a*religious – they yet spoke in a devotional language, in a pontifical voice, of nihilism, at worst and starkest, or, at best, of solipsism. I gripped a handrail and looked down at the exposed muddy bank, as Sebastian exclaimed, 'Yes! Yes!' He was ecstatic. 'Not even "existence precedes essence". Existence. Just that. Nothing else. Peel back the flesh to reveal meat and bone. Scream; no one will hear you.' It was as though everything I had believed was made paint, everything I had sensed made flesh in paint, everything I had thought taken to its logical extension, to its reductivist conclusion; this was the point to which my proud independence had taken me. The glacial thrill of this affirmation of 'I', desolate and solitary though it may be, dominated other considerations and emotions.

The irony of two solipsists communing in their physiological and aesthetic responses to Bacon's paintings was not lost on me: we were as close to each other then, as we revelled in the bleakest of revelations, as we had ever been. Two people happy together in the profound recognition of their fundamental, ultimate solitude; the happiness of the loneliest of life's long-distance runners. It was for this reason, I think, that I allowed Sebastian to accompany me back to my apartment, although I recall neither inviting him nor his asking to escort me home.

Only when I withdrew my front door key from my handbag did I think that this was the first time he was entering my home. Timidly,

I asked him to follow my example and to replace his shoes with guest slippers. My dislike of outdoor shoes and of naked or even socked feet in the house was greater than my embarrassment at asking visitors to wear guest slippers. He complied quickly, politely, masking, I feared, a smirk by bending his head to untie his shoelaces. I couldn't help but look at my apartment through his eyes and knew that despite the concessions I had made to a Western way of life, it would seem not quite Western to him. He followed me to the living room, past the kitchen that effectively divided the living and sleeping quarters. Not materialist, disliking clutter, unwilling to pay for a cleaner, I lived simply and comfortably; my only extravagance, outside of the clothes I wore for work, were books and some videos: I had bookshelves along a whole wall that would, one day, I was sure, be filled. Dozens of postcards I had bought in museum shops filled the spaces on them. Sebastian looked at the books appreciatively before following me into the kitchen where I made tea and where he picked up the smallest of the cookie-cutter men and lifted him to his eye before replacing him on the tiled window sill behind the mixer tap, giving me a knowing look.

'Nice view,' he said, and we stood, as the tea brewed, Sebastian in front of one three-quarter-length sash window and me in front of the other, looking out over the common where any of the joggers and the dog-walkers and the children and their parents looking up would have seen two people, each framed by their window, alone together. He nodded appreciatively out of the window. 'I can see why you chose this flat.'

No, not for the view, though I didn't say as much. Unremarked by Sebastian, dozens of telephone cables and wires streamed to and from a junction point on the outside wall below my window. Positioned there, I could close my eyes and travel all the way to Japan, to Sangenjaya, to home, entering, like a breath of air, my old bedroom, my old bed. I had noticed the ugly assemblage of wires and cables immediately and they had acted as my visual madeleine so immediately and profoundly that I wondered if I hadn't, at some subconscious level, been looking for just this as a feature of a new apartment. I hadn't taken in a word of what the estate agent had said subsequently.

We sat with my low glass table between us and I found comfort in the act of pouring him tea, my body registering the familiarity of the action, of my knees-together posture and my elbows-close-to-body movements. His eyes wandered around my sitting room, lingering on my books and videos. He looked around me to take the measure of me. And rightly so, I thought. Every book is a brick in the building I have become and every film a feature. My parents and the culture I was born into may have laid the foundations but the interior and exterior are mine.

Relaxed, on home ground, I thought this would be the time to press my advantage. The unfamiliarity of his presence here, in my home, the strangeness of the space he filled on my low sofa provoked me to forget my manners as host and to pose the question I had intended to ask him for some time. Taller than me, he appeared even bigger in my flat than he did elsewhere. I placed my cup and saucer on the table, tugged at my skirt and smoothed it over my knees and woollen stockings; I had thought them on the just–fashionable side of neutral, but now feared they might seem school–girly to him. 'So, you have seen my apartment and now you know everything about me,' I said coquettishly. 'But I know nothing about you.' The change from small talk was abrupt.

Sebastian just raised his eyebrows at me.

'Well?' I hoped he would see I was smiling.

'Can one really know anyone?' He seemed unsure of what I expected from him.

I declined to indulge in an abstract, intellectual discussion and made it personal. 'Are you married?'

I surprised him.

'Do you have a girlfriend?' To have brought him home and asked him, in the privacy of my domestic setting, these questions so unexpectedly in such a forthright way rattled him, I could see. 'Where do you live? Who do you live with? Do you have children? Siblings? Are your parents still alive? Do you believe in God? You see, I know nothing about you.'

'Mie, if I had been married, I would have mentioned it by now.' He narrowed his eyes.

I had upset him. I had become emotional. He said nothing and

I heard myself say, 'I'm sorry for the interrogation!' I hoped I had communicated the exclamation mark at the end of my statement, my attempt at levity. I felt like weeping and the anger I felt at wanting to weep compounded the perturbation I had brought upon myself.

'That's okay.' He too put his cup and saucer down. I made for the teapot but he shook his head. Where we had been reclining on our respective sofas, we were now both leaning forward across the battle-field of a coffee table and he spoke earnestly. 'You never asked. Any of these questions. You never asked once.'

'You never volunteered any of it.'

'You never volunteered anything, either.'

'You never asked.'

'I never asked because I respected your culture. And you. You didn't open the door, never once, so I never tried to kick it down.'

'You never even knocked. I couldn't ask because you were my superior. In the bank. And you never showed interest in people or in me. Only in ideas or in paintings or in books.' My voice tailed off as I recognised the injustice of my comments and the sentiment they betrayed.

'Don't forget finance, economics and the odd film,' he added gently.

An image came to me of the back room, the prep room, of my parents' shop when, on a Saturday evening, it had been scrubbed clean and disinfected and all the knives had been put away and the unsold meat returned to its rightful store room. The overhead electric light would bathe the walls of the room in an anaemic blue hue, but the floor stayed a pinkish gray. The room would seem devoid of life, with no indication of the activity, the endeavour, the humour or the anger, the normal range of human emotions and animal body parts that had filled it only hours earlier. The room would seem dead, as though past exhaustion or in suspension.

It took me all of my effort and my hands on my knees to force myself up, to stand. In lieu of the speech I was no longer capable of, I described abstract patterns in the air with my hands that communicated the fact, or so I intended, that I no longer had the energy for this. Deliberately, focusing on each small step, I entered my bedroom in which the setting sun's rays, interrupted by the light brume of the lace curtains, gave the room a subaqueous quality and only increased my sense of wading through a substance thicker than air. I stepped out of my slippers and lay down on the far side of my double bed. I looked at him, beyond the sunlit motes of dust above me, leaning against the doorjamb looking at me, and fell asleep.

When I awoke Sebastian was lying next to me, he too on his back and awake. Direct sunlight, brokered by the naked branches of oaks and beeches and by my drawn lace curtains, caressed the far wall as it edged towards the ceiling, so low was the sun. When I turned to look at him, he turned and looked at me.

'How long have I been asleep?'

'Twenty, maybe thirty minutes.'

'Is that all?' My sleep had rejuvenated me. I lifted a hand to push my hair from my eyes and allowed it, relaxed fingers splayed, to fall in the direction of his. I felt the back of his hand with mine, those long blond fine hairs, the backs of his fingers with mine that interlaced cautiously, delicately. 'The hand of friendship.'

'Friendship,' he said, giving no indication that he had noticed the slight, the raising of a barely imperceptible barrier. Then, 'So, you want to know more about me. Is this a good time to start?'

'It's a good place to start but as to the time...' I sat up. 'Please excuse me.' I was relieved to have a good reason to extricate my hand from his before we reached the embarrassing position of wondering what to do with them next. Leaving my bathroom only once the sound of the cistern refilling had ceased, I sat cross-legged on my bed.

Sebastian placed his hands on his stomach, stared at the ceiling and spoke. 'When I meet someone, at a party – wherever – I never ask them what they do for a living. Knowing what they do, what their profession is, only gives you the illusion of knowing them but, actually, you see them less, you see them through a veil, you bring to them your preconception of what a lawyer, banker, baker is; what that person really is, that becomes harder to grasp. So, of all the questions you asked, the only one that, if answered, would tell you anything about me, is the God one, to which the only honest answer I can give is, I don't understand the question.

'If I had to believe in anything, it would be in something like a life force – Spinoza called it *conatus*, the inner drive of every being to persist in its existence, but let's call it Life. Life wants only to persist through time, to survive, and we all – people, gorillas, crocodiles, amoebae, spiders, ants, birds, fish, germs – are Life's multiplications of its chances of continuance. Species are just rolls of the dice. Life is indifferent about which survives. Life doesn't care that the dinosaurs have died; there will be dead ends, blind alleys, but evolution will open other paths. Environmental destruction? Life doesn't care. Organisms that feed on carbon dioxide and higher temperatures will thrive. Ants and ivy may take over the world – well, that's Life. May humans become extinct, destroy themselves? Yes. Is that necessarily a bad thing? No, not from Life's perspective: more than any other species we have destroyed more species and so closed more doors, blocked more ends than any species before us. Every species seeks to protect itself and to propagate itself according to Life's programme. What's interesting about our species is that we, perhaps more than any other, have developed the fiction of the self in order to do so. We believe this little collection of cells that is us – you, me – to be important, worthy of protection and propagation and so, at the individual level, by maximising our own chance of survival, we do the same for our species'. Therefore, nothing matters. We, all we people, are one. We, all we species, are one. This is what I believe – what I really feel to be true.'

'Nothing matters.'

'Not really. Not in the long run. And not even in the short run unless you want it to.' Sebastian put one hand on my knee. 'I haven't upset you?'

I had been looking out of the window at the setting sun-lit clouds while he had been speaking, so that when I turned and looked down at him in the crepuscular room all I could make out immediately before me were the whites of his eyes floating above an indistinct, darker duvet. An emerging halo of ruffled fair hair restored structure to a face that returned my look with one of concern and, in part, I ungenerously thought, conceit.

'If nothing really matters,' he continued, 'we can embrace hedonism and, well, just enjoy ourselves.' Gently, enquiringly, he began stroking my stockinged knee; I saw rather than felt his action through my ribbed, thick woollen hose.

I caught his fingers and held them in mine before, my heart beating too fast to allow me to formulate an answer, I lifted his hand off my knee and placed it back with its twin on his stomach.

'Or we can do as existentialists propose and create meaning, invest our actions with a purpose of our choosing – which doesn't preclude simultaneously enjoying ourselves.' Slowly raising his hand and extending his fingers he placed them oh so deliberately on my knee again. 'In other words, we could take the fun very seriously.'

Unceremoniously, I raised both knees and clasped them so that his hand fell to the duvet. His citing a rehearsed philosophical position that I required time to consider compounded my discomfiture at having somehow allowed this situation to have developed. Sebastian, here, in my bedroom at dusk and with the upper hand. He, it would seem, knew what he wanted while I didn't. I rested my chin on my knees and raised a finger when he made to resume his advances; I needed some time to think about what he had said. I responded to some of it with my body, essentially, viscerally, refuting from my very heart what he'd said about the fiction of self. I knew that not knowing what I wanted was not the same as knowing what I didn't want. That my room was now in almost complete darkness and his features and mine too, I presumed, quite indiscernible gave me the required courage to talk candidly, and attenuated what physical attraction he possessed. I prepared myself to give the longest speech that he would ever hear me give.

'Who am I? What do I think? Let me tell you something about Japanese women, some things I have heard Japanese women say.' I began to list them and held one hand with outstretched fingers out before him.

'Having a relationship can get in the way of one's life.' I bent my little finger down.

'I don't want a boyfriend. I don't want to feel restrained.

'Couples in the foreign films I watch stay together forever but, in Japan, love fades when you have children and they grow up.

'Having a boyfriend is a hassle.' Only my thumb remained out-stretched.

'Mie, hold on,' he interrupted me. 'Don't start telling me who you are by telling me what other people think.'

'Well, maybe I think in exactly the same way that they do.'

'You don't. Or you wouldn't have said, *maybe*. Would you mind switching a light on? I don't think I can do this in the dark.'

I switched my bedside lamp on, which brought a degree of warmth and benevolence to the room. We blinked in the soft light, two crabs exposed on a summer's beach and content to forego shelter while the sun shone. Abashed, I was not so much uncomfortable for us to be revealed to each other together on my bed as embarrassed at how comfortable I felt. 'I had this big speech prepared but then you inter-rupted me.'

'Well, I'm sorry. Go on.' He raised himself on his elbows. 'Tell me what else you've heard Japanese women say.'

I said, 'When I see happy couples at Christmas I wish they would die.' I lowered my closed hand.

We looked at each other. The absurdity of that statement was greater than its misanthropy. I giggled and he chuckled. I convulsed as I snorted and I covered my mouth with my hand. He laughed expansively, chest out, head back and mouth open wide. Unbalanced, I fell onto him and allowed myself for a moment to rest my head on his chest, from which unusual angle the protrusion of his canines amidst his otherwise perfect teeth and the lush redness of his mouth confounded me. His arms flopped carelessly, caressingly around me. I saw myself a fly in a Venus flytrap, that scarlet-padded carnivorous plant that seems an aberration of nature, and I went rigid and opened my eyes wide to look up at him and he narrowed his to look down at me. His lower and upper eyelashes resembled the cilia that lace together when the trap shuts on its prey. We stopped laughing.

The adamantine sense of immobility I must have communicated, my dissemination from every pore of the anticipation of an unwel-come advance (must have) led him to open his arms wide, theatrically, and to rest them by his side before saying in a voice that did little to hide his frustration and, even, anger, 'Mie, do you know what you're doing? You bring a horse to water but you don't let him drink.'

He was right, of course.

I stood and walked to the window and looked out. I hadn't put my slippers back on but considered it awkward to look for them so I stood there, my back to him but watching him closely in the window's reflection. By changing focus, I could follow the red and white lights of the cars as they criss-crossed the common and traced patterns on the reflection of his face. The reflection of my ruffled hair clouded the sky in exaggerated imitation of the branches of the trees below it. I took satisfaction in the successful collimation of the tree branches with the common's tangential roads much as I had, years ago, when aligning plane trails and telephone wires, confirmation that my intended course of action was the right one.

Sebastian sat up too. 'Where do we go from here, Mie?'

My heart went out to him, not romantically, but sororally or maternally, as it would to a child for whom one had some responsibility or, at the very least, a deep reservoir of affection. I made a decision. 'I know where you are going.'

'Where?' His tone, as his reflection gazed at mine, was defeatist and melancholy.

I had intended to add, 'Home,' but sympathy and remorse mixed with mischief led to me to say, 'Why don't you go and see Sharon?'

Sebastian sat up straight and wore an expression of extreme surprise. 'What! Why on earth are you bringing her into this?'

I wasn't sure how to answer him; I had regretted mentioning Sharon the moment I had spoken her name. Confused, I brought my face close to the window, so that my expression might be concealed from him, and watched a cyclist dismount from his bicycle in order to cross at a pedestrian crossing. The red light on his bicycle pulsed in time with my heart. I had brought Sharon into this either to enjoy the petty thrill of sharing her secret, or because I considered her guilty of attributing the drift of our friendship to my promotion and resented her for it. Or a mix of the two. I said, as if by way of explanation, 'She can give you what you want. I'm sorry I misled you. But she can, you know.' I turned from the window to look at him directly. 'She's a stripper, you see.'

Sebastian had stood, but sat immediately down on the bed again, keeping his eyes fixed on mine all the time. In them I read incomprehension, disbelief.

'Or a lap dancer.' That sounded weak. My confusion matched his, as I realised that I didn't know the difference between the two and might have maligned Sharon. I gave him the name of her club, as though that would help him come to a clearer understanding of exactly what she was.

Sebastian's blue eyes lost their focus, they seemed to lose their colour and swim in the middle distance as though an original thought preoccupied him. He had blanched and in the bleaching light of the bedside lamp he resembled an albino, his tightly pressed lips his darkest feature. Eventually, he nodded and felt for his discarded guest slippers on the floor. He put them soles together, held them in one hand and stood again. I sensed the extreme effort he expended to turn his attention from Sharon to me. 'Mie,' was all he said, looking at me dolefully, and shrugged his shoulders.

I smiled fixedly at him.

'It's so disappointing that, after all this time, you can know me so little.' He waved the slippers in his hand half-heartedly at me. 'Or do you have this idea that "all men are the same"? I mean, really, I wonder what I've done to deserve this.' He smiled ruefully at me.

I gathered my slippers and followed him into the hall where I watched while he tied his shoelaces and shrugged his jacket on.

'I'm sorry,' I said and stood on tiptoe to kiss him on both cheeks. I understood his disappointment and frustration but felt no remorse at having been its cause; if anything, I was cross with him for having got this far with me. I opened the front door and stood by it.

'Bye, Mie,' he said resignedly, squeezing me by the shoulders.

I watched Sebastian descend the stairs, following his gradual effacement with each step, first his feet, his knees next, then his waist, his hand on the banister, his arm and shoulder, the mop of his hair last until he had disappeared entirely from view on the landing below. I heard the building's front door open and shut and, ever so quietly, unaware of the time and not wanting to disturb my neighbours, I closed my apartment door behind me and went to the window to monitor his progress across the streetlamp-lit common. My reflection, however, given the nocturnal landscape and internal light source, once again dominated the view and I found myself looking at myself, standing slim and straight, hands by my side, appearing to all the world like a bold, capital I.

Sharon

I was feeling a bit down, so Tony's gloomy 'Good evening, Sharon,' as he held the door open for me resonated precisely within me, as though he weren't announcing a welcome but a plague or a death.

'Pierre must be thinking of retiring him soon,' had said Melanie recently.

'Pierre must be thinking of retiring himself soon,' I had said.

I sat next to Melanie in knickers and bra facing my reflection in my dressing table's mirror. Three of its ten light bulbs had blown. There were nine such tables in the girls' dressing room, ninety-one bulbs in the room in all, including the one overhead light.

Melanie was complaining that her boyfriend's business was doing well and that he was pressurising her to leave the club. 'He says that it's not right for a businessman of his stature to have a lap dancer for a wife so if I want to marry him I'll have to stop. Can you believe it? He's a brickie with ideas above his station. He's very happy to have me dance for him.' She admired her painted face.

'If you follow Gaia out of here, I'm leaving too,' I said, looking at myself directly in the mirror to see if I could detect any insincerity.

'I mean, if I'm not good enough for him as I am…' said Melanie, and left her sentence unfinished.

'But I thought that's what you wanted,' I said. 'Marriage, children, the big house.'

'Yes,' sighed Melanie. 'But, you know, I've always been able to bring so much money to the table and then he'd be my boss and my husband and I'd lose all my, you know, independence. Anyway, there's a limit to how much longer I can keep on doing this. If he asked to marry me, now, as I am, then I'd give it up on the spot, but if he says I've got to give it up for him to marry me then I won't. But I can't very well tell him that, can I? How long do we have left, Sharon?' Melanie indicated the younger girls reflected in our light bulb-surrounded mirrors. 'Five years max?'

'Thank you so much for yesterday,' said Eva, a Spanish girl, coming up to me from behind and leaning over me to kiss me on both cheeks.

Her dark hair tickled my neck and her breasts kneaded my back. A drunk punter had refused to let go of her hand until I had talked to him and promised him all manner of things and had Tony bundle him into a cab. Where I had once looked forward to the admiring looks my customers would give me, I was now made happy by the need these young girls had for me. I had gone from ingénue to auntie in turn and didn't mind.

Attired in bikinis that were held in place by strings at the hips, at the neck and in between both bra–cups, thereby giving us several options when stripping, Melanie and I left the dressing room to greet our early customers.

I was in between dances when I saw Sebastian. My impulse was to run and hide, to regain the sanctuary of the girls' dressing room, but his eyes were fixed on mine. Pierre was insistent that girls not throw themselves at the men at the foot of the stairs but give them a moment to collect themselves, calm their beating hearts and overcome their trepidation, so I was unusual in making my way directly to him. I imagined myself walking down the trading room aisle as I made my way through the men seated on the pouffes and low comfy chairs, past the ice buckets on stands and the low tables, around the dancing girls. We stood facing each other, close, in order to be able to speak above the music.

'How long have you been here?'

'Long enough to see you dance.'

'Do you want to sit down?' I turned to find a seat.

He caught me by the arm and said, 'Why not go upstairs? It seems quieter there.'

I looked at his hand on my arm.

He let go of me.

'Give me a moment. If you find a table upstairs, I'll follow you shortly.'

I retrieved a cardigan from my locker, inspected my make–up and made my way to the office where I found Wanda getting ready to go home. 'Aunt Wanda,' I said, 'will you still be here in five minutes?'

'Yes, I think so. Why?'

'Do you remember that man I was seeing some years ago? The one from the bank?'

'Yes.'

'Well, he's just turned up and wants to talk.'

'Interesting!'

'I'm not so certain. Could you find me and liberate me if necessary?'

'Of course. How will I know if you want liberating?'

'You'll know.'

Sebastian had chosen one of the many unoccupied tables upstairs and was declining the attention of a new girl, who arched her eyebrows at me when I effectively dismissed her by sitting next to him.

'How long have you been working here?'

'Quite a few years. Once a week.'

'Even when we were seeing each other?'

I nodded.

He slapped his knees and rocked back on his low-backed armchair. 'I don't believe it!'

'What?'

'You think you know someone. Why didn't you tell me?'

'Did you ever ask me?'

'Oh, God, not this again.'

'What?'

He waved his hand as though to erase my question. We looked at each other.

'Is this your first time here?' I asked.

'Yes.'

'In fact,' it occurred to me to ask, 'why did you come here?'

'Why do you think?'

'What? You knew I'd be here?'

'Yes.'

'How? Why, when you can talk to me any day of the week?'

'Mie told me. That I'd find you here.'

'Mie! Oh well, I suppose she kept it quiet long enough. Do you see Mie out of the office then?'

He scowled. 'No!'

'But why come looking for me here when you can speak to me in the office?'

He didn't reply.

I giggled as I placed a hand on his knee and asked mischievously, 'Go on, tell me, are Mie and you seeing each other?'

'No!' Irritated, he swung his knee away from under my hand.

We were quiet a moment and waved away the offer of a drink. 'Actually, just bring us some still water, please,' I said to the departing waitress in lingerie. She gave me a strange look 'We are meant to encourage customers to buy champagne,' I explained to Sebastian.

He made a gesture that expressed something between indifference and a mild antipathy. 'Whatever.'

'So, you wanted to see me,' I said sombrely.

'Why?'

'Oh, come on.'

'Why? Why do you do this?'

I had no easy reply.

'Come home with me. This evening.'

'I can't,' I said, pulling my cardigan tight around me.

'I see,' he said. 'Is there someone else?'

'No.'

'Do you take,' and he waved his hand around the room, 'your customers home afterwards then, is that it?'

'Ouch! That was a bit below the belt.'

He was unapologetic. 'Then why not?'

It seemed cruel to tell Sebastian that the girl who had once climbed so willingly into his bed was not the woman before him today, and that he couldn't lay claim to her just because he thought she was. Looking away from him, my gaze took in the unoccupied pouffes that were like so many stepping stones in a sea of rippling lights. I was the same human being as the girl who had taken timid steps from stone to stone, but I wasn't the same person.

The waitress returned with the water that she poured into two glasses, and the bill that she placed on a saucer in front of Sebastian while presenting him with her full cleavage. He tried and failed not to stare.

'Have you been seeing a lot of blokes, then?' he asked, raising his head.

'Some.'

'Do you ever see the customers here? Out of here. As in a relationship,' he added hastily.

'No! I told you. We're not allowed to.' I passed him his glass and drank from mine.

'Did you ever see any other blokes while we were seeing each other?'

'You've got no right to ask that question!' I touched his knee with my hand again. 'What is this?' I asked gently. 'We don't see each other for years and then you come over all jealous.'

'Hmmph.' He dropped his eyes to the floor momentarily.

I looked at him closely. He looked tired, and I realised now that I examined him properly that he had aged, of course; and yet, paradoxically, his air was one of a disappointed boy whose toy had been placed out of reach. His fair hair was tousled, as though he'd just got out of bed, and fairer, bleached to the point of being nearly white in the club's reflected mix of coloured lights, and his clothes seemed tighter on him, as though he persisted in shopping for clothes of the same size as he had ten years ago. His trainers and torn jeans contrasted somewhat comically with his ribbed polo neck jumper and sheepskin jacket. His eyes, still blue but, I thought, unusually bloodshot, couldn't keep from moving over my shoulder. I turned in my seat to sit closer to him and afford him an uninterrupted view of the club's first-floor lounge area, in which the new girls served drinks and encouraged customers to the dancing floor below. He waved one hand in their general direction and said, 'It's enough to turn a man to crime.'

'What is?'

'All this,' he said. 'This. Downstairs. I mean, honestly. All this flesh. This meat. All this look but don't touch. How does a heterosexual man stand it?' A little bemused, clearly having no idea what to expect, he watched Aunt Wanda approach us.

I introduced them to one another.

Sebastian placed his glass on the table, stood and the two shook hands. 'How do you do?' he said, looking incredulous when I introduced her as Aunt Wanda, and embarrassed to have to adjust his trousers. He did his jacket up, as though out of courtesy on meeting her.

Wanda smiled knowingly and said she was off home and would see me later.

He sat back down and watched her depart with interest. 'I see it's in the family,' he said, his eyes still on her. 'Working in a place like this with one's aunt. I don't know. Does she? Did she? You know.'

I laughed and shook my head in turn. 'Oh no, she's an accountant. She helps run the place.'

'When I saw that slob.'

'Who?'

'The slob you were dancing for downstairs. He was salivating. I wanted to smash his face in.'

'No!'

'If he had touched you I would have done.' He flared his nostrils and clenched his fists exaggeratedly.

'What's got into you?'

'What's got into me? What hasn't got into me?'

We watched the girls and the customers at the bar making their way up- and downstairs.

'What about you?' I said. 'Are you seeing anyone?'

'No.'

'Have you been?'

'No. Not really. Not at all, in fact.'

'And that's the problem,' I said, unable to keep the smile from my face.

'You could say that.' He frowned.

'You're not getting any.' I said it thoughtfully, as though regretfully, and couldn't help but tease. I lay a finger on his knee.

He glared at me and, absurdly, I feared he might cry.

'Would you like to?' I said it slowly and very deliberately, two fingers on his thigh. An idea had come to me.

He looked at me incredulously. 'Sharon! Are you toying with me? I should never have come.' He couldn't help but turn his eyes to a beautiful Japanese girl in a thong and two star-shaped spangles for a bikini top who had sat down nearby with a man who appeared to be three times her age.

I raised my fingers to his chin and turned his head to face me. 'Would you like to spend the night with a kind, beautiful and very sexy friend of mine who has heard a lot about you from me and who said she'd like to get to know you?'

'Sharon!'

'Would you?'

'This is all doing my head in. Earlier today I went to a museum with a friend who took me home with her and who raised my expectations of – oh, never mind. Let's say, a deepening friendship. And this evening I find myself in a strip club getting propositioned by an ex-girlfriend on behalf of one of her friends!'

'Her name is Gaia. Gaia.' I gave him the name of Gaia's club and its address and had him repeat it. 'It's ten minutes in a cab. I'll call her, tell her you're coming.'

'So you really won't come home with me?'

'I won't go home with you.'

'And you really expect me to go and see this – this Gaia?'

'Yes.'

'You're kidding me.'

'No.' I had never felt more serious. 'You can each be my present to the other.'

'And on Monday, you'll walk to my desk with your little chits to sign in triplicate, you'll glide through the dealing room to me and we'll pretend none of this ever happened?'

'Yes,' I replied.

I stood while Sebastian settled the bill for the water and then I accompanied him to the velvet ceiling-to-floor drapes that marked the exit before moving to the window. On tiptoe and gripping the brass rail, from above the purple velour curtains, I saw Tony raise an arm above the crowds on the street and hail him a taxi. The exhilarating clamour of London's nightlife – its people and tourists, its car horns and bicycle bells – reached me through the closed window. Every night was a carnival. I watched Sebastian shoulder and sidestep his way around friends in groups and couples arm in arm. The taxi stopped at a red light. I fancied I saw Sebastian looking back, at me, but, what with the winking traffic and car lights and my and the other girls' reflections crossed by the many faces of revellers on their way home or to pubs and clubs, it was difficult to be certain whose overlapping face was whose.

Isabella

You entered the club and stood with the heavy wooden door open momentarily, framing you. The late autumn cold, the wind and the leaves followed you in and in the seconds between tracks I could hear the leaves quarrelling on the bare wooden floor. You seemed to be waiting for your eyes to adjust to the poor light and they met mine, fleetingly, before moving onto the next girl and the next before tracking back to mine.

You were exactly as Sharon had described you, your hair tousled, as though you'd just got out of bed, and achromatised to the point of appearing nearly white in the club's strip lights above the door and your clothes tight on you, as though they'd shrunk in the wash. You wore trainers that were old and jeans that were torn slightly at one knee and yet were clean and had not been inexpensive. A ribbed purple polo neck jumper and a sheepskin jacket betrayed your age. Your eyes were a striking blue beneath bushy pale eyebrows and long fair eyelashes.

I had come to notice these things, the material things. I had come to know the difference between a pair of jeans and a pair of chinos and the difference between off the shelf and made to measure, not so much in terms of how much they cost but of how much their wearer would pay or tip me. I noticed the cufflinks, too, and the heavy watches and the ties and the absence or presence of a wedding ring and would know what a girl's takings would be for a night. A suit, a shirt, a tie, a watch and cufflinks: a contemporary Venetian mask held before its owner like a Plato's form. But this was different, this set-up was different. You were new to this, you had different expectations. You were new to me; and the game, I had come to realise, was old to me and I was tired of it.

Godehard materialised next to you, welcomed you, took you by the elbow, indicating the stage, the bar, the lounge area, the private rooms beyond and told you, I know, of the entry fee, of the obligatory purchase of a bottle of champagne, of the cost of a dance and of your and a girl's liberty to negotiate whatever you and she wanted. He stayed your hand as it reached for your inside pocket; there would be time enough later to settle bills.

I observed you in the long mirror behind the bar as you wandered the bare floorboards, wondering what your move should be and when and how to make it. As you walked past me, I removed my handbag from the bar stool next to me and placed it on the bar. I knew you would sit there and you did. It's as if the removal of the handbag creates a vacuum that a man can't help but fill. That's the great thing about the handbag-on-the-bar-stool routine. If a girl doesn't like the look of the punter she keeps her handbag there, and more often than not he'll move on. If she does, she removes it and it's like reeling him in like a fish.

'Hello,' you said. 'Sebastian.'

'Hello.'

'Gaia,' you said.

'Yes.'

You asked Dieter, the barman, for the wine list that you perused with arched eyebrows before handing it to me open at the first page and saying, 'Please pick a champagne you like.'

I chose a relatively inexpensive one.

You nodded gratefully.

'Gaia,' you repeated. 'Is that a real name?'

'Yes,' I replied truthfully, though I knew that what you had said was not exactly what you had meant. 'So. Sharon. She's very fond of you.'

'Not fond enough, clearly.' You spoke more with resignation than with rancour.

Dieter produced the bottle and an ice bucket on a tray.

'Would you like to sit down with me in the lounge area?' I indicated it with an upward inclination of my head and eyebrows. 'I think we'll be more comfortable there.'

You said you would love to and stood, courteously moving your bar stool out of my way.

I looked at you in the mirrors as we glided silently by and saw you observing my back and my hips that I swayed to the music that was now Country and Western. I was wearing a black see-through strapless dress that was split up the sides all the way to my waist. In my glass six-inch high-heeled shoes I came up to your shoulder.

Dieter pursued us with the champagne flutes and the champagne in the ice bucket until we reached the last of a dozen brown leather sofas and smoked glass tables. 'I think you'll be comfortable here, sir,' he said obsequiously.

'I'm sure we will,' you replied. I liked that, that you were thinking of my comfort, too, and not just of your own.

You indicated a sofa and you only sat down once I had, tucking your leg up under you a bit so that you were naturally inclined towards me with your arm extended along the sofa back behind me. We were as close to each other as we could be without actually touching and, after I had filled the flutes and we had said 'Cheers!', I brought my flute to my parted lips and just held it there, my tongue's tip exposed to the wine's soft petillance.

I hoped the low light hid my imperfections: my poor complexion and skin quality. I had powdered my face but knew that the light source, positioned behind you and shining directly on to my right cheek, would probably not help me conceal it completely. That was the problem with my job: too little exposure to natural light. Over the years, this had taken its toll.

The bar was a long way from us, well at the other end of this long, low-ceilinged room as if viewed from the objective lens of a telescope, and it all felt very private, very intimate. Godehard was speaking to a punter while the other girls looked on without interest. I felt very pleased to have you and imagined the conversation I would have with Sharon when I saw her next.

'So,' you said, looking around you. 'This is an interesting place.'

'Have you never been here before?' I knew you hadn't.

'Never.'

'Ever to a place like this?'

You shifted in your seat. 'In Japan – well, they're different there, the *geisha* bars.'

'Sharon told me you'd been to Japan.'

You asked, 'So, how does this place work, exactly?'

'Didn't Godehard tell you?'

'That chap at the door? I didn't really take anything in that he said, frankly.'

I placed my champagne flute on the table and rearranged the top of my dress to better explain. 'Like this. We can sit and chat for a while, but then we can go into one of the private rooms for a dance that'll last a couple of songs.'

'And then?' you asked.

I could see my outstretched legs and feet in their glass shoes through the smoked brown glass table-top and waggled my toes.

'And then you go home with me. Come on,' I said and held out my hand.

You stood and indicated the champagne flutes. 'Shall we leave them here?'

I said you could take yours if you wanted to. You buttoned your jacket, middle button only, then took your champagne flute in one hand and my hand in the other, allowing me to lead you back the way we had come.

We weaved, you, me and our dull reflections, through the brown sofa suites, along the once polished floor to the bar area and to the adjoining private rooms. The lights were low and flattering to both the girls and the rooms themselves: they hid the dirt on the floor and on the benches' worn mauve plastic upholstery, rubbed bare by the clenched arses of so many punters. The seating area was horseshoe-shaped and surrounded by mirrors. You closed the mirrored door behind you and there we were in the pink gloom: hundreds of *you*s and *me*s: a stripper and her punter reflected to infinity from the waist up with hundreds of disco balls rotating slowly above us, duplicated and reduplicated past and future images of a man and a woman.

You said something and I replied automatically without taking in what you had said; I was thinking of what dance to give you. I invited you to sit down, then stepped in between your legs and moved them apart with mine. 'You must be comfortable and relaxed,' I said, and I ran my hand through your hair as I looked down at you. It gave me a strange sense of satisfaction, messing up your already ruffled hair. I held my hand to my nose and sniffed. It smelled nice, of apple and something else. Your hair and my hand were the only things that smelled nice in that room. You sat there, palms down either side of you, looking up at me expectantly. 'I said, relax,' I said. I swayed gently in time with a pop song.

'I said, this is all too weird,' you said.

I danced long and well. With the right person, a clean and courteous man, I could escape, withdraw into a song and into my body and so leave it and the moment. Away, I became more desirable. I could touch you but you couldn't touch me. I maintained contact throughout, my knee against your knee, a caress, my hand on your shoulder, the brush of my hair in your face, my bottom perched on your lap momentarily, fleetingly, full of promise that failed to deliver. You closed your eyes and opened them. You parted your lips and licked them. You shifted in your seat. We entered our fourth song and I knew that Godehard would be watching me closely on one of the monitors behind the bar by now; when the song came to an end the lights rose. We were both perspiring. The look on your face as you sat looking up at me was of a child coveting a sweet.

'What's so funny?' you asked defensively.

'Nothing.' I swept your hair back with both hands and patted it down. 'I've ruffled you.'

You stood and ensured your jacket was buttoned. 'That was, that was…' you said, lost for words.

I excused myself in order to towel down and to fetch a shawl, the worst thing about my job being the constant passage from cold inactivity to perspiration and back; there was always a girl with a cold in my place of work.

'The worst thing?' you queried.

'That and the lack of sunlight,' I said.

You said, 'Look, as you're going to get dressed anyway, why don't you get dressed once and for all and we can just, you know, move on? I'll settle up in the meantime.'

'So, tell me about Sharon,' I requested, taking your arm with one hand

and clutching my coat around my neck against the night air with the other.

'Sharon,' you reflected. 'She's a lovely girl. There. That's about it. You probably know her better than I do. How can you walk in those?'

'It's not far.' I kept flat shoes in my shoulder bag but stiletto heels allowed me to totter, to lean on my escort and to bring out the beau in him.

It was midnight and the streets were quiet. We made our way from pool of light to pool of light, Farringdon's streetlight-lit stepping stones. We stopped at a red pedestrian traffic light.

'That's a hive of activity up there,' you said, looking ahead. We started across the road.

'That's the meat market.'

We made our way through the press of traders and butchers, through thickets of pending carcasses and sides of meat.

'This place is fantastic!' You marvelled at the buzz and bustle, the lights and the shouts, the slabs and parcels of animals, the energy and the geniality that the meat market radiated. We stood to one side so you could look around you. 'It's like a cathedral.' You looked up at the ceiling, at the roof supports, struts and gird-ers. 'A Victorian cast–iron cathedral built in veneration of meat.' A side of venison on a running porter's shoulder obstructed your face from mine for a moment, a purple brush across my field of vision. 'It's frenetic!'

'You should have seen it before it was modernised,' I shouted. 'All this' – and I indicated the new overhead meat rail system – 'wasn't here then. It was a riot.'

'It's worse than our trading room! Or maybe I mean better. It's like your strip club. Flesh – meat on display. Fresh meat for sale! Sorry,' you added, but seemed too enthralled to really care that you might have offended me.

'Here we are,' I said.

As Frederica had observed, our punters rarely passed more than a cursory glance around our sitting room, whether out of cour-tesy or lack of interest, and, even when they did, I was indifferent to them, to what conclusions about the apartment's inhabitants they might draw. However, Sharon's introduction had changed the nature of our encounter; you were the friend of a friend. You wandered around, picked items up and examined them closely before replacing them; you admired the view that you guessed rightly would be of even greater attraction in daylight.

'You live here alone?' you asked.

I told you no, but that Frederica had met a man and was more out than in, so it felt to me as though I did.

'How lucky,' you stated, leaving me unsure whether you meant for me, generally, or for us, for this evening, specifically.

You declined a beer and a tea but accepted a glass of water.

'This is the second time today I've been in a girl's apartment,' you said to the window.

'Did you not get what you wanted the first time?' I asked your reflection coquettishly. I stood by you and we looked out over the London skyline, our reflections hanging in the night sky above the meat market in parody of the pigs on butchers' hooks being shuffled from lorry to stall below.

Turning from your reflection to you, I made a mental note to ask Sharon what had done it for her, what she had seen in you, to discover whether she had fallen for the obvious in you, your symmetrical features, your mane, your height, the perfectly straight nose, or for the defects that rendered you human: the slightly overly large ears, which was presumably why you wore your hair long, and the canine tooth that rested on your lower lip when you hadn't quite closed your mouth, that made you look boyish and cheeky, more endearing than frightening and more goofy than frighteningly good-looking.

'Shall I help you out of your coat?' I offered.

'It's a little chilly,' you protested.

I insisted. 'It will be warmer in the bedroom.' I removed your coat and hung it on the back of the chair. 'It's this way.' I pulled you by the hand but you resisted, kept your feet rooted so that our reflections in the window appeared arrested mid-dance.

'Should we, you know, agree terms or however you put it?' you proposed determinedly, as though intent on overcoming your timidity.

'No,' I said. 'No. Money doesn't come into it. Not at all. Come,' and I pulled you into the hallway and into my bedroom and closed the bedroom door behind us.

'Hold on,' you said, and paused to consider Cosmo's pencil drawings that I had tacked to the doorframe. 'You?' you enquired.

I shook my head. 'My brother.'

You nodded approvingly. 'Very good.'

No one had ever remarked on Cosmo's art to me and I was overcome with lapping waves of pride and gratitude.

You looked at Cosmo's pictures more closely and then at me, as though assessing me in a new light. 'Really good.'

I kicked my stiletto heels off.

'The same wonderful view,' you noted, 'and, yes, you're right, it is warm in here.'

Our reflections had followed us in.

'Yes,' I said, looking down at the cast–iron radiator that ran the length of the window that took up the entirety of one wall. 'We don't even need curtains.'

'Doesn't the daylight bother you?'

'No! I can't get enough of it. And there's no one to overlook us. Anyway, it's night now.'

You sat on the bed and I knelt to unlace your shoes. 'I can do that,' you said quickly, embarrassed.

I hadn't stripped provocatively but had undressed with my back to you and hung my clothes in the wardrobe and yours on the back of a chair. We lay in bed side by side with the duvet pulled up to our armpits as I imagined virgins might on their wedding night, or a married couple many years after theirs. From our low vantage point at some remove from the window we could no longer see Smithfield Market's roof but office blocks, silhouettes of irregular shape and height that bordered the river, St Paul's dome, the flashing lights of the radio masts in South London's more elevated suburbs and, before them all, our faces, hovering disembodied in pools of soft light and each framed by the massive window's vertical and horizontal crossbars like a diptych. I felt for you under the duvet and found your thigh and then your hand and held it.

'You'll forgive me if my mind is spinning,' you said, turning to look at me and laying one forearm across your brow. 'I've had two options expire out of the money and now.' You stopped and started again. 'I've had two rejections and now this. Not to mention extreme sexual provocation in two clubs, culminating in a dance stimulating enough to drive a man to commit an act of unspeakable savagery.' You squeezed my hand, I assumed, to convey the humour that your eyes failed to communicate.

'I'm sorry,' I said, and then, 'Well, your luck is in!' and I wriggled a little closer to you. We lay not quite touching, fingertips to fingertips was all, and yet I could feel the heat that emanated from you all the way down my right side, down my thigh, calf, ankle and foot. 'So who was foolish enough to rebuff you?' I asked, flattering you.

'Sharon, you know,' you replied. 'But I understand. To return to an old flame is a retrograde step. And besides,' you added ruefully, 'I didn't exactly try to woo her with flowers and charm this evening.'

'No?'

'No. I think I expressed all the subtlety of a caveman. If I could have hit her on the head and dragged her home after me, I would have.'

'How do you find her? I mean, what's she like in the office? I've always struggled to picture her there.'

'Much as she is elsewhere, I would think. Anyway, we don't work in what I would term a conventional office. It's more like the market down there. She's guileless, friendly, enthusiastic.'

'And the other? There was another rejection?' My little finger, as I held your hand, traced little circles on your thigh.

You flared your nostrils and grimaced, your mouth down at the lips, the tip of your canine on one side just visible. 'She's Japanese. A colleague of ours. She is the opposite, come to think of it, quite the opposite of Sharon. Everything that Sharon isn't intellectually and nothing that she is physically. She is as rigid as

Sharon is pliable, as frigid as Sharon is warm. To think,' you sat up a little, 'to think I had to visit her bedroom to learn that!'

'So your ideal woman,' I teased, 'would have a little of your Japanese girl in her and a little of Sharon?' Tracing circles on the inside of your thigh now.

You responded by turning to me and burrowed your face in my neck, inhaling deeply. 'That bit, that bit behind a woman's ear, the smell and taste of it, that's what I love,' you said.

'You kinky thing!' I exclaimed.

You turned fully, your right leg over mine now, your arm around my shoulder and both our hearts beating faster. Your head still buried in my hair, you clutched me hard. 'Your dancing,' you said, ignoring my teasing. 'I have never had to exercise such self-control. Are men really expected to behave when tormented so much?'

I laughed and stroked your hair. 'You're flattering me!' And flattening me. I adjusted my weight under yours in the language of slight body shifts, movements, touches that all lovers understand. I raised my knees and was surprised, of all the touches and sensations, to be aware of my big toes against the backs of your knees, as though they had been made to fit those tendon-edged hollows, and I looked into your eyes to read if you had read the amusement in mine and was overwhelmed by the intensity of their blue. I had the impression of swimming up to them, the bedside light filtering through the hanging, curling locks of your hair that tickled my cheeks and my neck, up from ultramarine depths, up, up into your eyes and through, higher yet, flexing and inflating forewings and hindwings, slowly but strongly, purposefully and evenly, the night's warm draughts carrying me higher, higher and out.

What do we look like to birds, bees and butterflies, seen from above? We look alike as we come together, separate, travel side by side for minutes or years, move in contra-direction, evade one another, lie side by side, lie on top of each other. Our identities blend, they change, they interchange, in intercourse they interchange and change back and change again; the coincidence of our bodies with our selves is striking, wondrous – miraculous. We lose and find ourselves at a steady rhythm. We are lazy: it's that much easier assigning one self to one body, that's all, it's less confusing and easier to follow and to keep tabs on, it's easier to advance the existence of, to have flourish, every little parcel of cells that comprise each one of us than to admit of the self as a fiction, as an essential and efficient narrative that enables the persistence of us, of Life. We are wired for deception, for Life's anabasis, advancement and promulgation, for our blind faith in Life. It is the flesh on our bones, It is the sugar in Mama's *bonbons*, It is the air in St Ethelreda's Church, the hanging Jesus Its best salesman. We congregate in villages, in towns and in cities where we hide in full view. Deception by numbers. At the meat counter in a supermarket in Paderborn, a red kidney-shaped ticket dispenser spewed numbered tickets out to Oma and me that we exchanged together with money for packets of offal, chops and sausages that Oma would have me carry home in cloth carrier bags, stained brown at the bottom from years of leaky meats. Look after the package. Don't drop it. Guard it with your life! Don't you know? You are the package you carry with you. Mama, I forgive you. Papa, I forgive you. You were wrongly wired, overzealously wired, your urge to multiply and go forth was too great, out of control, it was misplaced, misdirected is all. Mama, I cannot forgive you. Papa, I cannot forgive you. You haunt my every waking day, my every move with every lover. You crept into my garden and into my bedroom; you stole my innocence, poisoned my apple, corrupted my happiness, you severed me from my body as a baby's umbilical cord to its mother is cut. You made it impossible for me to love and to be loved without my seeing your face and hearing your hollow endearments. And those of your friends. You sold me too cheaply, Papa. That you were pinned to the worktop by Grandpapa as you pinned a butterfly to its board is no excuse, Papa. I must see your face, feel your breath, bear your weight: you colour my life not in pastels but in ochres, crimsons and blacks. You pushed and you shoved, there's pushing and shoving and then, only then do I arrive at a liberation of sorts: my butterfly, the butterfly I am, me. But now

I tire of myself, that me that is not the true me, not me in my entirety.

'Are you sleeping?' I repeated, a little louder.

'Not any longer.' You had fallen asleep on your back so you had only to open your eyes and turn your head a little to look at me, the tip of your side tooth just visible on your lower lip irresistible; I lowered my head and kissed it, kissed your lips, gently.

'What do you believe in?' I asked you quietly.

'Really?' you asked.

'Yes,' I whispered.

'Give me a clue,' you requested. 'Tell me what you believe in first.'

'It's not so much what I believe *in*, just more what I believe.'

'What do you believe?'

'That there's more than this and that there's nothing. That I'm nothing and everything. That I'm not just mind and not just body and that I'm not any more than either or the two of them combined. That you can't step in the same garden twice. That everything I have ever done or said was said or done by different versions of myself. That the selves I've left behind are more strange to me than strangers. What's so funny?'

'I'm not laughing at you,' you said defensively, still laughing.

'Oh, no?' I poked you in the ribs and you caught my hand and held it. We were still naked under the duvet. 'What do you believe in, then?'

You raised your head and rested it on your hand, looking straight at me, serious all of a sudden. 'I thought I believed in everything you said to begin with. I believe in choice. I believe in me. And I think I believe in you.' You released my hand and traced my lips with your fingers, inserting one in my mouth. I bit on the dry knuckle and held it. 'You can bite harder,' you said.

I did.

'Do you think that by eating me you can –'

'I can what?' I mumbled, sucking your finger.

'Acquire my power? My knowledge, my essence and *charisma?*'
You spoke ironically.

I bit harder yet.

'Ouch!'

I released you.

'I liked that,' you said, as through surprised at yourself, examining
and then rubbing your knuckle.

I could tell. 'Tell me what else you like,' I added more quietly, moving constantly a little besides you, to and fro.

'Do you want me to tell you? Do you really want me to tell
you?' and parting my hair with your tooth-marked finger, tucking a lock of my hair behind my exposed ear you whispered in
it, breathed into it, nibbled my earlobe, licked it.

'Oh, that!' I laughed. 'That! That can easily be arranged!' and I
threw the duvet back with one hand while feeling for you with the
other.

I have thrown back the duvet and face the end of the bed, the
window and beyond. What do you and I look like from above?
I know, as I flutter by. The duvet lies puckered, half on the foot
of the bed, half on the floor. The tops of my feet touch the
soft cotton of the sheet either side of your head, your blond hair
radiating from you as though electrified. My knees are by your
shoulders and my elbows are either side of your hips. The mat-
tress is firm but yielding, soft but supportive of me in this act
of supplication. Up, up I fly and around and around. I am dizzy
with titillation, with excitement, elation and exhaustion, with liking and love for Sharon, for you and for me. I suffer a revelation,
an epiphany of sorts so sharp in the joy it delivers that it's as
much a source of pain, the learning that I can love myself, that if
I don't love myself no one will. I'm airborne, carried higher on
draughts and by winds. At intervals, I rest and breathe. I feel the
tips of each of your fingers and thumbs distinctly on my buttocks.
The pale hairs on your legs are the finest of seaweed, your knees
the rocks that shift and shape over eons, the reefs that protrude
from the seabed at the lowest of tides. We came up out of the

sea and the mud, apparently. Grandpapa told me that butterflies pre–date *Homo sapiens* by tens of millions of years. Up, up and out I fly, floating in giddy happiness higher, higher. Out of the muck and the clay came the villages, the towns and the cities, few as big, as throbbing with self-importance, as London. There are the lanes, the streets and the avenues and there are the budding gardens, the bushy parks and the leafy commons; there are the houses, the shops and the offices with their stairs, escalators and lifts and the building sites with their elevator shafts, their pulleys and rising platforms and their cranes; there are the monuments, the columns, the spires – there are the gushing, pulsing fountains. The flooding river and its trickling tributaries are there. There its ponds and pools and drying puddles and there the city's gutters and drains and the sewers' stench surmounted by the smells of sap, of spring, of Life, of birth and rebirth. A hand alights on a bare shoulder; it's the touch of a stranger. The city exhales and rests before tilting at the rising sun. I push up on my hands now and straighten my arms, I inhale and lift my head. If I close one eye I can align the nipple of one reflected hanging breast to sit just above St Paul's massive pink-lit teat in the early dawn; they touch, my pendent nipple and the dome's Golden Gallery, a mirror image at the horizon plane. I respond to the light touch of your hand on my thigh and swing one leg over and pad on hands and knees to the edge of the bed where I sit, looking out. You sit up and join me there: we are superimposed on London's morning sky, side by side, impassive, reminiscent of Henry Moore's *King and Queen*. Together, suspended, floating above the now–quiet market, we look down over the city and back and in at the two of us framed by the giant window on a bed in an apartment in a city, the bedroom dimly pink-lit too and warm-looking. I look closely and am delighted to see your hand in mine. I can hear your heart beat along with mine, in time with mine and with the city's so that all pulses merge and I no longer know which throb is whose, yours, mine or the city's or all of ours, just that it's there, this rhythm, and that it's all of ours, it's the blood coursing through our veins, it's the commuters spilling and streaming in their thousands from their homes, from the Underground's tunnels and London's double–decker buses into schools and shops and offices. The busy sun warms our faces and streams through your halo of golden hair on the way to lighting our bedroom. I look again and see our hands have become wings that we flap and dry in the unruly sun and, leaving us behind in the warming bedroom, beat purposefully so we rise along with the city's millions of other waking butterflies.

There is a riot of bright, transparent colour there in the sky where we flutter and swoop, flutter and swoop and whoop, *We are one!*

Epilogue

It's like this. I am an options trader. This means that I see everything in terms of time to and probability and nature of outcome – in my personal as well as in my professional life. The one has leaked into the other. I tried explaining this to Sharon once and she kind of got it.

'So Pascal's bet,' she had summarised, 'is that you lose nothing by believing in God, whether he exists or not.'

To which I had said, 'Yes.' About to elaborate, I realised she had fallen asleep.

But Mie had really got it after she had stayed silent a moment and reflected. We were in a taxi in, of all places, Pascalstrasse, just north of Hamburg. 'It's not just that you lose nothing by believing in God but that you stand to gain an infinite amount if you gain everlasting life by believing. The argument is that from a risk and reward perspective one would be foolish not to believe.'

'Exactly,' I had said. 'No risk and infinite reward.'

And yet, yet, I didn't believe because, actually, the risk that I saw was one of personal obliteration, the evisceration of the very thing that made me me. We must consider not only the probability and the size of the outcome but the stake too.

From my study window, I look out over the garden and onto Isabella's butterfly pavilion. We're in the third year of her breeding butterflies here. That first summer, I was lying on my back in the grass playing with Sky when I looked up to see Isabella standing above us, a kaleidoscope of butterflies around her head. I reasoned then that if I remained married to her it wasn't because I had committed to so many years previously but because I wished to on that very day as I hoped I would on every day.

I can see Isabella move from breeding cage to breeding cage, observing, tidying. A butterfly has alighted on an eyebrow; she juts her lower jaw forward and blows it off. Others garland her hair, like, from a distance, a straggly daisy chain. She moves gracefully, despite being seven months pregnant with our third child.

Sky is at nursery school, Jess is asleep in his buggy by the pavilion door. Isabella is possessive; too much so, I believe: she never lets the boys out of her sight when they're at home. I think to myself that I should show more understanding and not take offence.

I don't like the names she has chosen for our children but, now that they are our children's, I like them more. I hope for a girl, now, after two boys, but need to have Isabella understand she must choose a name other than Gaia, a name that has different connotations for me than it does for her. From the start, Isabella insisted that we would have three children.

I trade from home now and Isabella works part-time as an art dealer, having begun with her brother's pictures and demonstrated a remarkable capacity to price a painting just where a purchaser will buy it. We go into London once a week or so, me to lunch with other traders or former colleagues and Isabella, when Sky is at school, to catch up with Sharon in the gallery, taking Jess with her. Once a month, we go in as a family and show Sky and Jess the sights and the museums, keen that the wonderful city be accessible to them. Its avenues and streets feel like the arteries and veins that comprise us. The human proportions of its buildings and public spaces reflect us and refine us, our humanity, our aesthetics, our relationships.

Occasionally, Sharon will join us; she knows all the short cuts through London's parks and the most secluded places. While she and Isabella chat, I entertain the boys, reviewing, all the time, my facile assessment of Mie as mind and of Sharon as body and of Isabella as person, perfect fusion of the two, and conclude, every time, that I'm being unfair to both Mie and Sharon.

Very occasionally, Kimberley joins us, when, by the end of the afternoon it will be me deep in conversation with her and Isabella running after the boys. Kimberley teaches English literature in a London university now and has a depth and breadth of reading I envy and find breathtaking. 'You can find the solution,' she says, wheezing, 'to most of life's important questions in a novel,' to which I nod vigorously, while Isabella only smiles.

Acknowledgements

My thanks to my wife, Adriana, and my children, Gabriella and Ludovic, for rejoicing when I sought to retire from gainful employment in order to write my first novel, for their love and support. My thanks to my friends and readers for, variously, their encouragement, their too kind and often detailed feedback and their contribution to my Unbound promotional video – Neil Burgess, Dido Crosby, Annie Eaton, Catherine Evans, Caroline Harding, Takeshi Imamura, Judy Luddington, Sophia Neville, my mother Amy Noble, Helene Schlichter, Laura Williamson and Nadia Williamson. My thanks to Amélie Nothomb from whose *Stupeur et tremblements* I 'borrowed' the cast of Yumimoto and to Chris Whiting for his tour of Robert & Edwards (butcher's).

My thanks to Xander Cansell who accepted this book onto Unbound's platform, to Annabel Wright and to Elizabeth Cochrane, my merciless structural editor. I'm also grateful to Gillian Holmes and Dan Smith, my diligent copyeditor and proofreader.

My very special thanks to my supporters – to those generous friends and strangers who funded this book and made its publication possible. It wouldn't have happened without you.

Patrons

Chiara Albertini
Antonietta Baldacchino
Charles & Sophie Bankes
Wendy Bliss
Jayne Buxton
Terry Cakebread
Adriana Cavalli
Albina Cavalli
Gia Cavalli
Sandro Cavalli
Brian & Kathryn Clapp
Ruth Clarke
Dido Crosby
Catherine Davies
Gary Dennis
Stathis Dimitriadis
Claire Durtnall
Annie Eaton
Sarah Fong
Elizabeth Frayling
Megan Halligan
Amanda Hamlyn
Sean Henaghan
Sarah Herrick
Pamela Honour
Fiona Hunter
F J
Pamela Jennings
Leandros Kalisperas
Ben Keisler
Esther Lecumberri
Vivienne Marshall

Anne McFarlane
Peter Mirzoeff
Linda Murgatroyd
Sophia Neville
Janet Nevin
Gabriella Noble
Ludovic Noble
James North
Jane Phillips
Scott Ransley
Tony Reiss
Kevin Restivo
Helen Rule
Billie Seymour
Isabel Stehn
Maria Street
Sally Tattersall
Almuth Tebbenhoff
Margaret Thirlway
Deborah Tom
Isaac Velasquez
Oliver Wheatley
Wendy Wheatley
Richard Williams
Olivia Williamson
Nadia Williamson
Barbara Zarzycki